Mekong Rescue

Mekong Rescue

David B. Freeman

Nissi Publishing
Roanoke, Texas

Published in the United States of America by Nissi Publishing, Inc., Roanoke, Texas.

ISBN: 978-0-944372-19-7

http://www.mekongrescue.com
http://www.nissibooks.com
http:www.dbfonline.com

Republic of South Vietnam
III & IV Corps

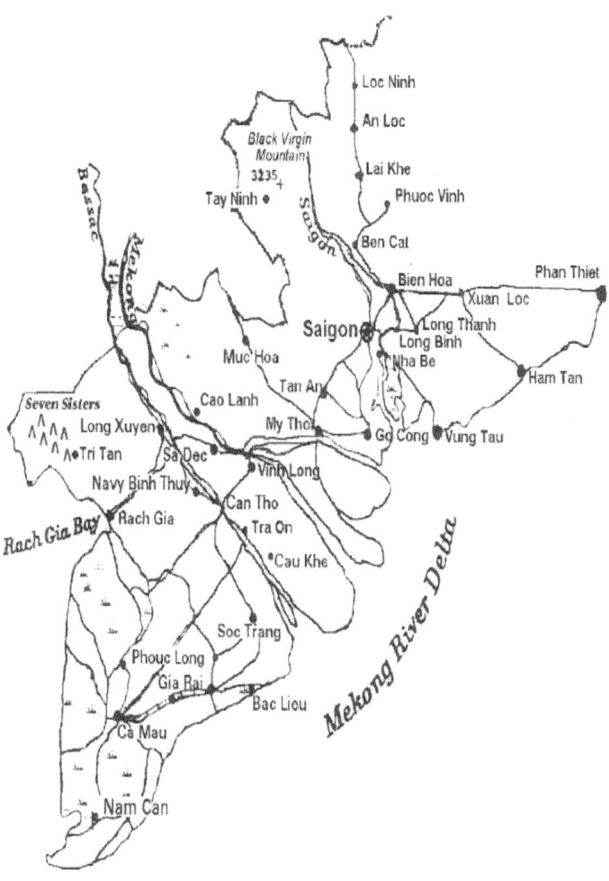

Dedication

This book is dedicated to the Dustoff pilots and crew members who flew in the Vietnam War. It is also dedicated to the Navy pilots of HAL-3 (The Seawolves) and VAL-4 (The Black Ponies) who flew out of Navy Binh Thuy and other locations in support of the Brown Water Navy.

ONE

Over the Mekong River near Cao Lanh, Republic of Vietnam, late October 1971

Navy Lieutenants Steve Cooper and Martin "Stump" Willis of the VAL-4 Black Pony Squadron circled their OV-10 Broncos over the Mekong River just after dawn, while below them a US Navy River Patrol Boat (PBR) marked their target. "Smoke is out!" the PBR radio operator called out.

Cooper keyed his mike, "We've got yellow smoke, Echo Two. Break. Pony One-Two, you take the first pass."

Willis didn't hesitate. "Pony One-Two, rolling in hot!" He banked his aircraft into a steep right turn toward the target. When the aircraft was aligned with the smoke, Willis leveled its wings and lowered the nose into a steep descent. With his left hand he flipped all six of the arming switches by his left knee from "safe" to "armed." The full load of ordnance, combined with the still, calm, morning air produced a delightful flying platform. It reminded Stump of riding downhill on a giant roller coaster.

There was no buffeting from thermals or wind gusts and it seemed he only needed to think of making a control input and the plane instantly responded. *This is worth getting up early for,*

Willis thought. It wasn't often he got to fly on "greased rails" in the hot tropical climate of the Vietnam Delta.

Willis double-checked to make sure the orange lights beneath his glare shield were illuminated, indicating his weapon stations were fully armed. Below him, wisps of early morning fog partially obscured the target area. Mixed with the thinning fog Willis saw the yellow smoke marking the VC hiding place. He had to trust that the PBR crew had marked the target accurately. On the Bronco's instrument panel, the airspeed needle quivered near the top of the green arc before edging into the yellow caution range. The wind noise increased and the controls stiffened. Stump kept his eye on the yellow smoke, expecting at any second to see a clear view of his target. The sampans were hiding beneath low hanging branches along the north bank of the Mekong River.

Willis waited until he was 500 feet above the river before firing two 5-inch Zuni rockets at the location marked by the smoke. He followed the rockets up with a burst of fire from his 7.62mm machine guns. Then he pulled the OV-10 Bronco up over the trees, climbing for a safe altitude. It was time for his wingman, Lieutenant Steve Cooper, to make his run.

"One-Two's out and arms safe. Coop, you're in," he radioed, switching his armament switches to the "safe" position. The radio was silent.

Stump searched through his overhead canopy for his wingman. Just a few seconds earlier, Black Pony 11 had been with him, orbiting at two thousand feet while waiting for Echo Two, the Navy PBR patrol boat on the river, to mark the target. Now Pony 11 was nowhere in sight.

"Black Pony One-One say your position," Willis called.

"On my run," Cooper responded. He should have been diving from altitude in clear sight of his wingman. That was

SOP—Standard Operating Procedure—designed to provide mutual protection and to lessen the chance of a midair collision. Yet, Willis had lost sight of Cooper. He leveled off and turned back toward the river. Even after the turn Willis could not locate Steve Cooper's aircraft.

In the cockpit of his own OV-10, Steve Cooper didn't have time for conversation. When Stump began his run, Cooper pointed his own aircraft to the east, away from Willis, and descended rapidly for the deck. When he reached treetop level, he turned toward the river and descended further until the tips of his props were just inches above the water. Tree branches wouldn't obscure the target from Steve; he was going in under them. The patrol boat was out of sight west of the target and not a factor. Pony 12 had cleared the area. Now it was his turn.

Steve willed himself to relax his grip on the controls. He felt his muscles tightening, rotated his shoulders, and moved his head from side to side, stretching the muscles in his neck. *This is just like cropdusting back in Mississippi*, he reminded himself. Sweat rolled down his forehead and into his eyes, but he didn't have time to wipe it. He had armed his weapons before reaching the river. His right forefinger was on the machine gun trigger, his thumb ready to punch off rockets. He rounded a bend in the river, and there was the target—so close he could see the surprise on the VC faces.

Cooper punched off four Zuni rockets as fast as he could press the button, then walked machine gun tracers across the water into the nearest of the sampans. He was immediately rewarded with at least one secondary explosion, maybe two, as the rockets impacted the boats. His adrenalin was flowing. This was the way to fight a war!

Suddenly, the Bronco was in the smoke and debris from the exploding sampans. The trees! Steve yanked back on the control stick and wrestled the Bronco hard over to the left, climbing and turning at the same time. His props chewed through tree limbs as the airplane clawed for altitude. It had been close, but it had been worth it. The sampans were burning, their cargo of ammunition and explosives blowing sky high. Charlie wouldn't use that load of ammunition against the good guys.

Stump Willis saw the explosion and shook his head. He had finally caught sight of Cooper just as his first rockets had been fired. From his position overhead, it looked like Black Pony 11 was on a suicide run into the tree line. Cooper was going to get himself killed if he didn't ease off. He'd been that way ever since he got back from R&R two weeks earlier. The guy acted like he was invincible, or that he didn't care.

Thirty seconds later, Cooper joined up off Willis' right wing. "Did you see that?" His voice was like that of a school kid, full of excitement. "There were secondaries everywhere. Charlie was carrying a load and I busted him."

"Yeah," Willis replied, cooly. "You got him all right." It wasn't the time or place to discuss Cooper's safety violations. He'd talk to him later at the club—try to warn him before the Old Man got wind of Cooper's antics and pulled him off flying status.

While in formation, they checked each other's aircraft for battle damage. Stump dropped below Steve's aircraft to look at its belly. There were tree limbs caught in the rocket pod pylons.

"You've got evidence stuck on your rocket pods, Coop," Willis told him. "Chief ain't gonna like it."

"Let's go to Binh Thuy to rearm, refuel, and get some breakfast," Cooper replied. "Chief will never see it." He was still coming down from the adrenaline high that had carried him into the inferno. He wasn't worried about the trees. Sure, it had been close, but he had been in control. The Bronco was like an extension of his body. It went where he willed it, almost without conscious thought. He was so comfortable with the airplane, it seemed as if he had been flying it all his life.

Willis shook his head again and taking up the lead position, turned toward Navy Binh Thuy, the Navy airstrip just east of Can Tho on the south side of the Bassac River in the middle of the Vietnam region known as the Delta.

100 miles away, east of Saigon

Hydraulic motors activated beneath the Pan Am 747's cabin floor, producing a series of whirring and groaning sounds that could be heard throughout the cabin. Midway down the right-hand side of the cabin, Eric Mohr—Warrant Officer, US Army—sat in the aisle seat of the outside section, listening to the sounds of the Boeing's mechanical systems. He imagined what was happening in the cockpit as the pilots extended wing flaps and slats to reconfigure the big jet for slower flight. The wind noise decreased and the sound of the engines dropped a few decibels. It seemed to Mohr the airplane was circling.

He looked around the cabin to see if other passengers were noticing the changes. It was a crowded flight with every seat occupied. At least two-thirds of the 300 hundred-or-so people on board were military: Army officers and soldiers in Class B khakis; a sprinkling of Air Force blue and Navy white adding color. The remaining passengers were civilians, mostly Oriental. Indeed, the passengers were beginning to stir throughout the cabin. The airliner was approaching its destination—Saigon, Republic of Vietnam.

Eric leaned over the two sleeping men between him and the window. Warrant Officers Brian Patton and Tom Zerbe were Eric's buddies from flight school. The airliner was flying over land. Eric guessed its altitude to be somewhere around 10,000 feet.

It had been nearly nine hours since their last fuel stop in Guam. Mohr had no idea what time it was locally; his watch was still on California time. During the previous eighteen hours, they had crossed the International Date Line and had flown through darkness and back into light again within just a few hours. His internal clock was totally confused, but it didn't matter whether he was on Saigon time or California time. He was tired of sitting, tired of sleeping, tired of waiting.

"Wake up, Zero, we're there." Eric said, shaking the sleeping warrant officer beside him. Tom Zerbe rolled over in his seat, turning his back to Mohr. On the other side of Zerbe, Brian Patton opened his eyes and looked out the window. A new day was beginning. Below, people were already fighting and dying.

More than half the passengers on the 747 were military. Some were veterans returning to the war who knew what was ahead. Others were first-timers who had no idea. Many of the civilian passengers were Vietnamese, on their way home from vacation or visiting family. For them, the war had been around so long they had learned to go on with their lives in spite of it. Civilian contractors, reporters and technical support personnel, all somehow connected to the war effort, rounded out the passenger manifest.

The military newbies experienced the jittery nervousness of heading into the unknown—an unknown some wouldn't survive. Most thought they were invincible. A few had an impending sense of doom, a premonition that they wouldn't be going home alive.

The three new Warrant Officer Aviators—classmates, fresh out of Fort Rucker and medevac pilot training at Fort Sam Houston—were among those who believed they led a charmed life. Each, in his own way, looked forward to the year ahead. They had trained for it and had volunteered for it. They were helicopter pilots—not just helicopter pilots, but medical evacuation pilots, who would fly unarmed Hueys into combat to evacuate wounded fighting men. They were following a proud heritage marked by Medal of Honor winners. Their profession had the respect, not only of the men on the ground, but of other Army Aviators. These other pilots—the ones who flew "slicks," the troop-carrying Hueys that inserted combat patrols into hot LZs, their M-60 machine guns blazing; the ones who flew the Cobra gunships that reigned terror on the Viet Cong with their rockets and mini-guns; and OH-6 Scout pilots who flew low over the treetops, uncovering enemy positions for the gunships—believed that medevac pilots were all crazy. But they did respect them.

The three new pilots—Mohr, Patton and Zerbe—were psyched up for the job ahead; a product of their flight instructors and the pride instilled in them at Fort Rucker and at Fort Sam Houston. They had graduated near the top of their class, a requirement for the medevac assignment. Now they were joining the Army's elite in the only place on the globe where Americans were involved in combat action. They were ready to get on with it.

Yet there were fears to be conquered. Where would they be stationed? To which unit would they be assigned? Would they be able to stay together? How would they react when shot at? These unspoken questions mirrored their inner fears. Their exterior shells were macho all the way. The sergeants, captains and chief warrant officers around them knew them for what they were—green, scared newbies. It was only in their own minds they were God's gift to aviation, ready to help America win the war. It never occurred to them they wouldn't be allowed to win it.

Eric Mohr's perspective was different from that of the others. Eric believed he had been sent to Vietnam to fulfill part of a Divine calling. Few of God's servants wore a uniform—far too few. Eric wore it willingly. Not only did it allow him to clearly follow what he passionately believed to be God's purpose for his life, but it allowed him to fly (his second greatest passion).

Among the "born again" crowd he hung around with in college, Eric's decision not to try to avoid the military was an unpopular choice. Even his wife Lynn had a hard time understanding it. The others, in their own eagerness to serve God, had avoided Vietnam by joining the reserves or by gaining deferments—the most popular being a ministerial deferment. To them, it seemed Eric had allowed himself to be carried along into the draft pool with no effort to stop it. He'd been a leaf on the water in the whirlpool of life and it had dragged him down the drain with no opposition from him. And they were critical of him for that. Never mind there had been a lottery and his number had been drawn. Never mind he had prayed and sought God's will as much as they had. It was as if he had crossed a line. They were on one side and he was on the other. Only Lynn, who had to accept his actions because she was his wife, accepted them as being in keeping with God's plan for his life.

As the plane continued to circle, Eric breathed a quiet prayer. *Lord, let me know what it is You would have me do here. Guide me to those whose lives I am to touch. Give me boldness to speak Your words to those You lead me to.* Though tired and apprehensive, he was alive with excitement. God had called him; God would use him; it would be an adventure!

Eric's thoughts were interrupted by a public address announcement. "Ladies and gentlemen, this is Captain Bergstrom. You may have noticed we have been over land for the past fifteen or twenty minutes. Currently, we are circling approximately fifty miles west of Saigon at an altitude of 10,000 feet. Ton San Nhut tower has advised us the airport came under a rocket and mortar attack just before dawn and the security forces are still in the process of clearing the area to make sure it is safe for us to land. Since we have enough fuel to remain airborne for awhile, we're going to wait out here until they give us the 'all clear.' I'll keep you posted."

The noise level in the cabin rose as the passengers reacted to the announcement. Welcome to the war!

Ton San Nhut Airport an hour later

Mattie Hill, already sweating from the heat and humidity of the subtropical morning, watched the Pan Am Clipper come to a stop a hundred feet from the terminal. She stood under a pavilion outside a ten-foot high chain link fence. The strap of her overnight bag cut into her shoulder. Her wrinkled blue and white striped dress, the standard uniform of a Red Cross "Donut Dolly," looked as if she had slept in it the previous night.

Mattie had, in fact, spent the night on a cot at the MACV (Military Assistance Command, Vietnam) compound wearing her dress. Arriving at Ton San Nhut Airport on a shuttle from Da Nang around 11:00 p.m. the night before, she had not wanted to risk trying to get a hotel room in Saigon at that late hour. She caught a ride with an Air Force sergeant to the MACV compound where she had slept in the ready room attached to the RTO (Radio-Telephone-Operator) shack. The RTO had awakened her at six, just in time to catch the military bus to the airport. There she hoped to meet her friend, Eileen Strickland, who was due to return from R&R in Hawaii and was expected to be arriving on today's Pan Am flight. Mattie heard about the mortar attack during her ride to the airport, but from where she had slept just a mile or two away, she had not heard any of the actual shelling.

Mattie felt perfectly safe among the protective, watchful eyes of most of the US soldiers she encountered. Still, she did not like traveling around Vietnam alone. She planned to join up with Eileen and go to Hotel Three, the main military heliport in Saigon, to catch a ride to Navy Binh Thuy. As soon as the tower operator put out the word he had two "Code 21" (female) passengers for the Mekong Delta, there would be plenty of ride offers. The girls had been in Vietnam long enough to know how to work the system.

The 747's engines were still spooling down as the Pan Am ground crew rolled two metal staircases up to its front and middle passenger doors. Men on small tractors pulled baggage carts under the plane's belly, and the huge baggage doors were opened. Baggage handlers scrambled inside the cargo bay and began tossing out bags and stacking them on the carts. American soldiers wearing jungle fatigues and holding M-16s lined both sides of an imaginary path that covered the shortest distance from the airplane to the terminal. The soldiers were all business. The smell of cordite from the earlier mortar attack lingered in the air.

Mattie tried to watch both doors of the plane as the passengers made their way down the stairways. Eileen had no way of knowing Mattie would be there to meet her, so it was important for Mattie to catch her friend's attention as soon as she stepped off the plane.

The passengers carefully made their way down the metal stairways and into the building. There was little conversation among them—the sobering knowledge of the early morning events made them anxious to get inside.

Eric noticed Mattie standing outside the fence, searching the faces of the passengers coming down the ramp, and nudged Zero, who grinned and elbowed Brian. Not beautiful, but attractive in a girl-next-door way, she was somewhat petite, with not-quite shoulder length blond hair and blue eyes. She was obviously an American girl. Vietnam couldn't be all bad.

Mattie saw the men looking at her and smiled. She was getting used to the attention and liked it. Among the coeds at the University of Alabama she had hardly turned a head. Here the competition wasn't as intense. She resumed her surveillance of the deplaning passengers as the three aviators walked by and disappeared into the terminal.

Inside the terminal, the arriving Pan Am Clipper passengers stirred up a great deal of activity. Civilians were met by family or friends. Of the people in uniform, those returning from R&R or on their second tour, located their baggage and moved out to the street to arrange transportation. The newbies, however, were lost. They were in Vietnam. Now what? Their questions were quickly answered by a muscular, black Army Staff Sergeant whose name badge said "Baer" and whose voice sounded like the vowels in his name were transposed.

"All right, listen up," Sergeant Baer shouted above the noise of the passengers milling about the terminal. "If you've got orders telling you to report to the 90th Replacement Depot, Long Binh, Republic of Vietnam, go right over there to the baggage cart against that wall (he pointed), pick up your bags, and get on one of the buses parked right out that door. (He pointed toward the street.) You don't have to go digging for your orders. If you're new to this tropical paradise and you arrived on that blue and white bird out there, that's what your orders say."

Approximately 150 soldiers turned *en masse* to move toward the baggage cart. The three warrant officers dropped back, not wanting to get caught in the crowd.

"When you get your bag," Sergeant Baer continued, "make sure it's your bag. It's got your name stenciled on it, remember? Its shape, size and color is the same as everybody else's, so don't go grabbing without looking."

Eric nudged Brian Patton and nodded toward the sergeant. "His last assignment must have been as a drill sergeant."

"Yeah," Patton agreed.

"You don't have to worry about getting on the wrong bus, either," Sergeant Baer's authoritative voice continued. "Any of the buses will do. They're all OD (olive drab), like your bags, like your blood, like the coffin they're going to send you home in if you don't pay attention to what you're doing for the next 365 days, and they're all going to the same place." He turned to answer a question from an individual who approached him—one of the individuals who, in any crowd, could listen to clear instructions, then ask again all the questions that had just been answered. Sergeant Baer rolled his eyes, summoned up a measure of patience, and turned to explain to the newby what he had just explained to the crowd. "Yes, you. Yes, pick up your bag right over there. Yes, get on one of those buses right out that door."

Mohr, Zerbe and Patton followed the shuffle of the crowd toward the baggage cart, holding back until there was a clear pathway to their duffle bags.

Out on the ramp, Mattie watched as the last of the passengers left the plane and made their way toward the terminal. Eileen was not among them. When the pilots and stewardesses descended the front staircase, Mattie accepted the fact her friend had not been on the plane. Undecided about whether to wait around for the next day's flight, or get back to her duty station at Navy Binh Thuy, she entered the terminal.

Zerbe saw her as she walked in. He nudged Patton, the only single one among the three warrant officers, and pointed her out. The Donut Dolly approached Sergeant Baer, who gave her his full attention.

The three warrant officers followed the other soldiers out to the street, where their senses were assaulted with that first impression of Vietnam that most of the men and women who served there would carry to their graves. It was a combination of heat and humidity that drenched their clothes causing the material to creep into armpits and crotches and any other crevice it could find to create breeding grounds for fungus rashes that would be carried a lifetime. It was the smell of diesel fuel, rotting fish, open sewers, burning feces and other indeterminate odors that combined to raise such a stench that God, in His mercy, supplied the rainy season to periodically wash the filth away. The noises here were a mixture of motor scooter and diesel truck engines and horns honking on a variety of vehicles as sing-song voices everywhere shouted unrecognizable phrases at one another. This was in Saigon. Elsewhere, these same sounds would exist, and added to them would be the sounds of firefights, artillery, jet fighters, helicopters, bombs, screaming and crying. It was an assault on their senses unlike anything any of them had ever seen, heard or smelled before. It was an introduction to Vietnam they weren't likely to forget, and this was only the beginning.

The first two buses were already crowded, so they made their way to the last bus. As they stepped aboard, they caught a glimpse of the American Red Cross girl boarding bus number one in the company of Sergeant Baer.

Within seconds, the doors were closed and the three buses started off, forming a small convoy. Inside, they were like prison buses, with wire mesh covering the windows. On the streets of Saigon, people were everywhere—on bicycles, on Hondas, in cyclos (rickshaws) and on crowded mini-buses selling or buying fruit and vegetables or other wares along the sides of the street. There were no defined lanes in the streets. Traffic went wherever it could. The right-of-way was determined by who had the biggest vehicle, the loudest horn, or could shake their fist in the most threatening manner. Children stood at the edge of the street, staring at the buses with their American occupants inside. There were no smiles, just vacant stares. The passengers wondered if the kids were going to start throwing rocks at the bus and if that was the reason for the wire mesh covering the windows. They were too naive to realize the children were just as likely to throw hand grenades as rocks, and that was the real reason for the wire mesh.

Navy Binh Thuy Airfield, 8:45 a.m. that same morning

The piercing sound of turbine engines turned every head on the airfield, as a flight of four OV-10 Broncos in close formation made a low pass over the runway, broke left maintaining a diamond formation and climbed steeply over the Bassac River. Navy Lieutenants Steve Cooper and Stump Willis stood on the ramp beside Cooper's OV-10 watching the flight of four climbing away in the still morning air. When the formation reached an approximate altitude of 5,000 feet, the aircraft turned back over the field and executed a perfect loop, their formation so tight their wings appeared to overlap.

"What do you bet that's Jake Herring leading that flight!" Cooper commented.

"Has to be," Stump agreed.

Jake Herring was a legend among the Black Pony pilots. He'd been a Blue Angel pilot a few years earlier when the Navy air show team was still flying F4 Phantoms. Why he was flying OV-10s in a close air support mission now was anybody's guess. He was a highly skilled and disciplined pilot, respected by the entire squadron. Jake occasionally worked with the other OV-10 pilots polishing their formation flying and aerobatic skills. This morning's demonstration with four planes was a practice for a special event. Their commanding officer, known affectionately as the "Old Man," was about to rotate stateside. Jake and his wingmen were practicing for a flyby tribute for the Admiral when he departed Navy Binh Thuy for his next assignment.

"Watch how they come over the top, Stump. That's a perfect loop—not flat on top, not falling out the bottom and the other three are staying right with him." Cooper was fascinated. "Man, I'd love to be in his back seat right now," he said.

"You can have that backseat stuff," Willis told him. "I get airsick if I'm not doing the flying."

"Yeah, I do, too," Cooper admitted.

The Black Pony flight made a second loop, and split off one at a time into a break for the traffic pattern.

The two lieutenants watching the airshow were contrasts in appearance. Steve Cooper stood six feet tall and was a muscular 180 pounds. His muscles were not a product of weight training, but of a lifetime of hard work and athletic participation. His curly blond hair and blue eyes served to accent even more the contrast between Steve and his wingman, Marty "Stump" Willis.

Stump, as his nickname indicated, was short of stature and somewhat chunky, though within the fitness requirements of Naval Aviation. Stump had close-cropped brown hair and brown eyes, and was anything but athletic. Both men were married, though Cooper had recently stopped wearing his wedding ring. As one would get to know them, it would become apparent their personalities differed as much as their appearance.

With the air show over, the pilots each went to his own plane. For a brief moment, Steve Cooper had been able to forget the nagging depression he had fought since returning from R&R a couple of weeks earlier. He had just finished a big breakfast consisting of steak and eggs at the Navy mess at Navy Binh Thuy, one of the few places in Vietnam where you could get real eggs. Before breakfast, he had flown a successful mission. After breakfast, he had a front row view as members of his squadron executed precision flying maneuvers that would impress even the toughest fighter jock.

One by one the OV-10s landed. When the runway was clear, it was time for Steve and Stump to go back to work. The emptiness Steve had felt since returning from R&R returned as he climbed the ladder into the cockpit of his freshly armed and refueled warplane. One of the local crew chiefs climbed up the ladder behind Steve to help him secure his shoulder harness and to hand him the safety pins from his rocket fuses. "Lieutenant, you've got to keep this airplane out of the trees if you want your rockets to fire," the man told him.

Cooper shrugged and gave the crew chief a two-finger salute and a nod to acknowledge he had been a bad boy. As the seaman stepped back, Steve lowered his canopy. After checking around to make sure everything was clear, the seaman gave Steve the signal to start his engines.

A few minutes later, as the four Broncos of Commander Jake Herring's flight pulled into their revetments, Steve Cooper and Stump Willis took the runway for their second sortie of the morning.

Long Binh, RVN, later that morning

Captain Brad Duncan, US Army Medical Service Corps, was in his office at the 24th Evac Hospital in Long Binh. His feet were on the desk, and he was smoking a cigar while reading the morning mail. When the phone rang, he grabbed it without changing position. "Duncan here."

"Captain Duncan, this is Sergeant Johnson at the 90th Reception Depot. You've got three brand new one-hundred-bravo-deltas over here." Duncan sat up at Sergeant Johnson's news, putting both feet on the floor and brushing cigar ashes from his shirt front. He noticed the buttons were starting to get tight.

"Yeah?" he said. He'd been afraid they weren't going to send him any more replacements now that some of the units were standing down. He could sure use three new men. By their 100BD military occupational specialty (MOS), he knew they were medevac-trained warrant officers. "Any second tour guys?"

"No, sir," Sergeant Johnson replied. "You got yourself three brand new wobbly ones, Captain." A "wobbly one" was a WO1—Warrant Officer One, the lowest officer rank in the Army.

"Figures," Duncan replied. "Have they processed in yet?"

"No, sir. They just got off the bus a few minutes ago, but I figured you'd want to know right away, what with what's been going on up around the Parrot's Beak."

"All right. I'll give them a couple of hours and then I'll be over to pick them up."

"Thank you, sir."

"Thank *you*, Sergeant Johnson."

What had been going on near the Parrot's Beak, and elsewhere in the regions just north of Saigon, was war. After three or four months of relative calm, Charlie was on the move again. And this time he had something new—shoulder-held, surface-to-air missiles. They were Russian-made SA-7s and they were knocking helicopters out of the sky like doves on the opening day of dove season. It was bad enough the US was losing Cobras and Scouts, but there had been two Dustoff crews shot down in the past 30 days. Duncan needed replacements at Long Binh, but they were also calling for help in the Delta where training the VNAF (Vietnamese Air Force) Dustoff pilots was taking its toll on the American pilots. The 57th Med Detachment didn't have enough experienced pilots to last out the next three months, not to mention the estimated six months the brass in Washington had decided it would take to complete the Vietnamization effort in the Delta. It would be tough deciding where to send these newbies. What he really needed were some second-tour aviators—some guys who could come up to speed as aircraft commanders pronto.

It was almost noon when Brad Duncan drove up to the quonset hut that housed the 90th Reception Depot. He'd spent the time since Sergeant Johnson's call on the phone talking with the commanders of the Medical Evacuation units assigned to the 68th Medical Group, trying to assess where the most pressing needs for the new pilots were. He wished he had ten more, but didn't anticipate more replacements arriving any time soon. The next AMEDD (Essential Medical Training for Army Medical Department Aviators) class was not scheduled to graduate from Fort Sam until after Christmas. Who knew what Washington's commitment to the war would be by then?

The 90th Replacement Depot had sleeping quarters, but most people were pushed through to their respective units as quickly as possible. Orders were checked, units notified and transportation arranged. Other than that there wasn't much the new arrivals had to do except sign for and pick up their TA-50 gear—their basic in-country clothing and web gear. Weapons and flight gear would be issued when they reached their respective units.

Mohr, Patton and Zerbe spent the morning with their in-processing paperwork. There was no indication of where they would be assigned. The buddies wanted to stay together but knew the chances of that happening were remote.

After having their paperwork stamped, stapled, folded and mutilated, and drawing their TA-50 gear, they were thinking about trying to find something to eat. One of the clerks, a Spec 4 with a colored tattoo on his left forearm and a gold St. Christopher's medal around his neck, brought Captain Duncan over to them.

"Good morning, men," Captain Duncan said, extending his hand. "I'm Brad Duncan, Aviation Officer for the 68th Medical Group. I'll be responsible for your assignments here. What do you say we go get something to eat and get acquainted?"

"Sure." They were game. "Should we grab our gear or leave it here?" Zerbe asked.

"Bring it on," Duncan replied. "We'll find you a place to stay over at Long Binh Dustoff until you get assigned. What he didn't tell them was it was undecided yet where they would be going. Two of them would probably be staying in Long Binh. The final decision would be his, but he wouldn't make it without an informal interview with each of them.

Brad Duncan was thirty-two years old, a dedicated soldier and a dedicated family man. He took his job as Aviation Officer for the 68th Medical Group seriously. This was his third tour in Vietnam. During the other two, he had been a Dustoff pilot. Now he was grateful to be flying a desk.

Duncan's primary responsibility was to provide support to the commanders of the helicopter ambulance units in the III and IV Corps military regions of South Vietnam. This included assigning qualified aviators, an asset getting in short supply now that the war was supposed to be winding down.

He drove the new men over to the Officer's Club that was shared by the 24th Evac Hospital and the 159th and 283rd Med Detachments, collectively known as "Long Binh Dustoff."

The O' Club Duncan took them to wasn't much different from any bar and grill you would find back in the States. It was air conditioned with a bar at one end and tables and chairs scattered around the rest of the room. A small stage was at the end of the room opposite the bar. Against the back wall stood a jukebox.

A few tables near the bar were occupied. Captain Duncan led the way to a table in a back corner of the room. A young Vietnamese waitress came and took their order for hamburgers and french fries, then passed the order through a window behind the bar to an older Vietnamese woman working the grill. After turning in the food order, the waitress brought ice-filled glasses and canned soft drinks to the table.

"So tell me, guys," Duncan began. "Where are you from?"

"Near Cincinnati," Zerbe said. Zerbe's jet black hair was cut in a flat top. Long, almost feminine eyelashes highlighted his brown eyes. He was short for a pilot, but well-built. His eyes drew Duncan's attention. They were so innocent now, so full of confidence and expectation. What would those eyes reflect in three months; in six?

"I'm from Shuqualak, Mississippi," Eric told him. He pronounced the name of the town "Sugar-lock." Eric was taller than Zerbe, but weighed less. His hair was brown, his eyes hazel, and he had a mustache, obviously grown since flight school.

Both Zerbe and Mohr were slightly older than most first-tour aviators Duncan had seen arrive in Vietnam. He guessed them to be twenty-two or twenty-three years old, and noticed they both wore wedding rings.

"What about you, Patton?" Duncan asked. Brian Patton was looking around the room lost in his own thoughts. His attention snapped back as he heard his name mentioned. He was younger than the other two, with curly brown hair and gray-blue eyes. He had a thoughtful, distracted look about him, as if his mind was occupied elsewhere.

"Syracuse, New York," Patton replied.

"I'm from Milwaukee, myself," Duncan told them. "I don't meet many people from Milwaukee coming through here."

"Sanders is from Milwaukee," Mohr said. "Greg Sanders. He should have been here within the last few weeks."

"Is he a medevac pilot?"

"Yes, sir. He was in the class ahead of us at Fort Sam, but got held up because of some kind of emergency in his family. He was supposed to ship out sometime last month."

"Well, I didn't see him come through here. He could have gone up north to Da Nang. There's a reception depot there that handles incoming personnel for the northern two military regions."

They continued with small talk, Duncan mentally assessing the men from their conversation and mannerisms. Two of the new men would stay in Long Binh and one would go to the Delta. Regardless of where they went, their situations would be dangerous. The guys who stayed in Long Binh would be flying in and out of areas that were currently alive with enemy activity. The one who went to the Delta would be doing a lot of night flying and would have to do some flying with his Vietnamese counterparts. He would have to grasp the mission concepts quickly and have the patience to work with the Vietnamese Dustoff pilots.

Right now the Delta was quieter than III Corps, but it wasn't likely to stay that way. There were good aircraft commanders in both units, but whoever went to the Delta would have to get up to speed faster. The unit was consolidating and losing some of its assets, and it was heavily involved in the Vietnamization of America's war effort.

The food arrived, and as they ate, Duncan described both locations, then asked the men if they had any preference about their assignments.

Mohr had a preference, but he was hesitant to make it known. He wanted to go to the Delta. He knew his brother-in-law, Steve Cooper, a Navy pilot, was stationed somewhere in the Delta, but he didn't know exactly where. Steve's letters, what few there had been, had not contained a lot of details.

Steve and Eric were married to twin sisters. But even before they had married, they had known each other in a different capacity. Steve, a Navy Flight Instructor at Meridian Naval Air Station in South Mississippi, had spent his off-hours as a civilian instructor at one of the local airports. Eric, who had learned to fly before joining the Army, had been one of Steve's students. That relationship led to Steve meeting, and subsequently marrying, Gail Gibson, who had originally been Eric's girlfriend. Now Eric was married to Gail's identical twin sister, Lynn.

When Captain Duncan mentioned the Delta Dustoff Unit was stationed at a Navy Airfield, Eric knew he wanted that assignment. It would be his best chance to be near Steve. Even though he knew he wanted to go to the Delta, he was hesitant to say so. One thing he had already learned about the Army is that if you're ever given the opportunity to make your choice of assignments known, it is almost certain your choice will be removed from the dart board before the dart is ever thrown. Typically, the Army sends you where you least want to go and doesn't send you where you most want to go.

Eric also knew he had a tendency to get ahead of God … to try to make God's will happen in his life. He was learning the hard way to relax and let God do His work and not try to make things happen that were beyond his control. For this reason he decided to let his two friends make their choices known first, and he would go along with whatever was left, trusting God to make it be the right assignment.

Patton and Zerbe didn't make that decision easy. The three young warrant officers had been through flight school and medevac training together and would have preferred staying together. Eric hoped they would both decide for the action of III Corps, but they volunteered nothing.

"I'll tell you what," Duncan said, as the waitress began cleaning their empty plates from the table. "Since you guys are undecided, I'd like to talk with each of you individually before making my final decision. Let's go over to the office and chat. Then I'll take you to Long Binh Dustoff and introduce you around."

As Captain Duncan pulled his jeep up in front of the 24th Evac Hospital a few minutes later, a Huey with red crosses painted on its nose and side doors was making an approach to the hospital's helipad. The four men got out of the jeep and stood beside it to watch the helicopter's arrival.

The rotor blades made a throbbing sound that vibrated nearby windows and matched the increased beat of the on-lookers' hearts as the pilot added power to slow the Huey's descent. The incredible noise and power of the Huey's engine could be felt as well as heard as the rotor wash swept over them—a hot blast of strong wind that caused them to hold onto their hats and close their eyes against the swirling debris. It was this type of arrival, with dust blowing everywhere, that had earned the medevac pilots the call sign "Dustoff."

The helicopter settled on its skids, the sound of the turbine engine decreased, and the throbbing beat of the main rotor was replaced by a swishing sound, as the rotor blades, now devoid of lift and turning at a slower rpm, sliced through the air overhead. Two crewmen jumped from the rear of the air-craft and motioned rapidly to the medical team waiting at the hospital entrance. The team ran out to the helicopter, ducking as they ran, even though the rotating blades were at least eight feet over their heads. They carried with them an empty litter, which they exchanged for the one the Dustoff crew unloaded from the helicopter with their patient on it. The patient was then hurried inside.

For Eric, Brian and Tom, watching the Dustoff crew at work was thrilling. Soon they would be the ones flying such helicopters—saving lives in the face of danger. Even Duncan was moved by the event, though he witnessed it many times each day. A part of him was flying that mission—flying all Dustoff missions—and always would be. As for the newbies, there was no way they could know that before this year was out, one of them would be flown to that very helipad with a bullet in his heart. At the controls of that helicopter would be another of the three, crying and hoping it wasn't as bad as it seemed.

As they stood watching, the pilot in the left seat of the medevac chopper looked over at them and touched his helmet in a friendly salute. He then looked around to make sure his crew was aboard and everyone else had moved away from the aircraft. Satisfied that they were clear to depart, he gave a thumbs up signal to his right seat "peter pilot," who picked the Huey up to a hover, and eased his cyclic control stick forward. The Huey moved forward, slowly at first, then picking up speed. The airframe shuddered as it passed through translational lift and the Huey started climbing. When it disappeared over the horizon, the spell was broken and Captain Duncan led the warrant officers inside.

He showed Eric and Tom the pool table in the rec room, then ushered Brian into his office. Mohr and Zerbe hadn't even finished a game of eight ball when Brian came back and told Tom the captain wanted to talk with him next.

Brad Duncan knew his policy of interviewing aviators and trying to match them with available assignments in III and IV Corps was unusual. Most military assignments were just names with MOSs matching staffing requirements. The circumstances that allowed him to have any say in the matter at all were unusual in themselves. There were four helicopter ambulance units currently under the administrative control of the 68th Medical Group. The 82nd and 57th Medical Detachments were in the Delta. The 159th and 283rd Medical Detachments were combined at Long Binh to cover III Corps. The two northern military regions, I Corps and II Corps, had two similar units each. Those were someone else's responsibility.

Because of the Vietnamization effort, in six months there would only be two detachments in all of III and IV Corps. Congress had decreed the United States was turning the war effort over to the South Vietnamese. From Duncan's perspective, it didn't appear the South Vietnamese wanted it.

After talking with Brian and learning he was single, Duncan subconsciously selected him for Long Binh. He detected in the young warrant officer a certain detachment that could be interpreted as a willingness to face whatever occurred with a nonchalant "what-the-hell" attitude. Long Binh it would be for Brian Patton. The CO of the 159th, Captain Bernie Johnson, would be able to integrate Patton into the unit. The two men were a lot alike.

Now Duncan had to decide which of the other two would have what it took to work with the South Vietnamese Air Force in the Delta, and which one would be best suited to helping keep Brian Patton alive for his entire tour. After talking with Zerbe for half an hour, Duncan still wasn't decided. It all hinged on his conversation with the third man, Eric Mohr.

Eric was uptight when he entered Captain Duncan's office. He tried not to be, even argued with himself that it was ridiculous. Whatever happened would be in God's hands. It was just that he had allowed himself to start hoping he would be stationed near Steve. It seemed that more often than not, when he got his hopes up about something, he was disappointed. He sat in the chair across from the Captain's desk, his legs apart and his hands grasping the edge of the seat between his knees. Duncan picked up on Eric's nervousness right away.

To him it was a sign this young aviator was taking this place seriously.

"So, Eric, you're married?" Duncan began the interview.

"Yes, sir." Eric replied.

"You miss her?"

"I sure do."

"How long have you been married?"

"Two years, sir," Eric replied.

"I've been married nearly twelve years," Captain Duncan said, leaning back in his chair, crossing his legs and pulling the cuff of his flight suit pants down over his boot. "This is my third tour. Some marriages don't make it. Mine seems to have gotten stronger."

"Mine will, too," Eric assured him.

"I hope so," Duncan said, then changed the subject. "So tell me, why are you here? Why not a deferment? Surely, as a married man, you didn't want to be drafted?"

"No, sir. I volunteered. But I was going to be drafted. My number was drawn early in the lottery, and I wasn't in school. Mostly it's the flying. My father is a commercial pilot. It's all I ever dreamed of."

"Well, you'll get your share of flying. But you know there are other places you could have flown without getting shot at."

Eric didn't know how much to tell Captain Duncan about his convictions, but decided he would open the door, then see what happened. "Well, sir, it's like this. I'm here because I believe with all of my heart I am pursuing God's calling for my life. The circumstances under which I joined the Army, got accepted into and made it through flight school, then got selected for medevac training were too extraordinary to have been coincidence. I'm here to fulfill a purpose, though I'm not exactly sure at this time what that purpose is."

Duncan swiveled his chair away from Eric and looked out the window. Was he dealing with a religious fanatic or someone with deep convictions? He was intolerant of the first, but had respect for the latter. The thought of getting into a religious discussion in order to determine where Eric was really coming from made him feel uncomfortable, but he did want to explore Mohr's motivation a little further.

"If you're sure you are here because God wants you to be, where do you think God wants you to be stationed?" he asked without turning around. Another Huey could be heard landing at the helipad on the other side of the building.

"I have no idea," Eric replied. "In fact, I don't even know enough about Vietnam to know how to pray about it. The only thing I do know is that my brother-in-law, who was also once my flight instructor and a friend, is stationed somewhere in the Delta. I would like to be near him if at all possible, but I don't know exactly where he is."

Duncan was interested. "What does he do?" he asked, turning to face Eric.

"He's a Navy pilot." Eric replied. "He flies OV-10s."

"That means he's either at Vung Tau or Navy Binh Thuy," Duncan explained. "As I mentioned earlier, Navy Binh Thuy is where two of my detachments are located—the 82nd and the 57th Medical Detachments. The 57th is the original Dustoff Unit—the one that's been here the longest. It'll probably be the last to leave. If I send you there, you'll be facing a much different challenge than if you stay here." He leaned over the desk on his elbows as he continued.

"The two Delta Dustoff units are currently co-located with the 3rd Surgical Hospital. That's a MASH hospital, which is currently located at Navy Binh Thuy, a Naval Air Station on the Bassac River, near Can Tho. The 82nd will be standing down within a couple of months and the 57th will have all of the Delta to cover. Currently, they're engaged in training VNAF—that's Vietnamese Air Force—helicopter pilots to fly medical evacuation missions. It's a tough assignment, because the Orientals don't value human life like we do. They're not prone to risk their own lives to save another life. To them, life is cheap. But, if a Vietnamese dies, they'll take any risk imaginable to recover the body. It has something to do with their belief in reincarnation. Most of them are Buddhists.

"The VNAF pilots don't fly at night. The American Dustoff pilots are flying with their Vietnamese counterparts on daylight missions which involve Vietnamese personnel. On those missions they're flying VNAF-owned and maintained Hueys. They are also putting up three crews a day to fly their own helicopters on any missions during daylight or darkness that involve American personnel. On top of that, they're still taking all of the Vietnamese missions at night, and that's the most dangerous part."

Eric thought of his instructors at Fort Wolters and their reluctance to fly at night, especially when it came to practicing night autorotations.

"The Vietnamese pilots are really good," Duncan continued. "Some of them have eight to ten thousand flying hours, and they all learned to fly at Fort Wolters and Fort Rucker, but they have little regard for the safety rules we try to teach them. They're likely to go anywhere and do anything, without regard to ATC instructions or aviation regulations.

The Delta is flat, but it covers a lot of land. Most of the southern portion of what is called the Cau Mau Peninsula is covered by the U Minh Forest. It's a tropical rainforest that covers hundreds of thousands of acres. You go down in there and we may never find you. The U Minh is crawling with Viet

Cong. For a while we left them alone in there. Now, there is a concentrated effort by both the Army and the Navy to shut down the VC supply lines that go in and out of the U Minh. That's part of what the Navy OV-10s are doing with their inland base there on the river."

Eric was listening with interest, but none of Duncan's explanation meant much to him. He had no frame of reference with which to compare what Duncan was describing. He wanted to fly, to gain as much experience as possible, and he wanted to make it home alive and in one piece. He would like to be near Steve. Most of all, he wanted to be where God wanted him, but he didn't know where that was. It wasn't like God spoke to him in a clear voice and said, "Go here, go there." For Eric, God's leading was more subtle and came through impressions and circumstances. Sometimes he wished God would speak to him more clearly.

Duncan stood up and rubbed the back of his head. "I've got some thinking to do," he said. "Let me take you guys over to the Dustoff Unit and find you a place to sleep. I'll let you know later where you're going."

TWO

Vung Tau, RVN, 7:00 p.m. that evening

The O' Club at Vung Tau Airfield was at the south end of the field, near the Navy hangars. Stump Willis and Steve Cooper joked with the other guys in the squadron as they walked in and took a table by themselves near the bar. At the other end of the club, a screen had been set up for the evening movie.

A Vietnamese girl took their order for shrimp and beer. Stump had mentally worked all afternoon on the speech he was going to give his wingman. Now that they were alone, he wasted no time.

"Coop, I'm worried about you," he began. "Ever since you got back from R&R, you've been a different person."

Cooper gave his friend an exasperated "I don't want to listen to this" look. But Willis continued, "You used to fly by the book—aggressive, but safe. Now, you're reckless. It's not just your life you're endangering. I'm affected, too. You fly as if there are no limits—on you, on your airplane, on your wingman. But there *are* limits. I don't know about you, buddy, but I want to go home from this stinking war alive and on my own two feet."

"Just what do you mean, *you're* affected? What are you talking about?"

"You." Stump told him. "You're supposed to be protecting my butt—mine and the guys in the boats. Instead, you're going after Charlie like some kind of kamikaze. You act like you don't have a wife and a daughter … and a wingman who's depending on you to get him back alive."

Cooper didn't want to hear any more. He tried to change the subject.

"You want to watch the movie? I hear it's that funny movie with Barbara Streisand and Ryan O'Neal—*What's Up Doc?*"

"Maybe later," Stump told him. "Right now I want to talk about what's eating you."

"What are you talking about?"

"Only you know. Something happened when you were away on R&R—something we need to talk about."

"There's nothing to talk about."

"Yes, there is," Willis said. "*Talk* to me. It's important for a pilot to keep himself mentally fit for the mission. You can't let personal problems get in your way when you're flying combat."

"There's nothing getting in my way."

"You can't convince me that's true," Stump told him as the waitress brought the beer. "I've known you too long. At least if you can't talk to me about it, go see Doc Hazlett."

Steve picked up his beer. "Let's go watch the movie," he said, as the projector started rolling. He got up and joined some of the other Navy pilots who were watching the movie at the other end of the room.

Long Binh, RVN, late the next morning

Eric Mohr, Brian Patton and Tom Zerbe were in the Long Binh Dustoff pilot's lounge shooting pool when Captain Duncan came in, accompanied by the Donut Dolly they had seen at Ton San Nhut Airport the day before.

"Mohr," Duncan said. "Get your stuff together. There'll be a helicopter from the 57th landing here in about fifteen minutes. You need to be on it when it leaves here."

Eric looked at his two buddies and shrugged. He hung up his pool cue and turned to go out the door, stopping long enough for Captain Duncan to introduce his companion. "This is Mattie Hill. She's stationed with the Red Cross at Navy Binh Thuy. She'll be riding down on the helicopter with you."

"Hi, Mattie," Eric greeted her.

Mattie extended her right hand. "Hello," she said. Being a product of the "Old South," Eric didn't like shaking hands with a woman using a man's handshake. Instead, he reached for her right hand with his left hand and gave it a gentle squeeze. Mattie smiled, recognizing the gesture, then turned her attention to the other two men who were approaching to be introduced. Eric went out the door to get his gear from the room where he had slept the previous night.

A few minutes later, Eric, Tom, Brian, Mattie and Captain Duncan stood outside of Dustoff Operations as a medevac

Huey landed at the Dustoff helipad. It made a ninety degree turn and hovered to a clear area between two revetments. There the pilot set the aircraft down with a slight bounce.

Captain Duncan started toward the ship, but stopped when the left seat pilot drew two fingers across his throat to signal they were going to shut down.

The Huey's engine speed decreased to flight idle. The medic and crew chief got out and stood beside the aircraft. The pilots remained in their seats, unfastening their seatbelts and shoulder harnesses and taking off their flight helmets, survival vests and flak jackets. After the required two-minute engine cool-down period, one of the pilots closed the throttle and cut off the fuel supply to the turbine engine. A minute or two later the big rotor blades coasted to a stop, and the pilots climbed out, piling their flight gear on their seats.

The aircraft commander was Chris Sanders, a tall 1st Lieutenant with a dark complexion, curly black hair and a friendly smile. The other pilot, a WO1, reminded Eric of a Texas cowboy. He was small and wiry, with a hint of a mustache and a faraway look in his eyes—not a Marlboro man, but still a cowboy. He was Gary Dickson. Mohr was not surprised when he learned during the introductions that Dickson was from El Paso. When Dickson turned around to walk back to the helicopter, Eric halfway expected to see his name engraved on the back of his belt.

Sanders sent his crew chief off to locate some transmission oil. The rest of them went over to the pilot's lounge to get a cold soft drink.

Thirty minutes later, Eric, Mattie and the Delta Dustoff crew were in the helicopter, en route to Navy Binh Thuy. Eric had said quick goodbyes to Tom and Brian, promising to keep in touch. Mattie sat in one of the crew chairs directly behind the pilots. Eric was put in one of the "hellhole" seats on the left side of the aircraft beside the transmission housing. It was his first time to ride in a Huey without the ear protection provided by a flight helmet. The sound was unbelievable. The high-pitched whine of the transmission added to the sound of the turbine engine and the beating rotor blades to produce a deafening roar.

The helicopter left Long Binh and skirted the southern edge of Saigon, following along the Saigon River for a while. Then the city was left behind and there was nothing as far as the eye could see but rice paddies and an occasional small village. The landscape was crisscrossed with irrigation canals laid out in straight lines, dug under the French administration in the late nineteenth century.

Conversation was next to impossible over the noise. It was just as well. Eric was separated from the others by the upright poles supporting the litters used for transporting patients. His isolation left him with nothing to do but gaze upon the countryside and think. He soon found himself thinking about his wife, Lynn. It was the first time since leaving San Francisco almost 48 hours earlier he had allowed himself to think about how difficult this year was going to be away from her. Now he was fighting an oncoming feeling of depression and despair. It was uninvited, yet he couldn't shake it.

He was 10,000 miles from his wife and his home and he couldn't go back until the Army let him. He was powerless to control his own destiny, making it even more important to trust God during the year ahead. He reminded himself of the Bible verses in the book of Philippians that had sustained him so often during flight school: *Do not be anxious about anything, but in everything, by prayer and petition, with thanksgiving, present your requests to God. And the peace of God, which tran-*

scends all understanding, will guard your hearts and your minds in Christ Jesus. He silently prayed to God to take the loneliness away and to give him a supernatural peace in its place.

Flying at 5,000 feet above the flat, treeless countryside, the reality of war seemed far away. Eric turned in his seat and studied the occupants in the Huey's cabin. He saw the girl, Mattie, talking with the crew chief. In front of them, in the cockpit, everything seemed routine as far as the pilots were concerned. Eric wished for a flight helmet—not only to block out the noise of the helicopter's engine and transmission, but so he could plug into the intercom and be part of the conversation.

Eric was loaded with questions. From time to time one of the pilots would change his ICS selector from intercom to one of the radio positions. Eric could see the pilot's lips move as he talked with someone on the ground. Were they in any danger? The flight *seemed* routine. In fact, except for the arrival at Tan Son Nhut and the medevac chopper landing at the 24th Evac helipad, nothing in Vietnam so far had seemed much different than the stateside military scene.

They had been flying not quite an hour when the helicopter began descending. Eric thought perhaps they had arrived at Navy Binh Thuy. He leaned forward in his seat to look out the big cargo bay doorway to see where they were headed. The Huey was on a long, shallow approach to a small compound on the northern bank of a river. This obviously wasn't the Navy airfield. It looked more like a refueling depot for Navy patrol boats.

When they landed, Eric was told it was a fuel stop called Nha Be and also a great place to eat at the Navy mess hall when the occasion warranted it.

The pilots remained in their seats with the engine at flight idle while the crew chief refueled the aircraft. The medic led

Eric and Mattie to a safe point approximately 50 feet away from the aircraft, where he told them to wait until they finished fueling.

Mattie turned to Eric. "Where are you from?" she asked.

"Shuqualak, Mississippi," he answered.

"Really!" Her eyes were wide with surprise.

"Yeah." Eric nodded and shrugged his shoulders, wondering what the big deal was.

"I'm from Livingston, Alabama!" she exclaimed, with a huge grin on her face.

"You're kidding," Eric said, fascinated. "We're practically neighbors. Did you go to college in Alabama?

"Graduated from the University of Alabama," she said. "How about you?"

"I went to Mississippi State, but didn't graduate."

"Hmm, good school," Mattie offered. "So, what do you think of Vietnam?"

"I don't know what to think," he said, honestly. "I've only been here a couple of days. I saw you at the airport yesterday morning when we got off the airplane."

"Yeah, my friend Eileen was supposed to be coming back from R&R, but she wasn't on the plane. I thought maybe she was on this morning's plane, but she wasn't there either. I don't know how I missed her. She's probably already in Navy Binh Thuy. I tried to call this morning, but I didn't get through to anybody."

"You can just pick up the phone and call?"

"Sure. We have phones. This is a modern war, you know. I mean we have helicopters, air conditioners, Coors beer and whatever else you might want. We may be fighting a war, but people here go to great lengths to make themselves comfortable when they can. Well, some of them do," she added with sadness in her voice. "I guess the grunts don't have it so good."

"How long have you been here?" Eric asked.

"Four months," Mattie answered. "It's been four great months. And I've made a lot of friends."

Something suddenly dawned on Mattie.

"Tell me your first name again." she said, touching the name tag above his left pocket and looking at it as if she was seeing it for the first time.

"Eric," he replied.

"You just came from Fort Sam, right?"

"Yes. Well, I went home on leave for a couple of weeks before coming over."

"Do you know a medic named Blake Sam?"

"Yeah. Do you know Blake?"

"Sure do."

"How?"

"He's stationed at the hospital near where I live."

"That's great," Eric said. "It will be good to see him again. But what made you ask if I knew him?"

"He's a Christian."

"Yes, I know." Blake had been part of a Bible study group Eric had attended regularly when he'd been at Fort Sam Houston. Blake left for Vietnam six weeks before Eric did.

"He told me—us, about a Christian Dustoff pilot he met at Fort Sam. He said you would be coming over soon."

"How did you know it was me?"

"Your name. It's spelled different than you would expect. It didn't dawn on me when I first met you, but just now I remembered that Blake told us your last name. Only I just assumed it was spelled M-o-o-r-e."

"Why was he talking about me?" Eric asked.

"I think he was pretty impressed with you," Mattie said. "He said you were very outspoken about believing in Jesus. He hoped when you came to Vietnam you would get to come to Navy Binh Thuy."

"You must be a Christian, too," Eric said.

"Oh, yes," she said, grabbing his arm and pulling him toward the helicopter where the crew chief was motioning for them to get back on board. "And you are here as an answer to prayer."

Mattie seemed to be genuine. Apparently there were others like her around. Eric silently asked God to help him seek them out. During most of his Army experience, he had met very few individuals who unashamedly and openly professed to be Christians.

When they reached Binh Thuy forty-five minutes later, Eric got a good view of the airfield from the air as the pilots circled to land from the south. Mattie, who had joined him in the hellhole after the refueling stop, described the lay of the land to Eric as they made their circuit. She had to shout in his ear to be heard over the sound of the helicopter's engine and transmission.

East of the runway, two large yellow hangars stood at the north end of the field. These were the Navy's maintenance hangars. Seven or eight gray OV-10 Broncos were parked in three rows of concrete revetments just south of the hangars. There were parking spaces for twenty of these aircraft in all. Two more of the OV-10s could be seen taxiing away from what appeared to be an armament loading station. Seeing these aircraft caused Eric's heart to beat faster with anticipation. Could it be that in all of Vietnam he was actually going to be stationed where Steve was? Captain Duncan did tell him that there were Navy OV-10s at another location called Vung Tau, but there was a good chance that Steve was stationed right here at Navy Binh Thuy!

There were other aircraft in the Navy area. Eight or ten black Hueys that looked like Charlie Model gunships were parked in smaller revetments just south of the OV-10s. Eric didn't understand why the helicopters were black and why they were parked at the Navy base of operations. He asked Mattie about them. "They're Seawolves," she told him. "Navy gunships." Eric nodded, though he didn't really understand. He'd never heard that the Navy used helicopter gunships.

The perimeter of the compound was easily distinguished by a high chainlink fence. Outside the fence were several rows of coiled concertina wire. The southeast quarter of the compound contained an ammunition storage area—several rows of underground bunkers with mounds of dirt piled on top of them, known locally as the ammunition dump. Mattie pointed out the Third Surgical (M.A.S.H.) Hospital, west of the runway, near midfield. The hospital was housed in a group of quonset huts. Just west of the hospital was a helipad marked with a bright red cross. Adjacent to the hospital, Eric was surprised to see a full-sized, above-ground swimming pool.

South of the hospital were several rows of two-story buildings. One section of these was the living quarters for the doctors and nurses from the hospital staff. Eric was pleased to learn the Dustoff pilots also occupied those quarters. The other section of buildings was the enlisted barracks.

In the same area were two white, 60-ft. house trailers and a number of one-story structures. Mattie pointed out the house trailers telling Eric that was where she and the other Donut Dollies lived. She also pointed out the PX, a large metal building facing the runway on the west side. Directly across the runway from the PX were the Dustoff facilities. One metal hangar and a couple of single-story buildings surrounded two rows of revetments made of concrete, approximately four feet high. Eight Hueys could be seen, all marked with the red crosses used to designate medical evacuation aircraft. An OH-58 Jet Ranger was parked alongside the runway. As they turned final, Eric noticed four more Hueys parked across from the Dustoff area. When they taxied by them after landing, he noticed these helicopters had Vietnamese markings. They also had the red cross markings of a medical evacuation aircraft.

As the Dustoff Huey cleared the runway, the two Navy OV-10s that had been taxiing out of the rearmament area moved into takeoff position on the runway.

THREE

Steve Cooper waited for the Dustoff Huey to clear the runway before calling the tower for takeoff clearance. "Navy Binh Thuy Tower, Black Pony One-One, flight of two, ready for departure."

"Black Pony One-One, altimeter two-niner-niner-seven, winds three-five-zero at eight knots, cleared for takeoff."

Steve taxied into position just to the left of the runway center line and applied his brakes. Stump Willis in Black Pony One-Two, taxied into position to his right and slightly behind him. "One-Two's ready," Willis called.

"Rolling," Steve advised and released his brakes. The two OV-10s rolled approximately half the length of the runway and broke ground together. Though they were heavy with fuel and armament, the powerful twin 715 horsepower Garrett turboprop engines propelled them skyward in excess of 2500 feet per minute.

"Black Pony One-One, contact Paddy Control, your discretion," the tower advised.

"Switching," Cooper responded. He moved his UHF radio selector switch to the number two position.

"Paddy Control, this is Black Pony One-One, flight of two, off of Navy Binh Thuy, en route whiskey sierra one-six-two-eight-eight-three, climbing to seven point five," he radioed, reading the mission coordinates from the briefing sheet clipped to the kneeboard strapped to his left thigh.

Ten miles west, inside an antenna-covered, olive drab trailer van at Air Force Binh Thuy, the radar controller working low altitude flights in the central sector of IV Corps responded to Black Pony 11's call. Leaning over his radar console, he searched for a new target near the Navy airfield.

"Black Pony One-One, squawk one-two-one-one and ident," he instructed.

Steve dialed in the discrete code on his aircraft's transponder and pressed the ident button. A blip representing Steve's aircraft momentarily brightened on the controller's radar display. The controller placed his finger on the blip to mark its position on the scope, then filled out a flight strip with the aircraft type and call sign, placing it on the status board to the right of his scope.

"Black Pony One-One, you are radar contact, ten miles northwest of Navy Binh Thuy," he advised the OV-10 pilot. "You have traffic at your seven o'clock position and three miles, two zoomies off Air Force Binh Thuy, now passing Angels Five and turning behind you. Should be no factor."

"Roger," Cooper replied.

"Black Pony One-One, say again your destination."

Steve checked the mission grid coordinates on his kneeboard again. "Whiskey-sierra-one-six-two-eight-eight-three," he responded.

"Stand by," the controller advised. He issued a command to the VNAF A-37s that had just passed behind the OV-10s, advising them to contact the high altitude controller on a different frequency. He then returned his attention to the Navy flight.

"Black Pony One-One, those coordinates are beyond my radar coverage. However, if you'll fly heading three-four-zero for approximately six-zero miles, that should put you in the general area."

Steve checked his map and concurred. They were headed to a small tributary of the Bassac River near the village of Chau Phu, on the Cambodian border. He glanced over his shoulder at Stump in the other aircraft. Stump gave him a thumbs up sign. They were now level at 7,500 feet, headed for a skirmish involving a Navy PBR that had followed several fleeing Viet Cong sampans up the small river after attempting to stop them on the larger Bassac River. It had been a trap. A few miles up the river, a VC ambush caught the Navy gunboat in a crossfire at close range. According to Steve's information, at least one US Navy patrol boat, and possibly two Vietnamese Monitors—small, but heavily armed and armored river patrol boats—were en route to help break up the firefight. The Seawolf helicopter gunships assigned to fly support for the PBRs had gone to Rach Gia to refuel and wouldn't be back in the area for at least forty minutes.

The firefight was in a narrow portion of the river with steep banks and high trees all around. The fixed wing aircraft wouldn't be able to get as close to their targets as the helicopters would have, but they were maneuverable and carried an impressive load of firepower. The patrol boat skipper was thankful they were on their way.

Before leaving Binh Thuy, Steve and Stump had each instructed their armorers to exchange their inboard rocket pods for 250 pound cluster bombs. If they weren't going to be able to make clear rocket runs at Charlie, they might be able to drop a load or two of bombs on them in a flyover.

Beneath the flight, a layer of broken clouds threatened visibility. But if the Ponies could get on station and find a break in the clouds, they would be able to work under them in close support of the patrol boats. The Bronco was well-suited for low and slow flight in tight places.

It would take about eighteen minutes for the Ponies to reach the site of the ambush. Steve called Stump on the tactical FM radio. "Let' go up the mission freq. Switching now."

A moment later, he attempted to contact the patrol boat on the tactical frequency he had been given by Flight Operations. "Delta Two, this is Black Pony One-One, over."

All he heard in reply was static. He recycled the radio frequency selector and tried again. "Delta Two, this is Black Pony One-One, over."

"Black Pony One-One, Delta Three copies. I think Two may be disabled. We're about ten minutes from his location. What's your position, over?"

"About one-five out," Steve replied.

"Push it if you can, Pony One-One. It sounded like they were in some pretty hot stuff when we last talked to them."

"Willco," Steve responded, willing his OV-10 to go faster. He eased over into a shallow dive, with Stump right on his wing. An agonizing fifteen minutes later, they were approaching visual range. The pilots had been monitoring the tactical channel used by the patrol boats. They knew the two Vietnamese Monitors were approaching and Delta Three had arrived at the site of the ambush. The original PBR was disabled with an undetermined number of injuries.

"Delta Three, this is Black Pony One-One. Do you have a medevac chopper en route for your wounded?"

"That's a negative, Black Pony, we haven't been able to communicate with Handlash Operations since we left the Bassac."

Handlash was the call sign of the Navy River Operations head-quarters at Binh Thuy.

Steve was concerned because he knew it would take a chopper at least forty-five minutes to get out there from Binh Thuy, maybe longer. "We'll give the Army Dustoff unit a call," he said. "Somebody give me a sitrep [situation report]. What do you need from us?"

"Stand by," he was told.

Stand by? They didn't know what they were doing down there. Obviously, the guys were shook. On his UHF radio, Steve said, "I'm going to take a look, Stump. You cover me from up here, and call the medevac request in."

"Wait, Steve. Let them mark a target for us. If we go in there shooting, we're liable to get some of the wrong guys."

"I'm not doing anything brash, Wingie. I just want to find out what's going on."

They could see the river, and Steve had found the coordinates on the map, but they didn't see any boats. Only short segments of the river were visible because of the rising terrain and high trees. There were low clouds, but they were scattered to broken and thin. Green jungle could be seen beneath them.

Steve planned to go over the river and descend through a hole in the clouds to try to locate the action. If he couldn't get one of the boats to mark targets for him, he would do it himself. After all, the Air Force and Marines used OV-10s as Forward Air Controller (FAC) aircraft. It was an ideal airplane for scouting out a situation.

He found a large hole in the cloud layer and punched through it. At approximately two hundred feet he leveled off, searching for signs of the firefight. He slowed the airplane to 100 knots and lowered 20 degrees of flaps for stability. The river snaked through the area in a series of "S" turns. The trees were approximately a hundred feet high and visibility on the river itself was generally less than a quarter of a mile because of the heavy jungle foliage.

"Any Delta, this is Black Pony One-One," Steve radioed on the Bassac River tactical radio frequency. "Can you give me a flare or smoke to mark your location."

"Black Pony One-One, smoke is out," came a reply after a slight hesitation. Steve searched but didn't see it.

"Behind you One-One," Willis called. "You've got goofy grape."

"Confirmed, Black Pony, it's purple smoke," came the call from the river boat. Cooper still didn't see it. He looked over both his shoulders, then brought the OV-10 around in a steep turn to the left.

Wham! Something hit his airplane. Immediately, there were two more hits. Wham! Wham! Steve jerked his plane upright and shoved the power levers forward. "I'm hit!" he yelled. Warning lights lit up his instrument panel like a Christmas tree. The right engine started losing oil pressure. From somewhere behind him, smoke was trickling into the cockpit.

Steve's first thoughts were to stabilize the airplane. His next thought, almost immediately thereafter, was to get the gunner who had shot him. He started pulling circuit breakers to isolate the fire. He raised the flaps and added more power. That's when he realized the right engine was smoking and oil pressure had dropped to zero. Pulling the right power lever past the detent, he feathered the prop. The plane was sinking, but as the increased power on the left engine took hold, the sink stopped. Steve started to turn back toward the area where he had been hit.

"Cooper, where are you going?" Stump yelled over the radio. "Get out of there!" As soon as he heard his wingman call that he had been hit, Willis started toward him in his own Bronco. What was important now was getting the crippled aircraft out of the hostilities and to a safe landing site. He couldn't believe Steve was turning back toward the area from which he had just taken fire.

"I'm going to get those sorry ..." Steve started. Suddenly, his aircraft shook violently as its side was raked by .51 caliber heavy machine-gun fire from the trees. His control stick was getting sloppy. Still, it was anger he felt more than fear. His airplane skewed to the right—towards the engine that he had shut down—and he saw flaming red tracers the size of baseballs coming at him from the trees. He was going down, but he would take that machine gunner with him. He armed his rocket launchers. Suddenly, his windshield was full of gray as Stump Willis dove in front of him, all four 7.62 machine guns blazing. Willis laid down heavy fire on the .51 cal's location, then followed up his machine-gun fire with a Zuni rocket that was right on target.

"Climb, Pony One-One, climb!" Willis yelled. "Drop your bombs now!" Willis was thinking for his wingman, who was letting himself be blinded by rage, even though he had his hands full with a crippled aircraft.

Steve shook out of it when he saw that Willis had destroyed the gun that had hit him. He turned his attention to flying his crippled aircraft, correcting the OV-10's trim and arresting its descent toward the river. He punched off the 250-pound bombs without arming them, allowing them to drop harmlessly in the water. The reduced weight enabled the OV-10 to begin a steady climb on its remaining good engine.

"Stump, you gotta stay and help those guys on the river," he told Willis.

"Getting you on the ground safely is the first priority, Buddy," Stump told him. Even as he said it, he was circling around to get a look at the damage done to Steve's airplane. Out of the corner of his eye he saw another PBR pull up beside the stricken one, his .50 caliber guns blazing toward a group of Viet Cong boats huddled against the western bank of the river.

"We've got things pretty well under control down here, Black Pony," Delta Three radioed. "If you've got some extra ordnance you want to get rid of, however, we could use it over against that river bank where we're concentrating our firepower."

"Go ahead, Stump," Steve said. "I've got things under control here."

"Get over to the Bassac, Steve, and follow it southeast. It's about forty miles to Long Xuyen."

Long Xuyen was the province capital, and it had a decent airstrip. Steve had already thought of it as a possible destination. He nursed his Bronco around to the correct heading. His airspeed was steady at 150 knots, and the left engine was holding. Fuel was leaking from somewhere, probably the right wing tank, outboard of the engine. Hopefully, he would have enough in the left tank to keep the one good engine running until he could reach a safe landing area. The navigation instruments were all out because of the fire and the pulled circuit breakers, but he had communications radios and engine instruments. He would make it.

Stump rolled in on the VC flotilla and let them have his remaining rockets and the 250 pounders. He got a cheer from the Navy river boats as he roared overhead. Then he joined up on Steve's right wing. What he saw made him sick.

"Pony One-One, slow your speed," he advised his wingman.

"What's up, One-Two?" Steve answered. "I'm afraid to go much slower with just one engine."

"I'm afraid you've got a lot more problems than that, buddy. Your right boom is nearly severed in two just ahead of the vertical stabilizer."

That news caused fear to grip Steve Cooper's heart for the first time. He was out of the heat of battle now. His airplane was crippled, but manageable. He thought he had it made. Now he knew that could change instantly.

The OV-10's twin tailbooms extend backwards from the engine nacelles and turn upwards into two vertical stabilizers. These are joined at the top by a single horizontal stabilizer, to which is attached the elevator used to raise and lower the aircraft's nose. Damage from the .51 caliber machine gun had nearly severed Cooper's right empennage, just ahead of the vertical stabilizer. The only thing that appeared to be holding it together was one or two of the aluminum stringers that provided support along the length of the boom. If it came apart, or even buckled, the OV-10 would be uncontrollable. It might not even be possible to eject safely.

"Steve, you'd better get out of there while you can," Willis told him.

Steve looked back trying to see the damage, but that portion of his airplane was blocked from his view by the engine nacelle. Bailing out over the jungle was not an option he wanted to pursue. At least not while he still had a measure of control.

"Let's see what happens," he told his wingman. "Is there any place closer than Long Xuyen where we can land?"

"Not that I can find," Stump replied. "Look, buddy, you hang in there. I'm going to get on the radio and get us some help. I'll be right back with you. If it gets shaky, you get out of there. You hear me?"

"Roger."

Willis wanted some help for his wingman and he wanted it right away. He had already called in a Dustoff mission and knew the Army medevac chopper should be en route to the ambush site to assist the wounded men on the PBR. He considered trying to divert them to Long Xuyen, but knew that would be selfish and unadvised at this time. Instead, he called Paddy Control and told the controller they had an emergency, then contacted Black Pony Operations on his FM radio.

"Pony Ops, this is Black Pony One-Two," he called. He continued to monitor guard and the Paddy Control frequency on his UHF radio, in case Steve needed him.

"Black Pony One-Two, this is operations," came the clear voice from Navy Binh Thuy.

"Ops, Pony One-One has been hit. His right engine is shut down and he has extensive damage to the right empennage. We're en route to Long Xuyen and we're going to need security and possibly medical help there as quickly as possible."

"Has Pony One-One sustained any injuries?"

"Stand by." Then, on the air-to-air frequency, "Steve, are you okay?"

"Yeah," Cooper responded.

"He's okay," Willis reported.

A few seconds later, Operations called again. "Black Pony One-Two, this is Ops. Pony One-Seven and Two-Three are on their way in here." Black Pony 17 was the squadron maintenance officer, Lieutenant Commander Jason Brandt. Pony 23 was Jake Herring, the squadron instructor pilot and probably the most experienced aviator on the airfield. The knowledge and experience in their collective heads would be valuable—if they made it to Operations in time. Meanwhile, Stump Willis was concerned about how much time his wingman might have before the Bronco came apart in the air. As a one-engine performer, the OV-10 was all right. Minus a tailboom, it would be nothing more than a collection of aluminum parts. He wanted Cooper out of there. But there were problems. Afternoon showers were developing and the clouds below them now obscured much of the terrain. They were level at fifteen hundred feet—the low clouds beneath them wouldn't give Steve much of an opportunity to pick a safe landing place after an ejection.

"Pony One-One, let's get some altitude and turn south where we can find some rice paddies."

"Okay, Stump." Despite his efforts to stay calm, Cooper's voice was beginning to sound strained. He wasn't really struggling with the plane. He had used the aileron trim to relieve the pressure of the wing loading as he banked slightly into the good engine. He had also cranked in a healthy dose of rudder trim and the airplane was holding its own. He started a steady climb, easing the nose up and adding a little more power on the good engine.

"Steady, Coop," Willis told him. "Don't make any abrupt control movements."

Steve acknowledged with a double-click of his transmit button.

Willis was starting to call Ops for an update on some help coming their way when his radio crackled. "Black Pony One-Two, this is One-Seven."

"Go ahead One-Seven," Stump answered.

"Give me a description of the damage to One-One's aircraft." Willis described to Commander Brandt what he could see of the damage to Cooper's airplane. Brandt conferred with Jake Herring and they came back with a verdict.

"Pony One-One, can you hear me?" Jake Herring called.

Steve could hear him, but when he tried to transmit on the FM radio, all they could hear was static. Willis called him on the UHF.

"Coop, your FM transmitter is apparently out. Can you read them?"

"That's affirmative," Steve responded, but his voice sounded weak. That radio was going, too. Willis dropped down below Cooper's aircraft for a look and could immediately see the reason. The FM antenna was dangling in the wind. The UHF antenna appeared to be intact, but there were large holes in the aircraft fuselage near the radio access panel. Who could tell what kind of damage had been done in there. He reported what he found to Black Pony Operations at Binh Thuy.

"Tell him to get out of there," Jake Herring instructed. "He's riding a loose cannon. If that boom severs, he will snap inverted and won't be able to get out. Tell him to get out now."

"Roger," Willis replied. "What have you got coming this way for search and rescue?"

"We're talking to Paddy Control on the land line," Herring told him. "They've got a fix on your emergency squawk. Two Seawolves are en route from Rach Gia to your location and two Ponies that were on Patrol near Sa Dec are heading your way for security. There's also an Army Dustoff ship en route to the PBR site. He'll be monitoring Paddy Control and will offer assistance if necessary."

"Steve, did you copy all that?" Stump asked his wingman. He thought he heard a two-click response, but he wasn't sure.

In his Bronco, Steve Cooper was making his own assessment of the situation. He appreciated all the help being offered by his squadron mates, but it was his responsibility to bring that plane back if he could and to make the final determination about what emergency action he should take.

The idea of bailing out from low altitude with a low cloud deck beneath him, and below that nothing but jungle, didn't appeal to him. Several miles to the south, he could see the Seven Sisters—the only mountains in all of IV Corps. They were seven small mountains—the tallest of which was twenty-three-hundred feet—rising up out of the surrounding rice paddies in the western part of Long Xuyen province. Steve knew the area around the Seven Sisters from working search and destroy missions with the US Army Special Forces. The mountains themselves were crawling with VC base camps and storage caches. But the rice paddies around them would be a fairly safe place to land during daylight hours. He could be picked up by the Seawolves or the Army medevac chopper a whole lot easier if he could get over those rice paddies. He turned south and continued his climb. He was now passing through two thousand feet.

Suddenly the left rudder pedal, against which he was holding steady pressure, gave way. His foot slammed against the forward firewall and the Bronco started skewing to the right. Then something else snapped! The Bronco pitched violently, then rolled inverted. Without hesitating, Cooper reached between his legs and pulled the handle on his ejection seat. The canopy blew and he was thrown straight down beneath the out-of-control OV-10, which was entering an inverted flat spin.

Willis saw it all. It happened so fast, he didn't have a chance to yell out a warning. Then he saw the ejection seat break loose and Cooper was hurled toward the ground. Stump banked to the right to avoid Cooper's spinning OV-10 and keyed his mike, "One-One's ejected. He's out of there. There's no chute yet!" He held his breath, waiting for the automatic deployment of Cooper's parachute. The ejection seat was upside down. He didn't know what would happen.

For Steve Cooper, things were happening in slow motion. He knew the tailboom had snapped and that his OV-10 had rolled inverted. He had no choice but to eject, but the ejection seat was not designed for an upside down ejection. As he was catapulted downward, he could see the clouds beneath him as if he were right on top of them. In reality, he had several hundred feet to go before he entered the cloud cover, but it was hard to judge the distance above the white background. He heard, then felt his chute deploy as it snapped in the wind. It jerked him upright just before he entered the clouds and the ejection seat fell away. He was totally disoriented in the clouds.

After a short ride through the white nothingness, it grew dark beneath him—trees! He grabbed at his shroud lines and spun around, looking for a place to land. Slightly to his right, he located a small clearing. He twisted and pulled and managed to steer in that direction. But he didn't make it. His feet struck the top of a tree, a branch caught his ankle and he was flipped face first into the foliage. The chute caught in the wind and drug him across the treetops for approximately ten yards before he came to rest in the tops of the trees. His right ankle was wedged in a fork in a tree limb and his right arm twisted behind him. With his left arm he managed to grab the knife from his survival vest and begin hacking away at the shroud lines, trying to cut himself free from the parachute.

He heard his plane crash a short distance away. He could hear Stump's OV-10 circling overhead, but he couldn't see it through the clouds. What he really needed was a helicopter, and to get on the ground. His arm hurt, and he had to get his ankle free.

FOUR

Navy Binh Thuy Airfield - that same afternoon

Most people wouldn't consider the control tower at Navy Binh Thuy Airfield an exciting place to spend an afternoon. But that is where CW2 Les Winters spent much of his time. He justified the time spent in the tower each day as part of his job as the Aviation Safety Officer for Binh Thuy's two medevac detachments. The real reason he hung out in the tower was to hide. His favorite nighttime hiding place was a bottle of Jack Daniels.

Winters considered himself a misplaced warrior, and he never missed an opportunity to make that fact known to anyone who would listen. He was a career soldier on his third tour in Vietnam. His first tour was in 1965 as a grunt. He returned in 1968 as a gunship pilot, flying Charlie Model Hueys in the Central Highlands. This time he arrived in country with an intense hatred for North Vietnamese and the Viet Cong. The hatred carried over to most South Vietnamese as well, including women and children. In Winters' mind, even they couldn't be trusted. He wanted to kill, maim, and destroy. He wanted to fly a gunship through the Central Highlands, flushing out Viet Cong strongholds and amassing a body count that would make any warrior envious. He wanted to prove that American fliers were a force to be reckoned with and to avenge his comrades killed during his last two tours. But he was stuck in Binh Thuy as a Safety Officer for a bunch of medevac pilots who flew around in unarmed Hueys, saving lives rather than destroying them.

That he came through his earlier tours unscathed remained a mystery to Les Winters. There were times he thought he was going to die. He saw grunts, pilots and crewmembers fall all around him, yet he came through mission after mission untouched. The thought sometimes crossed his mind that some higher power might have a plan or a purpose for his life. But when he considered what he had become, that thought seemed ludicrous, especially when so many better men had died and he was still alive.

When Winters learned he was being assigned to a medevac unit, he reported in with his orders in one hand and a request for transfer in the other. He made no bones about the fact he didn't want to be there. He was a warrior. He wanted to take lives, not save them.

But the Delta Dustoff units needed an Aviation Safety Officer, and after serving a tour as a primary flight instructor at Fort Wolters, Les Winters had attended the Aviation Safety Officer course at the University of Southern California, compliments of the US Army. The Army's plans to collect on that education included sending him to Vietnam as an Aviation Safety Officer. When he arrived in Vietnam, Binh Thuy was where they needed one. Binh Thuy was where he was sent, like it or not.

He didn't like it. He didn't like the Dustoff pilots and consequently, they found it hard to like him. He did nothing to learn the mission and swore he had no interest in ever making aircraft commander in a Dustoff unit.

For the most part, he kept to himself. But one of the young aircraft commanders, a young warrant officer from Virginia, was just too friendly and outgoing to be put off by Winters' belligerence. Stuart Chambers pressed in through Winters' defensive outer shell, and the two men became friends.

By October, 1971, Chambers had been in country for a little over six months. A natural flier who quickly gained the respect of his fellow pilots, he had been recommended for aircraft commander after just three months in country. He passed his AC checkride with flying colors, and became Dustoff 79.

After that, Stu began to change, taking what some considered unnecessary risks. He appeared consumed with the idea of completing any mission assigned to him, regardless of the circumstances. After flying as Chambers' peter pilot on a few missions, Les Winters reported to the Operations Officer, 1st Lieutenant Wade Daugherty, that Chambers was an accident waiting to happen.

Since Winters had done nothing to gain credibility with Daugherty, the Operations officer dismissed his concerns about Chambers as coming from a bitter, drunken has-been. Chambers continued to fly as an aircraft commander and was never put up for review by the unit IP.

The afternoon of October 28, Winters was in the tower as usual, watching traffic come and go. Things were generally quiet until Black Pony 11 ejected in the western part of Long Xuyen province.

VNAF Dustoff flights had been coming and going throughout the afternoon; some with Americans riding peter pilot and some with all Vietnamese crews. The transition to all-Vietnamese crews was gradually becoming a reality—at least during daylight hours. The Third-Up US Dustoff crew, which had left early in the morning on a patient transfer mission to Long Binh, returned mid-afternoon with a couple of passengers, a Donut Dolly and a replacement Dustoff pilot.

Navy Seawolf helicopters flew in and out all afternoon, refueling and rearming between sorties flown in support of the Navy's river patrol boats. The Black Pony OV-10s were in and out as well. They were covering river patrols and conducting search and destroy operations over the U Minh Forest with the Army.

Civilian operations were also a part of the typical daily routine at Navy Binh Thuy. A Shorts Skyvan operated by Continental Air Service made regularly scheduled passenger stops and package drop-offs each day around four o'clock. Continental also flew smaller twin-engine Dorniers, which operated more like charter operations. The Dornier had an unusual and distinctive look about it that took some getting used to. Unlike most twin-engine airplanes, the Dornier's engines were not mounted on the wings. Instead they were mounted on their own pylons that extended out of the side of the fuselage. The wings were above them, providing a parasol effect.

Air America, the CIA's airline, also a frequent user of the airport, contributed to the traffic as several of their blue and silver Hueys and fixed wing, turbine-powered Pilatus Porters came in for passenger drops or pickups. The Porters operated almost like helicopters, such was their short field takeoff and landing capability. Winters, who liked aircraft much better than he liked people, never tired of watching the air traffic come and go.

Navy Binh Thuy was also headquarters to a US Army Engineering Battalion, which had an OH-58 helicopter used to fly engineers to the various construction sites around the

Delta. The OH-58 left Binh Thuy a little after four o'clock for a look at a facility under construction a few miles up the river west of the airfield. It returned a few minutes later. The pilot told the Binh Thuy Tower controller the weather was too bad out that way for his passengers to get a good look at what they wanted to see.

The First-Up Dustoff crew received an emergency medical evacuation mission around four-thirty. The call came from the Navy, and was a request for assistance in evacuating wounded personnel from a PBR that had been ambushed near the Cambodian border. The aircraft commander was Stu Chambers, Dustoff 79. Soon after Dustoff 79 switched to the Paddy Control frequency, things began to get busy on the various radio monitors that were in the tower. Chambers and his crew were headed in the same direction as the OH-58 pilot who had turned around a few minutes earlier because of the deteriorating weather.

In the tower, a number of radio monitors were tuned to various channels that helped the tower personnel maintain an awareness of any events that might lead to a sudden increase in air traffic activity. One radio was tuned to the Paddy Control frequency used by the Air Force air traffic controllers to work the local sector, which included Navy Binh Thuy, Air Force Binh Thuy and Can Tho Army Airfield. Tactical FM radios monitored the operations frequencies used by Dustoff Operations, the Navy Black Ponies and the Seawolves. These radios operated quietly in the background, but served to give the on-duty controller advance warning of any tactical emergency flights that would originate from, or terminate at, Navy Binh Thuy.

Dustoff crews often received emergency medevac missions that required immediate departures with little or no prior notice. Also, many times during the day and night they dropped off patients at the Third Surgical Hospital helipad, which was located a few hundred yards west of the runway. The Dustoff pilots always called the hospital when they were a few minutes out to alert them about incoming wounded. The tower personnel were accustomed to clearing the traffic pattern when they heard priority one missions being called in on the Dustoff tactical FM channel.

Les Winters listened as Chambers picked up his mission details from Dustoff Operations a minute or two after becoming airborne. He knew Chambers would not have taken the time to get an updated weather briefing before departing on this mission, which had been called in as "urgent." The "urgent" designation, as opposed to "priority" or "routine," was used to indicate imminent loss of life or limb. The Dustoff radio in the tower had no transmitter, so Winters could not communicate to the Dustoff aircraft commander about the weather conditions out west that might prohibit him from safely completing his mission. Winters told the tower operator to pass the information along, but Dustoff 79 switched his UHF radio to the Paddy Control frequency before the tower operator had a chance to advise him.

Oh, well, it's nearly five o'clock, anyway, Winters rationalized. Time to go to the O' Club. Part of him was concerned that Stu Chambers might try something heroic, but stupid, and put his crew in danger. That part of him wanted to go to the RTO shack at Dustoff Operations on the other side of the runway, pick up the radio, and advise the young pilot about the weather conditions in the direction he was headed and caution him to be careful. But the cynical part of him figured Chambers would do what he wanted to do anyway, regardless of a warning from Safety Six. The cynic was winning the struggle and Winters was about to leave the tower when he heard Paddy Control acknowledge Black Pony 12's emergency transponder squawk and his announcement that Black Pony 11 had ejected.

Paddy Control's frequency became busy as Seawolves and Black Ponies were vectored to the point of last radar contact. Paddy Control also advised Dustoff 79 of the approximate grid coordinates. Winters stayed in the tower to follow the action.

Eric Mohr was oblivious to his brother-in-law's plight. For him the afternoon was filled with names, faces and impressions that would take him a while to put together. A few of the Dustoff pilots had been in Dustoff Operations when Eric arrived. Others were about their duties, either flying missions or working in the supply room, the hangar, or resting up for night duty. Around five o'clock, they all began to congregate in the Operations office as the normal work day drew to a close and the night crews prepared to take over.

Though everyone was friendly to Eric, he felt like an outsider. He sensed a camaraderie among the aircrews, both officers and enlisted men, and knew he was not part of it. There was a clear, though unspoken, distinction between his green inexperience and their seasoned understanding of the place, the time and the mission. No one said or did anything to make him feel like an outsider, he just did. He was an unknown; they knew each other very well. They were like family—laughing, joking, chiding one another and sharing anecdotes and experiences about which he had no knowledge.

They were kidding one of the pilots about getting chased out of a hot LZ by a tornado. Were they serious? Were they talking about a weather phenomenon, or was that some kind of weapon Eric was yet to face?

It would take time for Eric to find his footing with this group. In the days, weeks and months ahead, he would have to prove himself. Would he be able to do it? What would they think about his Christian testimony and his belief that he was in Vietnam on a God-ordained mission and that the US government had only served as an instrument to get him here?

A little after five, the night First-Up crew indicated they were going to the Navy mess hall to eat before it was time for them to preflight their helicopter and check the mission board for their missions. Sanders and Dickson, the two pilots who flew Eric down from Long Binh that afternoon, offered to take him over to the BOQ (Bachelor Officer Quarters) to find a room and stow his gear before they went to eat. They borrowed the CO's jeep and drove around the end of the runway and halfway back up the other side, where they stopped in front of a two-story, unpainted wooden building.

"Here it is," Chris told him. "Home."

The building looked like a rustic motel you might find at a ski resort in the Rocky Mountains. A concrete walkway went along both sides of the building and a full-length balcony extended down each side of the second story. There were twenty rooms on each floor, ten on each side. A latrine at the center of each floor doubled as a pass-through to get from one side of the building to the other. On the north side of the building, a stairway went up to the second story balcony. At each end of the building stood a concrete bunker about ten feet square and six feet tall, similar to the above-ground storm shelters you often see beside farmhouses in the American Midwest.

Around the base of the building, dirt-filled rocket canisters stood on end to make a four-foot high wall to offer some protection in the event of a rocket or mortar attack.

Dickson explained the living arrangements. "Most of the Dustoff pilots live in this building," he said, indicating the southernmost building. Between that building and the hospital were two more buildings, built from the same plans. Beyond the farthest one was the hospital. "Some doctors and nurses live in this building," Gary said, "but most of them live in the other two buildings." He thought again. "No, that's not true. For the most part, we have the upstairs in this building and the hospital people have the downstairs, but it doesn't have to be that way. It just kind of worked out that way. In each of the buildings, the women use the downstairs latrine, the men use the one upstairs, regardless of which floor they live on. There are three empty rooms in this building, two upstairs and one downstairs. You can claim whichever one you want."

They showed Eric the downstairs room first. There wasn't much to it, just an empty room with unpainted plywood walls. There was a hole in the outside wall where an air conditioner had once been. All of the occupied rooms seemed to have air conditioner window units that dripped puddles of condensation on the walkways. A green, mossy slime extending a few inches up the wall grew in those spots where the water dripped.

Upstairs, the first room they looked at was right at the top of the stairway. Eric liked it immediately. An elevated bunk against the west wall had a built-in seating area beneath it. There was a ceiling fan in the center of the room. A couple of bookshelves were on the back wall, easily reached from the bed. A small table stood against the east wall and there was even a chair.

The room was next door to the latrine, which Eric thought was an advantage. (He didn't know yet how early some of the pilots got up in the morning, how late they came in at night, or how thin the walls were.) The room's walls were also covered with unpainted plywood. A bamboo curtain hung on one of them, providing a wallpaper effect. The wall facing the sidewalk had a cutout for an air conditioner, but the hole was empty.

"What's the deal with the air conditioners?" Eric asked.

"Over at Engineering there's a guy who rebuilds them out of spare parts," Chris answered. "That's where everybody gets them. He charges about a hundred and fifty dollars for one and it's well worth it. When people leave, they sell theirs back to him and he sells it to the next guy. He's got himself quite a business going."

"I can imagine," Eric replied. His Nomex flight suit was dripping with perspiration and already chafing him under his arms. The little ceiling fan over the bunk didn't look like it would stir up much air. "So I can buy one?" he asked.

"Sure, we'll take you over there tomorrow," Chris replied. "I doubt he's there now."

Eric pretty much knew this was the room he wanted, but figured he might be surprised by the other one. "Let's go look at the other room," he said.

"It's on the other side near the end," Dickson said. They walked through the latrine, which had a screen door on either end. Along the right wall were sinks with mirrors. On the left was a row of commode stalls and an open shower with six shower heads. They went through to the other side and turned right. On this side of the building were the two white mobile homes Mattie had pointed out to him from the air. They were parked perpendicular to the BOQ building.

"That's where the Donut Dollies live," Chris told him as they walked along the balcony toward the end.

They stopped outside a bright red door, second from the end. Dickson jerked open the door, which stuck slightly, and motioned for Eric to look inside. The room was a mess! Trash covered the floor and the walls were painted in wild psyche-delic patterns of bright yellow and red.

"The last guy who lived in here was a 'Jesus freak,'" Dickson told him. "He was pretty weird—not your typical Dustoff pilot. He got busted for smoking marijuana. I think he's in the clink up at Long Binh. He was sure one weirdo."

Great, Eric thought. *Here I am trying to be a Christian witness and the last guy through here who called himself a Christian was a marijuana-smoking hippie. I wonder what they'll think of me when they find out what I believe?*

"I'll take the room on the other side by the latrine," Eric told him.

"Good choice," Sanders told him. "My room is right next door. I was thinking about moving into that one myself."

"You can have it."

"That's all right. I really don't want to go to the trouble of moving my air conditioner and refrigerator."

"You've got a refrigerator?"

"Yeah, most of us do. You can buy them at the PX for about a hundred dollars."

"Good deal." This place wasn't going to be bad at all.

After Eric put his belongings in the room, they drove around the airfield to the Navy mess hall where they had a meal of fried chicken, mashed potatoes and a variety of veg-etables. The meal was as good as you would find anywhere.

While at the mess hall, Eric looked around for signs of Steve or any other Navy pilots who might know Steve or could tell Eric where to find him. Maybe the timing was off, but there weren't many Navy people eating. There were no pilots that he could see. The Dustoff pilots ate rather quickly and headed back to the BOQ.

David B. Freeman

Eric was anxious to write Lynn and tell her about his assignment. He figured it would be at least ten days before he received any of her letters. That thought made him miss her even more. He sat down at the small table and started a letter, explaining to Lynn his first impressions of Binh Thuy. He wrote there was a good chance he would see Steve. Then somebody knocked. He put down his pen and opened the door.

The man standing there was a 1st Lieutenant. The name "Harris" was on his shirt, but Eric didn't remember his first name. He had noticed earlier that all the officers seemed to be on a first name basis. Even the two commanding officers, Captain Aubrey Scott and Captain Terry Green, were called by their first names.

Harris was tall and lanky, with a thin crop of slicked-down brown hair. His eyes said this place was a joke, he was too good for it, but he tolerated it anyway.

"Let's go," he said.

"Go? Go where?" Eric asked.

"To your initiation party. Where do you think? You didn't think you were going to get out of drinking the 'Green Mother,' did you?"

"Get out of drinking *what*? I don't even know what you're talking about."

"Well come on," Harris said. "You'll find out soon enough. By the way, I'm Hank Harris. You met me this afternoon in the supply room, but you probably don't remember."

"I remember meeting you. Thanks for helping me remember your name."

"You'll get to know us soon. We're a pretty tight bunch."

"So I gathered."

Eric really wanted to finish his letter, but he didn't want to appear anti-social his first day there. He reached for his flight suit shirt, which was hanging on the bedpost and put it on. "Okay. Let's go," he said, tucking in his shirttail and putting on his cap.

"That's got to go," Harris said, pointing to Eric's cap.

"I noticed you guys all wear maroon hats with 57th Med patches on them. Where can I get one?"

"Downtown Can Tho," Harris replied. "We'll take you there tomorrow so you can get one."

He was already halfway down the stairs. Eric followed, wondering what was ahead of him.

Long Xuyen Province

With the darkness settling in, Steve realized he wasn't going to get out of the jungle that night. His survival radio battery was getting weak, Pony 12 had returned to Vung Tau because of weather and fuel, and the Seawolves had given up on finding him beneath the low-hanging clouds. At least he was on the ground and in one piece. His ankle was twisted and wouldn't carry him very far, and his right shoulder was dislocated, but no bones were broken.

Steve slowly made his way toward the clearing he had seen when breaking out of the clouds. He found a place at the edge of the clearing under some brush, and after checking as carefully as he could for snakes, settled in to wait out the night. Charlie might be around; he might not. If anyone had heard or seen the OV-10 crash nearby and seen the parachute, they would be looking for him. He knew the Viet Cong paid handsome rewards for an American flier.

What he didn't know was that an ARVN Ranger patrol with a US Special Forces advisor was en route to his location on foot. They had observed his crash and his parachute from the side of Dop Chompa, the highest of the Seven Sisters, and had started his way immediately. They had approximately six kilometers to cover, much of it through bad guy territory.

When Pony 12 checked out, promising to be back at first light, Steve turned off his survival radio to conserve its battery. It had been off for nearly an hour and he had almost made himself comfortable for the night, when the unmistakable sound of a Huey's rotor blades could be heard south of his location. He had flares and he had the radio. Maybe one of the Seawolves had come back to get him. If he could make contact, he was sure the Huey could hover down into the clearing near where he was hiding. He reached in his survival vest pocket and pulled out the small handheld UHF radio.

"Aircraft near the Seven Sisters, this is Black Pony One-One," he called out on 243.0, the international aircraft emergency frequency.

"Pony One-One, this is Dustoff Seven-Nine," came the immediate, but weak reply.

"Dustoff! Boy am I glad to hear you," Steve spoke quietly into the UHF microphone, not wanting to attract the attention of any bad guys who might be looking for him. The Dustoff pilots were also not aware of the ARVN Ranger team who was looking for the downed pilot. The Dustoff Mission was not one that had been requested through channels, but one undertaken by the Dustoff aircraft commander on his own.

After picking up the wounded PBR personnel and dropping them off at the Third Surg, Chambers had decided to refuel and have a look for the downed Navy flier himself. He "hot refueled" without shutting down, then headed back up the river, informing Dustoff Operations he was just going for a "look see." When he departed Navy Binh Thuy, his crew's shift was scheduled to end in fifteen minutes. Now, he was approaching the area of the Seven Sisters after receiving radar vectors toward the vicinity of the downed aircraft from Paddy Control. The weather was really giving the helicopter pilots a problem. They were in and out of clouds, but the fact they were in radar contact with Paddy boosted Chambers' confidence.

"Can you hear our helicopter?" Chambers asked the downed flier. "How far away from you are we?"

"I can hear you. It sounds like you're a couple of clicks south of me," Steve replied.

"Can you mark your position for us?"

"I've got flares and the homing signal on the radio."

"Unable the homing signal," Chambers told him. The Army didn't have the capability to home in on emergency radio transmitters. That was a privilege that belonged to Air Force Search and Rescue, who were in full force up north where the fighters flew against Hanoi, but non-existent in the Delta. "The flares will do, though," he continued. "If you think I'm close enough, go ahead and pop one now."

Steve eased out from under the brush and into the clearing. He pulled the small flare handle out of his vest and mounted one of the red signal flares to it. He pulled back the sliding firing pin, pointed the flare gun into the air over the clearing and let the firing pin go. The flare shot up like a roman candle and burned for fifteen or twenty seconds before fizzling out.

"Flare's out," Steve called as soon as he fired it. The clouds were thick above and around it and Steve doubted it could be seen very far.

"No joy," came the answer a few seconds later. "Give me a direction to fly toward you and we'll try again when we get a little closer."

"Okay, fly north," Steve replied, "I was a couple of miles north of the Seven Sisters when I bailed out."

"That'll help us," Dustoff Seven-Nine told him. "We're talking to Paddy Control and they can help us with the coordinates, as long as they don't lose us on radar. They probably will if we get too low."

"Roger."

Steve turned off his radio to save battery power and sat back to wait. One minute he imagined he could hear the ship getting closer, the next it sounded like it was moving away. Maybe it was flying around in circles. He had a dozen flares. He decided to fire another one. He shot it straight up, then turned his radio back on to listen for the Dustoff ship's call. He heard something on the radio; it was very weak and he couldn't make it out. He held the radio up to his ear and keyed the mike. "Dustoff Seven-Nine, this is Black Pony One-One, how do you read?"

Silence. Off in the distance the sound of the Huey's engine increased, like it was pulling more power, like it was climbing or something. Then, there was the unnerving sound of something big and fast hitting the trees, followed by a loud whoomph, like an explosion or a flash fire, then silence.

"Dustoff Seven-Nine, how do you read?" The survival radio battery was gone. Steve leaned back against a tree and slipped into a sitting position, the realization of what had just happened making him sick to his stomach. As he put his head between his legs, a hand touched his shoulder.

FIVE

Navy Binh Thuy

The hospital O' Club was dark, packed and noisy when Eric Mohr and Hank Harris entered. A Gordon Lightfoot tune played in the background. The bar stools were full of patrons. The bulk of the room was filled with round tables, four or five chairs at each. Few of the chairs were vacant.

"All right! Our Newby is here!" came a shout from near the bar as Hank made his way to a table near the center of the room with Eric in tow. Several of the pilots moved aside to make room for them. Noting a distraction at the bar, Eric turned to see what was going on. The bartender was mixing up some kind of drink and everyone at the bar seemed to be giving him instructions, which he was apparently ignoring. It was of no interest to Eric, since he didn't drink. He turned his attention elsewhere, surveying the room for familiar faces.

Mattie Hill sat at one of the tables. Her companions were all female—probably the rest of the Donut Dollies. Most of the Dustoff pilots Eric had met that afternoon were present in the room. Eric figured the other patrons to be doctors and nurses from the Third Surg.

Both of the Dustoff commanding officers were there. Eric had been impressed by his short exposure to the two COs. They seemed to be down-to-earth guys. As he watched Captain Scott's interaction with his men, he pegged him as a reserved, but apparently respected leader. He was in his 30's, sandy-colored, thinning hair, hazel eyes, tough and wiry looking. John Denver's *Almost Heaven* came on in the background and Scott yelled out, "God's country!" From that, Eric surmised he was from West Virginia.

Terry Green, the CO of the 82nd, was a different man altogether. He was short in stature. He was also short in country, with something like a month to go. The men had been kidding him about going off flight status since he was so short. It was obvious Green was well-liked by his men. His face was friendly and open, his green eyes full of amusement. He had a thick shock of blonde hair, almost too long by military standards.

At the end of the bar, a CW2 sat with his shoulders hunched over his drink. A maroon Dustoff hat sat on the bar in front of him. He sat alone in the midst of a crowd. He was older than many of the others and almost bald. Eric's gaze stopped on him, and he wondered, *Have I met this guy yet?* The man returned Eric's gaze with a look that said, *heaven help you.*

What's his problem? Eric thought. Maybe the man was plastered. Was he by himself because he chose to be? In reality, Les Winters had only been there a few minutes and had just started drinking. He had stayed in the tower until the Navy called off the search for their downed flier for the night and Dustoff 79 reported he had successfully evacuated the wounded personnel from the PBR.

Winters was expecting Stu Chambers and his peter pilot, Ernie Baker, to show up at the club after getting off duty. Any minute now they should be walking in the door. This gathering was not only a welcome for the new Warrant Officer, but a send-off for Jerry Grant, one of the 82nd pilots who was DEROSing (Date of Expected Return from Overseas) the next day.

Grant had been the subject of a number of toasts since the party began. Now the attention was turned toward the newby, Eric Mohr. A group of Dustoff pilots with K. J. Madison in the lead, made their way through the crowd to the table where Eric was sitting. K. J., who had taken the lead in showing Eric around Dustoff Operations earlier in the day, was carrying the "Green Mother," a large glass filled with who-knows-what. The drink was unmistakably green. That was when Eric realized this was the drink the bartender had been mixing amidst much coaching. He felt trapped.

K. J. put a hand on his shoulder. "Stand up, newby," he said. Instead of standing, Mohr leaned back in his chair and looked at K. J. with a "what's this all about" look.

"This," Madison explained, "is a 'Green Mother.' It's the traditional welcoming drink for all new pilots in this outfit. You're supposed to chug it."

I don't drink, Eric thought, and he started to say it. But when he looked around the room, all eyes were on him, and they were full of expectancy. He caught Mattie's eye. She was smiling in anticipation along with the rest of them. So much for the look of disapproval from a fellow Christian that would have given him an out. What the heck, he thought. He made a quick mental assessment of his options. He could refuse the drink and come across as a goody-goody, but would that really help his witness? He had no alcoholic tendencies, so it wasn't something he was afraid of in a spiritual sense. During his early college days when he did drink, he found he had a pretty good tolerance for alcohol. It took a lot to make him feel drunk, so this drink probably wouldn't affect him very much. He reached for the drink. K. J. pulled it back.

"Stand up," he said, and the command was echoed by several others. As he stood, K. J. stood beside him, holding the drink and placing his other arm around Eric's shoulder.

"This drink is special," K. J. told him. "It's a mixture of everything at the bar, with a special touch from our good old bartender, Jerry." He pointed Jerry's way with the hand that was around Eric's shoulder, directing Eric's gaze as he did so. Jerry, the bartender, waved his towel in acknowledgement.

"I've got to chug it, huh?"

"You've got to chug it," they assured him.

"Well, here goes." Eric took the drink from K. J. and turned it bottoms up.

"Go! Go! Go!" the crowd chanted as the fiery liquid drained down his throat. It didn't taste half bad. In fact, it was kind of sweet. Creme de Menthe not only added the green color, but flavoring as well. Eric kept the glass turned up until it was empty. Then he brought it down and belched. A loud cheer went up.

Within minutes they forgot all about him and drifted back to their own conversations. He felt no immediate effects from the liquor, so he sat listening to the conversation among the pilots at his table. They spoke of recent missions and the general state of affairs between the Americans and the Vietnamese. It was not a conversation Eric could relate to, even though he was interested. Again, he felt left out.

He wanted to get to know K. J., who seemed friendly and helpful. K. J. was tall and lanky. His rust-colored hair was thin on top, combed over to cover a bald spot. He was a WO1, but older than Eric and older than many of the other WO1s Eric had seen. He was obviously well-educated. That he had been the ringleader in the Green Mother incident didn't phase Eric. It just confirmed what Eric had already decided—that K. J. was a leader, and probably someone who could teach him the ropes in his new assignment.

He wanted to meet Mattie's friends. He even wanted to meet the man at the bar who sat all alone—the man watching the door as if expecting someone.

Eric seemed unaware that most of the patrons in the bar were watching him out of the corner of their eyes to see what kind of reaction he would have to the drink. That it would have no effect on him was something they weren't prepared to accept.

Presently, Mattie came over and whispered in his ear, "Eric, you need to go outside and make yourself throw up that drink before you get sick. That was a pretty powerful drink."

"Thanks, Mattie, but I feel all right," he replied. "How about introducing me to your friends."

"Okay." She shrugged, thinking he was crazy to act macho when nobody really cared.

Around the table, the others were in animated conversation. They wouldn't miss Eric if he left. He stood up to follow Mattie to the table where she had been sitting with the other girls. As he walked past the CW2 at the bar, the guy turned and stuck his hand out. He had a cigarette dangling out of his mouth, a drink in his other hand and a glazed look in his eye. *He's drunk*, Eric thought, as he shook his hand out of politeness.

I'm Les Winters," the man said. "It's none of my business, but you ought to get rid of that drink before it does you in."

"That's what she just said," Eric told him, nodding toward Mattie, who stood waiting politely.

"Well, she's right. It's good advice." He turned back to his drink. That appeared to be all that Winters had to say.

78

Eric thanked Winters, then went with Mattie to her table, where she introduced the girls. There was Eileen (who had beaten her friend to Binh Thuy), Mary, Gwen and Margaret. He probably wouldn't remember all of their names, but would listen carefully and try to learn them over the next few days. He would have liked to have sat down to visit, but found himself suddenly overcome with drowsiness.

"I'd love to stay and get acquainted," he told them, "but I think I'd better turn in."

"I'm ready to go, too," Mattie said. "I'll walk back with you." Eric didn't detect the concern in her voice, but the others knew she wanted to make sure he got back to his room okay.

Outside, the evening air finally offered some relief from the heat. Eric was a little lightheaded, but mostly, he just felt sleepy. He wanted to finish the letter to Lynn before going to sleep, but wasn't sure he would be able to now.

It was a short walk to the BOQ and when they got there, Eric told Mattie he would walk her to her door. She insisted she would be okay and that he should go upstairs and go to bed. She told him again he ought to make himself throw up the drink before going to bed.

Eric didn't want to throw up, but he *did* want to go to bed. He was so sleepy the climb up the stairs seemed formidable. He made his way up them with the aid of the rail. Mattie watched to make sure he didn't stumble and fall. He opened his door and turned on the light, then waved to her that he was all right. She waved back, then went around the building to her own quarters.

Eric closed the door and fell on his bed, his clothes still on. The letter to Lynn would have to wait until morning.

He woke up around 3:00 a.m., his head spinning, his stomach churning. Thank God the latrine was right next door. As he got out of bed, his room started spinning wildly. He located the door and fell toward it, catching the knob before it moved out of the way. He inched his way through the door and hugged the wall until he made it to the latrine. There he fell on his knees and crawled across the floor to the nearest commode stall. *At least they didn't see me get sick*, he thought, as he hugged the commode, retching his guts out. As he heaved, filling the basin with green slime, he was thankful this was happening in the middle of the night when he was all alone. Then he heard a snicker and another and another. He looked up. Silhouetted by the single bare light bulb in the latrine's ceiling, a row of heads peered over the tops of the commode stall walls. It seemed that every Dustoff pilot at Binh Thuy was there watching him. They'd gotten their satisfaction after all!

He awoke for real a few hours later to the sound of water running in the sinks and showers next door. He snapped awake, and reached for his watch, realizing he was in a war zone and in the Army and something would be expected of him. Sleeping in would not be part of the program.

It was nearly 7:00 a.m. He had no idea what time he was supposed to report for work. He figured he'd better get with the program. Pulling on a pair of flight suit pants and grabbing a towel and his toilet kit, Eric opened the door to his room and headed for the latrine. On the walkway outside his room, he encountered Chris Sanders.

"Good morning, Chris," he said cheerily.

"It's not a good morning," Chris replied in a somber tone. "We lost a crew last night."

Eric was stunned. He mentally upbraided himself for being so insensitive, then realized that was ridiculous. There was no way he could have known. But last night? Last night had been full of festivities. There had been no indication anything was wrong. They couldn't have known. How did they find out? How come he hadn't found out? Had it happened later? Had he been sleeping when the rest of them had been awake, agonizing while some of their comrades had been in trouble?

Slowly, the realization hit him that this really *was* a war zone—not the casual, seemingly unthreatening environment he had experienced the past couple of days. He stood on the balcony watching as Chris and several of the other pilots descended the stairs, climbed into a jeep and drove off. They were fully dressed. They had things to do. He was late.

He went into the latrine, shaved and took a quick shower. He was all alone. When he came out of the shower with a towel wrapped around him, a young Vietnamese woman was standing at one of the sinks, washing an article of clothing in it. She glanced at him and went back to her work, as if it was perfectly natural for her to be in the men's latrine while he was there wearing just a towel.

"Newby," she said quietly as he walked behind her to pick up his shaving kit and head back to his room. He saw her smiling at him in the mirror over the sink. He didn't know what to say.

After dressing, Eric wasn't sure what to do. Had he missed breakfast? Was that where they were all headed? Should he go to Operations? That meant he would have to walk around the runway. The others had taken the jeeps. It was already hot. He had just taken a shower and put on a clean flight suit and already he was sweating.

There was no one around to ask. He figured his safest bet would be to go to Dustoff Operations. Someone there would tell him what to do. He'd just reached the bottom of the steps when a jeep rounded the corner of the building and skidded to a stop in a cloud of dust. At the wheel was Les Winters, the

CW2 Eric had seen alone at the bar the night before—the one who had told him to throw up the Green Mother before he got sick.

"You," Winters said, looking at Eric. "Get in the jeep and come with me." Eric climbed in. Something about the man's demeanor told him not to ask where they were going. The jeep raced around the end of the runway, through the Dustoff area, behind the Navy ramp and screeched to a halt in front of a building with a sign on it indicating it was a dispensary. A Navy officer wearing starched and pressed jungle fatigues and a black beret was waiting outside. He wore the rank of a Navy lieutenant, the equivalent of an Army captain. The lieutenant climbed in, and with neither man speaking a word, Winters sped off again, this time in the direction of Dustoff Operations.

There, Winters led them into a room that served as a crew lounge for the on-duty crews. In it were a pool table, a card table and a couple of bunks. Winters reached into one of the leg pockets on his flight suit and pulled out a stack of papers, which he plopped down on the pool table. Nobody was talking. Eric seemed to be the only one who didn't know what was going on. He assumed he would find out soon enough.

The two commanding officers, Scott and Green, came in. It was obvious they were waiting for someone else.

That someone arrived a few minutes later in the form of a red-haired CW4 accompanied by the 57th's Operations Officer, 1st Lt. Wade Daugherty. The CW4 wore Senior Aviator wings. He had age, he had experience, he was tough, and he was in charge. All of this Eric deduced from the way he walked into the room. Though technically the captains outranked him, they would take orders from this man.

"I'm Chief Warrant Officer Warren Guy," the CW4 began. "I see nearly everyone is here. Let's get started with the assignments. Captain Scott tells me we will be able to launch as soon as the people from Graves Registration arrive."

Terry Green pulled Eric aside as CW4 Guy began giving instructions to the men standing around the pool table. "I don't think you're supposed to be here," he said quietly.

Eric shrugged. "I'm only here because Mr. Winters brought me here," he said. "I don't even know what's going on."

"Just a minute," Green said. He walked around the pool table and whispered something in CW2 Winters' ear. If CW4 Guy was bothered by the interruption, he didn't show it. Winters nodded, and they both looked over at Eric. Green indicated to Eric that he should stay.

Mr. Guy looked at him. "Mr. Mohr, do you type?" he asked.

"Yes, sir," Eric answered.

"Good. You'll be our reporter. You'll keep up with all of our notes and prepare the final report for my approval. Do you understand?"

"I guess so," Eric said, hesitantly. CW4 Guy didn't look like the kind of man you would want to ask about what was going on. It was beginning to dawn on him anyway what this was all about. He looked at Winters with a look that said, "What have you gotten me into, and why haven't you told me what's going on?" Warrant Officers were supposed to take care of each other—even wobbly ones. Winters returned Eric's look with one of his own that said, "Get over it."

They heard a vehicle pull up outside. "See if that's them," Guy said to Lieutenant Daugherty, who stood closest to the door. Daugherty stuck his head out the door, then looked back inside and nodded. "Let's go," Guy told the group.

Outside were two enlisted men and two more men wearing green fatigues, with insignia on their collars that said DAC.

They were pulling quite a few backpacks out of a three-quarter ton truck.

"What's DAC?" Eric asked Winters quietly.

"Department of the Army Civilian," Winters answered. "They're from Graves Registration."

"Oh," Eric answered, as if that explained it.

On the flight line, two Hueys were warming up. The group moved toward them, split into two groups and started climbing aboard. In the absence of any directions to the contrary, Eric was going to get on the bird with Winters. But when he saw Winters drop back, he realized the man was staying behind. *What about me?* he wondered. *Am I supposed to be going?* His question was answered when Aubrey Scott took him by the arm and ushered him aboard the first helicopter. As he strapped himself into one of the hellhole seats, someone handed him a flak jacket and an M-16. The crew chief reached into an ammo box and handed him two full clips of ammunition. A couple of minutes later they were airborne.

Near the Seven Sisters

The two Dustoff helicopters landed just outside the village of Tri Tan, near the base of Dop Chompa. They couldn't land on top of the mountain because it was obscured with clouds. Low-lying scud could be seen across the small plain surrounding the mountains. The air was still, hot and humid. Near where the helicopters landed was a clump of trees. The men piled out and drifted toward these trees looking for shade and to engage in an old Army custom: hurry up and wait.

Eric decided it was time someone told him what was going on. He might be the junior man in the bunch, but they owed him an explanation.

He spoke to Captain Scott. "Sir, would somebody please tell me what's going on."

"Winters didn't explain it to you?"

"No, sir. He caught me when I came out of my room this morning and told me to come with him. Now I'm here. I heard we lost a crew last night. I'm assuming this has something to do with that."

"I'm sorry, Eric. You probably didn't even get any breakfast."

"No, sir."

"There are C rations in the helicopters. You're going to need your energy, and later you probably won't feel like eating." Scott got up and brushed off his pants. "Come on. let's see what we can find."

They walked over to the nearest helicopter and Captain Scott pulled a case of C rations from under one of the hell-hole seats. He opened it and handed Mohr two cans, one was labeled "Peaches" and the other "Pound Cake."

"You got a P-38?" Scott asked. Mohr shook his head. He didn't know what a P-38 was. Scott produced one from the dog tag chain around his neck. It was a small can opener. He used it to open one of the cans. "Look in the bottom of that case," he nodded toward the open box on the helicopter floor. "There should be one in there. Keep it and put it on your dog tag chain so you'll always have one with you."

Mohr found the can opener and opened his peaches and pound cake. Then he put it on his dog tag chain.

The two men sat in the cargo bay of the helicopter, dangling their legs over the side and eating the C rations while Scott brought Eric up to speed.

David B. Freeman

"Last night one of our crews was on a search and rescue mission, and they crashed into the side of that mountain. The US Special Forces advisor from Tri Tan took a team of ARVNs up the mountain at first light and located the wreckage. There were no survivors. We're the accident investigation team: you, me, Terry Green, Mr. Guy, Doc Hazlett—the Navy Flight Surgeon—and Les Winters."

"Who are the other guys—the DACs?"

"They are morticians from Graves Registration. It's their job to recover and identify the remains and send them home for proper burial. The two army specialists work for them."

"What about Winters? How come he didn't come with us?"

"Smooth talking, I guess. He conned his way into going over to Paddy Control to listen to a tape of the conversation between Paddy and the flight during the last few minutes before the crash. I'm sure he didn't want to go up on that mountain and find the body of one of his best friends." Scott gazed out across the open field at the mountain. "Can't say that I blame him, but Hazlett is in the same boat." Scott was speaking of the Navy Flight Surgeon who sat by himself a short distance away from the others, leaning against a tree with his eyes closed. "Doc Hazlett and Stu Chambers, the AC on the flight that crashed, were best friends. They spent all of their off-duty hours together. It's got to be pretty tough on him drawing this detail, but we have to have the flight surgeon on the board. Regulations."

"Are we waiting for the weather to clear?" Eric asked.

"The crash site is close to the top of the mountain. The ARVN Rangers are up there waiting to take us to it. As soon as the clouds burn off, the helicopters are going to airlift us to an LZ up there. We'll walk down hill to the wreckage." Eric nodded. This wasn't exactly how he had envisioned getting his feet wet in Vietnam.

An hour later, the general consensus among the pilots was that they could get into the LZ. They talked to the American advisor on the radio and he told them he could see blue sky looking straight up from the clearing on top of the mountain. They climbed into the helicopters. Everyone checked their weapons and gear as the pilots started the engines.

The two-ship formation made a steep approach into the LZ and hovered over the tall grass as the passengers jumped out and headed for the trees as if they were on a combat assault mission. At the edge of the clearing, Special Forces Major Hamilton Ray waited with his team of ARVN Rangers. Scott and Green conversed briefly with the major, then they began to make their way down the mountain.

The ARVNs took up the lead and trail positions and interspersed themselves among the Americans. One of the ARVNs motioned to Eric to take his M-16 off his shoulder and hold it at the ready position. *It's like playing army,* Eric thought. *I'm supposed to be an aviator and here I am, my second full day in Vietnam, traipsing through the jungle like a grunt.* They moved through the jungle on an existing trail. Whether it had been there before, or the ARVNs had cut it that morning, Eric didn't know. He was near the back of the group and observed with some humor they didn't exactly look like a combat patrol. The aviators all wore their aviator sunglasses, and were wearing Nomex flight suits rather than jungle fatigues. Several of them were taking pictures.

The major was a sharp contrast to the aviators. For his personal weapon, he carried a 12 gauge Winchester pump shotgun. He was dressed in jungle fatigues and wore a floppy bush hat that covered his short black hair. The major's eyes were at times brooding, the next minute bright with excitement as he talked about his men and his mission. His men were the Vietnamese Rangers he had trained and molded together into a highly effective combat patrol group. They had been on their feet, walking through the jungle and up and down the mountain now for at least sixteen hours, yet they showed no signs of tiring. The ARVNs were alert and ready for an ambush or booby traps; the Americans in their charge strolled along naively as if they were on an afternoon hike.

Slowly, they moved down the mountain, unable to see more than five or six feet into the dense foliage. Were they being watched? Would there be any Viet Cong around? It didn't seem a likely place to fight a war—too remote, nothing of value. For Eric, whose favorite pastime as a boy had been exploring the woods on his grandfather's farm, the trek through the jungle was just another exploration. The thought of being involved in a firefight didn't even cross his mind. They were going to find the wreckage of a helicopter. It was that simple. He looked around for signs of worry from the others. Only the ARVNs seemed alert, prepared for danger. Fortunately, none appeared.

It was almost an hour later when they began to smell the gruesome odor of charred meat. They came upon a huge boulder, eight to ten feet high and twelve to fifteen feet across. Behind the boulder, a Huey tailboom stuck up at an odd angle—as if it had been planted upright, then blown over. As they rounded the boulder, they saw the wreckage—what was left of it. It consisted of the tailboom and part of the engine. Everything else had been reduced to a pile of ashes, the product of a JP-4 fueled titanium flash fire.

Eric dropped back. The stench was sickening. The DACs and their enlisted helpers moved forward and knelt in the ashes. One of the civilians poked at a charred body with a gloved hand. There were four such bodies—torsos only—partial heads, no arms, no legs. The limbs had all been burned away by the intense fire. Captain Scott and Lieutenant Hazlett moved forward into the ashes, grim looks on their faces. Eric slipped behind the boulder and vomited. He heard someone else in the bushes doing the same thing. When Eric rejoined the group, CW4 Guy handed him a small package of graph paper and a pencil.

"Mr. Mohr, we'll need a drawing of the crash scene. Do you have a compass?"

"No, sir."

"Major Ray, can you get this man a compass?"

"Yeah, we'll get him one." A minute later an ARVN stepped up to Eric and handed him a lensatic compass.

"See that path through the trees marking the helicopter's flight path?" Guy asked, pointing at some broken tree limbs behind the helicopter tail boom.

"Yes, sir." Eric answered.

"Find out how far it extends, and plot its direction. I'm going to be sending the ARVNs out to scout for any parts that might have separated from the aircraft before it burned. They'll be instructed to call you over when they find something and not to move it. You chart it all. You don't have to move anything, unless you find something like a watch, a clock or some other instrument that might tell us something. I want you to graphically plot a top-down overview of the crash scene showing the location of the wreckage, the flight path of the helicopter and the location of any parts we find. Got it?"

"Yes, sir."

"Don't worry about scale or making it pretty right now. You'll get a chance to redraw it. Just make yourself good notes." He turned his attention away from Eric.

"Captain Green, let's see if we can find any instruments that didn't burn."

Eric set out through the jungle to make his chart, thankful to get away from the sight, though he couldn't get away from the smell of the charred bodies. He was a couple of hundred feet down the side of the mountain a few minutes later when one of the helicopters came overhead and hoisted up the crewmembers' remains in body bags so they could be flown back to Can Tho.

The morning wore on. The men worked in the almost unbearable heat. Eric worked on his chart. The ARVNs found a door and pieces of rotor blades. The helicopter had apparently traveled almost two hundred feet through the trees at an uphill angle before coming to rest against the rock. There was speculation that if the rock hadn't been there, the bird might have kept traveling, decelerating over a longer distance and perhaps not burning. But it was something they would never know. Eric finished his work and returned to the crash site.

The morticians seemed morbidly interested in the ashes. All four torsos had been lifted out in body bags. What were they looking for? Teeth, glasses, rings, something to help them identify the dead?

One of them stood up and addressed Captain Scott. "Sir, as best we can determine, there were only four remains here. Are you sure there was a fifth man on that helicopter?"

Scott nodded grimly. "Johnson was with them. He's not back at Binh Thuy and the RTO saw him get on the ship before they left. He told several people he was going to be flying with the First-Up crew yesterday, even though it was his day off."

"Well, he didn't die in this fire," the DAC told him.

"You're absolutely certain?"

"Yes, sir. Something would have been here. It doesn't make sense for there not to be some part of him here."

Eric shuddered. *How can they talk about a human being that way?* he wondered.

"Then we've got to search this mountainside," Scott said. "We can't leave him here."

"Sir," Lieutenant Daugherty said. "We've been searching all morning. Our best bet is to let the ARVN Rangers find him. They found the Navy flier last night."

"You mean my crew was out here searching for someone who had already been rescued?" Scott looked at Daugherty with a strange look in his eyes, one of anger and disbelief.

"No, sir, we don't know that." Daugherty answered. He let it go at that.

That answer didn't satisfy Scott. He walked over to Major Ray. "What happened last night?"

"We saw the Navy pilot eject yesterday afternoon," Ray explained. "We saw his parachute and we saw his plane go down, but we were several klicks away from him. We started toward him, but we had no radio contact with any of the fliers overhead, so we had no way of letting the Navy know we were in the area."

"And you found him?" Scott asked.

"Yes, sir," Ray responded. "It was after dark. We saw him shoot up a flare, then a few minutes later, another one. He was on his survival radio talking to the helicopter pilot. I eased up to his position carefully, so as not to get shot. Then we heard the helicopter crash."

"We took the guy on foot back to Tri Tan and the Navy picked him up at first light. Then we headed up here to find your helicopter. Some of the villagers saw the fire, so we knew where to start looking."

"Can your men find my soldier?"

"They can find him, Captain. May I make a suggestion?"

"Certainly."

"Authorize a reward of several thousand piasters. Say, the equivalent of about four hundred dollars."

"That'll work?"

"It will."

"Okay. It's authorized. Even if I have to pay it myself."

"Then you guys call in your helicopters and go home," Ray told him. "We'll have him before nightfall."

Scott looked over at CW4 Guy. "Are we through here?" he asked. Guy looked at each of the men on the team for confirmation. It appeared they all wanted to get out of there and felt there was nothing more they could do. Guy nodded.

"Let's get back to the LZ," Scott said. He turned to Wade Daugherty, who carried a PRC-25 radio on his back. "See if you can raise the helicopters."

They started back up the trail, the ARVNs falling in place ahead, behind and among the Americans. As they arrived in the clearing where they had been dropped off earlier, the two Dustoff helicopters circled overhead. One landed and picked up the first load. As it took off, the second helicopter landed and the remaining men climbed aboard. Eric scrambled for a hellhole seat, relieved to be leaving the jungle behind. As the helicopter climbed away, he saw Major Ray assemble his ARVN troops and head back into the jungle.

SIX

Navy Binh Thuy

Steve Cooper sat on an examining table in the base dispensary at Navy Binh Thuy. He winced as the corpsman pulled the bandage tight around his shoulder. The medical corpsman was treating his injuries in the absence of the flight surgeon, Lieutenant Steve Hazlett. In the treatment room with Steve was Lieutenant Commander Jake Herring, who had met Cooper at the helipad when the Seawolf helicopter dropped him off earlier. Herring indicated he would fly Steve back to Vung Tau later that afternoon. Cooper suspected there was a reason the Senior Flight Instructor had met him on his arrival at Binh Thuy, a reason that went beyond the fact that he had bailed out of a damaged aircraft the night before.

The injuries to Steve's shoulder and knee were not severe, but he would be grounded for a few days while they healed. Herring was apparently interested in making sure the episode had not affected Cooper emotionally. But more than that, it was his job to find out what was affecting this young aviator's judgment. Cooper's wingman, Lt. Willis, indicated in his report that Cooper had turned his damaged aircraft back toward the enemy gun, a gun which at that time was no longer a threat to anyone else. The prudent thing would have been to concentrate on flying his airplane away from the threat and to a safe landing. It was on that second pass that the aircraft sustained the critical damage that caused it to go down.

Some of Cooper's recent antics had become the talk of the squadron—flying too close to the trees, low level attacks on concentrated gun positions, pulling out of dives too close to the ground. This was an aviator courting disaster. Herring had to either turn him around or ground him.

"Well, sir, that about does it," the corpsman announced. He stepped back to look at the work he had done on Steve's shoulder. Doc Hazlett was a good man to work for. He let his medical corpsmen do a lot of the hands-on stuff. Consequently, they were good at their jobs.

"Does he need to wait around for the flight surgeon to get back?" Commander Herring asked the corpsman.

"No, sir. Not unless he needs a grounding slip."

"I think we can handle getting him some time off without having Lt. Hazlett authorize it."

"Then you're ready to go, sir," the corpsman said to Steve.

Cooper responded by slipping off the edge of the table and struggling to pull up the top part of his flight suit, which had been dangling around his waist.

"I can get you some pain killers, sir, if you'd like," the corpsman offered. Steve put his good arm in its sleeve, then pulled the remaining side of the flight suit over his bandaged shoulder.

"That's all right." He shook his head, then winced as he took his first step on the bandaged and swollen ankle. Herring reached for his good arm and the two of them made their way out into the hall and through the front door to the jeep Herring had borrowed to get them to the airfield.

Thirty minutes later, they were airborne in the Lieutenant Commander's OV-10, climbing toward the cooler air above 5,000 feet. Few clouds remained and the air was a vibrant blue. The morning rains had washed away the haze, leaving crisp, clear air behind.

Steve sat in the observer's seat immediately behind the pilot, and found himself enjoying the flight. It was the kind of afternoon pilots dream of when they have miles to cover and no passengers to impress. They could see the coastline and Vung Tau Bay from 30 miles away.

"How do you feel?" Herring asked his passenger.

"I feel all right … a little sore," Steve answered.

"Yeah, I expect so. A few days rest will do you a little good, I imagine."

"I'm not exactly looking forward to it."

"Why not?"

"Flying is what I do, sir. I'd rather be in the air than anywhere." Cooper answered.

"Coop," Herring began, then hesitated, carefully weighing his words. What he was about to say was important, and he wanted his words to have impact. "I've heard you're a pretty good pilot."

"I work at it," Steve answered, still waiting for the lecture he'd been expecting since the Commander had picked him up that morning.

Suddenly, the aircraft was on its back. It happened without warning and so smoothly that had it not been for the strain against his shoulder harness and lap belt, Steve would not have believed they were inverted. Yet they were upside down with the nose of the aircraft above the horizon, the wings steady, a perfectly executed aileron roll to inverted flight.

"Whoa …" Steve said. He was impressed.

"Close your eyes," Herring said. Steve did so. Immediately he felt the airplane rolling … one … two … maybe three times, then it stopped.

"Are we right side up or upside down?" Herring asked. Steve felt for the strain that would tell him he was upside down, but the combination of his torso harness and vertigo confused his senses and he honestly couldn't tell. Before he could answer, Herring asked, "Which direction are we headed?" Steve couldn't resist opening his eyes. They were upside down, but in a descent that counteracted some of the G forces. Vung Tau and the ocean were behind them. Herring was watching him in the small mirror mounted on top of the pilot's glare shield.

"Couldn't tell with your eyes closed, could you?" Herring prodded him, as he half-snap rolled the aircraft right side up.

Steve didn't get the point. "No," he said.

"That's how you've been flying, Cooper—blind. You're flying missions with your eyes closed."

"I don't get it," Steve said.

"There are more ways to see than with your physical eyes. You're letting anger at someone or something blind you. I've seen it before. It's fatal in our business."

Cooper remained silent, not wanting to admit how close to home Herring was hitting.

"You can work it out, whatever it is," Herring continued. "You have friends; now you have some time. You're grounded, and not just for physical reasons. You want to talk to me about it, I'm open. If not me, talk to somebody. Otherwise, come see me when you think you're ready to get back on flying status and we'll talk about it."

Angry? Maybe. Right now what he felt was resentment—resentment against Willis for ratting on him, resentment against Herring for reading more into the situation than was there, resentment against the VC gun that just happened to be where he made his slow turn, and resentment against Gail for … he couldn't think about that now. In the back seat of Herring's OV-10, he became an actor. If Herring wanted a contrite and humble pilot, Cooper would be a contrite and humble pilot—for whatever time was necessary to convince Herring to place him back on flight status.

Vung Tau

When the two aviators parted company, Steve thanked Herring for the ride and for the pep talk, telling the Commander he had given him something to think about. He avoided going to his room as long as he could, then went in to get a fresh change of clothes before taking a shower. They were there in the corner—the stack of letters. The ones on the bottom of the stack had been opened, the others had not. On the table were two more, today's mail, put there by Stump, the faithful friend. If only he knew, he'd have burned the letters before Steve ever saw them.

Steve knew there were pictures of Emily in those letters. Gail sent pictures in almost every letter. At two years old, Emily was changing every day. It was almost worth reading the letters to see what new discoveries their daughter had made, or what cute thing she had said. But even that hurt too much. If Gail was not to be part of his life, how could he hold on to Emily? It was too painful to think about. If only he were home he could take control. He could make things happen. But he wasn't. He was here and he would be here for six more months, and he was helpless to change the most important thing in his life.

He picked up the two new letters, then tossed them unopened on top of the pile. Emotion welled up inside him, and he felt his eyes burning and a lump in his throat. He grabbed a towel and a clean pair of underwear and headed down the hall to the shower. He unwrapped the bandage from around his shoulder, then let the warm water spray on it. He stayed that way a long time, the warmth of the water soothing his shoulder and mixing with the water from his face as it swirled down the drain and away … away from the necessity to deal with it. When he emerged from the shower, he was a reformed man. Willis would see it; Herring would see it, and soon he would be flying again.

Navy Binh Thuy

Eric tossed on his bed throughout the night. The tiny ceiling fan struggled against the hot, humid air in his room, but brought little relief. The small hole in the wall where the previous occupant's air conditioner had been was the only source of ventilation. It was totally inadequate. The hole did, however, do a good job of letting mosquitoes in.

Not only was the small ceiling fan over his bed no match for the heat and humidity of the subtropical Vietnam climate, but from the moment Eric put his flight suit on in the morning until he took it off at night, it clung to him like wet sandpaper. Though he had worked outdoors in the humid climate of

Mississippi most of his life, this was different. When morning finally arrived, Eric began his third full day in Vietnam uncomfortable, exhausted, and facing a series of challenges—the first would be to get an air conditioner.

Today, he also hoped to find someone who knew Steve Cooper. It occurred to him he should have asked the Navy flight surgeon. The Donut Dollies were another possibility. At mealtime, he planned to ask some of the Navy pilots. He had already asked around among the Dustoff pilots and none of them had recognized Steve's name.

Since the previous afternoon, Eric had been experiencing an uneasy feeling about Steve, and he wanted to find him soon. He felt it was possible that his main purpose in being in Vietnam was related to his brother-in-law, Steve.

Something else was bothering Eric. That he was different from the other pilots in the unit, and an outsider by virtue of his outspoken Christian beliefs, was a given. Yet, he wanted—needed—to be accepted by them, not just to have an effective witness, but to fit in with the medevac mission. Being picked for the accident investigation board was not going to help. On what normally would have been his first day on the job, he, an outsider, had been spirited off into the jungle to find the remains of one of their ships and the bodies of their comrades.

Upon returning to Binh Thuy, Eric had been told by CW4 Guy to remain apart from the other members of the unit until the investigation was completed. That's when he first learned why he had been picked. Because he didn't know any of the crew members involved, he could remain impartial. Guy didn't want Eric influenced by any of the other pilots' theories or defense of their friends who had died. He wouldn't have time to visit anyway. The other aviators weren't told this was the case, which left them free to arrive at their own conclusions concerning Eric's aloofness. It was not a good way to begin a relationship, especially one in which the mutual development of trust could mean the difference between life and death. Eric wondered now if he would ever be able to gain their trust.

It also didn't help that the one person Eric was allowed to spend time with was Les Winters, who was already an outsider. Eric found himself liking Winters, but it didn't seem anyone else did. Eric could tell there was a rift between Winters and the others, but he didn't know the cause. He didn't know about Winters' spoken disdain for having been assigned to a medevac unit. Now, it almost seemed Eric was unwittingly on Winters' side in whatever "us versus them" scenario was being played out.

"What's the deal between you and the other pilots?" Eric asked Winters while they were eating breakfast at the Army mess hall. The eggs were powdered, the bacon soggy. The Navy served real eggs. Eric would have much preferred eating there, not only for the better food, but for the increased chance of finding Steve.

"They don't like me because I'm different," Winters said. "But it doesn't bother me."

"What kind of different?" Eric asked. He understood being different.

"I'm a gunship pilot—a killer. I don't fit in."

"I bet they like gunship pilots when they're on a hot mission," Eric offered.

"Oh, they like them fine. They just don't want one being part of their unit; which is just fine, because I don't like *being* part of their unit." The way Winters said it indicated he was ready to move on to a different subject.

Eric just wouldn't let it rest. "Aren't you a school-trained Safety Officer?"

"Yep. That's why I'm stuck in this hole."

"Do you really consider it being 'stuck'?" Eric asked. "To me, it's a privilege to be part of the 57th."

"That's because you're wet behind the ears," Les told him. "Wait until you've been here a while. You'll be wishing you had some guns to shoot back with."

He doesn't know me very well, Eric thought. He let the conversation drop. Something else was bothering Les Winters, something probably Winters himself didn't realize. Eric made a mental note to pray for wisdom in relating to his new friend. They were, he realized, becoming friends.

When Eric considered the challenges facing him, he had to admit there had been one small victory. He had been exposed to what conceivably would be the most gruesome situation he would encounter all year in the form of the "crispy critters" (that's what the others called the burned corpses) they had discovered in the ashes of the Huey on the side of the mountain the previous morning. His stomach had reacted, but he had gotten over it and gotten on with the job. That was one hurdle behind him. To someone else it might not seem significant, but Eric had a weak stomach and had even fainted at the sight of blood in times past. He wouldn't have to worry about that any more. He could not imagine anything worse than seeing someone burned beyond recognition.

Mohr and Winters finished their breakfast and walked back to the BOQ. The investigation board was scheduled to meet at 10:00 a.m. and Winters had to make a trip over to Air Force Binh Thuy to pick up an audio tape from Paddy Control he had arranged to have copied the day before.

"I've got to pick up a jeep from Operations and go over to the Air Force base," he told Eric. "You want to ride with me?"

"Sure," Eric responded. "On the way, could we stop by the Engineers and find that guy that sells air conditioners?"

"No problem. You got cash? He only takes cash."

"How much?"

"The going rate is $150 bucks. He'll hit you up for two hundred. When he does, just walk away."

After borrowing the Operations jeep from Lieutenant Daugherty, they stopped by the PX so Eric could cash a check. It took only a few minutes more to complete the air conditioner transaction, which happened just as Winters had predicted it would. They put the unit in the back of the jeep; Winters promising to help Eric install it later. It looked pretty beat up, but the man plugged it in and ran it for him and it had put out cold air. It was a little noisy, but the noise would probably help Eric sleep.

By the time they exited the main gate at Navy Binh Thuy, they had only an hour to get back for the meeting. Winters hit the Vietnamese highway with the same passion Eric had seen the drivers use between Saigon and Long Binh a couple of days before. A loud horn, guts and a willingness to bluff, got you the right-of-way, unless, of course, a bigger vehicle was coming from the opposite direction.

For Eric, it was a chance for a close look at the indigenous population. Street vendors were everywhere. Some of the roadside stands reminded Eric of a kids' neighborhood lemonade stand back in the USA, only these were selling gasoline in one gallon glass bottles—fuel for the countless mopeds and Honda 50s that traversed the narrow highway. Eric wondered how much of the fuel had been stolen from the US government.

Other stands sold pineapples, coconuts, bananas and various vegetables. There were ice vendors and people selling chickens and goats.

Many of the Hondas on the road were driven by women dressed in white or pastel ao dais. Eric marveled at how the women all appeared immaculately clean in spite of their surroundings. Some of the women rode sidesaddle on the back of Hondas driven by men. They held on with one hand on the driver's shoulder and the other resting in their lap, their eyes ever watchful for the mud puddles that frequently appeared in the worn roadway.

Men stopped to urinate in the ditches along the side of the road; those same ditches that a few feet away someone else was washing clothes. Modesty and sanitation were apparently foreign concepts to the Vietnamese population on the street.

Women walked hand-in-hand or with their arms around one another. Eric did a double take the first time he saw this, but apparently it was a common custom, for as they drove along, he saw it frequently.

He watched the faces of the people as the jeep wove in and out of traffic. It was the same mix of expressions you would expect to see on any street in any country. Some were smiling; some were intent. Some laughed; some wore the look of grief or agony. Some faces stared devoid of expression, as if their owners had checked out, leaving only an empty body to cope with life as best it could. Others seemed to find hope, even merriment in the day-to-day transactions of their lives.

The jeep attracted little attention, except from the children. Whenever Winters was forced to slow for traffic, children swarmed toward the jeep, yelling, "GI! GI!" Eric was fascinated by them, for he liked children, but Winters not only ignored them, he accelerated away from them whenever he could.

The two men arrived at the Air Force gate and were motioned through by a Vietnamese military policeman. Winters drove down an access road parallel to the runway. Parked in rows of revetments beside the runway were many small two-place jets that resembled US Air Force T-37 trainers. They had side-by-side seating and were painted in camouflage, with Vietnamese markings.

"What are those?" Eric asked.

"Zoomies," Winters answered. "A-37s the Air Force donated to the Dinks." *Dinks.* That was Winters' word for the Vietnamese. To him, North or South, they were all the same.

They pulled up in front of a semi-trailer covered with antennas. Winters told Eric to wait in the jeep while he went inside. Eric watched as two A-37s took off and climbed away to the north. *They may be little, but they sure are loud*, Eric observed. The first two zoomies quickly disappeared into the haze and two more followed with bombs and missiles mounted underneath their wings. *They're off to fight the war*, Eric thought. This war was strange compared to how he thought war would be.

Except for the visit to the mountainside, the war was still something far away to Eric. People flew off to it, but they came back—to their air conditioners and clubs, hamburgers and french fries, steaks, clean rooms, maids, even a swimming pool—all the comforts of home.

Winters came out of the shack and handed Eric a cassette tape as he climbed behind the wheel. "Put this in your pocket and don't lose it," he said, as if talking to a little child. Eric unzipped one of the leg pockets in his flight suit and put the tape in it. Winters started the jeep and put it in reverse. He backed around in a cloud of dust, shifted to first and popped the clutch. He seemed in a hurry to get back, though they had at least 30 minutes before the meeting.

Vung Tau

Steve left the airfield, driving toward downtown in a jeep he had commandeered from the maintenance section. Up until now he had avoided exploring the much-talked-about local color, out of deference to his family. Now that things had changed at home and he had a few days off, he decided it was time to visit some of Vung Tau's beaches and "massage" parlors. Turning right on Tran Phu Street, he followed it toward the resort beaches some twelve miles away. As he drove past the market and away from the fishing village, he couldn't help but take in the scenery. To his left were mountains, their slopes dotted with Pagodas and the villas of well-to-do Vietnamese businessmen. To his right were beaches; beyond them, the fishing fleet and a scattering of US Navy vessels.

Vung Tau was on a peninsula seldom bothered by the war. An offshore oil industry flourished and a fleet of fishing boats went out at dawn and came back each evening. Much of the area was devoted to recreation. This was one of the few places in Vietnam—Dalat in the mountains being the only other one of note—where vacationers could enjoy beautiful scenery and exotic entertainment, without worrying much about the Viet Cong. It was commonly believed Viet Cong might be among the vacationers, taking their own break from the war.

Steve breathed deeply of the salt breeze coming off Vung Tau Bay and did his best to shut out the emotional pain he felt from being betrayed by Gail. During the previous two weeks, there had been times he almost convinced himself he could forget Gail and get on with his life. He had flying, the only thing he had ever really cared about before meeting her, and a promising career in Naval Aviation. After this tour, he hoped to attend the Navy Test Pilot School at Patuxent River. Then there would be no stopping him. But the letters kept coming every day, and when he closed his eyes, he saw Gail's face and the face of their daughter, Emily. Gail might not be his, but Emily was. It was a tough call to think of living life without her.

It wasn't just to see the sights and experience the pleasures of Vung Tau that caused Steve to leave the airfield, as much as it was to get away from the loneliness of his room and those letters. Even though he wasn't opening them, they haunted him. He knew what they contained—pictures of Emily, along with apologies and pleas for forgiveness from Gail.

Could he forgive her? If it was just an isolated incident, sure. But he believed unfaithfulness was in her nature. He had thought she would change for him, and it appeared she had ... as long as he was there. But as soon as he left the country .... a Navy wife couldn't be that way. He would always be leaving the country. No. He would have to get over her and get on with his life. Bac Dinh, the White Villa, would be a good place to start.

SEVEN

Navy Binh Thuy

Eric tried to swallow the lump in his throat. More than one man brushed a tear from his eye. Even the tough gunship pilot, CW2 Les Winters, was misty-eyed and silent. Warren Guy pushed the rewind button. "Anybody want to hear it again?" he asked.

Around the room, men were shaking their heads and avoiding eye contact. What they had heard had been enough—too much. They had just listened to the last five minutes of conversation between CW2 Stuart Chambers, Dustoff 79, and Paddy Control. Interspersed between Paddy's advisories to Chambers and Chamber's acknowledgement of those advisories was one side of the conversation between Chambers and the Navy pilot he was trying to rescue. That Chambers was focused on rescuing the pilot when no one else thought it possible was obvious. That he had lost something that no pilot should ever lose was also obvious. He'd lost situational awareness, the necessary ability to keep up with where you are in relation to hazards around you.

Just a few minutes before the crash, the radar controller had advised Dustoff 79 he was losing radar contact with the Huey.

The controller also advised the Dustoff aircraft commander that at his last point of contact he was seven miles from the tallest of the Seven Sisters and on a heading that would take him toward them. Seven miles. Chambers had acknowledged the warning and had even responded with his altitude—two thousand feet. The mountain was twenty-three hundred feet tall. Three hundred feet. Why had he not climbed? Why had he not turned around? Was he so sure he would see the Navy pilot's flare?

The men in that room would never know for sure what Stu Chambers had been thinking, or what his peter pilot had been thinking. Was the peter pilot blindly following his aircraft commander's lead? Had he been depending on Chambers to keep them away from the mountains? They'd apparently been in and out of clouds, yet neither pilot held an instrument rating. Both of them held only a "tactical" instrument ticket—one that was designed to help them get out of trouble should they inadvertently fly into clouds. It gave them no license to willingly flirt with IMC—instrument meteorological conditions (flying in the clouds).

The verdict would be pilot error. It could be nothing else. That's what the official Army record would show. And Captain Scott would be left to come up with his own story to tell the families about the crew members' heroic actions in the face of danger.

The group began to break up, slowly leaving the room. CW4 Guy pulled Scott, Winters and Mohr aside. Eric watched as Lt. Hazlett walked out the door. He wanted to catch him, yet Guy obviously had something on his mind.

"Captain, can you get this man a typewriter?" He addressed his question toward Aubrey Scott, while pointing at Eric.

"Sure," Scott replied.

"Please do it," Guy commanded. He turned to Eric. "Mr. Mohr, you'll need to work in your room or some place isolated from the other pilots in the unit. We'll have the civilians from Can Tho bring you the pathology reports on the pilots. Doctor Hazlett will supply you with a medical profile for each of the pilots. You've got your diagram, which will need to be done up as neatly as possible. This audio tape will need to be transcribed. There's a series of questions on the report form that you'll need to answer as best you can. I'll review it and make any corrections I deem necessary. When you get it all typed up, I'll work with you on the final revision. Then we'll get each of the board members to sign it. Can you do all of that in three days?"

"Yes, sir, I guess so," Eric responded hesitantly. It seemed an overwhelming task and it appeared to him they were dumping it on him. But he was the lowest ranking member of the board, and the only one without other duties assigned.

"Good. Then I'll see you in a couple of days. Gentlemen." He nodded and went out the door. The others followed. Outside, they stopped again to talk briefly.

Eric went outside hoping to catch Lt. Hazlett before he got away. Hazlett was just getting into a jeep driven by Lt. Daugherty. "Sir," Eric called out to him. Hazlett turned toward him and Daugherty released the ignition switch. "Sir, do you know a Navy pilot named Steve Cooper?"

For a brief moment Hazlett just stared at Eric. "How do you know Cooper?" he asked.

"He's my brother-in-law," Eric answered slowly, somewhat taken aback by the intensity in Hazlett's eyes.

"Then you didn't know?" Hazlett asked with surprise.

"Know? Know what?"

"That Cooper was the pilot Stu was trying to rescue."

"Steve? That was Steve?" Eric couldn't believe it. The world was small, but not that small.

"Yes, it was Steve Cooper," Hazlett answered. Eric couldn't read his expression. *Was Hazlett blaming Steve for the death of his friend, or was he just saddened at the meaninglessness of the deaths?*

"Where is he now?"

"I have no idea," Hazlett answered. He turned to Daugherty. "Let's go," he said. They drove off, leaving Eric with no real answers.

He started back toward the others, head down, discouraged. He heard a truck approaching and looked up to see a three-quarter ton truck, its gears grinding; the dust from beneath its wheels reminding Eric of the dust from a Mississippi back road. *Funny,* he thought. *It rains here and within an hour there's dust.*

The truck clattered to a stop just outside Dustoff Operations. Major Hamilton Ray, the Special Forces advisor from the mountains, piled out of the passenger door. Eric joined the others who were standing outside.

"We got your man, Captain," Ray addressed Captain Scott. He pointed over his shoulder at the back of the truck.

"Dead?" Scott asked with disappointment.

"Yes, sir." Ray affirmed. They all waited for an explanation. It was Timmy Johnson who had been missing—the youngest and possibly the best liked of all of the medics. Johnson had flown on this mission for kicks, for the thrill of it. He was off the duty roster, having just put in three days and two nights straight.

"We found him down the side of the mountain face down in a stream."

"How far down?" Scott asked.

"About eight hundred yards. He'd apparently crawled there, though we don't see how."

"He wasn't burned?" Terry Green asked.

"No, sir." Ray said. Eric had the feeling Green wanted to know more, but, at the same time, he didn't. They were all that way. They *had* to know, but they didn't *want* to know. Major Ray, having seen much in combat and not knowing the man, continued, "He was pretty well broken up. Our medic says both of his arms and both of his legs were broken. He thinks his pelvis was crushed, too. My guess is he was either thrown out when the helicopter first hit the trees, or he jumped out, thinking he'd have a better chance jumping into the jungle than flying into the side of that mountain."

"Do you think he survived the crash?" Scott asked.

"I wish I could tell you no," Major Ray said earnestly, "but he crawled quite a way. He was probably going for help."

"Could he have been alive when we were there looking for him?" Green asked grievously. Timmy Johnson was a 57th medic, but Green thought of him as one of his own. It was Aubrey Scott, however, who would be the one writing the letter to Johnson's parents.

"Your guess is as good as mine," Ray said.

They'd heard enough. Guy took over for them. "Can you take him over to the Third Surg?" he asked.

"Of course." Ray motioned for his ARVN driver to start the truck. He started toward it.

"I'll get your reward," Scott said to him.

"Don't worry about that," Ray replied. "I am the one who found him."

EIGHT

Meridian, Mississippi

Lynn Mohr pulled her pickup into her sister's driveway, shut off the engine and remained in the cab. *Please, Lord,* she prayed, *give me wisdom to know how to minister to Gail.* Earlier that morning, Lynn had received a phone call from her sister, Gail, who was upset because the mail had arrived, and still no letter from Steve. As for Lynn, she had just that morning received her first letter from Eric. He indicated he might be stationed near Steve, but had not yet seen or talked to him. Lynn shared that information with Gail over the phone hoping to encourage her, but it only contributed to her depression.

Eric's letter had been mailed the afternoon after he had been on the mountain probing the wreckage of the downed Huey. At the time he mailed it, he had no idea it was Steve they had been trying to rescue.

Lynn wrote Eric right back, telling him about the problems occurring between Steve and Gail, and encouraging him to talk to Steve as soon as he could. She also told him another bit of news she knew he would welcome—the fact that almost two weeks earlier, Gail had given her heart to the Lord. This was something that for the past two years Eric and Lynn had earnestly prayed would happen.

Sitting in her truck cab, Lynn reviewed the events leading up to the time of Steve's marriage to Gail and her own marriage later to Eric. Eric's maternal grandfather raised Tennessee Walking horses. The twins' father, Ernie Gibson, was a professional show horse trainer who ran a training stable just south of Meridian. Eric often accompanied his grandfather when he went to watch Ernie Gibson work his show horses on the track adjacent to his barn. The twins had known Eric since they were in junior high, but their only contact was during the summer horse show season, or during the occasional trips Eric made with his grandfather to the training stables during the off-season months.

That had changed when they went to college. Eric went to Mississippi State University at Starkville. The twins started school at MSCW, Mississippi State College for Women, at nearby Columbus, but they transferred to Mississippi State after their first year so they could live with their aunt to help defray the costs of having two girls in college. Ernie Gibson's business was successful, but during the off-season his revenue stream experienced enough ups and downs to make it a struggle to put both girls through college at the same time.

Arriving at Mississippi State, the Gibson twins were pleasantly surprised to discover Eric Mohr in some of their classes. He was a friendly, easy-going guy they both enjoyed being around. Having Eric there helped make their adjustment to the new school less traumatic.

Gail, as she had done with other guys before, played up to Eric in an attempt to get him to fall for her. That was just something she did. Lynn didn't understand it, and didn't approve of it, but was powerless to change it. Though identical in appearance, the twins were far from identical in personality. Lynn was quiet, thoughtful, serious, yet with a sharp sense of humor. She was always helpful, ready to rescue anyone in trouble.

Gail, by contrast, walked on the wild side. She was impetuous, unpredictable, and, when it came to men, she was always falling in love. She fell quickly and deeply, got physically involved, got hurt, bounced back, then started the cycle all over again as if she never experienced any emotional scars from the episodes. Lynn had preserved her virginity, opting to save it for her husband after marriage. Gail had given hers up early and seemed to have no regrets.

Gail had been successful in winning Eric's attention. Even now he was very fond of her, but in a different way. That was not something that bothered Lynn, because there was no doubt in her mind that what she and Eric shared was a genuine love upon which they could build a lifetime. It was a commitment kind of love, a Christ-centered love, a love that went beyond passion and emotions.

Lynn had known Gail was setting Eric up for a fall, and found herself drawn more and more toward Eric's side in the breakup she knew was inevitable. She was drawn even deeper into the impending conflict when Gail came up with a scheme to get out of a promised concert date with Eric so she could go out with someone else. The "someone" was a man she had met through Eric.

Eric's father was a corporate pilot who flew a jet for a packing company. He had encouraged Eric to take flying lessons and had even recommended a flight instructor. That flight instructor was Steve Cooper, a Navy pilot who instructed in the Navy's primary jet training classes at Meridian Naval Air Station during the week and freelanced at some of the local small airports on weekends and summer evenings. In keeping with her *modus operandi* for wrapping a man around her fingers, Gail Gibson showed enthusiastic interest in Eric's flying. He offered to let her ride in the back seat during one of his flying lessons, provided his instructor had no objections.

Steve Cooper took one look at the vivacious blond with the spirited eyes, tanned skin and well-proportioned body, accented by the mid-thigh sundress she had chosen to wear that day, and had no objections. During the lesson, he offered most of his explanations to the enthusiastic and charming blond riding in the back seat, rather than to the student pilot he was supposed to be instructing. Eric was too busy trying to master accelerated stalls and crosswind landings to notice the chemistry developing between his girlfriend and his flight instructor.

A few days later, Steve Cooper asked Gail to go out with him on a night when she already had a date with Eric. He wanted to pick her up at the Starkville Airport and fly her someplace "special" for dinner. Gail asked Lynn to pull a "switch," and go with Eric to a concert in her place. It was something they had done before and gotten away with—not with Eric, but with other guys. At times, it could be fun. But Lynn refused at first for two reasons: one, she liked Eric—maybe too much; and two, she was certain that Eric and Gail had become physically involved, and she didn't want to be caught in a situation where Eric would expect something of her she wasn't ready to give.

Gail persisted. It was just a concert. There would be no opportunity for "hanky-panky." Finally, Lynn gave in. Maybe it would be fun. She had wanted to go out with Eric, even before he and Gail started dating, but he had never asked her. This would be her chance. Perhaps sometime during the evening, she would tell him she was not Gail and that Gail had in fact betrayed him and was even at that moment out with his friend and flight instructor, Steve Cooper.

The evening did not go as planned. Eric picked Gail/Lynn up at their aunt's house to take her to the concert, but knew from the moment he reached for her hand in the car before they arrived at the concert hall that it was Lynn with him rather than Gail. He didn't know why they had done it, but he knew they had switched. He decided to play out the charade to see where it led. When they were stopped at a traffic light, he pulled his date to him for an impulsive kiss. Lynn hesitated slightly, almost flinched, before returning his kiss. It wasn't a "Gail" kiss; it couldn't be a "Gail" kiss, for Gail kissed with abandon. To Lynn, a kiss was something sacred, something to be guarded, then given freely only when the time and the person were right. This was happening too fast for her, so all she could offer was an imitation. It didn't fool Eric a bit, and he drove the rest of the way to the concert in silence.

Oh, no, Lynn thought, *what have I done? I really care about this man. It's not right to trick him.* "Eric," she started to say as he searched for a parking place.

He shushed her, then pulled the car into an available space and pulled her toward him. He took her face in his hands and looked into her eyes. Lynn shivered even now as she remembered that look. Eric had looked through her and into her soul. His eyes searched hers; searching for a motive; searching for the person beyond the charade. Then he kissed her; at first a gentle, tender kiss on the lips. Then caressing the back of her head with his hands, he kissed her again, deeply. Her hesitation left, for she knew that he was kissing her, Lynn, not her sister Gail, and she responded with feelings of her own.

"Hello, Lynn," he said, when he released her.

She felt weak, almost faint. She put her hands on his arms for support and leaned her forehead on his shoulder. "Eric ...."

He lifted her head and put his finger to her lips. "It's okay," he said. "I'm glad it's you." She nodded and wiped a tear from her eye. She had not wanted to hurt him.

"Where is she?" he asked.

"With Steve Cooper, your flight instructor."

"I'm not surprised," he said. If he was hurt, he didn't show it. Then, in a lighter vein, "Do you want to go to this concert?"

"Not particularly."

"Me either." She thought that was strange, for she knew he loved music.

They drove out of town and to his grandfather's farm, some thirty miles away. On the way, they saw a meteorite shower producing hundreds of "shooting stars" in the southern sky. When they reached the farm, Eric pulled up at one of the pasture gates, opened it, and motioned for Lynn to drive through. Once the car was inside the fence, he fastened the gate, then slid behind the wheel and drove down a small dirt road until they came to a hillside overlooking a pond. They got out of the car and walked. They walked and talked and sat and watched the stars until it was time to get Lynn back to her aunt's house. She was pretty sure they had fallen in love that night. She knew *she* had. For Eric, it may have taken a little longer, but they had fallen in love—so much in love that when Gail announced to them a couple of months later that she was pregnant and that she and Steve were getting married, Lynn did not see a hint of pain in Eric's eyes.

That had all occurred three years earlier. Shortly thereafter, Eric and Lynn had both accepted Christ into their lives at a Campus Crusade for Christ rally. Two years ago, they had gotten married. Until Vietnam came along, it had been a marriage made in heaven.

Eric and Lynn shared their new-found faith with Steve and Gail, but were met with indifference. They didn't need God, they said; they had each other. They were caught up with their passion for each other and for their little daughter, Emily. Religion was a crutch, a figment of people's imagination—weak men and women who could not stand on their own strengths. Thanks, but no thanks.

For Gail, that position had now changed. Two months earlier she had encountered an old boyfriend, and in a time of emotional weakness aggravated by Steve's prolonged absence, she gave in to temptation and went to bed with the man. She was ashamed after she did it. She wasn't the old Gail; she was a married woman and a mother, and she loved her husband. It was wrong, and she knew it was.

A few weeks later when she met Steve in Hawaii for his R&R, she confessed to him what she had done, hoping for forgiveness and a cleansing from the guilt she felt. It didn't happen that way. Instead, Steve reacted by tuning her out. He wouldn't touch her the rest of their time together. He wouldn't even talk with her about it. It was as if he couldn't wait to get back to the war—that cursed war that had been the cause of their separation in the first place.

Gail was totally distraught. She came back from Hawaii and drove straight to her sister's house on the farm at Shuqualak. What a time that had been! Gail poured her heart out. Lynn shared the gospel with her again, and for the first time, Gail was totally open. She gave her heart to Jesus, trusting Him to forgive her for her sins and to restore her peace and her joy.

Gail couldn't wait to write Steve and tell him what had happened. In letter after letter she poured out her heart, her excitement, and her new-found joy to her husband. She asked for his forgiveness, pledged her undying love and loyalty, and told him she would do anything to make it up to him. Jesus had forgiven her, couldn't Steve find it in his heart to forgive her, too? In answer, she received nothing. Had he even gotten her mail? Had he opened it? Had he read it? Was he okay? She didn't know. She needed help, her faith was slipping. This morning she had called Lynn.

Now Lynn was there. Together they would pray this thing through. Lynn slipped out of the pickup cab and went inside to comfort her sister.

NINE

Navy Binh Thuy

Navy San Quentin—that's what it seemed like to Eric. His room became a prison; the compound, a prison yard. It was that way for four days. Four days in which the world—the war—passed him by while he labored over words, over regulations, over procedures and syntax, and over the growing sense of loss that even he, a stranger, felt because of the waste of five lives on an impossible and unnecessary quest. It had been the decision of one man; the others had followed him blindly. It could just as easily have been Eric or any of the other medical evacuation pilots. They all made mistakes. Some he knew now could be fatal.

There was no mail—not enough time had passed for Lynn to have received his first letter or to have sent him one in return. There was no association with the other men in the unit, except for Les Winters who stopped in from time to time to look over Eric's progress and to offer him companionship when it was time to eat. Thank God the air conditioner worked.

They left him with a manual typewriter (he had learned to type on an electric), a stack of forms and the army regulations pertaining to "Reporting, Investigative—Aircraft Accidents."

Throughout the first day, they brought him pictures, pathology reports and medical reports. It had been up to him to transcribe the contents of the audio tape and to complete his graphical sketch of the crash site and to put the entire report together in the proper report format.

About mid-morning the first day, a quiet knock came at the door. Hungry for company, Eric got up to open it. Before he could reach the knob, it turned and the door opened slowly. There stood the Vietnamese girl he had seen at the sink that first morning. She stood just outside Eric's door with two others: one younger and baby-faced, the other slightly older and very pregnant. They were all short, with shining round faces, jet black hair and almond eyes. They wore simple pajama-like clothing.

"I am Minh," the familiar one said, leading the other two into the room by the hand—one on each side of her. "This is Baby-san, and Mama-san." She nodded toward each as she introduced them. They smiled shyly. Their names fit—baby-face was obviously a young teenager and the other a mother-to-be. She had to be at least seven months along. "We rork for you," Minh said.

"Rork?"

"You know … rork … shine your boots, make your bed, do laundry … rork!"

"Oh." Now he understood. "Work."

All three nodded enthusiastically. It would seem that only Minh spoke English.

Eric had not been briefed about this arrangement. "How much?" he asked.

"Three hundred P," Minh said. That didn't seem like much to Eric. As best he could calculate, that was something like seventy-five cents.

"Three hundred piasters?"

"Three hundred P," Minh affirmed as the others nodded. "Each. You pay one week."

"So, I pay each of you three hundred piasters a week and you clean my room, make my bed, do my laundry, and shine my boots?"

"You smart GI," Minh announced. She was picking at him, the same sense of humor she had displayed the first morning when she laughingly called him "Newby." Even now her eyes twinkled with humor. *Good, someone to spar with,* he thought. He liked a good sense of humor.

"Okay," Eric said, thinking the deal was concluded. But it wasn't. Not quite. Minh pulled on his arm, bending him toward her. She put her hands on his shoulder and pulled him down further so she could whisper in his ear.

"You buy for us things," she whispered, as the other two turned away shyly, biting their lower lips and finding his ceiling fan extremely interesting.

"What kind of things?" he whispered back to her.

"Soap," she announced. He nodded. "Tide," she said. He nodded again. She pulled him closer and put her lips right to his ear. "Kotex," she whispered. He couldn't help it. He put his arm around her waist and hugged her. She was so cute—like a little girl, though she wore a tiny wedding band and was probably in her late twenties. She hugged him back, then pushed him away. "You buy at PX," she said.

"Sure." Now the deal was done. It began a beautiful relationship between Eric Mohr, the country boy from Mississippi and these three peasant girls from Vietnam. They cleaned his room, shined his boots, made his bed, and washed his clothes. They tugged at the hair on his arm when he was shaving or had come out of the shower, and played with the hair on his chest. Their men had no body hair, so his was a novelty to them. He treated them kindly, and they loved him for it. They worked hard and he gave them each the equivalent of about seventy-five cents a week. He was frequently tempted to give them extra, but Les Winters warned him that doing so would play havoc with their economy. He bought Tide detergent, bath soap and feminine napkins at the PX for them from time to time. The other pilots paid them as well. They worked for everyone in the BOQ, so the 300 piasters a week added up.

The women had passes to come on the base and work for the Americans, so apparently they had been checked out and weren't Viet Cong. There were stories, however, that they didn't show up for work on days the VC attacked the compound. Eric didn't know; so far they were only stories.

Whenever he bought them items from the PX, he had to give them a note so they could take the items out the front gate without being accused of stealing. They couldn't take out too much or they would be accused of trafficking in the Black Market. They could get away with just enough for their own personal use. It was a system that had apparently been worked out long before Eric arrived in Vietnam.

The second day of his isolation, Minh knocked on the door quietly, and again without waiting for him to answer, came in to gather his laundry and his spare boots. She went over to where he was typing and put her hand on his shoulder. "How you say your name?" she asked, pointing to the name tag sewed on the flight suit shirt that was hanging on the back of his chair.

"Moore," he said.

She repeated it. "Moore."

"My first name is Eric," he told her.

"Moore," she repeated. Then she picked up the Bible that lay on the makeshift desk he had crafted out of scrap plywood. "Christian?" she asked. He nodded.

"Me, too," she said smiling.

"Really?" That surprised him. He thought the Vietnamese were mostly Buddhists.

"Uh huh," she nodded. "CMA."

"CMA?"

"Christian Missionary Alliance."

It was not a group he had heard of, but she settled his doubts quickly. "I love Jesus," she said.

"I do, too," he assured her. First Mattie, now Minh. The family was coming together. Plus, Blake Sam was here somewhere. He would have to find him when he had the chance.

Three days later, the report was finished. Then CW4 Guy got hold of it and it took Eric the better part of two more days to finish it again to Guy's satisfaction. On the last of those two days, the reward angel brought him two rewards.

Coming back from breakfast, he saw the Donut Dollies getting into a Navy jeep.

"Wait!" he called. He hadn't seen them all week. Mattie turned to greet him. The ride from Long Binh and the walk back from the O' Club after the "Green Mother" had made people assume they were friends. Funny how people make those associations. Maybe it was because she had told them he was a Christian. Whatever the reason, the others got into the jeep, leaving it to Mattie to see what he wanted.

He had a simple question. "Are you girls ever around any of the Navy pilots?"

"Sure." Judging by her answer, it should have been obvious.

"Do you know a guy named Steve Cooper?"

"No, I don't. Is he stationed here? Eileen knows a bunch of the Seawolves."

"I'm not sure where he's stationed—maybe here, maybe Vung Tau. He's a Black Pony. He was shot down a few days ago, and they got him back, but I don't know if he was hurt or not."

"Maybe he's at the Third Surg," Mattie offered.

"I hadn't thought of that." How could he have been so dumb? The Third Surg was right next door.

"It's worth a try." Eric realized the others were waiting for her, but he wanted her to take his request seriously in case Steve wasn't at the Third Surg. "He's my brother-in-law, and I'd like to find him, to find out if he's all right."

"We'll ask around," Mattie said. "We're flying out this morning on a Navy CH-46. We'll be going to Cau Mau, Bac Lieu, Soc Trang and Vung Tau during the next couple of days. The Black Ponies are here, but I think there are some at Vung Tau, too. I'll check."

"Thanks." He felt a little better, but couldn't believe he had overlooked the obvious. The Third Surg hospital was right next door. All he had to do was walk over and ask.

The second ray of sunlight appeared just as the girls drove off: mail call. He had hoped for at least one letter from Lynn, but there were four, *and* one from Gail. The hospital would have to wait. The letters came first. He sat down on the steps of the BOQ, checked the dates on Lynn's letters and opened the oldest one first.

Lynn's letters were full of love, but also of news about Steve and Gail. She told him of Gail's conversion, of her act of adultery and her confession to Steve, and of Steve's reaction when he heard about it. She encouraged Eric to pray for them both,

and to try hard to locate Steve and talk to him about forgiveness. He read Gail's letter last.

Dear Eric,

I'm sure Lynn has told you about my accepting
Jesus. On the one hand, I'm so excited, yet on the
other, afraid. I'm afraid of losing Steve. I told Lynn
it was okay to tell you what I did, so I'm sure you
know by now. It seems that telling Steve was a
mistake, though I felt at the time it was the right
thing to do.

I know he is hurt, but I just can't stand the thought of
him rejecting me totally. Can you find him and tell
him how much I love him and how much Emily and I
need him? I know you can share the love of Jesus with
him.

If you talk with him, please let me know how he is doing. He hasn't written me at all since we were together
in Hawaii.

Gail

Eric glanced over the letters a second time, pausing to
re-read some parts of Lynn's, then stuffed them all into the
right calf pocket of his flight suit. He walked the short distance to the 3rd Surg. This was his first visit to the Army
hospital and he was awed by its size. True, it was a mobile
hospital, but it had obviously been set up at its current location long enough to appear permanently situated. The hos-

pital was housed in at least twenty rows of quonset huts, all interconnected. He approached the south door. There were no signs or markings and he wondered if it was a staff entrance. A volleyball net was set up in the yard and a volleyball game was in progress. The players were all young Vietnamese men; some really just boys. Most had an arm or leg missing. Others had an eye covered or an arm in a sling or some type of cast. Crutches were in abundance, yet the game was as lively as any Eric had seen.

The sight saddened him, yet at the same time he found it fascinating. It was recreation, true, and he guessed rehabilitation as well. But it was something more. It was a symbol of the sickness of a war that left so many maimed in a land where even had they been whole, their lives would be a constant struggle. Yet, there they were, playing and laughing and making the best of what life had to offer. Maybe they were trying to forget. At least their war was over. Or was it? Wouldn't their lives now be consumed with the struggle to survive in a culture that probably knew little in the way of charity?

The game was a brief respite from real life. Their objective was just to get the ball over the net. Never mind about surviving in a war-torn economy where resources were scarce and mercy non-existent. That would come later. After watching a minute or two, Eric went inside.

The door opened into a long hallway, with doors spaced evenly along either side. He walked toward the center of the complex, stopping to look through the first door he passed. He was looking into one of the quonset huts, which was apparently a ward in the hospital. Rows of beds lined either wall, with patients in most of them. Arms and legs were suspended from various pulley arrangements, bandages covered large portions of their bodies, IV's hung from poles beside many of the beds. Here, too, the faces were Vietnamese. Why had he thought this was an American hospital? Eric continued down the hall, looking for someone he could ask about Steve.

Near the center of the complex, he came upon a young woman in fatigues bending over a counter to pick up a clipboard which appeared to contain some type of medical records. "Oh," she said, as she straightened up, caught off guard. "I didn't see you." She was an Army nurse, a second lieutenant, maybe 5' 5", a little heavy for her height, dark brown hair pulled back in a pony tail, and deep brown eyes, with long dark lashes.

"I didn't mean to startle you," Eric said. "I'm trying to find out if someone is here in the hospital."

"American or Vietnamese?"

"American."

"The other end of the building." She pointed down the hall opposite from the direction he had come.

"Thanks." He started to go.

"Wait," she said. She held the clipboard against her chest with her left arm and stuck her right hand out for a shake. "I'm Lisa Sneed. I live below you."

"Oh?" He hadn't seen her before … unless she was there at the club that first night. But then, there were so many people there that night.

"Minh, your hootch maid, told me you're a Christian."

"That's right," he said, surprised, yet glad in a way it was getting around. He had rather people know that about him than wait for him to tell them. *But why would she bring it up? And why did she know who he was when he didn't know her?*

Lisa seemed to read his mind. "I saw you at the club that night they had you drink that stupid initiation drink. I've seen you in the mess hall a time or two. Minh couldn't wait to tell me you were a Christian after she talked to you about it."

"You're a Christian, too, then?"

"Yes!" She nodded enthusiastically. It was then Eric noticed the joy in her eyes … the kind of joy that *should* be in a Christian's eyes. He was probably losing his with his discouragement about not flying and not finding Steve. In fact, he knew he was.

"My parents are missionaries," she continued.

"Really?" That was interesting. Somehow she didn't fit his image of a missionary kid. He wasn't sure what his image of a missionary kid was, just that she wasn't it. "Where?"

"Malaysia," she said.

"Then you're used to being around Oriental people?" It was both a statement and a question.

"Kind of," she acknowledged, "but I spent a lot of my life in the States."

Eric was delighted to find another Christian, but he might be just a few minutes away from finding Steve. He had to know if he was here.

"I would like to talk with you some more," he said, "but right now I really need to find out if this guy is here."

"Sure. I'm sorry. Listen. Do you want to get together for some Bible study and prayer some time? My friend Fran is a brand new Christian, and there's this guy here—he's an orderly—who keeps talking to us about getting together.

Now he was *really* interested, but he still wanted to find Steve. Already he was prioritizing his missions.

"I'd love to! I could use some fellowship."

"You would!?" She was excited.

"Yes." he nodded.

"Then we've got to get together. You go find your guy. I've got to get back to my ward. I'll talk to the others."

"Okay," he answered.

"Okay," she nodded, and went off down the hall.

Eric went in the opposite direction, but he struck out. Steve was not at the Third Surg; never had been. Eric was back at ground zero. But his visit hadn't been a total loss. He had met another Christian and learned of two more. The body of Christ in that particular area was coming together. He didn't know it, but in the days ahead, he would be extremely dependent upon their prayer support.

TEN

Navy Binh Thuy

Terry Green and Eric Mohr strolled toward the Huey, wearing survival vests over their flight suits and carrying their flight helmet bags in hand. Since this was to be a local training flight, they had foregone the uncomfortable "chicken plate" armored chest protector vest normally worn on all missions. Approaching the aircraft, Green motioned to Mohr, "You take the bottom, I'll take the top."

It was Eric's first time to fly since arriving in Vietnam. Captain Terry Green, the 82nd's CO, also doubled as the unit IP. Since the 57th's Instructor Pilot, 1st Lieutenant Rob McElroy, was on R&R, Green had offered to give Eric his in-country check ride so he could begin flying missions.

This practice of splitting up the preflight inspection duties with the aircraft commander inspecting the rotor system, leaving the first pilot, or peter pilot, to inspect the lower portion of the aircraft was common. By choosing to do the preflight inspection on the top portion of the aircraft, the ACs were exercising their prerogative to inspect what they considered the most important mechanical part of the Huey: the rotor system. Held together by imbedded straps of banded steel and an elaborate array of nuts and bolts, the whole thing was held on by one giant nut called the "Jesus Nut." It was called the "Jesus Nut" because if it came off, regardless of what you believed about Jesus, you were on your way to meet Him.

They started the check ride late in the day, about an hour before dark, because most of Eric's flying would be done at night. Green climbed to the roof of the Huey using the hand and foot holds aft of the right side pilot's door, and Eric retrieved the bound checklist from its storage compartment behind the cockpit center console. He opened the book and began preflighting the bottom portion of the Huey starting at the left-side pilot's door.

Green looked down as he watched Eric methodically start at the beginning of the checklist. "Hey Mohr," he called. "Put the checklist down and check this Huey out like your life depended on it—because it does."

Eric looked up at him with a questioning look. He'd been taught in flight school to always use the checklist.

"I'm not saying don't use the checklist," Green explained. "But use it to check yourself, not as a primary aid. You need to learn to inspect this Huey because you know what every inch of it is supposed to look like, not because some book tells you how to do it. The aircraft itself can serve as a checklist. You start at one point and you look at everything. If something doesn't look right to you, get somebody to check it out."

Eric shrugged, and put down the checklist. His father probably knew everything there was to know about the Sabreliner he flew for Deep South Packing, but he still used checklists. That's okay, he would do it Green's way. Green was the IP. Of course, Green could be testing him. But Green wasn't using a book on his preflight and it was obvious he was checking the rotor system over carefully. Eric watched for a moment as

Green pulled on every connection, checked every nut, checked the safety wires holding all of the connections tight, and examined each surface for cracks or separations. Eric would do the same when he inspected a rotor system. And, he would do the same now with the bottom of the aircraft, checking more than just fluid levels and for leaks or loose connections. He set about to check the Huey over carefully.

He was only halfway around the fuselage when Green climbed down to join him. Together they finished the lower portion of the preflight inspection, then climbed into the cockpit. Here, Eric had more to learn about the Dustoff way of doing things.

"Our engine start procedures are very important, and we follow the checklist here, but with a slightly different twist," Green explained after they had strapped into the two pilots' seats. Green was in the left seat and Eric in the right. Green continued. "We make a lot of rapid departures. Our goal for getting off the ground on an emergency medevac is two minutes. That means a lot of the pre-takeoff checks must be done ahead of time.

"The duty crews preflight their aircraft when their shift begins. When they finish their preflight, even if they don't have any missions pending, they get into the aircraft and go through the pre-start and starting checklists. They start the engine and check out all of the systems. When they are satisfied the aircraft is ready to fly, they shut it back down. Then they go through the starting cycle again up to the point where they're ready to pull the starter trigger. They set the throttle just past the flight idle detent. They leave the starter/generator switch in the start position; everything is ready to go, except the main fuel switch and the battery switch. When they get a mission, the right seat pilot starts the engine and brings everything up to speed while the left seat pilot straps in and puts on his helmet. The crew chief mans the fire extinguisher during start, then climbs in and straps himself in. By the time the engine is up to speed, the left seat pilot should be ready to go. He'll take the controls, while the right seat pilot puts on his seatbelt and shoulder harness, flight helmet and gloves. It may seem awkward to you at first, but within a week it'll be second nature. Our normal time off is actually about a minute and twenty seconds.

"In flight school, you typically flew only one flight a day. Here you'll be flying the same aircraft all day, or all night as it may be, and you'll know if there is anything wrong when you shut it down between sorties. So you don't necessarily get a chance to do a full preflight between flights. In fact, you rarely do. Any questions?"

About a million, Eric thought. He shook his head.

The IP knew Mohr was too green to know what was ahead of him. Today, his wings were shiny and he was full of the confidence they psyched him up with in flight school. If he made it through the next three months, those wings would be growing moss. In the next two hours, it was Green's job to see if the young pilot had any kind of control touch and if he still remembered to bottom the collective and point the nose toward some reasonable facsimile of a landing place when the needles split during a simulated forced landing. He wanted to make sure Eric still remembered his training and the emergency procedures he had practiced daily while in flight school. Other than that, it would be up to the 57th's aircraft commanders to mold Eric into a combat pilot.

During the next few months, Mohr would learn to put a Huey into places so tight they wouldn't cover half of one of the "instructor only" confined areas in flight school. He would learn how to point the Huey up, down and sideways, anywhere necessary, to avoid being shot down. He'd turn it around every axis it had and some it didn't. He'd push it past VNE (velocity never to exceed) and haul loads that were 3,000 pounds over maximum allowable gross weight. He would learn to fly tactical approaches that made it seem as if the aircraft was plunging to certain destruction, then pull it out of the dive at the last minute and plant it on a postage stamp. He would learn to use the aircraft's torque in a tactical departure that would spin him up to a safe altitude like a corkscrew at more than 2,000 feet a minute. These were the things his ACs would teach him. For now, it was Green's job to give Eric a standard, by-the-book check ride: standard autorotations, low-level autorotations, 180-degree autorotations, hydraulics-off landings, anti-torque running landings and night orientation. When Eric had put on his flight helmet and Nomex gloves and had buckled his seat belt, Green said, "Let's go flying."

Green called out the commands as Eric went through the startup checklist. Once the engine was up to speed and he was getting ready to lift the Huey to a hover, Green held his hand out to stop him.

"One of the hardest things you'll do here is to hover one of these birds in and out of these revetments."

Mohr looked at the IP with a "you've got to be kidding" look. That statement deserved more explanation.

"Oh, I know it looks simple, but don't say I didn't warn you." Green said. He sat back in his seat and motioned for Eric to please continue.

It was important to Eric that he impress the IP. Because his father was a professional pilot, he had been around flying all his life. Though he had only learned to fly within the past two years, it was something he knew he could do well. After a shaky start in flight school, he had graduated at the top of his class. Maybe the other Army pilots were flying just to get out of being a grunt, or as a stepping stone to a military career, but for Eric, flying medical evacuation missions in a helicopter was the most important thing in the world next to his relationship with God and his wife. He had to excel. He'd gotten off to a rocky start with the Dustoff pilots at Binh Thuy because of his isolation during the accident investigation, and because the word had been spread by those who had been in his room and seen his Bible and Christian books that he was a religious fanatic. It was an unfair label. Religion had nothing to do with trusting in Jesus and developing a relationship with Him, but in their minds that was not the case. Eric wanted to gain credibility with the other pilots so he could be an effective witness. But that wasn't all of it. He was like everybody else, with the possible exception of Les Winters. He wanted them to like him because it hurts to not be liked.

Eric eased the collective pitch lever up until the Huey was light on the skids. That's one thing he remembered from flight school. When the helicopter breaks ground, it's going to try to move over the ground, rather than remain stationary over the spot from which it was lifted. Even if the rotor system was perfectly level, the Huey's natural tendency was to drift backwards and to the right. Wind would also have an effect.

He'd been taught by his IPs at Fort Rucker to get the aircraft light on skids, and anticipate where it's trying to drift before you actually break ground. Then you can adjust the cyclic before you break ground to keep the aircraft in one spot.

In theory, it was supposed to work. When Eric pulled the Huey up, he had his hands full. The cyclic was all over the cockpit like it had been during his first days trying to learn to hover a TH-55 at Fort Wolters. "Don't say I didn't warn you,"

Green said, grinning as he watched Eric fight the turbulence caused by the downwash of the rotor system bouncing off the four-foot high concrete walls of the revetment. The revetment had three sides, and the only way out was backwards. Eric was sweating beads of perspiration as he struggled with the Huey that seemed to have a mind of its own. With a great bit of effort, he managed to ease it backwards out of the revetment. When he was clear of the concrete barriers, the hovering became easier. At this stage of his flying experience hovering was never really easy, but with experience it would get easier.

The check ride lasted nearly two hours, one full fuel load. They flew most of it at Can Tho Army Airfield where there was a grassy area beside the runway upon which they could do their autorotations and running landings without grinding down the Huey's skid shoes. At dusk, the runway lights were lit—not electric lights, but oil smudge pots lit by torches. At Green's direction, Eric moved from doing emergency procedures on the grass to practicing night takeoff and landings on the paved runway.

As the sky darkened, Terry worked with Eric on keeping oriented at night, pointing out some of the local landmarks. During his traffic patterns, Eric tended to angle toward the runway on final rather than line up with it from the base leg of the traffic pattern. Green knew if he didn't correct this problem now, Eric would have a lot of difficulty making approaches to poorly lit confined areas in the field at night. "Where are you looking when you turn final?" he asked.

"At the end of the runway," Eric answered.

"Which end?"

"The approach end."

"Ah," Green observed. "Then that's your problem. Look at the far end of the runway when you turn final. It'll give you a better perspective." Eric made that slight adjustment and amazingly, it worked.

His flying was a little rough—after all it had been nearly five months since he graduated from flight school—but it was safe enough and Green signed him off, satisfied he was ready to go on flight status.

The next morning, Eric went to Operations and asked Wade Daugherty when he would be put on the duty roster. Daugherty looked up from his desk as K. J. Madison walked in and asked K. J. if he would take Eric and explain the duty roster to him.

"Sure," K. J. answered. He led Eric over to the wall map of the 57th's Area of Operations (AO).

"When you come in at night," K. J. explained, "this board will normally be covered with missions. During the day, there rarely are any because we can handle the missions as they come in. At night, it's a different story."

"We put up four crews a day," he continued, as Eric made a pretense of studying the map, which at this point made little sense to him. "There are two First-Up crews, one during the day and one at night. They each pull a twelve-hour shift and get a lot of flying during that twelve hours—especially the night crew. The Second-Up crew is on for 24 hours and flies routine missions. They back up the First-Up crew when they get more than they can handle or when they are out of the area. Then there's a Third-Up crew who handle routine patient transfers and are available for emergencies when both First-Up and Second-Up are committed. That was a Third-Up crew who picked you up in Long Binh the other day after they made a routine patient transfer from the 3rd Surg to the 24th Evac.

"When you hit the duty roster, you'll fly Third-Up first, which is also a twenty-four hour shift. Lot of times you don't fly at all when you're on Third-Up. Rarely do you fly at night.

Most of the Third-Up missions are what we just call 'ash and trash'—admin missions. The next day, you'll fly Second-Up. Again, most flights are routine and happen during the day, but Second-Up is more likely to be sent out on an emergency medevac mission if First-Up is already engaged. If Second-Up goes out on an emergency medevac, then the Third-Up crew is alerted and put on standby."

"One of the First-Up shifts begins at 7:00 in the morning; the other, 7:00 at night—that's 1900 hours, officer time. When you come off Second-Up, you pull First-Up duty the next night. You'll get a lot of flying on that shift, usually eight to ten hours. Then, you're off for twenty-four hours and you pull First-Up Day. The next day you normally start all over again. It's a different rotation for the ACs and peter pilots because the aircraft commanders also fly with the VNAF Dustoff crews. What happens is a guy gets pulled off the normal roster for a week and flies with the Vietnamese every day for that week. Then he goes back on the regular roster and someone else gets the pleasure of riding around in the VNAF ships."

"Most of the ACs are flying in excess of 120 hours a month. Frankly, we're ready for some relief. We've been counting on some of the peter pilots making aircraft commander soon, and have been working hard with them to bring them up to speed. The loss of Stu Chambers and his peter pilot, Ron Elliott, hurt in more ways than one. Elliott was scheduled to take his AC check ride the day after he died."

Eric listened to the explanation, alternating his attention between the map and K. J. He understood most of what he was hearing, but as of yet, he couldn't put himself in the picture.

K. J.'s comment about Chambers and Elliott brought something to mind that had been nagging Eric about that crash. It was something mentioned, but glossed over during the accident report. Les Winters had made the discovery and informed the others, but it didn't go into the report.

The 82nd and 57th had twelve Hueys between them—six assigned to each detachment. During the preceding several months, those aircraft, as they went in for their 1200-hour inspections, were being retrofitted with crashworthy fuel systems. Winters had taken extra time to explain this to Eric, who had never heard the term before. A crashworthy fuel system was one that had been designed to minimize the risk of fire. The fuel bladder, which was rubberized to begin with, was coated with an inner lining of sealing foam that would close off most punctures to prevent fuel from being spilled. The fuel line connections were all replaced with breakaway, self-sealing connectors designed to break loose in the event of stress, closing off all connections automatically, thus preventing fuel spills from a fuel line rupture.

Eleven of the aircraft had been retrofitted. The only one remaining to be done was the one the ill-fated crew had been flying that night. There was the possibility that if the aircraft hadn't burned, the crewmembers would have survived.

Was it destiny that caused them to be flying that particular Huey? If so, did they all have a destiny—some to live and some to die? What was his destiny? Eric couldn't explain it, but he knew deep in his spirit he was not destined to die in Vietnam, that he had a life beyond that year in combat. Perhaps it was spiritual knowledge as explained in chapter twelve of First Corinthians. Whatever it was, that knowledge would affect how he flew and how he related to those around him on a daily basis during the coming months.

When Eric was on the duty roster a day later, it was with Hank Harris. Eric's earlier observation concerning Harris' dour outlook on life was reinforced during the routine flight they made to Poly Olay Island, off the southern tip of the Cau Mau peninsula.

Throughout the flight, Harris was a constant barrage of criticism. Not toward Eric—he hardly acknowledged Eric was there—but toward everything else. To Harris, everything about the war and how the US was conducting it was wrong. Everything about the 57th Med Detachment and how it performed its missions was wrong. If they would only listen to him, he would straighten them out. He knew how things should be done. It was obvious. Why didn't everybody else see things the way he did?

They stopped for fuel at Cau Mau both coming and going, and they dropped the patient off at the Third Surg. That meant there were five takeoffs and five landings. Harris let Eric fly some of the time en route, but made all of the takeoffs and landings himself. He did very little in the way of training the new peter pilot except to show Eric how and when to obtain artillery clearances when flying through the various military sectors that were marked on the map.

Eric was careful not to ask Harris many questions so as not to give him another topic to go on about. But there was one question Eric did ask. "How many days do you have left?" translated: "*how many days am I going to have to put up with this negative, critical spirit?*"

"One-hundred-seventy-three and a wake-up." It was the only thought Harris had expressed all day that might be considered positive.

Great, Eric thought, then immediately chided himself for being drawn into wrong thinking. What Hank Harris needed was to know about Jesus' love. He needed something to give him hope. He broached the subject as they sat in the Huey after the flight waiting for the engine temperatures to stabilize before shutting off the main fuel.

"Hank, you brought up a lot of issues while we were flying today—a lot of things that are wrong. Do you ever think about trusting God to change them?"

"God!" Harris was incredulous. "God! There's no God."

"Oh, that's where you're wrong."

"Yeah," Harris indicated with a flick of his wrist. "There's a God. That's why we've got this stinkin' war."

"God didn't have anything to do with starting this war," Eric told him.

"Then what good is a god, if he can't prevent wars or sickness or poverty?"

"God exists, but He doesn't cause all those things. In fact, if men would listen to God, those things wouldn't happen at all."

"Yeah, right."

"It's true," Eric insisted. "God gave us laws. We have problems like wars and sickness and poverty because people don't obey His laws."

"That sounds like such a simple solution," Harris told him, "but it's a fairy tale. There's no God, or if there is, He doesn't care about us."

"You think He doesn't care about you," Eric said, "but He does care. That's why Jesus died on a cross."

"Jesus Christ," Harris said. He didn't say it as worship or with consideration, he said it derisively.

"Yes, Jesus Christ. He loves you; He died for you; and you curse Him. It's not surprising your life is so miserable."

Harris' response was to close the throttle and shut off the main fuel switch. "Let's get out of here."

ELEVEN

Vung Tau

The girl grabbed her flimsy dress and left the room without stopping to put it on. On the way out, she ransacked Steve's wallet, taking from it not piasters, but military payment certificates—MPC, which she could parlay into greenbacks on the black market. He watched her, but did nothing to stop her. Fortunately, she didn't take everything he had. She took her price, maybe a little more for him being such a jerk. The whiskey had done nothing to help him forget; it had only made him more angry. The whore had tried in vain to arouse him, but even her professional techniques had produced no results. All Steve could think of was Gail. Gail with him. Gail in the arms of another man. *Was she as passionate with him as she is with me?* he wondered.

The Vietnamese prostitute had the body of a little girl and the mouth of a sailor. There was nothing about her that Steve found sexually appealing. Would he never be any good for anyone else after loving Gail?

The girl couldn't even pass for a good companion. She apparently knew only three English words—all vulgar. After he kicked her out, Steve lay on the bed watching the ceiling fan's shadow in the dim light and trying to get drunk enough to fall asleep before morning. He didn't make it.

When the sun finally appeared, its morning rays pushed their way into the room through the slats in the shudders, making the image of a ladder on the wall. Steve stared at the ladder, his mind filled with a myriad of contradictory thoughts until one thought began to push aside the others. *You can go up, or you can go down. It's up to you.* He was already down and still sinking—crushed by a heavy weight. He had tried to push the weight aside, he really had, but it was still there. Maybe time would heal the hurt—time and flying. Time and killing Viet Cong.

Slowly he dressed and went downstairs. The ground floor was deserted. A loaf of bread sat on a sideboard in the dining area. He tore off a handful of it on the way out the door. The jeep was where he had left it in the parking lot behind the villa. He dug the keys to the steering chain lock out of his pocket, and unlocked the chain before climbing slowly in the seat. His arm hurt, his neck was stiff and his leg would barely take his weight.

After leaving the villa, Steve drove east on Ha Long Street. He pulled off the road and stopped in front of the old French fortifications. Inland, a giant statue of Jesus stood on the side of Nui Nho Mountain. Steve looked at the statue and in his mind riduculed the people who had put it there. *Jesus. That's all Eric and Lynn ever talked about. Jesus. Jesus. Jesus. If Jesus is so real, why isn't He here now? Why didn't He stop Gail from ruining our marriage? Jesus doesn't care. You only have yourself. You think you've found someone to share your life with. You treat that someone with respect and even create a new life with them, and you still can't trust them. You only have yourself—no God, no soulmate, just yourself.*

He drove further along the road, letting it take him north along the seaward side of the peninsula. He parked the jeep beneath the shade of a palm along Bai Sau Beach. He got out and climbed a small mountain overlooking the beach. There were places he had to make his way around thick underbrush to get to the top. The sun was already hot overhead and he quickly worked up a sweat.

After a few minutes, Steve found himself on a high perch overlooking the South China Sea. There was a stiff breeze coming off the water and he stood facing it, letting the wind blow in his face. He couldn't remember when he had felt so lonely—felt so much pain. He could actually feel it in his chest and it kept on relentlessly, like he was in the jaws of a giant "C" clamp with some unseen force twisting it tighter and tighter, until he thought his chest would be crushed. He closed his eyes and saw Gail laughing ... saw her in the arms of a faceless man, then another and another and another ... the parade continued.

In his mind, he saw Emily running toward him, calling, "Daddy! Daddy! Daddy!" He started toward her and fell ... tumbling end over end toward the ocean. But he never reached the bottom. It was all happening in slow motion. He wiped his eyes with his sleeve and found himself still on the mountain, the morning sun reflecting off the water, seagulls swooping down after their prey. A marine horn blew, and he turned to watch a large junk across the bay, a Navy cutter in pursuit. The men on the junk were shouting, their voices carrying across the water. Sailors stood on the bow of the cutter, the waves splashing on their faces as they waited to board the junk to make sure it wasn't taking supplies up the river to the Viet Cong.

Steve had a strange, detached thought while watching the sailors in action: *the saltwater would be destructive to their weapons, making it imperative they clean them thoroughly when the mission was over. Life was like that. You did what you were supposed to do, and were attacked from time to time by rust, decay and the elements. You went on, you recovered, you cleaned up, and got ready for the next mission. He could do that.*

If only he could call upon Eric's Jesus. If only he could believe He was real—that Jesus was alive, that He cared, that He could, or would, fix things. Maybe if he could believe …. But no, it was just a fairy tale. Life was what *he* could make of it. With or without Gail, he would make something of it.

For a brief moment, Steve thought of jumping off the mountain onto the rocks below, but that was a quitter's way and Steve Cooper was no quitter. Determined to pull himself together, he started back down the mountain.

Around noon, Steve was sitting on the veranda of the Thang Muoi Restaurant drinking tea and eating boiled shrimp. Two pilots wearing gray flight suits with Black Pony patches on their shoulders bounded up the front steps. They took off their aviators' sunglasses and scanned the porch until they located Steve.

The one in front was Sid Kerr. When he saw Steve, he headed toward him. Behind him was Stump Willis, Cooper's wingman. Kerr was a lieutenant whose assignment prior to Vietnam had been as a Primary Jet Instructor at Meridian Naval Air Station. He and Steve worked together at Meridian and attended the OV-10 transition course in Southern California at the same time. Everyone liked Kerr. He was a friendly guy who always seemed to have the time to listen when a fellow flier needed someone to talk to.

Kerr's ambition was to become a doctor. While in Vietnam, he spent much of his off-duty time studying to pass the entrance exams for medical school. He was shorter than Steve, about 5'9" with curly brown hair, lots of thick hair on his arms and legs and a barrel chest. His eyes were close set, brown and searching. Sid Kerr was a man who didn't just live life. He analyzed it and constantly adjusted his personal flight plan to take advantage of the most it had to offer, within the parameters that made sense to him.

When they got to the table, Stump pulled out a chair and sat down. "We saw your jeep outside. We've been driving along the beaches looking for you."

"What's up?"

"It's Herring." Stump said.

"Jake? What about him," Steve asked.

Stump looked at Kerr, waiting for him to break the news. "He crashed and died yesterday," Kerr said.

"Jake Herring?" Cooper looked back and forth at the two faces, not believing what he was hearing. Nausea hit him in the gut. He pushed his plate away and leaned forward, his elbows on the table, his face in his hands. He felt bile moving up into his throat. He took a sip of water, then stuck his hand in it and wiped the dampness across his face. *Not Jake Herring!* "What happened?"

"Nobody really knows," Sid explained. "He was with some of the guys in the Gulf off Rach Gia. They were doing ninety-day carrier quals on the USS Coral Sea. After his three landings, he went up to altitude and pulled the Bronco into a hammerhead stall. They said he let it fall off into a spin and then just kept spinning. No recovery, no chute—he just spun it right into the ocean." He emphasized the crash by popping his right fist into the palm of his left hand.

"How high was he?"

"High enough," Kerr answered. "At least 5,000 feet."

"That's crazy," Steve said. "Not Jake Herring. You shove the stick forward, stomp opposite rudder and a Bronco's out of spin in less than a quarter of a turn. It takes 200 hundred feet. Five hundred, max, if you're not paying attention."

"Yeah, we know," Stump agreed. "It is crazy."

Kerr elaborated more. "We may never find out what really happened. The bird went into the drink. Divers from the carrier recovered his body, but the bird is still at the bottom of the ocean."

"I just don't believe this!" Cooper toyed with the idea they were making this up, but that would be too cruel of a joke. "Why didn't he punch out?"

"They said it was so hazy there wasn't any horizon." Kerr's eyes were intense. He was trying to come to grips with it, too. "Maybe he just didn't know how low he was."

"That doesn't make sense; not with Jake Herring. He was too experienced to let something like that happen."

"This is a war, Steve. Nothing makes sense."

"Yeah, but to die doing aerobatics? Not Jake Herring ...."

There was really nothing more to say. Steve motioned for his check, then stood up unsteadily. "You all right?" Sid asked, reaching for his arm. Steve shook him off.

"Yeah, I'm all right. Where are you guys headed?"

"We're going back to the airfield," Stump said. "We were looking for you."

"Okay, I'll follow you."

"I'll ride with you." Stump volunteered.

"Fine with me. You drive."

They were on Truong Cong Dinh Street, headed back to the airport, Kerr's jeep ahead of them, when Stump remembered something he was supposed to tell Steve. "There was a Donut Dolly asking for you this morning."

"A Donut Dolly? Who was she?"

"Sid knows her. She's from Binh Thuy."

"What did she want?"

"She said there was somebody there looking for you—an Army pilot. I think she said he was a relative." Steve racked his brain. *It could only be Eric. Was he out of flight school already?*

"Did she say what his name was?"

"Sid knows. You need to talk to him when we get back to the base."

When they reached the airfield, Steve caught up with Sid before he went inside.

"Stump said you talked to a Donut Dolly who was asking about me."

"That's right," Kerr replied. "Mattie Hill. She's a friend of mine. I forgot to mention it, but she'll be eating with us tonight at the club. You can see her there."

It was still early in the afternoon. Steve had Stump drive him to the hangar to check out the new OV-10 he was going to be assigned when Herring decided it was okay for him to fly. Now there was no Herring. Who would make that decision? Hazlett? Hazlett was not the one who grounded him.

Steve passed the afternoon watching the maintenance crew perform a 100-hour inspection on the OV-10. He talked with the armorers about how he wanted the weapons stations configured. When it became obvious he was keeping the crewmen from their work, he walked out to the flight line and watched the traffic, which was unusually light for the time of day.

There was no breeze and the tarmac was hot. When a crew van came by, Steve caught a ride to the dispensary. There he had the bandage on his shoulder rewrapped and the one on his ankle removed. Then he went to the O' Club for a cold beer. A couple of the other pilots were there and the conversation centered around Jake Herring's death. Nobody could understand it; it seemed so senseless.

A few minutes after five, Steve went back to the BOQ for a shower and some clean clothes. He lay on the bunk for a few minutes and found the lack of sleep catching up with him. He was sound asleep an hour later when Stump Willis and Sid Kerr came by to get him for dinner.

The O'Club was crowded. The Donut Dollies were there, six of them. When the pilots came in, one of them left the group she was with and came over to them. Sid introduced Mattie Hill to Cooper and Willis.

"How y'all, doing?" she asked. Her southern drawl painfully reminded Steve of Gail.

"I understand you know somebody I know," Steve offered.

"Yes," she answered. "Eric Mohr. He's your brother-in-law, isn't he?"

So it was Eric. "Yes!" Steve said. "What about Eric? Where is he? Is he here?"

"He's at Navy Binh Thuy," Mattie said. "He's been looking for you."

"Navy Binh Thuy? What's he doing at Binh Thuy?" He looked at Stump and Kerr. "What Army units are at Binh Thuy?"

Mattie spoke up. "Dustoff," she said. "He's a Dustoff pilot."

Dustoff, of course. Eric would want to fly medevac. Steve turned to Stump. "Let's go, Wingie. You've got to fly me to Binh Thuy."

"Not so fast, buddy. Why do you think I had time to go around looking for you today? My plane's down. Besides, we can't go running over there tonight. What would we tell Ops?"

Steve turned to Kerr. "Don't look at me, buddy," Kerr told him. "I've got the zero dark thirty patrol in the morning. Besides, Binh Thuy isn't going anywhere. In fact, I just heard we'll probably be moving over there ourselves by Christmas."

"What? You're kidding?" This was news to both Cooper and Willis.

"Nope," Kerr replied. "It's the straight scoop. We're moving to Binh Thuy with the rest of the squadron. I've got more news. Rumor has it we'll all be home by April."

April. That was when Steve's tour was due to end anyway. It wouldn't buy him any time. But if Eric was at Binh Thuy, things would be different. Somehow within the next day or two he would find a way to get over there and see him.

Steve turned to Mattie to ask her more about Eric, but she and Kerr had moved off to a table by themselves and appeared to be engaged in an intimate conversation. *Watch her,* Steve found himself thinking, *she'll turn on the charm to hook you, but then watch out.* Was he getting cynical?

TWELVE

Binh Thuy

The first night Rob McElroy was back from R&R, Eric flew First-Up Night with him. McElroy was a big man, a former college football player, with thinning blond hair and gray eyes that alternately smiled and worried. His manner with Eric was instructive, but laced with impatience. To Eric, it seemed McElroy expected him to grasp concepts that exceeded Eric's limited exposure to the Dustoff mission. Perhaps McElroy was irritated at having to fly with a newby his first night back in the field, or perhaps it was just the normal pressure that came with being a flight instructor in a combat zone. Whatever Eric was sensing from McElroy, he was determined to impress the IP and learn what he could from him.

There were eleven pending missions on the board when they checked it at the beginning of their shift. Eric was baffled. His concept of a medevac mission was "they called, we went." He couldn't fathom how missions could stack up like they had. McElroy told Eric to copy down the mission details while he went outside to help the crew prepare the aircraft.

When Eric went out to the aircraft a few minutes later, he found the crew chief and medic loading medical supplies.

McElroy was on top of the Huey inspecting the rotor system. Eric did the lower walkaround. While the pilots finished their preflight inspection, the two crewmen washed blood off the aircraft floor from the afternoon's missions.

In contrast to the flights with Hank Harris, McElroy was perfectly content to let Eric fly. In fact, Eric flew almost the whole night. It was a night filled with new experiences.

For the first mission, they headed north across both rivers—the Bassac and the Mekong—into a dark, sparsely populated area west of My Tho. McElroy gave the mission coordinates to Paddy Control who provided radar vectors to the area. As they approached the pick-up site, McElroy contacted the ARVN unit on the ground to determine the unit's exact position, the nature of their wounded and to get a description of the landing site. They flew without external lights so as not to attract ground fire. Judging by the lack of radio traffic, there were no other aircraft around to be considered collision threats.

The American advisor assigned to the ARVN unit handled the radio on their end. He described the landing site as a clearing with sufficient rotor clearance and no brush or stumps. There were trees on the north and east sides of the clearing making an approach from the southwest advisable. The wind was out of the north, so there would be a quartering headwind. Departure from the clearing would have to be back out the same way due to hostile elements to the north and obstacles to the east. The landing site was marked by a flashing strobe light held by an ARVN soldier standing at the north end of the clearing.

McElroy coached Eric through the approach, but let him do all of the flying. He instructed Eric to make a base leg, then turn to a northeast heading that would take them directly toward the strobe light. Eric made a steep approach.

"If you lose sight of that strobe light," McElroy instructed, "stop descending immediately. That means there is a tree or something in our flight path."

Eric felt as if they were descending into a black abyss. He could make out few visual cues, so divided his attention between the cockpit instruments and the strobe light. At least four times during the approach, Eric wanted to abort, but McElroy kept coaching him down. The IP called out airspeed and altitude continually as both steadily diminished. The strobe light's position remained fixed in the chin bubble until the last hundred feet when McElroy turned on the Huey's powerful landing light to illuminate the landing area. It looked small, what Eric could see of it, but there was the ARVN holding the strobe light and beside him another man, an American, motioning them down with hand signals. At McElroy's urging, Eric continued the Huey's approach all the way to the ground and bottomed pitch.

"Do that slowly," McElroy said, as Eric planted the Huey. "You never know what's under you. It could be wet and we would get stuck. It could be uneven. Sometimes there's a stump or a rock under one of the skids. It's best to hold it light on the skids and settle your way down easily."

"Okay," Eric acknowledged, his heart racing, his adrenalin pumping. He felt like they were in a giant black bowl with the darkness hiding who-knew-what kind of unseen threats. People were being loaded into the back of the helicopter—wounded people. That's what they were here for. Eric wasn't afraid of being hurt or killed, but he was afraid of screwing up.

"Let's go, sir," came the call from the back. The crew in the back had kept up a constant chatter during the entire approach.

"You're clear on the left, sir."

"You're clear on the right."

"Tail's clear."

 "Looks okay here."

Their instructions and McElroy's calm advice had kept Eric company on his first night combat landing. They were a team.

Eric glanced over at McElroy for the okay to depart. Across the darkened cockpit, illuminated by the dim red lights from the instrument panel, McElroy looked like some type of space creature in his flight helmet and with his survival vest and armor protection on over his flight suit. He had the clear visor on his flight helmet down for extra protection in case of flying shrapnel if they came under fire. Eric had forgotten his. It was too late now, but he made a mental note to pull it down on the next approach. Both hands were full as he prepared to lift the Huey to a hover. They'd been in the clearing for maybe twenty seconds. McElroy had turned the landing light off immediately after they had touched down.

"Let's go," McElroy said. "Pick it straight up until the tail is clear, then do a pedal turn to the right and take us out of here, back out the way we came in."

In the back, both crew members were working on the patients, making sure they were breathing and that critical bleeding had been stopped. They interrupted their work long enough to clear the aircraft.

"Tail's clear left."

"Tail's clear right."

Eric joined the chatter. "Coming up." He lifted the Huey straight up and kept it coming up until McElroy told him it was okay to turn.

"Okay," McElroy said. "Bring your tail to the left."

"Tail's clear left," came the call from the back.

"Tail's coming left."

He was disoriented, the blackness crowding in. "Airspeed!" McElroy called. Eric dumped the nose. Too much, but he quickly realized it and concentrated on his instruments as he adjusted the Huey's attitude for a normal climb. Which direction? Around him was nothing but black.

"How're we doing back there, guys?" the AC asked the crew. He was not aware of Eric's disorientation.

"Two are critical, sir—a chest wound and a head wound. The others are stable." They had four patients in all.

"My Tho?" McElroy asked the medic.

"Yes, sir."

Eric was fighting vertigo. He was practically on instruments, with very little in the way of outside references. The aircraft was under control, but he felt on the edge of losing it. McElroy seemed unconcerned. He scanned the instruments and noted some corrections that needed to be made.

"You can back off on the power, and pick up the airspeed. Bring us around to one-one-zero on the heading. My Tho is the largest of those two villages over there." He pointed at villages in the distance whose lights glowed in the darkness. "The one to the south," he said. "The other one is Ben Tranh. Over there," he pointed off their right side, "is Dong Tam. My Tho has one of the province hospitals where we drop off ARVN casualties." McElroy's apparent confidence in Eric caused him to swallow his nervousness and work to get things under control. He mentally coached himself through the process of setting up a good visual scan of the instruments, avoiding any abrupt control movements, and thinking through what he was doing. The helicopter responded as if it understood his lack of experience and made allowances for it.

Eric made the landing at My Tho, guided in by McElroy. There was a helipad just west of a canal that ran north/south through the village. The pad was not lit, but was easy to find as they flew up the canal from the Mekong River at low altitude and slow airspeed. The landing was uneventful and an ambulance alerted by the sound of their approach came from the nearby hospital to meet the helicopter.

Leaving My Tho, they had fuel enough for another mission. This one was at the edge of a rice paddy that made for an easy approach. Eric actually saw starlight reflecting off water below and didn't have the same boxed-in feeling he had experienced on the earlier mission. Once again, McElroy let him do all the flying. They landed—not to a flashlight, but to four small fires built to form a "T." The approach was made along the base of the T. Here, they picked up three patients, who they also took to My Tho. Then it was time for fuel.

They refueled at Binh Thuy, rechecked the mission board for priorities and took off again, this time to the west. While making an approach to the strobe light used to mark the area, they were fired at by small arms. Tracers cut across the sky as AK-47s followed the sound of the aircraft. McElroy delayed turning on the landing light until they were below the trees and almost on the ground. Eric held the Huey light on the skids while the patients were quickly loaded. McElroy pointed and they went out straight ahead, avoiding the small arms fire.

These patients were taken to Vinh Long. From there, the Dustoff crew flew north across the river to a small outpost that had been under attack. The enemy contact had been broken and the pickup of several wounded soldiers was fairly routine.

By daylight, Eric had logged 7.9 night combat hours and was exhausted. The crew went to breakfast together at the Navy mess hall and Eric took the opportunity to get acquainted with the medic and crew chief he had been flying with all night. He was impressed by their professionalism and their enthusiasm for the job. In his mind, they were the real heroes of the Dustoff mission—the guys in the back who provided medical assistance to their patients.

After breakfast, Eric looked forward to a shower and his bed. He assumed McElroy would do the same. The two crewmen mentioned something about washing out the aircraft before they knocked off. Eric was proud of them. The crew before had left them with a bloody cabin; this crew wasn't going to do the same.

The hootch maid, Minh, slipped into the room quietly while Eric was sleeping and gathered up his dirty clothing and boots. Before going to sleep, Eric had put 300 piasters on the table by the bed and Minh picked them up and tucked them into her pocket. She picked up the framed picture of Lynn that Eric had on the table and looking first at the picture, then at the sleeping warrant officer, she muttered a silent prayer of protection for him. She put down the picture and slipped out the door, closing it quietly behind her.

THIRTEEN

Vung Tau

"Wake up, Wingie! You're ungrounded!"

Steve Cooper struggled from his bunk to the door of his room and flipped the latch. He fell back onto the bed as the door opened and Stump Willis came into the room. Willis was chipper and alert. It was still dark outside.

"What time is it?" Cooper threw his arm over his eyes to shield them from the light as Willis flipped the switch.

"It's oh-three-thirty, buddy, and you're due at the flight line at four-fifteen."

Steve Cooper lowered his arm and looked at his wingman with a quizzical look.

"Technically, you never were grounded," Willis told him. "We've got a mission to fly and I'm your back seat."

"What do you mean 'back seat'?" When flying reconnaissance missions, the OV-10 was often flown with an aerial observer in the back seat of the tandem cockpit, but not during ground attack or close air support missions, and rarely with a qualified pilot in the back seat. Single pilot missions were the order of the day.

159

"My ship is down for maintenance; yours is up; I know the AO; I'm riding with you."

"You're keeping an eye on me, you mean?"

"Well, it's been a few days since you've flown," Willis acknowledged, "And on your last mission you got busted out of the sky. Ops thought it'd be a good idea if I kept you company."

"Figures. I'd probably make the same decision myself." If it had been anybody but Stump Willis, Cooper might not have felt the same. As it was, he simply shrugged it off, glad to be flying again. He was confident that with Willis as his "back seat" he could fly as the mission required, not by some by-the-book, conservative, save-your-butt rules handed down by the brass sitting on their cans in Washington or on some aircraft carrier in the middle of the Pacific.

"What's the mission?" he asked.

"The NVA and Viet Cong have a big push going on north of Saigon. Supplies are coming down the Ho Chi Minh trail by the truckload. There's also a lot of stuff getting into the Delta from the South China Sea. They want us to continue working the Mekong and the Bassac, but today we're starting to move into the heart of things down in the U Minh."

"The U Minh?" Cooper interrupted. "The Army is working the U Minh with the Ponies from Binh Thuy."

"Yeah," Willis agreed, "but the Army is putting in more guys than ever, and they're short on air cover and asking for our help. We've got a green light for search and destroy in certain areas. Plus, we'll be working with some Loach pilots who don't have enough Cobras to back them up."

"What about the Seawolves?"

"They're working it, too. But they're primarily working with the boats on the canals."

"The PBRs are working canals?" This was news to Cooper. Normally, they worked the rivers. It was too easy for one of those twenty-eight foot boats to get too far up a narrow canal, then run into an ambush and have no room to maneuver.

"Yeah. The PBRs and the Vietnamese boats, too." Stump explained. "They're working the canals with the Seawolves flying cover and they've been stopping a lot of the traffic, especially at night."

"The PBRs and Seawolves are working the rivers and canals at night?" Lots of things had suddenly changed.

"They have to. The Viet Cong are moving at night, and too much stuff has been getting through."

Steve found himself getting excited at the thought of getting some combat action. He was up and putting on his flight suit. "So what are we doing this morning?"

"We fly to Vi Thanh before first light and work our way up the Ganh Hoa River toward Rach Gia. Radar from offshore patrol boats picked up a flotilla heading into the mouth of the river last night, but they didn't have a shallow draft boat available to pursue them. An Army Mohawk was called in to follow the VC with infrared during the night. Technically, we know right where they are. Come daylight, we should have a surprise for them."

"Let's go, then!" Cooper was already out the door.

Forty-five minutes later, they were airborne. Steve shifted around in his seat trying to get comfortable. The strap of the shoulder harness and the weight of his survival vest pulling against the shoulder hurt, but it was pain he could live with.

The Bronco was loaded for bear, with twelve Zunis and twenty-eight 2.75 rockets. In place of the 7.62 machine guns, a mini-gun was installed on one weapons pylon and a twenty-millimeter cannon on the other. Even with the airplane fully loaded—two pilots, full fuel and heavy armament—the climb was exhilarating as Steve snapped the aircraft's nose up and felt the landing gear fold into the wheel wells. The lights of Vung Tau twinkled beneath them as they passed over the peninsula and headed across the bay in the crisp early morning air.

Steve checked in with the radar controller. "Paddy Control, Black Pony One-One with you off Vung Tau, climbing to five point five to Vi Thanh VFR." Even though it was still dark, Steve didn't request radar vectors, due to clear skies and excellent visibility.

"Black Pony One-One, this is Paddy Control. Good morning. Squawk one-two-one-one and ident."

"Roger." Steve set the code in his transponder as requested and settled back in his seat. Soon he was at 5,500 feet. He eased the nose over, reduced the power levers to cruise setting and rolled the elevator trim forward until the control stick offered no resistance in his hand. "Beautiful morning," he commented to Stump over the intercom.

"It is," Stump agreed. He was impressed with the way Steve had retained his control touch during his time off, but refrained from telling him so, lest he get the big head. The guy already had an ego; why fuel it?

"Black Pony One-One, you're radar contact eight miles southwest of Vung Tau," the controller informed him.

"Roger." Steve flexed his fingers, then rocked the wings from side to side just to get a feel for the OV-10's wing loading with the new armament.

"I wish we had a place for a weapons test," he told Stump, knowing it wasn't practical over land.

"Would be nice," Stump replied. He envied Steve the cannon and mini-gun setup and was already planning to request a similar setup for his own plane.

As the aircraft approached Vi Thanh, Steve contacted the Army Mohawk on the air-to-air frequency they had been assigned during the mission briefing.

"Overseer One-Nine, this is Black Pony One-One."

The voice came back deep and calm, the product of a good radio and a seasoned pilot, "Black Pony One-One, this is Overseer One-Nine, good morning."

"Good morning. I understand you have a target for us," Steve said.

"We have the target's location pinpointed, but it's unconfirmed as a hostile at this time and we have no clearance to fire. The mission commander is on Fox Mike thirty-eight-forty-five, call sign Rattlesnake Six. Let me know when you're ready to copy the grid coordinates."

"Go ahead." Steve pulled a grease pencil from his clipboard and smoothed down a place on his plastic map case to write down the coordinates as they were given to him.

"You'll find the target at whiskey romeo two-five-two-seven-five-zero."

"Whiskey romeo two-five-two-seven-five-zero," Steve repeated as he copied down the coordinates. Stump could have helped, and in fact was copying the coordinates down as well, but Steve was so used to flying solo, he'd forgotten how to use someone else's help.

"You got it," the Mohawk pilot confirmed. "This plane turns into a pumpkin at first light. I'm out of here."

"So, long One-Nine."

"You, too, One-One. Happy hunting."

Steve punched up the new FM frequency. Voice traffic was heavy on the channel and he waited for a break in the action before announcing to the mission commander he was on station. The gray light of dawn slowly replaced the darkness as details of the terrain below began to emerge out of what had only moments before been a black void. First to become visible was the dark outline of trees and fields. The new light began to reflect off canals and the river, enabling the pilots to orient themselves in the AO. Steve looked around for other traffic and caught a glimmer of movement below them over the river. It was a scout helicopter—a Loach. A Command & Control Huey was supposed to be somewhere in the area. This was an Army mission. The Navy was just there to provide additional firepower.

"Rattlesnake Six, Black Pony One-One is on station, armed and ready," Steve announced when he got a chance to jump in between the conversations going on between the scouts and the C&C ship. There was a lot of excitement about something that had apparently happened just before they'd switched onto the frequency. Steve couldn't put the pieces together.

"Black Pony One-One, this is Rattlesnake Six, stand by. We'll be back with you in a minute, if you can stay on station."

"Pony One-One, Roger." Steve eased the Bronco into a left-hand orbit, maintaining five thousand feet. The helicopters were all well below him. An Army colonel in the C&C ship was running the show.

"What do you think is going on, Stump?" Steve asked over the intercom.

"I don't know, man. It sounds like they may have a downed aircraft. There's a Dustoff ship on the frequency, and a couple of Knights. They're Cobras, aren't they?"

"Yeah, I think they are. I guess we'll have to wait and see what's happening." Steve caught a glimpse of something and tightened his turn. "Look," he said, "Over the river. There are the boats."

"Yeah, and there's a Loach hovering right over them. Listen up on Fox Mike. There's something going on."

They heard the word "friendlies," then an announcement by Rattlesnake Six that the primary mission was canceled. He was marshalling resources for a rescue mission west of their present location, closer to the coastline south of Rach Gia.

"Black Pony One-One, this is Rattlesnake Six. It looks like it's going to be a scrub on the primary target, but we've got another situation developing a few klicks west of here. We have a downed Loach at whiskey romeo eight-seven-zero-seven-zero-two. The crew is under fire from elements on the ground. There's a Dustoff ship trying to make the pickup, but on the first pass they came under intense fire and had to break off. We could use your help."

"Roger, on my way," Steve responded. He rolled out of the turn, heading west. He pulled the map off his kneeboard and refolded it to uncover the new coordinates. In the back seat, Stump was locating the coordinates on his own map. Below them, they could see the C&C ship and the two Loaches heading west, the sun at their backs.

A few kilometers west

It was toward the end of a long night when Dustoff 77—
Rob McElroy and his new peter pilot, Eric Mohr—were diverted to a rescue mission south of Rach Gia. A scout team
consisting of two OH-6 Loach helicopters had come under
fire just as they had begun patrolling at first light. One of the
Loaches had been shot down. The other had attempted to pick
up the downed crew and had also been shot down. The second
crew had been picked up by a Huey slick, but the first one was
still on the ground. The crew was visible from the air, but any
aircraft that tried to approach it came under intense fire from
the Viet Cong.

When the Dustoff crew arrived, it was obvious they were
the ones most qualified to make a rescue attempt. McElroy
was flying. The Loach was in a clearing. Sporadic small arms
tracers could be seen firing upon the Loach from a treeline
approximately fifty feet away. A Huey slick flew up and down
the treeline at about two-hundred feet, the door gunners on
either side alternately raking the enemy positions with their
M-60s. The other aircraft under the C&C's control were still
a few klicks east.

McElroy waited until the slick started moving down the
treeline away from the Loach before making his move. He flew
directly over the Loach at two thousand feet, and slowed the
Huey to forty knots. As the airspeed needle quivered around
forty, McElroy shoved the cyclic control forward and bottomed

the pitch. The Huey's nose suddenly pointed straight down and the aircraft dropped rapidly toward the earth. McElroy rolled the descending aircraft around in a three-hundred-and-sixty degree turn. As they plummeted earthward, G-forces pushed Eric back in his seat. He didn't know a Huey was capable of such maneuvers.

Within seconds, they were at treetop level. Mac hauled back on the cyclic to slow the aircraft and stop its descent. They were almost on top of the Loach. There was no place to land on the side of the Loach away from the bad guys, so McElroy attempted to set the Huey down between the Loach and the treeline. He didn't make it. An intense barrage of fire came toward them, so intense that to stay there would have been suicide. The crew didn't have to call the incoming fire. It was everywhere. Pieces of plexiglass flew around in the cockpit as bullets pierced the windshield over the Dustoff pilots' heads. Several metallic thunks indicated bullets impacting the airframe as well.

Unwilling to put four more people on the ground with another disabled aircraft, McElroy kicked the Huey's tail to the left, putting his side of the aircraft toward the incoming fire. Eric saw the two downed crewmen near the Loach. They were so close! One was standing beside the aircraft firing with a pistol toward the treeline. The other manned the mini-gun mounted in the Loach's rear door. McElroy pulled pitch, shoved the stick forward and raced southward away from the area.

When the Huey's speed reached a hundred and ten, McElroy jerked back on the cyclic, soaring the helicopter into the air at over two thousand feet a minute. No words had been spoken during the pickup attempt. The action had been too intense. The C&C radio broke the silence.

"Dustoff, this is Rattlesnake Six on Guard. Come up thirty-eight-forty-five Fox Mike."

Eric switched the frequency. As soon as the new numbers were dialed in, McElroy checked in with Rattlesnake Six.

"Rattlesnake Six, this is Dustoff Seven-Seven."

"We saw what you just did, Dustoff. It was a good try, but we've got to do something different. I've got two Cobras and a Black Pony with me. We're going to give you some gun cover before you go back in there.

Calmly, the mission commander in the C&C ship outlined a plan. In the right seat of the Huey, Eric Mohr was evaluating his reaction to what had just occurred and it surprised him. He was either too dumb or too naive to realize the danger they had been in. Either that, or the peace of the Lord had really enveloped him. The events of the previous minute or two had happened so fast there had been no time for fear. Even though McElroy had done all of the flying, and had been fully in control of the mission, Eric's own instincts had been fully alert, taking in everything that had happened. He'd never seen the type of maneuvers McElroy had executed in the Huey. But he'd stayed with him mentally, monitoring the airspeed and power settings to insure they hadn't been exceeded. He'd been fully aware of everything that was happening throughout the mission. Maybe he *did* have what it takes to be a Dustoff aircraft commander. He'd have to learn some of the tricks of the trade, but at least he hadn't been overcome with fear.

He glanced up at all the holes and cracks in the windshield. Some of the knobs had been shattered on the overhead panel, but the engine instruments were still in the green. And no caution lights were illuminated. Apparently nothing critical had been hit.

McElroy keyed the intercom. "You guys all okay?"

"Yes, sir," came the response from the back.

Roy looked over at Eric. "You ready to go again?" Eric nodded. The next thing McElroy did blew Eric's mind. "You've got it," he said.

It was the last thing Eric expected. He was going to fly on this next attempt! McElroy outlined what they would do and to Eric it seemed simple enough. They would make an approach toward the Loach from the south, keeping as far away from the treeline as they could, but paralleling it so they could make their approach to the only open area available. At this angle, Eric's side would be the one closest to the enemy. He hunkered down in his seat and pulled at the armor plate that offered limited protection from the side, making sure it was all the way forward and locked. He shifted his chest protector up to cover his neck. He rehearsed the plan in his mind.

The Black Pony OV-10 (could it be Steve?) was going to fly a cross pattern ahead of them, using his rockets, cannon, and mini-gun to suppress fire from the treeline. The Cobras, one on either side of the Dustoff ship would accompany them on their way down. The Cobras were both armed with 2.75 rockets.

Rattlesnake Six gave the command to begin the mission. Acknowledgement came from each of the aircraft commanders.

"Black Pony One-One."

"Knight Two-Three."

"Knight Two-Six."

"Dustoff Seven-Seven."

McElroy coached Eric into position. Following McElroy's instructions, Eric turned north from a position a half a mile south of the downed Loach and began his approach toward the open area just east of the aircraft.

"Keep your speed up," McElroy instructed. "Stay hot all the way to the ground." Here's where Eric was unsure of himself. Stopping a Huey took some planning. Normally, it was a progressive stop, with the helicopter gradually slowing throughout its approach. This would be different. He couldn't overshoot. He felt himself tightening up, although he knew that would work against him. He shifted in his seat and forced his mind to concentrate on the task at hand. The gray OV-10 swooped in front of them, its nose pointed at the treeline. Its guns were blazing and rockets streaked away from under its wings with flashes of light and puffs of smoke. As the rockets impacted into the trees, wood and debris flew everywhere. A Cobra appeared just off the Huey's right side, about a rotor width away. Another one was on their left, slightly below and ahead of them. Eric concentrated on the landing site. *Would bullets hit the aircraft again? Would he stay cool? Would McElroy have to take over?* He made constant adjustments to the collective pitch. He was anything but smooth as they closed on the open area beside the Loach.

Fire from the treeline resumed as soon as the Navy Bronco had passed over it. The pilot came around for another pass. This time he flew slowly, picking his targets, firing first the cannon, then the mini-gun, then a salvo of rockets before the plane was over the treeline and climbing back to altitude. Eric could see the outline of the pilots in the tandem cockpit as they flew in front of him.

The Cobra on the Dustoff ship's right broke right and began pulverizing the treeline with rockets, walking the impact point up and down the enemy location. The Cobra on their left did a pedal turn and flew sideways as it accompanied the Dustoff ship toward the Loach. Its turret cannon pounded the VC position relentlessly. Eric could almost feel, as well as hear the thudding of the cannon. He could see its shells ejecting from the smoking turret. For a brief moment, he thought he was going to fly into the Cobra's line of fire as he continued his approach toward the Loach. But as Eric kept descending, the Cobra leveled off, remaining above them. The two men on the ground must have been out of ammo, for they were no longer firing, but were waving their arms at the approaching Huey. McElroy continually called out airspeed and altitude as he coached Eric, "Okay, slow it down." Eric hauled back on the cyclic and the Huey started to balloon upwards. "Not too much," Mac coached. They were a team. The guys in the back were calling fire, but most of it was not being directed at them, but at the Cobras.

When they were fifty feet off the ground, a Cobra swept in front of them and unleashed a massive salvo of rockets toward the VC. The Cobra gunship appeared to be suspended in the air in front of the Dustoff Huey, then it turned away, leaving only smoke-filled air in its wake. Evidence of firing was everywhere. Flames erupted in various places along the treeline. As they approached the ground, Eric remembered to hold the Huey light on its skids. McElroy's hands were also on the controls. More fire erupted from the treeline. Eric saw bullets impact the ground in front of them, but miraculously none of them reached the aircraft. Movement was felt in the back—a jostling of the airframe as the two downed crewmen jumped aboard. "Let's go!" yelled the Dustoff crew chief. McElroy shook the controls. "I've got it!" he said. Eric felt the movement, and released his grip.

"You've got it," Eric replied, but kept his hands close to the controls, just in case. They zoomed up. Not out and up, but up—straight up. Eric watched the power meter. The needle stopped just short of the redline at 50 pounds of torque. The indicated airspeed was close to zero. They were spinning, corkscrewing to the left, as the rate of climb indicator pegged at nearly three thousand feet a minute. For the first time since the mission began, Eric was disoriented, like that first night coming up out of the darkness west of My Tho with almost no visual references at all. He felt the Huey's airframe shudder under an intense strain. Then it was over. McElroy decreased the power and eased the cyclic forward, accelerating normally. He offered the controls back to Eric. Suddenly both pilots found themselves being pounced upon as the grateful Loach crew hugged them and pounded them on the back, promising all the drinks they wanted when they got back to the base.

It felt good! A successful mission—a tough mission—and Eric had actually flown a big part of it! He looked up again at the damaged windshield and overhead console as he settled the Huey into normal cruise and pointed it toward Binh Thuy and the Third Surg. He was maturing as a Dustoff pilot. He could do this mission.

The flight to Binh Thuy took almost thirty minutes. The crew chief and medic chattered the entire flight as they relived the excitement of the moment. McElroy leaned back against the left side of his seat and watched Eric for some kind of after-mission letdown, some evidence of fear, some indication the man was real, not a robot. You didn't throw a green newby into an intense fire situation and not get some kind of emotional reaction. Quietly, in his own way, Eric also wondered about the calmness he felt. Scriptures were running through his mind. *"You will keep him in perfect peace, whose mind is stayed on You." "Even though I walk through the valley of the shadow of death, I will fear no evil, for You are with me." "Perfect love casts out all fear."*

Could it be those scriptures were really working for him? Could it be the peace of God had kept him in perfect peace in the midst of danger? If so, what a witness! It was solid evidence that Christianity—serving Jesus—worked as advertised. He understood it perfectly. He had yet to see how little the others understood it.

FOURTEEN

Navy Binh Thuy

Mohr and McElroy left the Huey in the hands of the crew chief and the maintenance officer, who were still going over it to assess the battle damage. The medic also stayed behind to pack up his gear. The pilots had seen enough. No major components had been hit, but the bullet holes were grim reminders of how vulnerable they had been. A different angle and the bullets would have hit flesh rather than plexiglass and aluminum.

Eric was exhausted. The mission in the U Minh had come at the end of a night in which he had already logged over seven hours. The final total for the twelve-hour shift figured in at 9.4 hours of combat flight time, eight of them during the hours of darkness.

Mohr had "lost his cherry" and that would call for a celebration, but that could happen later. Right now, all he could think of was a shower and bed.

K. J. Madison offered to drive Eric andMcElroy to the barracks. They climbed in the jeep—McElroy in the front, Eric in the back. "Those were two happy dudes you guys brought in this morning," Madison offered.

"They should have been," McElroy answered. "A few more minutes on the ground and they'd have been overrun."

"I've never seen two more thankful guys. You're sure heroes to them."

"Just doing our job," McElroy replied. "You know you'd have done the same."

Madison accepted the fact. Looking over his shoulder, he ribbed Eric. "Lost your cherry, huh? There are guys who have been here six months and haven't been hit yet."

Eric didn't have an answer. He knew K. J. was baiting them for a story; he wanted to hear one himself. He leaned forward, hoping McElroy would make a comment. McElroy had been quiet, almost reflective since the mission. Eric knew McElroy had something on his mind, but so far the IP had kept his thoughts to himself. What Eric really wanted to hear was praise from McElroy, but he'd take criticism for that matter. Anything would have been better than nothing. Eric was pleased with his own performance, but the IP's silence intimidated him. He kept quiet, saving his questions for later.

Eric had no idea whether his reaction to coming under fire had been normal, abnormal, spectacular or anything else. He wanted to know. He also wanted to know what those stunts were that McElroy had put the Huey through when he had been flying.

When they got to the barracks, the hootch maid, Minh, was in the upstairs latrine washing clothes. The two men went to their respective rooms and within two minutes were back, towels wrapped around their waists and their dirty flight suits balled up in their hands. Minh took the flight suits, then gave Eric an exasperated look as she pulled his belt out of the belt loops and threw it at him. Then she went through his pockets one by one, shaking her head. She handed him some change

and a pocket knife, accompanied by a muttered "choi oui …."
As he turned away from her, she beamed him a broad smile.

Eric set the items on a ledge and stepped into the shower.
The warm water began washing away the aches and stiffness
from the long hours in the Huey's armored seats and the irritation from the sweaty flight suits. Feeling better, Eric asked
McElroy about the approach and departures the IP had made
back at the LZ.

The IP in McElroy warmed to the topic in spite of his
fatigue. "We'll work on those tomorrow when we're First-Up.
I doubt we get many missions during the day, so I can show
you the Dustoff tactical approaches and tactical departures.
The approach I flew today is one most of the guys use in the
daytime when the LZ is hot and there's no gun cover." He adjusted the water temperature, then started lathering his arms
and shoulders. "The first departure, the one where we flew out
low-level and zoom climbed with the cyclic, is one most of
the guys use. That straight up corkscrew departure is kind of
unconventional and a lot of the guys are afraid of it. I learned
that from Ernie Moss."

"Wasn't he a Dustoff Medal of Honor winner?"

"That's him."

"You flew with Ernie Moss?"

"I met him when he was in country about six months ago.
He flew with each of the Medical Service Corp IPs and taught
us some of the tricks that helped keep him alive through two
extended tours as a Dustoff aviator. We're supposed to pass
them along."

"This morning was the first I've seen of them. In fact, I've
never even heard about them." Eric dropped his soap and bent
over to pick it up.

"Well, you've been flying mostly at night. The other ACs and I have been talking about it and we've been planning on showing them to you as soon as we had a chance to fly some daylight missions. It would have been me, or K. J., Chris, Wade Daugherty or Captain Scott. You just got to see them for real this morning before having a chance to practice them."

"Hey, why did you let me fly when we went back in the second time?"

"We'd already been fired at," McElroy answered, turning off his shower and reaching for the towel that hung over the stall. "You didn't panic, so I figured it was time to let you make an approach under fire. Besides, with all of those gunships, I didn't think we'd be receiving much in the way of fire." He straightened up after drying his legs and wrapped the towel around his waist. "Usually, when there are Cobras around, the bad guys shoot at them and leave us alone. They know we can't shoot back, so they spend their resources trying to eliminate the guys who can hurt them."

Eric turned off his shower and reached for his own towel. "I need to practice those maneuvers until I feel confident. They sure didn't teach them to us in flight school."

"They helped keep us alive this morning," McElroy said.

"That they did." Eric waited for the other man to walk out of the shower ahead of him. "Thanks," he said.

"Thanks?"

"Yeah, for keeping us alive this morning."

"You're welcome," McElroy said. He'd felt better about Eric after the conversation. Maybe Mohr was real after all. He had been concerned about Eric's apparent insulation from the reality of the dangers they had faced, but hadn't been able to put his concerns into words.

In his room, Eric slipped on a clean pair of briefs, turned the air conditioner down to its lowest setting, and collapsed on his bunk. He slept until mid-afternoon, then woke up hungry. It took a few minutes for the room to come into focus. His watch said it was three-thirty. His flight suit hung on the wall, clean and pressed. His freshly-shined boots were against the wall on the floor beneath it.

A few minutes before five, Eric walked into Operations, his flight suit drenched with sweat and his freshly shined boots covered with dust. He'd walked around the runway to get to Operations from the BOQ, hoping the whole time someone would come along in a jeep to give him a ride, but no one did.

A waist-high room divider split the Operations office into two sections. When Eric walked in, Gary Dickson, Chris Sanders and Hank Harris were lined up with their backs to the divider, with K. J. Madison and one of the medics, Jeremy Gray, standing a few feet across from them, effectively making a corridor. Eric's first thought upon opening the door was that he was about to run a gauntlet. Then he saw what was happening. Flies zoomed up the corridor while the men grabbed at them with their hands. "Five!" yelled Dickson, as he caught one. "I'm an ace!"

"Okay," K. J. said. "Aces on this side." Dickson crossed the hall to join K. J. and Gray, leaving Harris and Sanders on the other side. Mohr came through the door, stirring up another bunch of flies. "You," K. J. instructed. "Over there." He motioned for Eric to join Harris and Sanders.

A single fly came down the corridor, knee level. "Look out!" Sanders yelled. "Low level."

"Those suckers are getting smart." Hands swatted the air as the fly flew past, but it escaped. A few more flew through, and Eric made contact with one, almost letting it go, but closing his hand on it at the last minute. The flies were sluggish due to the heat.

"All right!" Harris yelled. "Our newby got one!"

"He's not a newby anymore," K. J. said. "He lost his cherry this morning."

"That's right," Harris acknowledged. "Sounds like a celebration to me."

"Agreed," said K. J. "Let's go to the club."

They started piling out the door when Aubrey Scott's voice shouted from within his office, "Wait!" Scott came out. With him were McElroy and Daugherty. "We're closing up shop and coming with you."

"Who's got First-Up tonight?" McElroy asked.

"Payne and Dickson."

"Where's Payne?" CW2 George Payne was the 57th's Maintenance Officer. Even though he had a full-time job maintaining the unit's Hueys, he also had to pull regular duty as an aircraft commander.

"He's in the hangar, making sure they patch all the holes you and Eric put in 706 this morning." Daughtery explained.

"Somebody better go tell him he's got First-Up," Scott said. "He's probably forgotten it."

"I'll go," Dickson said. "It's about time for us to preflight anyway. You guys have a good time."

"Don't worry." Several of them pounded Eric on the back as they made their way to the jeeps.

"By the way, Eric," Wade Daugherty said. "There was a guy here looking for you this morning. A Navy pilot. Said he used to be your flight instructor."

Eric stopped short and turned to Daugherty, irritation in his eyes. "Why didn't somebody come get me, or tell him where to find me?"

"Take it easy, man. He said he didn't have much time, but that he'd see you Saturday night."

"Saturday night?"

"You haven't heard?" K. J. interrupted. "The Donut Dollies are having a party, and we're all invited. Some of the Navy guys from Vung Tau are coming, too. I thought your friend Mattie would have told you about it."

"I haven't seen Mattie all week."

"You're working too hard."

"Tell me about it," Eric said, letting his irritation go.

They went to the Engineers' Officers Club. Eric had figured out the routine. The Hospital O' Club was for drinking and playing cards. The Navy O' Club was where you went when you wanted steak and lobster, and when there was a jeep available to get you there. For entertainment, it was the Engineers' O' Club, where there was either a movie or a floor show every night. Some of the floor shows were quite good, featuring bands from America, Korea and the Philippines. Both the Hospital O' Club and the Engineers' O' Club were within walking distance of the BOQ, but the latter seemed more popular with the Dustoff pilots.

This particular night there was a band, and it was a good one—a Filipino band that specialized in music by Frankie Vallee and the Four Seasons. Their most requested song was "You're Just Too Good To Be True" which they performed so well they got a standing ovation. That triggered several encore performances.

Beer flowed freely, but Eric was not the only one drinking Cokes. Several of the pilots were on duty, either Second or Third-Up and had to stay away from alcohol. Les Winters had heard about the celebration and deviated from his regular nightly visit to the Hospital O' Club to join the other Dustoff pilots in congratulating Eric on his first encounter with having his aircraft hit by enemy fire. Winters sat quietly and toasted along with the others, but otherwise had very little to say.

K. J. had prepared a surprise. He reached into the leg pocket of his flight suit and brought out a new maroon baseball cap with a 57th Med Detachment patch and WO1 bar sewed on it. He presented the cap to Eric, telling him it was about time he joined the rest of the unit in proper uniform and got rid of that OD hat he'd been wearing since he'd arrived in Binh Thuy.

Talk turned to the morning's mission. McElroy described it in great detail, making sure to point out that Eric had been flying when they picked up the downed flyers. The question, "How'd it feel, Eric?" came from a couple of them at the same time. It was not like they didn't know. Some of them had experienced it; some of them hadn't. But they wanted to hear about *his* reaction.

"How did I feel? I don't know. I was too busy to think about it." He took off his new cap and ran his fingers through his hair a couple of times. He looked to McElroy for help. "Mac was flying when we took the hits, and I was glad he was." He gestured with his hands—the pilots' disease. Eric's hands told the story of the nosediving tactical approach, the low-level departure and the zoom climb. The ACs knew the maneuvers and nodded in understanding as Eric described them. "The way he went in and out of that LZ—man, have I got a lot to learn." They'd all been there. Some had forgotten they'd ever been newbies.

McElroy picked up the story. "When we went back in, Mohr was flying. He did a good job, too." Eric was thankful for the praise, but knew he'd been rough on the controls and that McElroy had coached him throughout the approach. It was McElroy who had made that awesome departure from the LZ.

"I noticed you didn't seem to be afraid." McElroy baited Eric. He wanted to hear a valid explanation.

"Afraid? No, things happened too fast."

"I mean later." Mac was giving him another chance.

Eric realized he was being set up, but decided to tell it like he saw it. "I felt like we were under the protection of God." His words just hung out there, as if the music had stopped, and all conversation throughout the room had ceased. He catalogued their reactions, seeing everything in slow motion. Harris turned away in disgust, muttering the name of Jesus under his breath. That was an expected reaction, though a painful one. It hurt him to hear the name of Jesus uttered as profanity, and he wondered how even callous people could do it. McElroy sat back in his chair and started examining his boots. Only K. J. and Sanders continued to look at Eric, either out of politeness or because they wanted to hear more. Les Winters stood up and emptied his glass. Eric glanced up at him. Winters communicated a message to the young pilot with his eyes—*boy you've done it now.* He shook his head and left the room without saying a word.

Eric tried to redeem the situation. "Listen guys. I know you probably had a bad experience with that guy who was here before me that you all called a 'Jesus Freak.' I can assure you that I'm not like him. But I do believe in God. I do have a relationship with Jesus Christ, and I do trust in Him to protect me."

"That's the biggest bunch of crap I ever heard," Harris started. K. J. held up a hand to stop him.

"Let him alone, Hank," K. J. said. There was an awkward moment or two of silence, a staredown, with Harris looking away first. K. J. changed the subject. "I'll drink to that," he said, pounding Eric on the back. Soon the conversation turned back to flying, but Eric was no longer part of it.

He left the club a few minutes later. For a while he had felt like one of the guys. Now he felt very much alone. It wasn't Harris' ridicule that bothered him. He'd expected that. It was how quickly the others had changed the subject. Did they not even care about God? Were they afraid to think about God, even here in a war, where they needed His protection more than ever? There'd been a glimmer of interest from K. J. and Chris Sanders, but it sure faded quickly.

When he left the party, Eric felt a pressing need to be alone for a while. He wanted to write Lynn and tell her about the day's events and to let her know he would be seeing Steve soon. He couldn't believe that Steve had come looking for him that morning and he had missed him. At least Steve knew he was here and sooner or later they would get together.

He wanted to tell Lynn about God's protection, and to assure her he really was in God's hands. He wanted to spend some time in prayer, thanking God for His protection and seeking wisdom about how he might have better handled the conversation back at the club. He also needed to go to bed. He was still extremely tired and the next morning he and McElroy were on First-Up Day.

As he walked up the road toward the BOQ, a silent reminder of his own past came to mind. Maybe God put it there to help him understand the others and their reactions. He'd been about twelve years old and at a Boy Scout camp along the Leaf River in southern Mississippi. He and several of the other boys in his scout troop had gotten into a discussion about God. A deep fear had come over Eric during that discussion—not so much a fear of God, but a fear of the unknown. His vision of God was somewhat limited in those days. He and his family attended church and Sunday School on a weekly basis. He'd learned about Jesus, or at least thought he had. In his understanding at the time, believing in Jesus was like having an insurance policy. They'd told him at church that if you didn't believe in Jesus you were going to hell. If you did, you were going to heaven. Hell was a bad place, hot and full of suffering. Heaven was a good place. So, to avoid hell, he believed in Jesus.

That was in his head. It was the belief of a child, and maybe it was all right for the time, but that summer thinking about eternity in either heaven or hell was terrifying. Life on earth could be pretty boring at times. His image of heaven was that of a place where everyone was an angel who floated around on a cloud playing a harp. The thought of doing that for eternity was as terrifying, maybe even more so, than spending eternity in hell. Now he knew better. His whole concept of Jesus, salvation and eternity had been so wrong! How many others suffered under the same delusions? How many others experienced the same fears when thinking about God and eternity? How many others failed to search for the truth because they thought they already knew it and it wasn't worth knowing?

He walked past the hospital and along the west perimeter road until he reached the north gate, then turned around and walked back along the inside road east of the hospital. Eventually, he found himself standing in the road outside Mattie's door and noticed the lights were still on. On impulse, he climbed the steps and knocked. Eileen Stewart opened the door, wearing a robe and brushing her hair. "Hi," she said. Then called over her shoulder, "Mattie. Eric's here." She motioned for him to come in.

It was Eric's first time inside the Donut Dollies' place. They lived quite well, he noted—all the comforts of home. Mattie came up the hall from one of the back rooms, also wearing a robe, her hair in curlers. "Eric?" She looked embarrassed.

"Hi," he said. "I just haven't seen you in a while, and wondered how you're doing."

"I'm okay." She was obviously caught off guard by his visit, but not entirely displeased. Eileen excused herself and went to the back.

"Can I get you some coffee, a Coke or something?" Mattie asked, moving toward the kitchen area.

"No. I just left the club. Thanks."

She sat down in one of the kitchen chairs, inviting him to join her. "We have a curfew," she said. "Actually, we're supposed to be in by ten-thirty and no visitors."

Eric looked at his watch. It was ten fifteen. "I guess I'd better be going, then."

"No. It's okay. You can stay a few minutes. There are some things I've been wanting to tell you about."

"I heard about the party this Saturday."

"I wanted to tell you about it, but I haven't seen you."

"I've been pretty busy. Once they started me flying, they really started me flying."

"I can imagine." She hesitated a minute, forming her words. "Eric. I met somebody when I was at Vung Tau last week. His name is Sid Kerr. I want you to meet him."

"Okay. Why?" He sensed the reason, but waited to hear her say it, not wanting to jump to conclusions.

"I think he's kind of special. I'd like for you to give me your opinion, too."

"Is he a Christian?"

"I don't know. I don't think so."

"Then my opinion is that he may be a great guy, but you shouldn't get involved with him."

"Eric!" Her eyes pleaded with him.

He sat down. "Mattie, it's a classic trick of the devil—one of the oldest and most used, and yet Christian girls still fall for it." He went on to explain, seeing a mixture of hurt and curiosity in her eyes. "When a girl, a single girl, gives her heart to Jesus, one of the most effective ways the devil can render her life ineffective is to get her married to a non-believer. I've seen it happen again and again. Not only do they become ineffective for the Lord, but in most cases, their lives become miserable."

"I'm not marrying the guy."

"If you're dating him seriously, marriage is a possibility. It's usually best to avoid even getting started."

"That's not what I wanted to hear," Mattie said. But in her heart she had suspected that's what Eric's response would be.

"I know," Eric answered. "And it's really none of my business, except you asked."

"You're the only spiritual leadership I have here, other than Chaplain Wallace. And I have a sneaking suspicion he would tell me the same thing." And then she added, "He's one chaplain who really knows the Lord."

"That's unusual," Eric said.

"What? A chaplain knowing the Lord?"

"Most of the chaplains I've met are like most preachers."

"What does that mean?" She asked. It was a sincere question, not defensive at all.

"It's my opinion that if you walk into eighty percent of the churches in America, you won't find real Christianity. You might find a social organization with a lot of rules, but you won't find Christianity—not the Bible kind of Christianity."

"What makes you say that?" Mattie asked. "Do you really believe that?"

Eric had her interest. Apparently it wasn't a concept she had considered.

"Well, I grew up going to church, but I didn't find anything there that made me want to be a Christian."

"What kind of church was it?"

"It was Methodist. But from what I can tell, the Presbyterians, the Baptists or Episcopalians, they're all about the same."

"Well, I wouldn't know about that," Mattie said. "My family didn't go to church at all. I found out about the Lord from a friend in college who started reading the Bible to me. My family was Catholic, but we didn't go to church and we certainly didn't read the Bible."

"Funny," Eric said. "I learned about Jesus in college, too. There were a bunch of kids there who were really excited about being Christians. It wasn't like anything I ever saw in church. I have to admit that now that I *am* a Christian, I've been in churches where there seems to be life, but now I know what to look for. If I didn't know there was something beyond what most of them have, I wouldn't look in the organized church to find the answers to the great questions of life."

"That's interesting," Mattie said. "I don't guess I've thought much about it, but I would have thought that most churches are basically Christian."

"They probably were a hundred years ago. But just because our grandparents knew what it meant to be Christians doesn't mean we do. I think a lot of churches are filled with people who only go there because their parents or families have always gone there and they don't know anything different. Tradition can be a powerful force." Eric leaned back in his chair and crossed his legs. He was really getting into the discussion, though it had taken a strange turn from Mattie talking about a guy she was dating to the state of the church in America. "I find it interesting that when Jesus was on earth, the two things He went up against the most were tradition and organized religion. To Him, those two things were worse than the things everybody knows are sins like stealing, lying or committing adultery."

"Why?"

"My guess is it's because tradition and religion deceive people and pull them away from the truth. If you're stealing, you know you're doing wrong. But if you're going to church, you may think you're doing the right thing, when in fact you are believing all the wrong things about God."

"That's sad," Mattie said. The conversation seemed to be depressing her.

"It is," Eric agreed. "And you know what? The people who are supposed to be Christian leaders, but don't teach the truth about God and Jesus, have a lot to answer for."

"I guess they do," Mattie agreed.

It was time to go. "Be careful, Mattie," Eric said.

"I will, Eric. It's just that I'm twenty-six-years old and my options are not as good as they once were."

Eric stood up. "God has someone for you. You have to believe that."

Eric moved toward the door with Mattie beside him. "You're coming to the party Saturday, aren't you?" she asked.

"Sure. Of course."

"Sid said he'd bring your brother-in-law with him."

"Thanks for looking him up."

"You're welcome." She hugged him briefly before he went out the door.

* * *

First-Up Day was quiet. True to his promise, Rob McElroy taught Eric the techniques of the Dustoff tactical approaches and departures. They practiced them north of the Bassac River, not too far from Can Tho, at a rubber plantation with a few clearings in the trees. Mac indicated the place was relatively secure, but he cautioned the crew in back to stay alert and he made sure Eric never made an approach into the same area twice.

What Eric enjoyed most about the morning was the low level flying. Flying a Huey at 110 knots at treetop level was thrilling and usually frowned upon by the brass. Now he was doing it under the protective authority of the unit IP in the name of combat training.

They didn't practice the corkscrew departure. Instead, McElroy explained the basics of it to Eric and told him to save it until a time when he really needed to get out of a tight space with minimum exposure to ground fire. It sounded simple enough: a 40-knot attitude, 40 pounds of torque and full left pedal when you cleared all obstacles.

Eric wasn't sure what a 40-knot attitude looked like. Attitude means the relationship of the helicopter's fuselage to the horizon. At a given power setting, a certain tilt of the rotor results in a given airspeed every time. You learn what a ninety-knot cruise attitude looks like by watching the distance between the tip of the rotor plane and the horizon. An experienced pilot could fly a Huey at ninety knots all day without looking at the airspeed indicator. But what McElroy had described as a forty-knot attitude really looked more to Eric like a zero-knot attitude or straight up.

During the afternoon, they sat around the crew lounge and played cards with the Second-Up crew, Chris Sanders and Les Winters. Eric wondered what they would do about the God thing. Would they harass him about it, or would they have questions. They did neither. The conversation never moved in that direction.

On Friday, Eric flew Second-Up with Chris Sanders. While the First-Up crew was on a run to pick up an injured American near Soc Trang, the Second-Up crew got a mission. An ARVN patrol with an American advisor had been ambushed near Sa Dec. Some of the ARVNs had been wounded and the American had been shot in the ankle.

When they were on short final to an outpost camp along a canal that ran west out of Sa Dec, a Viet Cong stepped out of the bushes and opened fire at them with an AK-47. He shot low, but they heard a "chink" as a bullet hit what Eric and the crew chief both thought was one of the skids. Chris, who was flying, broke off the approach and announced they were returning to Binh Thuy to check out the aircraft. Eric questioned him.

"Aren't we going to pick the guy up?"

Chris' response was an angry glare. His jaw muscles tightened as he increased power almost to the redline and nosed the Huey over, picking up speed. The Huey had a moderate one-to-one vertical vibration at 105 knots, the rotor system obviously not trimmed for that speed, but Sanders pushed it even faster. It wasn't what Eric would have done at all, but he wasn't the aircraft commander. He looked over his shoulder to catch the crew chief's reaction and got an "I dunno" shrug in response.

They'd been only fifteen minutes away from Binh Thuy when the "hit" occurred. All gauges continued to read normal. Eric was concerned about the wounded men on the ground. But the Huey's right front seat might as well have been empty. From the time the bullet, or whatever it was, struck the aircraft, or maybe from the time Eric challenged Chris about aborting the mission, he became a nobody—a peter pilot occupying a seat, but with no part in the mission. Chris flew the aircraft. Chris worked the radios. Chris informed the ground unit at the pickup site they were aborting the mission. He contacted the artillery advisor in the sector for artillery clearance back to Binh Thuy. He contacted Paddy Control for radar flight following and advised the controller the aircraft had sustained a hit and had "unknown" damage. He contacted Dustoff Operations on the FM frequency and advised them he was returning after taking fire and needed maintenance to meet them on the ramp to check out the ship. He contacted the tower when they were close in and after he landed, he hovered quickly to the maintenance ramp outside the hangar. Once they were safely on the ground, Eric became part of the crew again—Chris told him to shut the aircraft down.

They combed every inch of the Huey, looking for the impact area. None could be found. Maybe someone had dropped a can of C rations or an ammo clip in the back of the helicopter. Maybe it had been a loose seatbelt banging against the side of the fuselage. No one had observed either. Maybe it *had* been a bullet ricocheting off a skid or something. If so, they never found any evidence of its impact.

Inside, Eric was fuming. *The whole reason they were there was to evacuate wounded personnel; not to panic every time someone shot at you!* It was only later, when eating dinner with Les Winters, that Eric learned that Chris Sanders was still a "cherry."

When Saturday arrived, Eric was on the roster for First-Up night. He tried to trade with Dickson, with Winters, with any of the other peter pilots so he could go to the party, but he got no takers. He was going to miss the party—he was going to miss Steve again.

By late Saturday afternoon, he'd lost his peace over it and was inwardly steaming. To make matters worse, he would be flying with Chris Sanders again; Sanders, the cautious one; Sanders, the conservative one. Sanders who wouldn't risk anything to save anybody.

Late that afternoon, Eric watched the Navy ramp for arriving OV-10s from Vung Tau. It was quiet in the Navy area, almost totally shut down. Nobody wanted to work that Saturday night.

Even the mission board was quiet. Maybe they would have no early missions and he could at least go to the party for a while. The girls had a phone so the RTO could reach the crew at their place. If they took a jeep, they could be ready to launch within five minutes of getting a call.

But at a quarter to seven, they got a mission, and it was called in hot. That meant they had to have gun coverage, which on Saturday night might take a while to get. The options were the Knights at Can Tho, the Vikings at Vinh Long, the Seawolves or the Black Ponies. The RTO had no luck raising any of them, so he called in Wade Daugherty while Chris and Eric took off to have a look.

It was not the same Chris Sanders that Eric had flown with the day before. This mission was called in with seven wounded after the Viet Cong had pillaged a small village near My Tho. Among the wounded were reported to be Vietnamese women and children.

Chris worked the radios. He let Eric fly. The darkness and the idea of landing to a flashlight, a strobe light, a small fire or a handheld flare no longer intimidated Eric. His night vision was adjusting. He'd learned to use his peripheral vision and to compensate for the lack of outside references by relying on both his instruments and coaching from the ground and from the crew.

There were no electric lights in the village, just a few lanterns and some small cooking fires. The local ARVNs identified a small landing area a couple hundred yards away from the village, on the side opposite from where the VC had fled after their attack. When twenty minutes had passed with no indication that gun coverage would be available, Chris elected to try the mission anyway. He let Eric fly the approach while he monitored the airspeed and altitude. Eric kept it smooth and steady, in spite of a quartering tailwind that tried to kick the Huey's tail around to the left. At about a hundred feet, he flipped on the landing light and quickly adjusted the beam with the cooley hat switch on top of his cyclic grip. Eric saw the wounded huddled beside a rice dike and made his approach to the ground to minimize the blow-by caused by the rotor wash.

As soon as they were down, Chris took the controls. The crew in back jumped out to load the wounded. Eric scanned the area, looking for signs of enemy activity. Seeing nothing, he turned his attention to the patients being loaded. Two of them were kids, one shot in the hand, another in the leg. Then the crew loaded a very frightened pregnant woman onto the bottom litter directly behind the crew seats. Her pelvic area was covered with blood and she was holding her lower abdomen.

"It looks bad, sir," the medic, Ronnie Powell, advised Sanders. "We've got a pregnant woman back here with gunshot wounds in the pelvic area. She's conscious, but going into shock." There was a hesitation while he checked her out. "I think the baby is still alive."

"Are we clear to go?" Sanders asked.

"Clear up left."

"Clear up right."

Eric gave the thumbs up that everything was okay with the engine instruments. Chris lifted the aircraft smoothly and accelerated, turning back toward the direction from which they had come. No shots were fired.

In the back, the crew turned on the red-filtered cabin lights. Eric watched as Powell began wrapping the woman's wounds with a bandage wrap. The medic made a figure eight, wrapping it around the woman's legs alternately and pulling it tight over the wounds in her pubic area. Though there was fear in her eyes, she didn't scream, she didn't cry, she just bore it. Eric's heart grieved for her and her unborn baby.

"The Third Surg, sir," Powell advised Chris, who was already headed in that direction. Usually Vietnamese patients were transported to a Vietnamese hospital in the closest city of any size that had one. But the medic knew this woman needed the kind of emergency care only the Third Surg could handle.

Eric called the hospital on the FM radio and told them they were inbound and advised them of the status of the patients the best he could tell. The hospital was only fifty kilometers away, about thirty miles, but it seemed to take forever to get there. Eric obtained their artillery clearances and advised Paddy Control of their intentions, but other than that there was nothing he could do to help.

The medic and the crew chief had their hands full. Chris had his hands full of controls. He didn't need navigational help for he knew the way and the landmarks were clearly visible in the moonlight. Eric could only sit there. Then it occurred to him—he could pray. He could pray for the woman and her unborn child. He could pray for the children and the others who had been wounded. Quietly, he began praying on their behalf.

Sunday morning, Eric slept. Sunday afternoon, he went to the hospital to check on the patients they'd brought in the night before. He saw Lisa Sneed, and she took him to the room where the pregnant woman slept. The doctors had delivered her baby by Caesarian during the night and both mother and child were in recovery and were expected to be all right. "Yes!" Eric thanked God. "Lisa, you should have seen that woman last night. She was so trusting when our medic was working on her. I don't know how she did it. I'd have been screaming my head off."

"They're an interesting people that way," Lisa responded. She changed the subject. "I went to the Donut Dollies' party last night. I guess you know Mattie Hill is a Christian. There were two other guys at the party who were Christians." She pulled at her pony tail as she talked, pulling it over her left shoulder and wrapping it around her hand. "One was the chaplain from over at Can Tho Army Airfield. The other was a civilian, an older guy who lives in a house in Can Tho. I don't know exactly what his job is, but I think he's with the CIA or something."

"What about the Navy guys from Vung Tau? My brother-in-law, the guy I was looking for here that day I met you, he was supposed to come."

"Oh, they didn't make it. Mattie was really disappointed, too. I think there's a guy she kind of likes who was supposed to come, but they didn't make it."

"Yeah, she talked to me about a guy over there, but he's not a Christian."

"Bad news," Lisa said.

"Yep," Eric agreed. "Bad news."

Steve hadn't been at the party, so Eric hadn't missed him after all. He was curious about this chaplain he kept hearing about and also about the civilian guy from Can Tho who was a Christian. He decided to go see Mattie and find out about them—but after lunch. Right now he was hungry.

The hospital mess hall was out. He'd eaten there when Winters was his only companion, but not since. The Navy mess hall was all the way across the airfield and there hadn't been any jeeps in the BOQ area when he'd gotten up, so it was the Engineers' O'Club for an American-style burger.

It was Sunday afternoon and the place was almost deserted. But Les Winters was there. That meant Eric had a choice. He could eat alone, or he could eat with Winters, which might be worse if Winters was drinking and brooding over his misfortune at being assigned with a bunch of "boy scouts" as he called the Dustoff pilots.

Eric sat down beside Winters, who gave him a once over. There was no invitation to talk in his Winters' expression, but Eric wanted to talk. He wanted to talk about the woman—the pregnant one with the bullets in her gut. Saving her life and saving the life of her baby was what Dustoff was all about. As far as Eric was concerned, he'd been in country less than a month and with the rescue of the downed Loach crew and the mission with the pregnant woman, it was worth it if he went home today. If he could have Lynn here with him, he'd just as soon stay until the war was over.

"Cooked your goose with that God stuff the other day," Winters told him.

"Oh really? So I'm an outcast for being a 'Jesus Freak' and you're an outcast for being a 'killer.' Which one's worse?"

"I dunno. Furthermore, I don't care." He turned up his glass, drank it empty, then looked around for a waitress.

Les said he didn't care, but Eric knew that deep inside, he did. Everybody cares what people think about them. They might put up macho exteriors, even erect walls to keep people out, but they care. The walls are erected for emotional protection. People don't want to be hurt, so they isolate themselves from those they think can or will hurt them. You let it go far enough and you isolate yourself from everybody. That's what Winters was trying to do. Eric wasn't going to be pushed out.

"You care," he said.

"No, I don't," Winters declared.

"Yes, you do."

"Hey, man, you're as stubborn and hardheaded as I am, you little squirt."

"That's what my mama always told me," Eric admitted. He raised his hand to signal the waitress that he really did want something to eat. She was leaning on the end of the bar with a bored, vacant stare, smacking bubble gum. It was an American habit that seemed totally out of place on the pretty Vietnamese face. When Eric caught her attention, she came over, painting an "I want a big tip" smile on her face.

Eric ordered food and Wes ordered a refill for his drink. Then Eric started telling Les about the patients he and Chris had brought in the previous night and how the baby had been born and the mother and baby were both going to live.

"Don't want to hear about it," Winters declared.

"You're kidding?"

"Nope. Just another Dink woman and another Dink kid. You'd have been better off letting them die."

Eric was stunned. "Les, you can't really mean that?"

"Sure I do."

"Oh, come on."

"Seriously, why shouldn't I? They'd just as soon kill you as look at you."

"A mother? A little baby? Don't be ridiculous."

"The mother, yes. The baby? Give the kid a few years. They hate our guts."

"Minh, Baby-san, Mama-san—they don't hate our guts."

"What makes you so sure?"

"The way they act, for one thing."

"They're Orientals. They can put on a smiley face for anybody, then when you turn your back, run a knife through your guts and never stop smiling."

"What makes you hate them so?" Winters' thinking was totally foreign to Eric. Even before he'd become a Christian, he couldn't have fathomed that kind of hate or bitterness.

"I've seen them do it. I've seen a little kid walk right up to you with a smile on his face and drop a live hand grenade in your pocket. They hate us, Eric."

Eric attempted to change the subject. "So, where in the real world are you actually from?" he asked.

"Abilene, Texas," Winters replied.

"Not too far from where Gary Dickson is from, huh?"

"You ever been to Texas?"

"Of course. I went to flight school at Fort Wolters."

"Then you ought to know that Abilene and El Paso aren't anywhere close to each other. In fact, hardly any place in Texas is close to El Paso."

"Yeah, I guess you're right."

They spent the rest of Eric's meal talking about things that were less confrontational—airplanes and helicopters, subjects of interest to them both. Then Eric decided to go find Mattie and find out why Steve and her friend hadn't showed up for the party. When he left Winters was ordering another drink.

Vung Tau

Steve Cooper didn't make it to the Donut Dollies' party in Binh Thuy because he was holed up in his room with a severe case of strep throat. Sid Kerr's reason for not going was less forgivable. He'd simply forgotten about it. A carrier pilot offered him a chance to take an A4 flight out to his aircraft carrier for a weekend break and Kerr forgot everything to make that flight.

Cooper's sore throat had started earlier in the week and by Thursday when Lt. Hazlett held sick call in Vung Tau, Steve couldn't even swallow his own saliva. He showed up at the dispensary carrying a cup to spit in. Hazlett gave him a shot of penicillin and sent him to bed.

Back in his room, pain and fever prevented him from sleeping. Thoughts of Gail and Emily came crowding in and he broke down and started reading her letters. He read her pleas of forgiveness and something within him was moved. She sounded genuine. Letter after letter, she was consistent.

He read the letters, a few at a time, spreading the pictures of Gail and Emily out on his desk. When he could sleep, he slept fitfully. Each time he woke up, he read a few more letters before drifting back to sleep. He lost all awareness of time, leaving his room only to go to the latrine or take an occasional shower.

Sunday morning he read the letter in which Gail told him she had accepted Jesus. A strange sensation enveloped him while reading those words. He didn't know what it was, but it was unlike anything he'd ever experienced before. It was as if another presence were in the room with him—an unseen presence, but not an evil one. It was good; it was love; it was truth, it was assuring him that everything would be all right.

He didn't know why he knew, but he knew that Gail's experience was real, that there was something to it, something more than superstition or emotion. He decided to write her, but it would have to wait. Overcome with drowsiness, he lay down on his bunk and drifted off into a deep and peaceful sleep—the first in a long time.

FIFTEEN

Navy Binh Thuy, Mid-December

Lisa Sneed met Eric at the bottom of the BOQ stairs. "Eric, if you can get a jeep, there's five of us, counting you, who want to go to Can Tho Thursday night."

"Five?"

"Well, there's you, Mattie Hill and my two friends from the hospital, Blake Sam and Nancy Pettis." Lisa counted them off on her fingers as she named them.

Blake Sam—the man with two first names. Eric had been so busy he had not had a chance to look Blake up. It would be good to see his friend from San Antonio.

"I talked to Captain Scott about the jeep and he doesn't have any problem with us taking it, if we can park it in a secure area," Eric said.

"I would think Russell Lamb lives in a pretty secure place, considering the business he's in," Lisa observed.

"Are you sure he's CIA?" Eric found it hard to believe a CIA agent living and working in Vietnam was also a Christian.

"No. Nobody knows for sure. But that's what everybody thinks. He doesn't talk about it, but Chaplain Wallace thinks that's what Russell does for a living."

"We should probably allow at least an hour to get downtown and find the place," Eric said. "Can you and the others be ready to go by six?"

"Sure. Will you check with Mattie?"

"I already have. She'll be ready."

"Good, then it's all set. See you Thursday." She turned to leave.

"Let's meet right here," Eric called after her. She nodded before disappearing behind a bunker.

Eric couldn't believe he was finally going to have an opportunity for some real fellowship. Trying to be a witness to the Dustoff crews and struggling with the burden he felt for Steve and Gail was getting him down. He didn't realize how much it had meant to him to have Lynn as a regular prayer partner. He looked at his watch. Five-fifteen. He'd better get something to eat and get over to Operations. He wondered where Harris was.

"Let's go, kid." His question was answered quickly as Hank Harris kicked open the screen door to the latrine and started down the stairs. The relationship between the two men could probably best be defined as "mutually tolerant." Harris was the unit supply officer and Captain Scott had decided Eric would be next in line for that position. Though Harris still had nearly five months to go in country, Eric was now working in the supply room during his non-flying hours so he could learn the routine. The two men had engaged in a number of conversations about Christianity, most of them turning into philosophical debates. At least Harris was willing to tolerate Eric's beliefs as long as he could categorize them as a value or belief system. But he obviously wasn't ready to face the reality of a life-changing relationship with the Creator of the universe. That was too much for his clinical mind to absorb. Eric found the debates challenging because they made him go back to his room and dig through his Bible for answers to the challenges Hank Harris presented. The fact that Eric usually came up with a suitable answer didn't really matter to Harris, who had determined in his mind to be dead set against anything having to do with what he called "religion." That didn't stop Eric from trying.

Harris and Eric took off in the CO's jeep. Dickson and K. J. flagged them down as they were getting ready to leave the BOQ and the four of them headed for the Navy mess hall to eat. After dinner, Hank and Eric went to preflight and check the mission board. It was Eric's second or third time to fly First-Up with Harris, and he felt he was beginning to gain the lieutenant's respect as a pilot, even if he wasn't getting any closer to winning him to Christianity.

They flew some easy missions early in the evening. Just before 11:00 p.m., Dustoff Operations received a call for a medevac from a unit in contact a few klicks north of Cao Lanh. Harris told the RTO to put in a request for guns, and they headed in that direction, with Eric at the controls. Just a few seconds earlier, Harris had been giving Eric and the crew a discourse in the Mormon religion. From that discussion, Eric gained a better understanding of the disdain Harris seemed to have for anything related to God. Being from Salt Lake, Harris had grown up in a protestant family in the middle of Mormon country. Because of the serious aspect of the new mission, he turned his attention toward the task at hand. Eric was flying, so Harris worked the radios.

"Paddy Control, Dustoff Seven-Two."

"Go ahead, Seven-Two."

"Seven-Two's got a new mission at whiskey-sierra-seven-one-three-six-zero-two."

"Stand by." There was a slight delay as the radar controller plotted the coordinates on his scope. "Dustoff Seven-Two, fly heading three-four-five for twenty-two miles. Are you going to stay at fifteen hundred?"

"Roger. Three-four-five for twenty-two miles." Eric turned slightly to the left, picking up the new course. He was actually at twelve hundred feet, so he added power to start a slow climb back to the altitude they had reported to Paddy Control.

Harris was now on the FM radio calling for artillery clearance. "Sa Dec Arty, this is Dustoff Seven-Two, direct Binh Thuy to Cao Lanh at fifteen hundred."

"Dustoff Seven-Two, Sa Dec Arty, reporting no activity at this time, over."

"Roger, Sa Dec. We'll catch you on the way back down."

Harris switched the FM radio back to the Dustoff Operations frequency. "Ops, this is Seven-Two. How're we doing on the guns?"

"Seven-Two, we've got a pair of Snakes out of Vinh Long working. They estimate thirty minutes until airborne."

"Roger." Thirty minutes was too long to wait. He keyed the intercom to talk to the crew. "Maybe this mission will be secure by the time we get there. You can't ever get guns at night any more."

That was true. Apparently, until just a few months earlier, Cobras and Charlie Model gunships had been in abundant supply throughout the Delta. It hadn't been that way at all since Eric's arrival. Dustoff regulations were specific about using gun coverage. If a mission was called in as "secure," meaning the pickup site was in friendly hands and the threat of enemy activity against the Dustoff aircraft was minimal, the aircraft commander had full discretion about when or when not to attempt a mission. If the mission was called in as "hot," however, that was an indication the unit which had called in the medevac was either in contact with the enemy or enemy elements were in the area and the safety of the medevac crew could not be guaranteed by the ground unit. The aircraft commander was forbidden to attempt a hot mission unless he was accompanied by gunships to provide covering fire.

In recent months a pattern had developed. A ground commander in desperate need of medevac support would call in a mission as secure, even if it was not, because he knew gun coverage was getting hard to obtain and the "hot" designation on a mission would insure an automatic delay.

In contrast, if the injuries were slight and the area relatively secure, the mission was often called in as "hot." Why make the Dustoff crew take unnecessary chances? Besides, the ground-pounders loved to see the Cobras in action. The Dustoff aircraft commanders had seen this often enough they now had an understanding of the situation. Secure missions were hot, and hot missions were not.

The fact this mission had been called in as hot, made Harris and Mohr think it probably wasn't. Still, they had to wait for the guns, unless when they got in the area and talked with the ground commander, they determined the tactical situation had changed. If the ground commander assured them his unit was secure, they could make the pickup, guns or not. It was a scenario the Dustoff crews saw played out all the time.

During the short flight to Cao Lanh, Eric thought about how he could break through to Hank Harris. There was so much the lieutenant was missing with his calloused approach toward life. If Harris could unlock the bitterness he seemed to feel toward all of the circumstances surrounding his life, perhaps he could find something to make life worth living.

It seemed to Eric that Harris just existed from one day to the next, with nothing to look forward to.

He wondered about Harris' wife. He knew Hank was married, but he never talked about his wife. It was as if he had stepped into a cell called Vietnam for a year to "do his time" and would start living again when the year was over. Silently, Eric asked God to show him a way to penetrate the shell Lieutenant Hank Harris had erected around his life.

They flew over the village of Cao Lanh, then turned due north. Eric checked the coordinates on the map. They were close to the coordinates that had been given as the pickup site. Harris was on the FM radio with the ground unit. The Cobras had still not launched from Vinh Long.

"Zebra Six, Dustoff Seven-Two."

The voice came back clear and strong and obviously American. "Dustoff Seven-Two, this is Zebra Six, go ahead."

"Dustoff Seven-Two is approximately five clicks south of your location. What's your tactical situation?"

"Contact was broken about fifteen minutes ago, Dustoff Seven-Two. We've got seven wounded—two critical."

Eric knew Harris was thinking about how they could pull the mission without the guns. Waiting around until their fuel was critical before attempting a pickup was not a good idea. Plus, the guys on the ground needed medical attention now, not an hour from now. It had already been more than twenty minutes since the first call for medical evacuation had been received by Dustoff Operations. Harris keyed the radio microphone switch. "Where are the bad guys?" he asked.

"They broke off to the west of us, Dustoff."

"Would you say that your site is currently secure?" He was coaching the guy to change the mission status. It worked.

"Roger that, Dustoff. We're currently secure."

Harris told Eric, "Start descending. I'll get him to give us a marker. Keep the lights off." Eric double clicked his mike to indicate he understood. He loosened the friction on the collective pitch and eased the lever down slightly. The Huey's blades began to pop as they always did in a reduced power descent.

Harris flipped his ICS switch over to the UHF radio. "Paddy, Dustoff Seven-Two is on site, we'll call you off."

"Roger, Seven-Two. You guys be careful."

Harris answered with a double click, then switched back to FM. "Zebra Six, this is Dustoff Seven-Two. Tell me about your landing site and what you've got to mark your position."

"Dustoff, this is Zebra Six. It sounds like you're a couple of klicks south of our location. We're on the south side of a canal that runs east and west. The landing area is clear of trees as long as you approach parallel to the canal. If you approach from the east you should remain clear of the bad guys. I can give you a strobe light when you're ready."

"Stand by on the strobe. What are your winds?"

"They're out of the north, about eight to ten miles per hour." That agreed with what Hank and Eric had observed about the winds earlier on their other missions and with the active runway back at Binh Thuy.

On the intercom Harris asked, "Everybody ready?"

"Ready left."

"Ready right."

Eric scanned the instrument panel, then keyed his mike. "Ready. Instruments are in the green." Harris gave no indication of taking over the controls. "I see the canal," Eric added as the dim outline of the canal became visible. He was sure it was the one. It was the only east-west canal in the area five klicks north of Cao Lanh. They were now at one thousand feet. Eric added some power and held it steady. He slowed to eighty knots and turned the instrument lights down to their dimmest setting. Just before reaching the canal, he turned to parallel it.

"Okay, Zebra Six," Harris called. "Give us your strobe."

All four of the crewmen searched the area below. Within seconds, they saw two strobe lights, both on the south side of the canal and about a half mile apart!

"I've got two strobes, Zebra Six," Harris called. "Can you show me a flashlight?"

Two strong flashlight beams shown in the air, waving around at the unseen Huey. "Let's try a flare," Harris radioed. Immediately there were two flares. Obviously the VC were monitoring Zebra Six's radio frequency.

They flew over the area and Harris signaled Eric to circle back for another approach. Eric banked left, entering a race track pattern that would bring the Huey back around on a westerly heading south of the canal.

Harris tried again. "Let me have a small fire, Zebra Six." It took a few seconds for the fires to kindle, but within a minute there were two small fires along the canal, still approximately a half mile from each other.

"I'm getting two of everything, Zebra Six," Harris railed. His previously calm and unemotional voice was beginning to show signs of stress. Eric was just as bewildered. There had to be some way the good guys could show their position. In the daylight the ground units used colored smoke to mark the landing site. They would pop a canister of smoke without identifying the color. When the Dustoff crew spotted the smoke, they called the color and the ground unit would confirm. That way the VC could be on the frequency, but they couldn't anticipate the signal. The best they could do was guess and if they happened to hit it right, the good guys would keep trying 'til they fooled them. At night, it wasn't so easy. You had to identify your method of marking the LZ, and as in this case, the enemy could duplicate anything they heard.

Eric brought the aircraft around to the east and lined it up on a heading that would take them toward the fires, both of which could be seen in the clear night air. They were about a mile east of the easternmost fire. Harris was determined to identify the correct site. "Okay, Zebra Six. I've got two fires along the canal. Which one are you, the one to the east or the one to the west?"

"The bad guys broke off to the west, Dustoff. We're the one that's toward the east."

"You're sure about that?"

"Roger that."

"Okay," Hank said slowly to his peter pilot. "Start making your approach toward that first fire, but be ready for action if it's the wrong one."

"Okay," Eric said. "What about the landing light?"

"Flip it on when you need it, but wait as long as you can. Leave the position lights and the rotating beacon off."

"Okay. Pre-landing looks good. Here we go." Eric decreased the torque to fifteen pounds and eased back on the cyclic to slow the Huey. He picked up the correct sight picture in his chin bubble and began milking off both airspeed and altitude as he approached the fire. His peripheral vision was tuned to look for obstructions and the crew in back were hanging out their doors, watching for obstacles or hostile action during the approach.

At two hundred feet, Eric flipped on the landing light. Suddenly, fireworks lit up the sky as tracers from a variety of weapons were fired at the aircraft. The tracers were a combination of red, green and orange. It was an amazing sight, and at once an indication to Eric of God's protection. The bullets seemed to converge at a point approximately twenty feet in front of the

Huey's windshield, then deflect, as if there were a giant invisible shield in front of the aircraft. Eric felt a tremendous peace come over him. God truly was protecting them. He flipped off the landing light and arrested their descent by adding power. He nosed the Huey over to pick up airspeed. Harris' reaction was typically low-keyed. "Nope, Zebra Six," he radioed. "Yours is the fire to the west."

Eric picked up the sight picture for the other fire as they flew toward it and started a standard approach. He again decreased power to fifteen pounds of torque and started a gradual slowing of the Huey's forward motion. This time when he turned on the landing light, they were met by nothing but the waving arms of the American advisor on the ground.

Can Tho - A Few Days Later

Russell Lamb lived in a two-story house on Vo Than Street, not far from the Market District that fronted the Can Tho River. Eric had to park on the street, but the jeep was visible from the second-story garden patio where the group was meeting for the Bible study and fellowship. Two other military jeeps were parked there already. Lamb shouted something in Vietnamese from the rooftop to a couple of local street urchins, then assured Eric the jeep would be safe.

The house was not unlike others on the street—two story in back with a garden patio area on top of the first story near the front of the house and overlooking the street. As the sun went down, a breeze stirred the air and the setting was not at all unpleasant. An elderly Vietnamese mama-san served snacks and soft drinks, while a very attractive young Vietnamese lady wearing diamond-studded gold earrings and with an immaculately coiffured hairstyle stood by Lamb's side holding on to his arm. Lamb introduced her to his guests as his wife, Vanh.

Russell Lamb had been in Vietnam for twelve years. His knowledge of the people and their customs was that of a native, no doubt aided by his marriage to a local woman. His rumored role was that of the local CIA station chief. His actual role was something none of the guests actually understood. One thing was certain, he was an intriguing man. The first thing Eric noticed about him were his eyes. Piercing blue eyes smiled out of a handsome, rugged face. His hair was solid white, full and thick. The eyes, it is said, are a mirror of one's soul. If that is the case, then Russell Lamb's soul was full of something you would not expect from a CIA agent—love. Eric was caught off guard by this. He turned his attention to Mrs. Lamb's face. Except for the color, her eyes were the same. Eric decided this was a couple who would be worth getting to know. Obviously something had happened in their lives to bring them into a close walk with God.

After a few minutes of eating snacks and getting acquainted, the group began to take their seats in a circle of chairs that had been arranged on the garden patio. Eric glanced over the railing to check on the jeep, then took his seat. Mattie took the seat next to him and the others from Binh Thuy sat nearby. Lisa Sneed sat on his right. Beside her was the other nurse, Nancy Pettis, and beside Nancy, sat Blake Sam. Also in the circle were Chaplain Cameron Wallace and several men he had brought with him from Can Tho Army Airfield. Chaplain Wallace opened the session by leading the group in a familiar worship chorus. Lamb stood up and went into the room that adjoined the patio. He came out a moment later with an acoustic guitar. He held it up, scanning the group for a volunteer who could play it. Eric started to reach for it, but one of the men from Can Tho who was closer, beat him to it. Eric sat back, content to let the other man play.

They sang more songs. Most were familiar to all who were present because they were choruses sung in a variety of Christian circles. The atmosphere was one of worship and Eric closed his eyes to enjoy the warming presence of the Lord. He was at the same time aware of the love and support flowing from those around him.

After a few minutes, Chaplain Wallace gave members of the group the opportunity to share with the others how God was working in their lives. The stories they told were encouraging. When it was Eric's turn, he had two stories to share. One was of the flight a few nights earlier in which he and Hank Harris had flown into a wall of enemy fire which had obviously been deflected by an invisible angelic shield.

"I had hoped the obvious nature of the miracle would have demonstrated to Hank Harris the reality of the presence of God. It didn't appear to affect him, however."

"You never know," Russell Lamb offered. "God worked miraculously in my life many times before I was willing to acknowledge it." His pretty wife, Vanh, nodded in agreement and smiled a knowing smile.

"That's true," Cameron Wallace added. "You never know how God is working on a man or a woman's heart."

"There's something else I want to share," Eric told the group. "A few nights ago, I was in my room, by myself, singing and praising the Lord. Suddenly, the door burst open and Chris Sanders, who lives in the room next to mine, came in and started looking around. 'Who's in here with you?' he asked. 'Nobody,' I told him. He acted like he didn't believe it. Then, because it was obvious I was by myself, he became real serious. He said, 'I heard three-part harmony coming from this room.'

and he meant it. Guys, I can't even sing one part on key and Chris was certain he heard three voices coming from my room and they were singing harmony. Those of you who know Chris know that he's a pretty pragmatic sort of guy and that he is not into anything that might be considered mystical. I can only say that the angels must have been singing with me."

"Wow!" Nancy Pettis said. The others nodded in agreement and wonder. All of them appeared to believe his story, not finding it at all unusual.

They sang a couple of more songs, then Major Wallace taught a short lesson on trusting God when circumstances seem to be against you. He reminded the group of Joseph, who had been sold by his brothers into slavery in Egypt, had risen to power in Pharaoh's Court, then had been thrown into prison falsely because he had spurned the advances of Pharaoh's wife. Many years later, he had risen to the place of second in command of all of Egypt. God had worked throughout all of Joseph's circumstances for his good.

Mattie was right about Cameron Wallace. He was not a typical clergyman in the way Eric had come to think of them, but a man who really loved God.

After the Bible lesson, members of the group were invited to share their prayer requests. Mattie asked for prayer for salvation for her friend, Sid Herring. Eric asked the group to support him in praying for his brother-in-law, Steve Cooper—that his marriage would be restored, and that he would come to know the Lord. Several of the others had similar requests about friends or loved ones. About nine-thirty, the group broke up.

The jeep jostled them through the streets of Can Tho and along the road back to Navy Binh Thuy. Its occupants engaged in animated conversation about the meeting they'd just attended. The five were becoming acquainted in a deeper, more supportive sense than they had known before and were beginning to realize the kind of support they could be for each other.

Behind the wheel, Eric had a nagging feeling he should be concerned for their safety. After all, they were five American military personnel, unarmed and in a land that was for all practical purposes hostile. To him, the darkness held unseen dangers of ambush, yet the others seemed totally unconcerned and trusting. He tried to lighten up, but the sense of responsibility stayed with him until they were safely inside the gate at Navy Binh Thuy.

He dropped Mattie off first because of her curfew. The others, who all lived nearby, stayed in the jeep as he drove around to the other side of the BOQ and parked it. Lisa and Nancy lived on the lower floor of the BOQ, just beneath Eric, and Blake lived in the enlisted quarters about two hundred yards down the path toward the hospital. When Eric switched off the jeep, they just sat in it for a few minutes.

"What do you think?" Lisa asked. "Do you think we can do this again?"

"I sure hope so," Blake answered. "This was so neat." He was young and full of enthusiasm. In spite of the fact that he was an enlisted man, he was obviously a close friend to Lisa and Nancy.

"I'm sure we can," Eric added. "But we don't have to go to Can Tho. There's at least five of us who can get together right here. Who knows? We might start something that will interest the people we've been witnessing to."

"That's true," Lisa said. "When could we do it?" The others looked at Eric as well, waiting for him to make a commitment.

He mentally went through the duty roster. He was off the next day, which was Friday, then started the rotation again on Saturday. That meant he would probably be available

Saturday and Sunday nights, but definitely not Monday night and probably not Tuesday. "It's either tomorrow night or next Wednesday for me," he said.

"Tomorrow night, my place," Lisa announced.

"What about Mattie's place?" Eric asked. "Doesn't she have more room?"

"I'll check with her," Lisa said. "Hey, I wonder if Minh would want to come?"

"I don't know if she can stay on the compound after dark," Eric said.

"Why not? There's nobody who checks their passes when they go out the gate."

"Agreed, but they might if she left at nine or ten o'clock," Eric pointed out.

"We don't know if she can stay, but I'll ask her," Lisa said. "If it's a problem getting her out the gate, we can take her."

"Okay." They all agreed that Lisa should invite her. None of them knew how much the little Vietnamese woman prayed for them, nor how much she needed fellowship as she suffered quietly through the difficulties of her own life.

SIXTEEN

Shuqualak, Mississippi

Emily Cooper chased the white chicken across the yard, squealing with delight. The hen ducked under the pasture fence, and scooted across the bare ground to the shelter of the feed trough, flapping her wings as if by some magic they could produce enough lift to make her fly. Emily was only temporarily stopped by the fence. She dropped to the dirt and started to climb under the bottom wire.

Immediately, she was swung into the air as Gail Cooper grabbed her daughter by the seat of her britches with one hand and with the other grabbed the suspenders of her denim overalls and lifted her high. Totally caught off guard by her mother's stealth, the toddler squealed her pleasure as she soared through the air, round and round until her mother became so dizzy she could hardly stand. As Gail eased her daughter to the ground, she pretended she was going to chase the little one back to the house. Emily took off running, but promptly fell down. She let out another squeal of laughter and her mother fell laughing onto the grass beside her. The two of them lay flat on their backs and watched the sky spin.

Lynn Mohr watched her sister and niece from the front porch of the farmhouse, proud, envious and thankful. Steve had written. Their prayers were being answered. It would only be a matter of time until the healing was complete and Steve, Gail and Emily could get on with what God had planned for their lives.

Recovering from dizziness, mother and daughter got to their feet, brushed off the loose grass clinging to their clothing and raced each other to the porch. Of course, Emily won. Inside, Gail flopped into Eric's recliner and watched with a mother's pride as her twin sister took Emily to the bathroom. A twinge of guilt took its stab at her as she realized Steve had missed Emily's potty training, along with so much more of her delightful discoveries of new and exciting things to know and talk about in life. It seemed the little one knew about everything there was to know about being a little girl, except having a father come home from work every evening to pick his little girl up, put her on his lap and let her wrap him around her little finger. Oh, well. Only four more months. And now that Gail knew Steve would be coming home, four months seemed like enough time to prepare for it. It would be different. So much had changed.

"Want some ice cream?" Lynn asked Emily as they trooped across the living room toward the kitchen. Gail abandoned her thoughts and got up to follow. Ice cream could heal anything.

A few minutes later, as the three of them sat around the kitchen table eating—or in the case of Emily, playing with—their ice cream, Lynn addressed her sister on a more serious note. "I can't believe it has been almost two months since Eric went to Vietnam and that he and Steve are so close to each other, but they haven't gotten together yet."

"I know." Gail thought it strange, too, but had not yet considered the spiritual implications of the fact.

Lynn enlightened her. "It's as if there is some kind of spiritual barrier to their getting together."

"What do you mean?" To Gail, everything that happened had always had a natural explanation. It was only within the last few weeks she was beginning to discover the spiritual realm and the battles waged there.

"You know there's a battle for Steve's soul," Lynn explained. "If he's around Eric, he's going to hear the truth. Satan doesn't want that."

Satan. Just a few weeks ago, Gail would have rebelled at the thought of a real being called Satan. A myth. A fairy tale. But now she was reading the Bible, and the same Bible that explained to her about faith, about salvation, about Jesus, spoke of Satan. If Jesus was real, and she knew He was; if faith and salvation were real, and she knew they were; then Satan must be real also. It would explain a lot. This new outlook on life sure did explain a lot of things that had previously been mysteries. At the same time, there were so many more mysteries that came out of an awareness of such an awesome power as God at work in your life.

"Then we just need to pray that they get together," Gail said. The fact that Steve had finally responded to her letters was indication enough that God did answer her prayers.

"Agreed," Lynn said. "But there's something else we can do. You write Steve and tell him everything we know about where Eric is: his unit number, where his room is, where he works when he's not flying, where he eats, stuff like that. I'll write Eric and tell him the same stuff about Steve."

Gail interrupted. "Steve hasn't actually told me much about those things."

"Well, we know what his call sign is, and what his unit designation is. We know where he lives. We'll just tell him what we know."

"Okay," Gail conceded, "but we still need to pray."

"Absolutely."

Navy Binh Thuy - A Few Days Later

Eric stood on the balcony outside his room and squinted into the bright afternoon sunlight. He went back into his room and picked his Ray Bans up off the table by the bed. He couldn't believe it. It was two days before Christmas and lying on top of the concrete bunker at the end of his building were three American women wearing two-piece swimsuits and soaking up rays from the tropical sun. On the sidewalk below, Sgt. Massey, the barkeeper from the Hospital O' Club was grilling steaks on a grill made from an oil drum. People in civilian clothes—doctors, nurses, Dustoff pilots and Donut Dollies—milled around drinking beer or soft drinks and waiting for the steaks to get done.

Most of the people had put in a full day's work and were now unwinding, getting into the holiday spirit. They were keeping their minds occupied rather than think about missing Christmas with their families. The cookout was part of it.

It was hard to think about Christmas when the temperature was in the high nineties every day. It was hard to think about Christmas, when everyone knew work would continue as usual. There would be no two-week shutdown for Christmas, no relief from putting up the duty crews, no relief from guard duty. The VC didn't celebrate Christmas.

Eric had worked the night before and slept nearly all day. Now he was stiff, thirsty and hungry. He started down the steps, noticing that his Levis and pullover knit shirt were starting to get tight on him. Was he really gaining weight in Vietnam? It was the Navy mess hall that was doing it. That, plus no one ever thought about or mentioned physical training here in the real war.

Eric heard his name called and recognized the voice as belonging to Lisa Sneed. She was one of the girls on the bunker. He bounded the rest of the way down the steps and toward the bunker. Nancy Pettis was there, also. The third girl he didn't know.

"Come on up," Lisa said. The bunker had a six-inch ledge around it about midway up. Eric grabbed a handful of ledge and shinnied his way up. He brushed the concrete dust off his hands and sat down beside Lisa as she made room for him on her beach towel.

"Eric, this is Alice Brewer." Alice, a short-haired brunette with long legs and a deep tan, raised her head and a hand and gave Eric a friendly wave.

Lisa whispered in his ear, "I've been praying almost constantly since the other night," she said.

Nancy nodded enthusiastically. "Me, too," she echoed.

"That's great." They were immersed in the love of God, and so excited about having His power at work in their lives. Eric sat with his arms around his knees. He nodded toward the grill where Sgt. Massey was flipping the steaks. "What's going on here?" he asked.

"You know about the vets?" Lisa asked.

"The vets?"

"Yeah, the veterinarians. It's their job to inspect the meat that goes to the mess halls. Your CO, Captain Scott, traded a helicopter ride to Saigon for a couple of cases of 'condemned' steaks, and now we're having a party."

"It's for everybody?"

"Sure is."

"Then I'm going to get in line. I'm starved."

"We're going, too. But first we're going to get dressed. Help us down, will you."

He helped them down, averting his eyes as he did so. Too much female flesh and his wife was too far away. The girls were innocent enough in their desire to work on their suntans, but sometimes even Christian girls seemed unaware or uncaring about the effect they had on a man's hormones. He forced himself to look away as they bent down to put on their flip-flops before walking across the grass to their rooms. He missed his wife.

He went over to one of the ice chests and pulled out an iced-down can of Coke. A line was starting to form at the grill, so Eric grabbed a paper plate and took his place in line.

The Next Morning

Gary Dickson had made aircraft commander, leaving Eric and Les Winters as the only non-AC rated pilots in the unit. Today, Eric was flying Third-Up with Dickson. They had pre-flighted the aircraft before seven, then went to breakfast at the

Navy Mess Hall. On the way back, they stopped to watch two OV-10s land and taxi into the fueling and rearming area on the Navy ramp.

"Wait a second," Eric said, as the two aircraft rolled to a stop and the canopies were raised. He watched as the helmeted pilots went through their engine shutdown procedures, then raised the visors and unsnapped the chin straps on their flight helmets. As the pilot closest to them lifted off his helmet, Eric shook his head and turned his attention to the other one. Slowly the helmet came off. The hair was blond, the profile right. It was Steve! "Come on, Gary, that's my brother-in-law." Eric was already moving toward the aircraft, breaking into a jog. Dickson waved him on, electing to follow at a slower pace.

Steve stepped over the side of the cockpit and searched for the mounting steps with his boot. Eric stopped near the Bronco's big propeller and waited for Steve to set foot on the ground and turn around. Steve descended slowly, feeling for each recessed step with his toes. When he set foot on the ground, something about the Bronco's turret gun caught his eye and he bent to examine it before turning around. He hadn't seen Eric approach.

"Steve!" Eric said. Steve jumped, then turned around.

"Eric!" They embraced and pounded each other on the back.

"I was beginning to think I was never going to find you," Eric said.

Steve stepped back and looked at him. "A full-fledged Army pilot, huh? So somebody finally was able to teach you to fly?"

"I can fly rings around you, buddy." Steve started to protest, when Eric added, "at least in a helicopter."

"I don't doubt it," Cooper shrugged. "Helicopters aren't supposed to fly, anyway, so it takes one of you weirdos to keep one in the air. So how have you been?"

David B. Freeman

"Couldn't be better," Eric replied. "Except for missing Lynn."

"Know what you mean, buddy. I can't get her twin sister off my mind, myself." Willis approached from the other aircraft as Gary Dickson joined them. The introductions were made, then Steve asked Eric, "Have you eaten breakfast?"

"Yep, but I can eat again if that's where you're going." He looked at Gary for approval.

"Fine with me," Dickson said. "I know where to find you if anything comes up." It was Christmas Eve and they were Third-Up. Hopefully, there wouldn't be any missions.

Over breakfast, Steve told Eric the news. "Our unit is moving here between Christmas and New Year's."

"Are you kidding me? What a deal. Think I can fly with you sometime in your OV-10?"

"I think that can be arranged. You've got to get me some helicopter stick time, though."

"I thought you didn't like helicopters." Eric put down his coffee cup and looked Steve straight in the eye. It was a habit he was beginning to pick up from Les Winters.

"I don't. But I've got to be able to say I flew one once so I can justify not liking them." Steve's eggs were nearly gone. He pushed what was left of them into a pile with his fork and knife, then scooped them into his mouth.

"As soon as I get to be an aircraft commander I'll see if I can swing it."

"When will that be?" Steve was buttering another biscuit.

"I'm not sure. I've been here two months. Usually you make AC in three. I think they're a little concerned about me, though, so I'm not sure what's going to happen."

"Concerned? What do you mean concerned?" Steve had been Eric's first flight instructor. He knew Eric had the talent

222

to be an excellent pilot. He put down his fork and slid his tray to the side.

"It's not about my flying," Eric told him. "It's because they think I'm weird."

"You are. Everybody knows that."

"I'm not kidding, Steve. They think I don't have a grasp on reality because I'm not afraid when we get shot at or when we think we're going to get shot at."

"You're not?"

"I don't know how to explain it, but I know I'm not going to die in Vietnam; that I'm going home in one piece."

"Lots of guys know that. They die." Steve thought about Jake Herring and his senseless death. "Some people you think would never die, die."

"Everybody's going to die sometime. I'm talking about here in this war. I guess I'm not afraid because the peace of God comes over me."

"I've got to talk with you about this God thing," Steve interjected. "It seems Gail has gone and gotten religion, too."

"Yeah, I heard." Eric warmed to the subject. He couldn't contain his excitement about it. "But it's not 'religion,' Steve. It's a personal relationship with Jesus Christ."

Steve held up his hand to stop Eric before he got started. "I know, I know. You've told me all of that before."

"But it's real, Steve."

"I've got to admit," Steve said, leaning his elbows on the table and looking at Eric sincerely, "that I believe what has happened to Gail is real."

"Of course it is!" Eric was emphatic. "She wrote me. Plus, Lynn has been keeping me posted. What's this deal about you not responding to her letters?"

"That's all over now. You heard what she did?"

"Yeah. And you've been a saint all your life?" One thing Eric knew was that forgiveness was what Christianity was all about.

"No. But I've been faithful since I've been married."

"You know Gail, Steve. She's weak in that area. That guy knew it and took advantage of her."

"Who was it?"

"She didn't tell you?"

"No."

"Probably thought you'd do something drastic, like drop napalm on him, or something."

"The thought has crossed my mind."

"Wouldn't fix anything. The key is forgiveness. You've got to forgive her, Steve. And him, too, for that matter; then put it behind you."

"I didn't think I could do that, for a while," Steve said, honestly. "But now I think I can. I'm willing to give it a try—her, anyway. I'm not sure about him."

"Well, that's a start. What are your plans for Christmas?"

"I don't know. I guess I don't have any plans."

"Can you spend the day here with me? We can talk over old times, watch a couple of movies, maybe play some chess."

"You'd risk playing chess against me? I thought you learned your lesson last Christmas."

"I've gotten better," Eric said.

Stump Willis approached the table. He had politely found somewhere else to eat while the two men visited, but now it was time to go to work. "We've got to go, Steve. The Riverines are pounding the island at Tra On and they need us to bust some bunkers."

"On my way, Stump."

Steve stood up to leave. Eric took a last swallow of coffee and got up from his place across the table from Steve. "Be careful, brother."

"I'll do it. See you tomorrow?"

"I'll be here. I'm on duty, but it's Second-Up and I doubt we'll do anything."

"I'll try to move some of my stuff down if I can find out where I'll be staying. See you later." He and Willis started to walk off.

"Wait, man," Eric called. "I'll walk out with you. I've got to get back over to Dustoff Operations, anyway."

SEVENTEEN

Navy Binh Thuy - Christmas Day, 1971

It was easy for Eric to get out of bed, though many of the guys would be sleeping in. He hadn't slept much all night, in anticipation of Steve's visit. He and Dickson had to pre-flight by seven. After that they could go back to bed. The First-Up Crew would be preflighting also. The Third-Up crew wouldn't preflight unless the other two crews were both out on missions.

Steve planned to be at Binh Thuy by noon. The Navy mess hall was putting on a feast for Christmas: turkey, dressing and all the trimmings. Most of the Vung Tau pilots were coming over; many to scout out living arrangements and start moving their personal gear.

Both of the 57th's jeeps were outside the BOQ area when Eric made his way downstairs around six-thirty. There had been no one in the showers or latrine. He wondered if something had changed and they were all sleeping in. Or, were the other crewmembers going to miss their preflight deadlines?

He went back upstairs and knocked on Gary Dickson's door. Gary met him sleepy-eyed. "What time is it?"

"It's six-thirty." Eric checked his watch again to make sure.

"Give me a minute."

"Sure. Who's First-Up?"

"Chris and Capt. Scott, I think."

"Think I'd better wake them? Nobody else is up."

"Wouldn't hurt."

Eric went to Captain Scott's room first and knocked. There was no answer. He went to Chris Sanders' door. Chris was just coming out, his shaving kit in hand. "Morning, Eric."

"Hi Chris. I was just coming to make sure you were up. Where's Capt. Scott? Isn't he flying with you?"

"He traded with Wade."

"Well, Wade's not up either. Think I ought to go get him?"

"Yeah. We've got to preflight, even if it is Christmas."

Wade Daugherty, a married man, was living with a nurse in the adjacent building. Eric didn't like it, but it wasn't any of his business. He thought he knew which room they were in, but wasn't sure.

"Do you know which room he's in?" Eric indicated the other building over his shoulder.

Chris pointed. "Second one from the end on the other side."

"Thanks."

Eric started that way, then saw Wade Daugherty come around the corner of the building. Daugherty came next door to the Dustoff BOQ and climbed the stairs to the latrine, stuffing the shirttail of his flight suit into his pants. Pulling his belt from over his shoulder, he started looping it through the belt loops on his pants. "Merry Christmas," he said as he reached the second floor balcony.

"Merry Christmas," Chris and Eric responded, though neither had illusions of it being very merry.

Eric went downstairs to wait in the jeep. He climbed into one of the back seats and allowed his thoughts to drift to Christmas back home. They would have opened presents at the Mohr's on Christmas Eve. He and Lynn would have then gone to Ernie Gibson's house for Christmas dinner. The year before, Steve, Gail and Emily had been there, too. It had been a blast watching the one-year-old tear open her presents. This year would certainly be different, but at least he and Steve could spend it together. He thought of Gail and her newly found faith in Jesus and how different Christmas would be for her if she really understood the significance of Jesus' birth.

His thoughts of home were interrupted when the others piled into the jeep. It didn't feel at all like Christmas. The temperature was already climbing and their flight suits were already damp from the humidity. Daugherty started the jeep and backed it around. They headed toward the flight line, leaving a trail of dust behind.

The pilots unanimously elected to skip breakfast and go back to the BOQ after making sure the aircraft were ready to fly. Some felt a little guilty about leaving the RTO on duty all alone, but the thought of a few extra hours of sleep quickly purged the guilt.

Back in his room, Eric couldn't sleep. He was keyed up for Steve's visit and at the same time lonely for his family. He sat at his desk to write Lynn a letter. A soft knock came at the door.

Minh pushed the door opened and peeked inside. Seeing Eric at his desk with the light on, she slipped inside and closed the door behind her. She was not dressed in her usual pajama-like outfit. Instead, she wore an American-style dress cut above the knees. Eric had never seen her wearing anything but her work clothes.

"All GIs sleep," she said.

"Minh, what are you doing here? It's Christmas!" Eric was shocked to see her. It never occurred to him the hootch maids would show up on Christmas.

"My family not celebrate Christmas. Only me," she said. "Everyone else Buddhist."

"I didn't realize," Eric began. "Baby-san, Mama-san, are they here, too?"

She nodded.

"You could have stayed home and celebrated Jesus' birthday," Eric told her. It pained him that she was having to work on Christmas.

She shrugged. "No one to celebrate with."

"I'm sorry," Eric said. Then, brightly, "Merry Christmas!"

"Merry Christmas, Mohr." She moved closer, a tear in her eye. Eric reached out to her and took her hand. She stood next to him, relishing the human touch. Eric felt the warmth, too. "Tell me about your husband," he said.

"My husband far away. Up north." She pointed. She held her head down, embarrassed for him to see her crying.

"How long since you've seen him?"

"Two year."

"Two years?!"

He couldn't believe it. He was in the same country.

She nodded.

"Are you sure he's all right?"

She shook her head no, tears flowing now. Eric stood up and held her to him. She put her arms around his waist and snuggled tight. It was a moment she needed, but it was a short moment. She pushed away and brushed the tears from her cheek with her

229

hand. Eric felt great compassion for the little woman. He realized he had done little to reach out to her. She'd been invited to some of their Bible studies, but had not been able to come, or maybe had not felt comfortable in coming, he didn't know which. He reached for his billfold and pulled out several one hundred piaster notes. He handed them to her. "Merry Christmas," he said. She pushed them away shaking her head no.

"Please, Minh. I want you to take it." She hesitated. To her, it was a lot of money. It was hard for her to comprehend how little it was to him. She hesitated, then searching his eyes for confirmation, reached out for it tentatively. He nodded and put it in her hand, closing her hand around it. "Take the day off, please," he told her. "No one really cares. Most of the guys are just going to be sleeping in today, anyway."

"You sure?"

He nodded. "I'm sure."

"GIs not get mad?"

"GIs won't get mad," he assured her.

She leaned over and kissed him on the cheek. "Cám ón" (thank you), she said and slipped out of the room.

Eric felt saddened by the encounter. He was a stranger in a strange land; how much stranger did she feel—a Christian in the midst of a Buddhist country and a Buddhist family. He promised himself he would pray for her often. Two years since she'd seen her husband—two years, and he was right here in Vietnam!

He turned back to writing Lynn's letter, describing for her the encounter with Minh and the emotional effect it had on him. He wrote her that Steve was coming to spend the afternoon with him and would be moving to Binh Thuy within a few days. He told her how much he missed her and how he was already looking forward to R&R in April or May.

The phone on the wall in the latrine next door rang. After four rings it was still ringing, so Eric decided maybe he'd better answer it.

He snatched the receiver off the wall phone. "Mohr here."

"Mr. Mohr, this is Eddie, the RTO. We've got missions and I need all three crews. There's a serious medical emergency in Rach Gia."

Eric hung up the phone, then went down the hall beating on the doors of the on-duty pilots. "Dustoff! Dustoff!" he called. "All duty crews, let's go!" Men scrambled from their rooms, pulling on flight suits and lugging helmet bags and weapons. It was almost 11:00 a.m.

During the next four hours, everything but taking care of their patients was forgotten as the Dustoff ships made two trips each to Rach Gia and back to transport Navy personnel who were in various stages of food poisoning. It was shrimp—Gulf of Thailand shrimp that had somehow spoiled. Some of the men were near death. The total number of patients transported by mid-afternoon was twenty-six. A doctor from the Third Surg told Captain Scott later that at least six lives had been saved by the prompt and expert medical attention provided by the Dustoff crews. Stomach pumps were used on most of the men who were brought to the hospital. It had been a true medical emergency, and it was handled professionally by all involved: the medical personnel on site at Rach Gia, the Dustoff medics and flight crews and the staff at the Third Surgical Hospital.

Steve arrived at Binh Thuy a few minutes before noon and went directly to the mess hall where he expected to find Eric. When there was no sign of Eric by 12:30, he became concerned. Leaving the mess hall, he walked across the OV-10 ramp and through the Sea Wolf revetments to Dustoff

231

Operations. There the RTO told Steve that all three of the Dustoff crews were going to miss Christmas dinner because they were all flying missions. K. J. Madison was in operations monitoring the progress of the flight crews. It was not a requirement that he do so—just an obligation he felt. If they were out there working on Christmas day, somebody ought to be in Operations supporting them in case they needed anything.

Steve visited with K. J. awhile, then the two went to eat. After their meal, K. J. drove Steve over to the Dustoff BOQ so he could wait in Eric's room until Eric returned.

Eric's room was cool and quiet, and Steve's first thought was to take advantage of the day off to catch up on some sleep. A book on the table beside the bed caught his attention. It was a small paperback entitled *How to be a Christian Without Being Religious*. For some reason, he found the title interesting, so he sat down to browse through the pages. Within minutes, he was engrossed in the book, amazed at how easy it was to read and how much he understood the scripture verses quoted in the book. According to the introduction, the book was a paraphrase of the Apostle Paul's letter to early Christians who lived in Rome—the Book of Romans from the New Testament.

What Steve read wasn't anything at all like what he thought Christianity was all about. There was a message here, and Steve understood it. It was not a message about a vengeful, angry God who stamped out people like you would stamp out ants at a picnic, but about a loving, caring God who made a supreme sacrifice to show His people how much He loved them. According to this book, people for the most part were totally indifferent to God, caring little for His concern for them. Was he that way? Of course he was. In his own mind, Steve had convinced himself that there was no God, or that if there was,

He didn't involve Himself in people's lives. Eric believed differently, and it seemed to work for him. Now Gail believed differently, and judging from her letters it was something she felt very strongly about. But could he accept it? It went against everything he had based his life upon. He believed in self-sufficiency, in taking care of your own, in making it in life based on your own skill, dedication and hard work. Were these beliefs inconsistent with believing in God? He didn't know, but something was definitely tampering with his belief system.

He put the book down and looked around the room. There was not one, but four Bibles, all in different translations. There was a shelf full of books about God, about Jesus, about living the Christian life. He certainly didn't want to become a religious fanatic like Eric. He picked up the *How to be a Christian* paperback book again. Something jumped out at him. "The wages of sin are death. But the free gift of God is eternal life through Jesus Christ." What was this sin thing? Being bad? The book said it was separation from God. He needed to know more.

As he read, Steve's skin began to crawl—something he called the heebie-jeebies. He had to get out of the closed-up room. There was a presence there—a presence not unlike the one he had sensed in his own room when he had finally begun reading Gail's letters and especially when he read the one about her accepting Jesus Christ as her Savior. He laid the book back on the table and opened the door to bright sunshine.

Leaving the BOQ, Steve walked toward the hospital. As he rounded the corner, he heard splashing and yelling and laughing. He couldn't believe his eyes. There was a full-sized swimming pool, right there in the middle of the Vietnam Delta! He watched as American men and women, apparently the doctors and nurses from the hospital, dove, splashed and swam in the pool. It made him think of his family and how Emily had been afraid of the water when he and Gail first took her swimming. He was her father. It was his job to teach her to swim and he had almost let himself fall into the trap of not being there.

He turned at the sound of a Huey approaching and realized there was more than one. The people in the pool heard the choppers, too, and as a group began moving to the edge of the pool, drying off, picking up towels, shoes and clothing and heading toward the hospital. The approaching Hueys were a signal that playtime was over, and it was time to go back to work.

Steve watched as the first of the Dustoff Hueys landed on the hospital helipad. The pilot made a faster-than-normal approach and set the big helicopter down with a slight bounce. Crewmembers jumped out of the back of the helicopter and began unloading people. Some of the passengers who could walk were clutching their stomachs. Others had to be carried on litters. Medical personnel from the hospital came out to help, some still wearing their swimsuits.

After it was unloaded, the first chopper lifted, and a second one came in swiftly, disgorging its own set of patients; some helping the others as they hobbled toward the hospital emergency room. A third helicopter appeared and circled, waiting for the helipad to clear. The first helicopter landed on the runway a few hundred yards away and hovered to the Dustoff ramp. Steve wondered which of the three Eric was flying. He'd better get over to Operations if he didn't want to miss him.

As Eric set the Huey down in its revetment and rolled the throttle back to the flight idle detent to let the engine temperatures stabilize, he looked at his watch. It was three-fifteen. Had Steve waited for him? Had he missed the feast at the Navy Mess Hall? If so, it was worth it. The guys they had picked up in Rach Gia had been in bad shape. Many would not have made it without rapid transportation to the hospital and the IVs the Dustoff Medics had used to treat them for shock. It was hard to believe. You come to Vietnam, and what almost kills you is not the Viet Cong, but some lousy spoiled shrimp from the Gulf of Thailand.

As Eric climbed out of the aircraft, Steve walked up, dusty from the walk around the airfield perimeter.

"You *can* fly a helicopter, huh?" Steve chided him.

Gary Dickson, sitting in the other pilot's seat, leaned across the console toward Eric and Steve. "No, he can't," Dickson said. "He just rides around with me while I fly. I keep trying to teach him, but he ain't learnin' nothin'."

"He couldn't learn anything from me either, when I was his flight instructor," Steve said.

Eric took the joking in stride, glad to be in the presence of friends and still feeling good about the job they had done. "Think there's any food left?" he asked. "I'm starved."

"Heck yeah, man," Steve retorted. "It's the Navy. We eat all the time."

"Let's go get some."

"I'm game."

"I'm coming, too," Dickson said.

Together they headed to the Navy mess hall.

After a splendid dinner of turkey and dressing with all the trimmings, Steve and Eric walked out to the flightline and sat on one of the revetments to talk. Steve was full of questions about God, but he wouldn't ask them. Instead, they talked about flying, about their missions, about getting home alive, about Gail's unfaithfulness and how it had affected Steve, and about his decision to forgive her. Eric sensed something was going on inside his brother-in-law, but wouldn't push him. He'd been guilty of that in the past. Near the end of the day,

Steve indicated he wanted to get back to Vung Tau early and spend some time cleaning up and writing Gail a letter. Before he left, he promised to try to get Eric in on a mission hop within the next few days.

EIGHTEEN

Over the Bassac River, East of Can Tho

The OV-10 was powerful and agile, and as far as Eric was concerned, it might as well have been a jet. He was in the back seat behind Steve, wearing a torso harness to help counteract the G-forces and a Navy flight helmet, loaned to him by Sid Kerr. The Bronco was not air conditioned, a surprise to Eric. The Army Cobras were air conditioned; he'd just assumed the Navy OV-10s would be. He was wrong. Vent air poured in around his feet and through small side vents, but the clear plexiglass canopy magnified the sun's rays, and the heat was oppressive. Because of their low altitude, thermals buffeted the airplane, making the ride even more uncomfortable. Sweat poured down Eric's back and under his armpits, and he had to keep wiping his forehead to keep the sweat out of his eyes.

Steve jockeyed the Bronco's controls to keep his aircraft in position relative to the other airplane. They were tucked in close to Stump Willis' wing, following Willis down the Bassac River. Their mission was to be part of an organized raid with ten River Patrol Boats sweeping the channel behind the six-mile-long island that lay near the north bank of the Bassac River between

Tra On and Cau Ke. The island was a stronghold held by the Viet Cong and a refuge for the sampans that crossed the river at night transporting supplies and ammunition.

The Riverine forces had staged a similar assault a few weeks earlier and had taken a beating. That day they went in the narrow channel early in the morning and spent the better part of the day fighting. This time they were going in during the afternoon, hoping to bust open some of the bunkers along the shoreline and put a stop to the crossing of the Bassac that would be attempted after dark.

Eric had mixed emotions about being along on such a raid. It was a killer mission, plain and simple. The OV-10s were loaded with bunker-busting Zuni rockets and would be targeting any bunkers from which the patrol boats were fired upon as they swept the channel. A pair of Seawolf helicopters were also along to fly cover over the boats. Steve promised Eric there would be plenty of action.

Stump's voice came over the UHF radio, "I've got the flotilla in sight, One-One. Let's go upstairs and cool off a bit until they get underway."

"Sounds good to me," Steve replied. Willis pointed his aircraft skyward. Steve eased back on his control stick and added power to follow, still in tight formation. Less than two minutes later, they were orbiting at 5,000 feet. Steve dropped back a few hundred feet from the other OV-10.

"Want to fly?" he asked Eric.

"You know it," Eric responded, reaching for the controls. "What sight picture do you use for staying in formation?"

"Line up his left vertical stabilizer with the front of his right engine nacelle and keep that angle. Use power, not pitch, to maintain the angle. You've got the controls." Steve raised his hands, a gesture that indicated Eric was flying the aircraft.

The plane's controls were sensitive, not unlike those of a Huey. Eric fought the tendency to over-control as he struggled to maintain the proper position.

"Watch out," Steve advised. "He's turning toward us." Eric reacted by snapping the control stick to the left. What he should have done was simply to reduce power and bank slightly. Willis had the flight in a left-hand orbit, and that put Steve's and Eric's aircraft on the inside of the turn. Because he was already out of formation, Eric dropped back and keyed the mike. "One-One's switching to echelon right." Steve was impressed. It was the right thing to do. On the outside of the orbit the pilot of the trail aircraft wouldn't have to work as hard to keep from running over his leader. He'd have to stay alert and add power to keep up in the turns—a far less difficult task.

After crossing behind Stump's aircraft, Eric added power to move back into position. He almost ran Willis down. Steve reached for the controls, but Eric backed off just in time. They made three or four orbits, and Eric was starting to get the hang of keeping the airplane in the right position without constantly fighting it. The FM radio came to life.

"All units, this is Handlash One. Commence operation."

"There they go," Steve said.

Eric felt Steve's hand on the controls and released his. "You've got it," he said. Steve banked the aircraft sharply so they could see the river below them. The patrol boats, grouped in pairs, were entering the canal under speed. Each pair of boats was spaced approximately three hundred yards behind the pair ahead. Two Seawolf helicopters flew right above the lead pair of boats.

"One-Two's starting down," Willis announced. Steve acknowledged with a double click of his mike. They began their gradual descent, widening their circle to move up the channel with the boats.

Suddenly, an excited voice yelled out. "Delta One's taking fire from the island!" At the same time, the boat's forward and rear gunners opened up with their fifties, raking the shoreline.

"Handlash One, this is Delta Two. We're under fire also. Requesting an airstrike on the bunkers south of our location." Though he tried to sound calm and professional, you could hear the tension in the radio operator's voice.

"Black Pony, One-One, this is Handlash One. That's your target. Do you need a marker?"

"That's a negative, Handlash One," Steve advised. "Target's in sight."

Steve keyed the mike on the air-to-air frequency. "Stump, you take the lead. Let's give them a north-to-south pass in tandem. I'll be off your left wing. Two hundred's the deck."

"Roger," Stump said. "North to south, two hundred's the deck." To provide a safety margin, two hundred feet above sea level was as low as the OV-10s were going to go. That would give the helicopters room to maneuver beneath them. The helicopters would be concentrating on Viet Cong in the open and suppressing small arms fire aimed at the boats. The Ponies were going to try to bust open the bunkers so the helicopters and boat crews could clean them out.

Steve flipped the switches to arm his weapons. Both OV-10s dove toward the island, one slightly behind the other, both picking up speed. Eric's adrenalin was pumping. His seat was slightly higher than Steve's so he had excellent visibility over the pilot's shoulder during the dive. The two pilots spread out so that they were approximately a hundred yards apart. Steve adjusted his power and raised his aircraft's nose slightly to keep from overtaking his wingman as they lined up on the bunkers.

With his bird's-eye view of the action, Eric had nothing to do but sit and watch. He could clearly see the bunkers with their heavy machine guns firing upon the boats. There were several of them close together, approximately fifty feet in from the shoreline. The boats were returning fire. Eric was ready to see those bunkers busted open.

At five hundred feet the altimeter was still unwinding and the airspeed indicator needle was hovering near the redline. Eric swallowed to clear his ears and remembered to pull down his clear helmet visor. Stump's aircraft started firing. Almost immediately Eric heard and felt rockets leave from the outboard wing nacelles of their own airplane. Two streaked away, then two more right behind them. The Zunis left a trail of fire and smoke as they converged toward the bunkers. Before they impacted, Steve pulled out of the dive. The resulting G forces crushed Eric back into his seat, and he fought to keep from passing out. He heard Steve announce "weapons safe" on the radio and saw him flipping switches. With a swift motion, Steve inverted the aircraft so he could get a look below and behind them at the damage they had done. While he was doing all of that, Eric was barely hanging on to consciousness.

"It looks like yours were right on, Stump," Steve told his wingman. "Mine went a little long."

"I concur," Stump acknowledged. "You fired a little late." He switched radios. "Handlash One, Pony One-Two, flight of two coming back around."

"This is Seawolf Three-Six," one of the helicopter pilots interrupted. "I'm on the target." No question it was a helicopter. You could hear the rotor's vibration in the background noise of the radio.

Stump acknowledged and led the flight into a wide circle. They watched while the Seawolf pilot did a tight turn that put his left door gunner in position to blast the bunker with his machine gun. Viet Cong scattered from the bunker and were easily picked off by the gunners from the river boats.

A minute or two later, the mission commander announced, "This is Handlash One. This one's a clean sweep, men. Let's move on to our next objective. Break. Pony One-Two, could you keep a watch on that church around the next bend? If we take any fire from it, level it."

"Level the church?" Stump asked.

"That's a roger, Black Pony One-Two. That church is a free-fire zone. It's not what you think it is."

"Pony One-Two, roger."

It was an easy target, but a church? Stump made a low pass by the building. Steve hung back to see what would happen. Nothing. The Broncos shot back upstairs for a little cooler air as the PBRs reformed into their formation pairs and started moving upstream. The two Seawolves made a low pass over the village where the church was. Everything seemed quiet below.

Suddenly, a B-40 rocket was fired from the steeple of the church, hitting the lead patrol boat and shattering its bow.

"This is Pony One-One. It's my shot," Steve called as he whipped his Bronco around toward the church. Eric saw the Viet Cong with the rocket tube in the window, getting ready to fire again. One of the Seawolves approached the church from the other side.

"Pony One-One, I got him," the Seawolf pilot radioed.

"You pick up the pieces, Three-Six. I've got a Zuni with his name on it."

"Roger." The helicopter turned away. Steve armed his rockets, pointed the aircraft's nose at the steeple, then pressed the button on his control stick four times. Four rockets shot from under the weapons pods, two from each side, and converged on the church steeple. Their impact left nothing but splinters. The Seawolf capped off the attack by raking the lower part of the building from end-to-end with his 50 caliber machine gun.

Eric had become totally engrossed in the firing at the church and found himself cheering its destruction. When it was over, his thoughts turned to the crippled patrol boat and its crew. He twisted in his seat to locate it and found the boat dead in the water, its stern sticking up in the air at an odd angle. Another PBR pulled up alongside. Several men scrambled off the stricken boat. The entire forward deck was gone. There was no way the gunner who had manned the front fifty could have survived. Suddenly, Eric had no stomach for the operation.

Killing the Viet Cong didn't bother him. Maybe it was because of their cruelties and the fact they were the "bad guys." Maybe it was prejudices he had inherited from years of hearing about Americans being killed by the Viet Cong. He didn't like aggression, and he didn't like communism, and he'd seen the results of Viet Cong raids too often. When the B-40 from the church tower hit the river boat, retaliation was on Eric's mind, as much as anyone else's. But the men on the river were another story. They were Americans. They were fighting for freedom. He suddenly wanted to be in his Huey, the savior, the guy who took them out of there when they were wounded. He was ready for the assault mission to be over. But it wasn't.

The stricken boat was left behind, its remaining crew safely on board the other craft. From the FM radio transmissions Eric learned they'd lost one man, and two others had been wounded. The wounds were not serious, and the mission would continue.

Four more times the OV-10s struck out at bunkers on the island. At least four more times the riverboats came under fire. Then two of the boats beached at a village that had been leveled by the Navy forces. The Seawolves hovered overhead for a couple of minutes before having to leave for fuel. Cooper and Willis played guardian angels from above. The sailors amassed a body count. They were vindicated, the loss of their comrade avenged. It was growing dark. Another mile and they would be through the channel and past the island. That distance passed without further incident, and the battle group made its way toward Binh Thuy. It was the last day of 1971.

A new year begins

January's missions consisted of the normal slow days and busy nights for the Dustoff crews. The 82nd was now totally gone, their six aircraft flown to Saigon and turned in for reassignment. The 57th, their six helicopters, fourteen pilots, eight medics and eight crew chiefs, along with maintenance and supply personnel, had the entire Delta to cover. The pilots were no longer flying with the VNAF Dustoff crews.

Two new pilots arrived in January: Danny McCloud and Kelly Smith. McCloud was another southerner—a Louisiana rice farmer. Kelly Smith was from Texas, the son of a career Army officer.

Eric began to anticipate making aircraft commander, but learned there was a faction against him. AC recommendation came by unanimous consent of the existing ACs. Wade Daugherty and Hank Harris had reservations about Eric, though they offered no constructive criticism, no specific areas he could work on to overcome their objections. He felt it was entirely personal and had nothing to do with his flying ability or his knowledge of the mission.

The entire Black Pony squadron, VAL-4, was now located at Navy Binh Thuy, along with HAL-3, the Seawolf helicopter squadron. Both units were making plans to stand down within the next two to three months. Meanwhile, they were being heavily utilized by both the Brown Water Navy and the ARVNs to help stop the flow of supplies from the Delta to the communist troops north of Saigon.

Steve and Eric found little time to spend together because of their work schedules. They did manage an ongoing chess tournament, which they committed themselves to playing at least one night a week. Eric flew at least two nights each week, often three.

Mattie was seeing a lot of Sid Kerr. Eric got to know the man and found himself liking him, but did not change his opinion about his and Mattie's relationship. Kerr was not a Christian—not even close. His belief system was humanistic and did not acknowledge a need for God. He believed man was the sole source of solutions to the problems that plagued society. His philosophy really became apparent during a medical transport mission that Eric and Chris Sanders flew. They took a medical team from the Third Surg to one of the small villages near Bac Lieu to provide medical treatment to the local population. Sid Kerr rode along because of his interest in medicine.

The village was remote and its inhabitants literally lived in grass huts. The doctors and nurses set up a makeshift clinic under a tent canopy. The villagers came to have open sores treated, infected wounds bandaged, teeth pulled, abscesses checked, broken bones set. Sid Kerr was horrified by what he saw. Eric, on the other hand, saw something entirely different. He saw a people who were making the most of what they had, and in many ways seemed comfortable with their lifestyle. He didn't see misery on their faces. Instead, he saw a lot of laughing and smiling; he saw friendships, and he saw appreciation for what the American doctors were doing. The two men shared their observations and Kerr got indignant. "You can't honestly believe these people can be happy in these circumstances! They're not healthy. They live in poverty."

"Oh," Eric replied, a little too argumentatively, "so you propose to heal them and give them better places to live and better clothes and then they'll be happy." He was thinking of Hank Harris and Les Winters and others who had all those things and weren't happy. In fact, many of these poor villagers seemed to be more contented with life than many well-to-do Americans Eric had known.

"It's a start," Kerr told him. "Practically anything would be better than this."

"Sid, happiness comes from within."

"That's bull. You can't be happy when everything is stacked against you."

"That's simply not true," Eric replied. "The Bible stresses the fact that inner peace comes from trusting God and has nothing to do with a person's outward circumstances."

"The Bible," Kerr scoffed. "So these people trust God and look what it gets them: grass huts, a little bit of rice and no medical attention, unless we bring it to them."

"I don't know whether they trust God or not. Most likely they're Buddhists."

"It doesn't make any difference. One god is just the same as another."

"No, Sid. That's where you're wrong." Eric was disturbed by what he was hearing—not because he was hearing it, but because Sid Kerr could be so deceived. "There is one true God, and one way to reach Him. That's through Jesus Christ."

"That's the problem with you Christians. You've got such a narrow view of things."

"Jesus Himself said, 'Wide is the pathway to destruction and narrow is the gate to life and few there are who find it.'"

"Not a very loving God, if you ask me," Kerr challenged.

"A very loving God," Eric responded. "He provided the way to eternal life. It's not His fault so few choose it."

"Well, you can pray for these people all you want to, but I'd rather treat them with medicine and help them learn how to become more productive and make a better life for themselves."

"There's nothing wrong with doing both," Eric said quietly. Kerr didn't respond. It was obvious he was ready for Eric to change the subject.

Eric knew after his conversation with Sid that Mattie didn't have any business getting serious about him. He also knew that there was probably nothing he could do to dissuade her.

The group of Christians from Binh Thuy and Can Tho met together one evening in a mess hall at Can Tho Army Airfield. After the meeting, Blake Sam and Eric were talking. He wanted to know when Eric became a Christian.

"I grew up going to a small Methodist church in a rural community in Mississippi. I thought I was saved. I guess I did believe in God, but He wasn't real to me. I was in college when I really heard for the first time what it meant to acknowledge that I was a sinner and needed God's grace. I heard a message about how God loved me and had a plan for my life. Something inside of me responded to that message and I asked Jesus to be my Savior. As a Baptist, you probably heard all about that a long time before I did." Blake nodded.

Eric continued, "I started going to a weekly Bible study on the campus and I also started reading the Bible on my own. It really came alive to me." Blake was listening intently. He didn't interrupt; and he wasn't distracted. Eric had his full attention. They talked late into the night.

NINETEEN

Navy Binh Thuy - Late February, 1972

"I heard we might be going home early," Steve Cooper said, pushing open the door to the briefing room.

Stump walked in ahead of him. "I heard that, too," Stump said. "In fact, Commander Kelly indicated last night we may get standdown orders within two weeks."

"Think that's what this is all about?"

"I don't know."

Several Black Pony pilots came into the briefing room behind them. Others were already there. They entered in small groups, talking, joking and jesting in the manner typical of airmen who have trained, fought and cheated death together. An afternoon briefing of the entire squadron was unusual. The fact that this one was being attended by the Seawolves added to the mystery. Was it because they were going home early, or was something else up?

Near the front of the room, Lt. Commander Brandt, the Maintenance Officer, was writing names and numbers on a

chalkboard. Lt. Commander Stu Kelly, the Operations Officer, stood over a table near the blackboard, pouring over operational maps of the Vietnam Delta. With him was Commander Matthew Reagan, the Commanding Officer.

Two weeks. Steve thought about what it would mean to go
home. Did he still want to stay in the Navy? Test Pilot School
didn't seem as attractive as it once had. He didn't realize how
much Jake Herring's death and his own experience of being
shot down had affected his attitude about a flying career until
he thought about how he no longer felt driven to make it to
Patuxent River. Foremost on his mind now was patching up
things with Gail and being a father to Emily. His career would
have to come second.

The HAL-3 Squadron, the Seawolf helicopter pilots, sat together near the back of the room.

The guy next to Steve nudged him and nodded toward the
helicopter pilots. "Any idea why we're meeting as a group?"

"Nope," Steve answered. "I hope it's about going home."
He and Stump sat down near the middle of the room. Sid
Kerr was already seated on the row in front of them. "What's
happening, Kerr?"

Kerr half turned in his seat and spoke over his shoulder.
"I think they want us to go out with a bang before we leave
here. I heard something about a massive sweep through the U
Minh. The ARVNs apparently want our support while we're
still here."

So that was it. It made sense. If the Navy really was leaving
the Delta, they were leaving a lot of work undone. As far as
he could tell, the Viet Cong still owned what they wanted of
the U Minh and he'd heard it was worse up north. The U.S.
wasn't going home because they'd won the war. They were going home because the politicians back home were giving up on

it. The thought was enraging, especially in light of the deaths of so many. Pulling out before the job was done would make those deaths senseless.

The Ponies had been lucky. Except for Steve being shot down because of what he had come to realize was his own stupidity and Jake Herring's death for whatever reason, there had been no tragedies among the squadron in recent months. The Seawolves hadn't fared as well. Several had been shot down, and at least one helicopter had crashed killing the entire crew because of a mechanical failure. Now that they were close to going home, Steve hoped the brass wasn't about to do something stupid.

A sharp rapping sound echoed through the room as Commander Kelly banged his pointer rapidly on the small podium in front of the room. "Gentlemen, let's get started," Kelly said. He waited a few seconds for the room to quiet down and he had everyone's attention.

"As you can see, the Seawolves have joined us this afternoon. Tomorrow we will be participating in a joint mission under the operational control of the Army IV Corps commander. Commander Reagan will be responsible for Naval air support. Commander Nelson, the HAL-3 Squadron commander, will be responsible for the individual Seawolf assignments, but all requests for Naval Air support will be coordinated through VAL-4, Black Pony Operations." He turned toward the base commander. "Commander Reagan."

Reagan stepped up to the podium. The fact that Kelly deferred to Reagan was just a formality. His was a figurehead position when it came to missions. Both he and the men under his command knew it. Kelly would be running the operation. "I've asked Commander Brandt to give us an update on aircraft availability. Commander Brandt."

"Thank you, Sir." Brandt, who was still standing in front of the chalkboard, began. He had written a list of aircraft tail numbers on the blackboard. Beside the numbers were pilot assignments. Many were not the aircraft usually assigned. Steve's regular aircraft was not on the list. "As some of you may have heard, we've gotten the word that parts of the unit may be standing down early. That means the aircraft that are approaching hundred hour inspections will not be inspected here, but will be flown to the carrier for transport to the Philippines.

"Of the sixteen aircraft currently assigned, four are down and will not be made operational. The four at the top of this list have ten or less hours to go until they are in for their hundred hours. We'll be flying those aircraft first, then deactivating them. The remaining eight aircraft will be used for the rest of our time here.

"You can see the initial pilot assignments here on the board. As these aircraft are flown into the standdown phase, the pilots will be reassigned to other aircraft that will do double duty."

Reagan took over. "Thank you, Commander Brandt. Commander Kelly will now brief you on the operational details of the mission. Stu." Reagan sat down in an empty chair in the first row of seats.

"Thank you, Sir." Kelly turned to face the group. "Beginning at oh-six-thirty tomorrow morning, Operation 'Clean Sweep' will begin with an airmobile assault in this area north of Bac Lieu, and another on the western edge of this region." Kelly pointed out the areas on a map he had clipped to an easel. "These assaults will consist of ARVN troops transported by US Army Assault Helicopter Companies out of Can Tho and Vinh Long. The Army is short on gunships, so the Seawolves will be providing gunship support for these insertions.

David B. Freeman

"Once on the ground, the ARVNs will sweep northwest through here." He traced the routes with the pointer. "And north through here, Vietnamese river patrol boats will be covering enemy withdrawals on the lower Song Cat River as far as Xa Xa Phien.

"Kerr, you will have FAC duties tomorrow and will be working primarily with the American advisor attached to the ARVNs at Vinh Binh. That's an ARVN Special Forces patrol. The U.S. Contact will be Major Hamilton Ray, call sign Hunter Six."

The name was familiar to Steve Cooper. It was Ray and his ARVN Rangers who had pulled him out of the jungle in Long Xuyen province a few months earlier.

"The Black Ponies will be working in flights of two to provide air support. Targets will be identified by ground units or the FAC and cleared through the Clean Sweep C&C. A free-fire zone will exist in grid squares whiskey-romeo-four-zero-five-zero and south of the plantation in whiskey-romeo-three-zero-three-zero. Your mission times, frequencies, call signs and holding coordinates will be posted in the morning at oh-four-thirty. The Seawolves will be joining the air assault forces at Can Tho Airfield at oh-five-hundred.

"Refueling for the helicopters will be available at Bac Lieu and Vi Thanh. Fixed wing refueling will be available at Cau Mau, Soc Trang and Navy Binh Thuy.

"Tomorrow will be a long day, maybe the last such day we'll spend in this place. Let's make it a good day, and let's make sure nobody gets hurt. Keep your heads up, stay alert, and don't do anything stupid. Remember, those are ARVNs down there, not Americans. We don't need any heroics. Any questions?"

Kelly scanned the room for raised hands and saw none. Behind him, Commander Brandt was making some final adjustments to the numbers he had on the board. When he saw there were no questions, Kelly ended the briefing. "Dismissed. Turn in early tonight men, and get a good night's sleep."

It was chess night. Eric would be coming to the mess hall to eat, then to Steve's room for their weekly game of chess. They'd have to knock off early. With a four-thirty mission posting and a full day's flying, Steve wanted to get a good night's sleep. Now that he and Gail were communicating in their letters and he felt confident things were going to be all right between them, he found he could sleep when he needed to.

It helped that Gail had not been browbeating him with her religion, but she was sharing some of the changes that were coming about in her life. Steve believed there would be no more incidents of infidelity. Two more weeks and he would be with her if the rumors were true. Judging from Brandt's plans with the aircraft and Kelly's comments about the next day's mission being one of the last of its type, there must be something to the rumors.

Eric was late for dinner because he and Chris Sanders had flown an ash and trash mission to Long Binh. By the time he got to the mess hall, Steve had already eaten, but he hung around until Eric finished. Afterwards, they both headed toward Steve's room and the chess board.

On the way to the room, Steve told Eric they had to knock off early because he had a big mission planned for the next day. Eric suddenly had a sense of foreboding.

"What kind of mission?"

"It's some big assault the ARVNs are doing down south. We're providing air support."

"Over the U Minh?"

"Yes."

To Eric, this revelation was like a warning light on the instrument panel. Immediately, in his spirit, he felt something would go wrong. He shared his concern with Steve, "You know in the Army, when a guy is short, down to two weeks or less, they take him off the duty roster. That's because so many times, when a guy gets killed, it's during his last two weeks in country."

"Yeah," Steve said. "I've heard that stuff. But we don't really know for sure if we're going home in two weeks. Besides, the whole outfit is flying tomorrow—the Ponies and the Seawolves. It's going to be a big show. There's no way to get out of it."

"I wonder why we haven't been alerted?" Eric asked as they arrived at the room. "I'm flying First-Up tomorrow, and I haven't heard anything about a big operation being planned."

"I don't know, but there is," Steve said, opening the door. "Let's play chess. You need to knock off early, too, if you're flying First-Up."

"Yep, I guess you're right. It's your turn to be white."

Their opening moves were familiar—cautious, each setting up a classic defense. In chess, they were evenly matched. Of the thirty games they had played since the first of the year, each had won fifteen.

Steve tended to keep his personal life to himself. He was not very open with his feelings and emotions. Eric, on the other hand, wore his heart on his sleeve, often speaking his thoughts out loud while pondering both sides of an issue. This often gave his friends the impression that he was wavering or doubleminded concerning the topic under consideration, when in fact he just had not made up his mind.

Tonight the roles were reversed. Steve felt the need to talk about things that were bothering him. Eric, on the other hand, was quiet and subdued, trying to understand his reactions to learning that Steve was flying a big mission the next morning. *Flying potentially dangerous missions is what we do. Is the Holy Spirit warning me, or is it just my emotions?* If it was God, Eric felt he wasn't being a very good listener, not knowing what his feelings meant or what to do about them.

Steve began telling Eric about the changes in his thought processes. "I just can't believe it, Eric. For years all I've ever wanted to do is fly. I wanted every rating I could get, every aircraft qualification I could gather. I wanted to go to the Navy Test Pilot School. I wanted to fly fighters. But now, something has changed."

Eric moved a pawn. It was a safe move, but gained him no ground. "What do you mean?"

"I don't know. I feel like I'm changing." Steve studied the board, almost made a careless move, then took it back. When he finally did move, it was innocuous.

"Change is something we all do," Eric said, "especially in a war zone." Eric felt inadequate. Steve was opening a door, and Eric didn't know how to step through it or even if he should.

Steve paused to gather his thoughts. He was in unfamiliar territory. Eric waited quietly, pretending to study the chess board. Silently he prayed for Steve and for wisdom in choosing his words. Was Steve opening his heart to God? After a minute or two of silence, Steve said, "I think what affected me the most was when Jake Herring flew into the ocean."

"You mean the guy who was doing aerobatics and didn't recover from a spin?" It was something the entire aviation community in the Delta wondered about.

"Yeah. He was too good a pilot to let that happen. It made me feel so …" he searched for the word, "mortal."

"I felt like that when I took part in the investigation of that Huey that crashed on the mountain," Eric told him.

"That one got to me, too," Steve said. He looked up at Eric; the chessboard no longer important. "You do realize it was me they were out there trying to rescue? And I didn't have any business being on the ground. It was my own stupidity that caused that—their deaths, too, I guess."

"You can't take the blame for that. That aircraft commander made some bad decisions."

"I know. But he wouldn't have had them to make had I not been out there."

Eric didn't respond. What was there to say? He looked at the chessboard, not really studying it.

"There's something else," Steve said. "It's Gail. I almost let my pride come between us."

"That's understandable. You were hurt."

"Yes, I was. But I've done plenty of things in my own life to hurt others. She didn't do it to hurt me. She just got caught in a weak moment."

"That's a mature way to look at it. You been reading the Bible or something?"

"Me? No, that's your department. But I guess some of what Gail has been writing to me has been making sense."

"What has she been telling you?"

"Well. That we need God—that I do, that she does, that we do together."

"What's your response been?"

"I don't know. You know this business of needing God goes against everything I ever believed. But I have to admit something has happened to change her. It's apparently changing me, too. I don't think it's just Gail's influence, either."

"God does tend to change a person," Eric said, glad the subject of God had come up and that Steve had mentioned it first.

Steve was thinking of an earlier time. "I saw you change when you went through this religious thing and figured it was just a fluke. Frankly, I didn't want to be like you." He realized what he'd just said. "Oh, don't get me wrong. There are things about you I admire. But … we're different."

"Don't worry, Steve. I'm not insulted. Besides, trusting God won't make you like me. It'll just make you more like *you* than you are now."

"What does that mean?"

"If God created you, He knows more than anyone what makes you tick. He knows how to bring out the best in Steve Cooper—how to help you be the best father you can be, the best husband you can be, even the best pilot you can be."

"I don't know about all that stuff," Steve said, "but I do know I want to make things work with Gail, and I don't want to go out there tomorrow and do something stupid."

"Are you afraid?" The question just slipped out. Eric hadn't even been thinking about it. But it did bring an unspoken area out into the open.

Steve took a few seconds to answer. It wasn't something he wanted to admit. He nodded. "Yeah, I guess I'm afraid."

"Of what?"

"I don't know. I just don't feel right about tomorrow."

"Are you afraid of dying?"

"I don't think about that much. I guess I think more about messing up, about letting someone down."

That didn't sound like the confident, almost cocky Steve Cooper that Eric knew. Something *was* changing him. Eric took a bold step. "You know what? I think we ought to pray."

That was too much for Steve. " No, you can do the praying when you get back to your own room. I'm ready to knock off and get a good night's sleep. Tomorrow I plan to be careful."

They were on two different wave lengths again. Steve was thinking in the natural. Eric wanted so much to steer him toward the spiritual, but Steve simply dismissed it.

257

Eric assumed it was the direction the conversation had taken that caused Steve to suddenly decide he needed to be alone. But it wasn't Eric's conversation that made Steve feel uncomfortable. It was the simple fact that Steve had never prayed in his life, and he didn't want to admit that he didn't know how.

Eric stood up. "Should we leave this game and pick it up later, or do you want to put the board up?"

"Let's leave it." Steve said. He wanted no part of anything that would indicate tomorrow wouldn't be business as usual.

"Good night, then. Please be careful tomorrow." It was all Eric could say. He wanted Steve to see the light. He wanted him to see God revealed. He wanted to know that Steve would have God's presence and protection with him on the missions he would fly the next day. But it was Steve's decision, not something Eric could force.

TWENTY

The Delta

It was too early for the monsoon season, yet the storms came. They swept in from the northeast bringing thunder, lightning, blowing rain and air cooler than any of the Delta pilots thought possible in the subtropical climate of Southern Vietnam. Strong winds rippled tin on the roofs; water swirled through cracks in windows and doors. During the night, air conditioners and fans were switched off, blankets were fetched out of duffles, and still the men were cold. Few slept well. At least two hardly slept at all.

These two were at opposite corners of the compound: one in the well-built quarters of a Navy officer, the other in a standard-issue Army BOQ, compliments of Pacific Architects and Engineers—a twenty thousand dollar building for which the Army undoubtedly paid in excess of $100K. Each of the men tossed and turned with his own thoughts. The storms outside were a perfect match for the storms within. Each felt helpless against the coming day. Each told himself a thousand times, "I must sleep." Each continued to toss and turn. Each attempted to quiet the intruding thoughts. One quoted Bible verses; the other called upon his own intestinal fortitude which had always been up to the challenge before.

It was not that danger was unknown to them or that either had shown any particular fear of it before. It was not that they were afraid of battle. It was a new fear that troubled them, and for each it was a different fear. For the first time, they had knowledge of a mission hours beforehand. For the first time, they had an inner awareness that something would be different about this day. For the first time, each felt there was more at stake than ever before.

Their alarms, set to awaken them early, were unnecessary. Those alarms, when they did go off, simply marked the transition from "waiting" to "action." The men moved through their morning ritual—cold, shivering, anxious for the coffee awaiting them in the mess hall and the heaters in their respective aircraft. It was pitch black outside—black and blowing, black and wet, black and loud. The dawn was still an hour away.

When Eric and Chris paid for their breakfast at the end of the line at the Navy mess hall, they saw Steve, Stump Willis and Sid Kerr sitting at a nearby table. There were empty seats, so they walked over. Steve looked up, surprised. "Eric! What are you doing here this time of morning?"

"When I got back last night, Chris informed me we were covering your mission. We'll be staging out of Vi Thanh."

"Figures. With this much activity, I guess it pays to have Dustoff around."

"We'll be there. Just don't need us," Chris said, half joking, half serious. He sat down and moved his bacon away from his eggs. Eric sat across the table from Steve. He put down his tray and took a swig of coffee.

"I'm actually not flying until around ten," Steve said. "In fact, I'm thinking about going back to bed if I can find a couple of extra blankets."

Eric shivered. "I know. What's the deal with this weather?"

"It's not supposed to get this cold until around late March or early April," Kerr said.

"Anybody gotten a weather briefing?" Chris asked.

"Yeah," Kerr answered. "It's supposed to clear off after first light. There'll be patchy clouds around during the early morning. It'll be windy all day."

"Just like a cold front back home," Stump commented.

"Yep. So much for this tropical 'air mass' weather system that doesn't have any fronts," Stump observed.

"What time are you guys supposed to be at Vi Thanh?" Steve asked Eric and Chris.

"Six thirty. Normally we don't start our shift until seven. We're getting an early start today."

"How many Dustoff birds will there be?"

"Only one," Chris answered. "We'll have two more back here on standby if we need them."

"I hope you won't," Steve said.

"Me, too," Chris agreed.

The Dustoff pilots ate hurriedly. Even so, before they finished, Kerr left to prepare for his flight. Stump was not far behind him. Steve finished his meal and walked with Chris and Eric to their jeep.

"Be careful," Steve told Eric as they were about to drive off.

"You, too," Eric said. He still hadn't shaken that feeling that Steve would be facing something unusual, perhaps extremely dangerous that day, and Eric was helpless to prevent it.

The preflight was no fun in the cold darkness. For once, Eric was glad it was Chris who was the AC instead of him until Chris sent him up top to inspect the rotor system. *The "Jesus Nut" inspecting the "Jesus Nut"* Eric thought. Was Chris indicating his trust, or was he simply wanting to avoid the cold up on the cabin roof where there was no protection from the wind?

Eric took his flashlight and inspected the rotor system and the transmission housing as if his life depended on it. By the time he climbed back to the ground, his fingers were numb. Chris was finishing up the bottom, and the crew chief was buttoning up the access covers.

Light preceded the sun and cast silvery shadows off the numerous patchy low clouds. Overhead, a high stratus layer was beginning to show signs of thinning. Visibility outside the clouds would be good, but there were a lot of low clouds in the area.

As Eric was putting on his bullet proof chest protector ("chicken plate") and survival vest, Chris said to him, "You fly left seat today." Eric looked up, surprised. The left seat was the domain of the Dustoff aircraft commanders, though it was not the command position in a Huey by design. The bulk of the instruments were on the right-hand side of the cockpit. But the left seat had fewer obstructions and therefore afforded excellent visibility. At some time in the past, the Dustoff ACs had started preferring it. Now it was an almost universal custom. *Was Chris preparing him for command, or was there a simpler reason? Perhaps the fact there was weather around and a chance of encountering IMC—instrument meteorological conditions— that made Chris want the right seat with its array of navigation instruments.*

Eric didn't argue. He picked up the rest of his gear and walked around to the left side of the aircraft. Soon they had the engine running and the heater on. Finally, they were warm. It was the first time Eric had even thought about a heater since arriving in Vietnam a few months earlier. Today it seemed like a different world.

During the flight to Vi Thanh, a beautiful sunrise appeared off to their left. The sun peaked above and below gray clouds, coloring their edges with a red hue. A few rain showers were still about. The winds blew strong and steady. The nose of the aircraft was canted almost twenty degrees left of their course over the ground to compensate for the wind blowing off the South China Sea. They checked in with the C&C just before landing near the south end of the dirt and grass airstrip at Vi Thanh. Then they settled in to wait. A nearby tent housed a command center.

The radios in the tent were alive with action. Insertions were being made; gun cover was blasting away at enemy positions; ARVNs were advancing; the FAC was calling in targets. Yet there were no American casualties. The Dustoff crew longed for action, while at the same time hoping it wouldn't happen. For them to get any action, someone else would have to get hurt. So they waited.

The sun warmed the morning, the battle noises were distant, and sleep beckoned the crew. They found places to stretch out—on litters, in the hellhole, on the cabin floor, and they slept the sleep of soldiers who catch naps that last minutes, but bring the rest of hours as the time of waiting slips by.

Suddenly the cry, "Dustoff!" came out of the tent. An American aircraft had gone down. The crew sprung into action. The rotor tiedown was released and the main rotor rotated ninety degrees. Switches were flipped, the throttle twisted and set. Chris yelled "fire in the hole." The crew yelled "Clear!" There was the popping of igniters, the "whoosh" of JP4 pouring into the turbine chamber and igniting, the whine of the transmission, the blowing dust as the chopper lifted, and the Dustoff crew was off to fulfill its mission.

"Hammer Six, this is Dustoff Seven-Nine, off Vi Thanh."

"Dustoff Seven-Nine, mission at whiskey-romeo-three-seven-two-five-five-six. We have a downed OV-10."

Eric's heart missed a beat. Indian country and an OV-10 down. He looked at his watch. It was nearly eleven. Not Steve!

"Dustoff Seven-Nine, roger."

Eric was at the controls; Chris on the radio.

"Give me a heading!" Eric cried. He realized his voice sounded excited. Wasn't that what the ACs warned about?

Chris gave him a sideways glance. "One-ninety-five," he said. Chris rechecked his map, measuring the distance with his finger. "Twenty-two klicks." Eric nosed the Huey over. It was doing a hundred and ten and shaking.

"Hammer Six, Dustoff Seven-Nine, what have you got?"

"Not many details yet, Dustoff. We're heading that way. Let's go up to channel three and talk to the FAC."

"Roger, switching."

"Black Pony Two-Three, this is Hammer Six. I've got Dustoff Seven-Nine on the frequency also. Who's down?"

"It's Pony One-Two," Sid Kerr responded. "Aircraft's on the ground, no chute. I'm overhead now."

No! Eric's heart sank. *Not Black Pony 12!* He willed the Huey to go faster. Twenty klicks—ten minutes, anyway you cut it.

"He was able to slow the aircraft before hitting the trees," Kerr was saying. "He may be all right." Then, a change in his voice. "Stand by! They're swarming the aircraft! I'm going in!" He was off the air doing God knows what. Not knowing was killing Eric. *Come on! Come on!* Eric coached the Huey, which was shaking all over as the airspeed needle hovered at the

VNE (velocity not to exceed) redline. Still, Eric wanted it to go faster.

Sid Kerr made a low firing pass at the Viet Cong who had appeared out of nowhere and were now climbing onto Steve's aircraft. He couldn't fire directly at them for fear of hitting Steve or igniting the downed Bronco, but he laced the perimeter with mini-gun fire. As he swept over Steve's aircraft, he whipped his own Bronco into a tight left turn to come back around. He lowered the nose into firing position. The VC had the canopy open and were pulling Steve's limp body out of the seat, dragging him over the wing. What could he do? He passed overhead without firing.

"They've got him!" Kerr cried. "The VC just pulled Pony One-Two out of the aircraft!"

Eric cut in, "Is he alive?"

"I don't know," Kerr responded. "I'm coming back around." He swept back over the site low and slow. He could see nothing. "I can't find him! I can't find him!" he yelled. He was furious that he couldn't do anything to help. If there'd been a place to land, Kerr would have been on the ground, fighting off the VC with his hands. "Where are you guys?" he cried.

"Hammer Six is about two north," came the response. The Huey was coming in just above the trees. Much too low for safety, but they wanted to know what was going on. Ahead, the Huey pilot could see the FAC OV-10 circling the area.

"They're gone," Kerr lamented.

"Oh, no! They must have gone underground," came Hammer Six's response.

Eric couldn't believe it! Steve went down and the VC had taken him out of the aircraft. They had to do something. He was still at least five to ten minutes out. It seemed an eternity.

Hammer Six hovered over the downed OV-10, his door-gunners alert. He scouted the nearby trees. There was no downed pilot, no VC, no visible life at all. Kerr flew over the area in a disciplined pattern. He wanted to cover every inch of terrain. When the Dustoff crew arrived on station, they found a hovering Huey, a low and slow OV-10, a slightly damaged OV-10 on the ground and no one in sight on the ground.

"I'm going down there, Chris," Eric said.

"Don't be stupid. You're not going to fight off a VC regiment with your M-16 and a thirty-eight special."

"I've got to try to find him."

"Look, we'll get Major Ray to hunt for him."

"It may be too late."

"He can do it. For you to go down there would be suicide."

"Well, where is Ray? How are we going to find him?"

Chris was sympathetic. He knew of the relationship between Eric Mohr and Steve Cooper, and he could put himself in Eric's place. He'd want to be down there, too. He keyed his mike. "Hammer Six, Dustoff Seven-Nine. Where can we contact Hunter Six?"

"Stand by." They waited. It seemed like forever.

"Dustoff Seven-Nine, this is Hunter Six, over." The voice brought Eric a measure of confidence. Here was a man who knew what he was doing.

Eric didn't wait for Chris to answer. He keyed his mike and said, "Hunter Six, this is Dustoff Seven-Nine. What's your location, over."

"I can't give that to you in the clear, Dustoff."

"We need to talk to you."

"Stand by a minute." There it was again, the waiting. It only took a few seconds, but it seemed an eternity to Eric.

"Dustoff Seven-Nine, I can meet you at Kien Long in two-zero minutes, over."

Twenty minutes! "We'll be there. Out."

Not Far Away—Underground

When Steve regained consciousness, he was disoriented. He found himself face down in mud. A cloth bag was over his head to serve as a blindfold. His hands were tied behind his back. From somewhere nearby he could hear voices arguing in Vietnamese.

His bladder was full. Somehow he had to relieve himself. He had no idea how long he had been unconscious. His head hurt, and his previously dislocated shoulder had been damaged again. He raised his head and shouted to get his captors' attention.

"Hey! I've got to go to the bathroom." The arguing stopped. Someone hit him across the back with what felt like a knotted rope, yelling the Vietnamese equivalent of "shut up."

Steve *really* had to urinate. He tried to get up on his knees. It was extremely difficult because of the way his arms were tied. Wham! The rope struck him again. There was more yelling and screaming. He urinated, not from fear, but simply because he couldn't hold it any longer. He felt the warmth along his legs and wondered when the chafing would begin. At least it was beneath him and they couldn't see it. He needed something to rest his head on to get it up out of the mud. There was nothing.

With his head twisted sideways, his hands tied behind his back and his knees drawn up under him, Steve could see a pinpoint of light through the material covering his head. Otherwise, it was dark all around. He wondered if they were standing right over him, waiting for him to move so they could strike him again.

He could hear dripping sounds, and the sound of their voices was muffled, as if they were in a cave. Perhaps they had taken him underground. The U Minh was known to be laced with underground tunnels.

Steve knew he had to escape, but because he was blindfolded, he had no idea who or how many were watching him, or the location of any possible avenues of escape. Someone must be searching for him, but could they find him? How long would it take? He couldn't just lie there; he had to have a plan.

Kien Long Airstrip

The strip at Kien Long was totally deserted. The Dustoff crew shut down to conserve fuel and waited in the aircraft near the south end of the strip. A few locals from the nearby village made their way to the airfield, satisfied their curiosity that it was just an American helicopter, then went on about their business. Eric checked his watch often. Twenty minutes might as well have been twenty hours. Steve could have been killed in seconds. He tried to pray; he had to pray; it was all he could do. His prayer was simple: *Lord protect Steve until we get there.* He would not accept the possibility of them not finding Steve and setting him free.

Ray and his rangers were nowhere to be seen. Eric began to doubt they would show up. He was anxious to get back to the point where Steve had last been seen. He had spotted a road a few hundred yards north of the downed OV-10. The strip of forest led north toward the Cai Loi River valley and south toward the village of Kien Long. Five klicks east and five klicks north, there were rice paddies. The VC would be in the woods, most likely heading north.

Eric was a farm boy, a hunter. His dad made his living flying airplanes, but the rest of the family were all cattlemen with hundreds of acres of land, much of it in pasture, much of it forest. Eric could follow a trail. With some help he could locate Steve and break him free before the VC moved him to the north where they might never find him. *Come, on, Major Ray! Please get here soon!*

"Chris," Eric implored his AC after fifteen minutes, "this is taking too long. Let's go back up there."

"No, Eric. Major Ray said it would take him twenty minutes to get here. It hasn't been that long. Besides, what can *we* do?"

"I could follow them; find out where they took him. We could call on the ARVNs for help, maybe even get some Americans down here."

"Give it a few more minutes," Chris said. At just that moment Ray appeared out of the jungle at the other end of the strip, accompanied by a dozen heavily-armed ARVN Rangers. Eric jumped out of the helicopter and started off at a jog to meet them. Chris followed, signaling the crew chief and medic to stay with the aircraft. Ray and his group remained near the edge of the woods, cautiously advancing along the airfield's perimeter. When they saw the two pilots jogging toward them, they stopped to wait, remaining in the shadows.

Eric jogged up to Major Ray, out of breath. "Sir," he began, then stopped to breathe, bending over, resting his hands above his knees. "Thanks for coming."

Ray surveyed the young pilot. He recognized him from the excursion to the top of Dop Chompa, but didn't remember his name. When Eric straightened up, Ray read his name tag and rank from his flight suit. "Hello, Mr. Mohr." He waited for Eric's explanation.

Eric took a few deep breaths, then began to tell the story. "An OV-10 went down just southeast of the bridge on the road that goes northeast from here up toward Vi Thanh. The pilot was Steve Cooper, the guy you picked up near the Seven Sisters a few months ago after he'd bailed out. He's also my brother-in-law. Another Black Pony flying over saw the Viet Cong drag Steve out of the airplane. I think he's alive. We're hoping you can help us find him."

Ray knew about the downed aircraft. It had been all over the net, and Hammer Six, the C&C, had briefed him. "What makes you think he's alive?"

Eric stopped to consider the question. It had never occurred to him that Steve might not be alive. "I don't know," he said. "The other pilot—the one who saw him go in—said the aircraft was traveling at slow speed when it hit the trees. The aircraft didn't appear too badly damaged from the air. If he was dead, why would they have taken him?"

Ray shrugged. "Only one way to find out. Can you take us up there?"

"Sure."

Chris had come up behind Eric and was listening to the conversation. "I don't know that we can take all of you at once," he said. "That's a pretty heavy load."

"There's thirteen of us, all in combat gear," Ray said. "But twelve of us are ARVNs. They don't weigh much."

"We can take them," Eric said, turning to stare Chris down. It was no time for being super cautious. Chris eyed Eric warily, but said nothing. Now he was seeing some of the ability to make combat decisions that Chris and the other Dustoff aircraft commanders had been waiting to see. They started walking toward the helicopter.

Ray pulled a map out of his back pocket and handed it to Eric as they walked. "Exactly where is that aircraft?"

Eric took the map and studied it a moment, locating Kien Long and the Cai Loi River. "Here," he said, pointing. "It's right here, just southeast of this bridge." Ray nodded. He knew the area.

When they were all on board, Chris lifted the Huey, confirmed that it would hover, then accelerated down the strip into the wind. When it passed through translational lift, the Huey began climbing. Eric felt some relief. At last they were doing something. "You're clear around left," he said, checking his side of the aircraft for traffic.

"Coming left." Chris leveled off at fifteen hundred feet and followed the road northeast toward the crash site. In back, Major Ray borrowed a flight helmet from the medic and plugged into the ICS. He got on the FM radio, talked with Hammer Six and worked out some air support for their reconnaisance on the ground.

The problem Chris had was where to set the Huey down. The road offered the most possibilities, though it was pretty well covered with a canopy of trees. They located Steve's OV-10, then flew up the road looking for a place to set down. They had traveled almost a klick north before Chris found a place he could slip the heavy Huey into.

It was a hover down, but they made it in spite of the load. When the Huey settled on its skids, Eric started unbuckling his seatbelt.

"Where are you going?" Chris demanded.

"You know I'm going with them."

"We can't stay here."

"Then get Tim up here to fly with you." Tim was the crew chief and like most crew chiefs had gotten his share of "stick time" during his months in Vietnam.

"You're part of my crew," Chris told Eric. "I'm responsible for what happens to you."

"Look, Chris. If it was your brother-in-law, you'd be going to look for him."

Chris started to argue, then thought better of it. Eric was right. If it was *his* brother-in-law, he would be going. After all, this is a war, and you can't always follow the rules. The enemy certainly doesn't.

"Okay, but be careful. And take my grease gun."

Eric nodded, then reached across the console and lifted Chris' .45 caliber M3 submachine gun from where it hung on the back of his seat. "Thanks." He also took his own weapons— an M2 carbine and an M-79 grenade launcher—and joined up with Major Ray's outfit. Tim Edwards, the crew chief, climbed into Eric's seat.

The Ranger patrol watched as the helicopter hovered slowly out of the hole. When it cleared the trees, it flew off toward Vi Thanh.

Leaving the road, Ray entered the woods with Eric right behind him. One of the Vietnamese Rangers moved out in front of them; the others took up positions beside and behind them. They moved through the thick subtropical forest with care, all eyes alert. It took them approximately thirty minutes to reach the airplane. The ARVNs spread out around it, setting up a defensive perimeter, while Eric and the Major climbed up the side of the fuselage and looked into the cockpit.

The cockpit was intact, and there was no blood. Eric was satisfied that Steve was alive when taken out of the aircraft. The trail was not as easy to follow as Eric thought it would be.

There were very few places in the surrounding jungle where a footprint would make an indentation. Most of the ground was covered with foliage. They did find an indication of something, or someone, being dragged, which they followed for twenty or thirty feet. Then the trail disappeared into the thick forest. Eric was discouraged. Ray methodically checked the area. One of his Vietnamese companions was a Kit Carson Scout who knew what to look for in the brush. Together, Ray and the Scout combed the woods surrounding the plane until they found what they were looking for—the entrance to an underground tunnel.

Eric stared at the small hole. "No wonder they disappeared so fast."

"Yep," Ray commented. "They've practically got underground cities around here. There's no telling where he is now, or how far they've taken him."

"What do we do now?" Eric wanted to know. "Can't we follow them?"

"I can send a man in that hole," Ray told him, "but he wouldn't find your man. He'd find a network of tunnels with unmarked turns. They'd be a step ahead of us the entire way. We don't have enough men to cover all of the entrances that might be connected to that tunnel."

"Are you telling me it's hopeless?" Eric asked.

"We won't find him this way, son," the Major replied, putting a hand on Eric's shoulder.

"So I'm supposed to give up?" Eric's frustration was apparent. Ray understood it, wished he could work a miracle for him, but knew he couldn't. The underground tunnels of the U Minh were just too much of a maze for him and his small group to expect to cover. There would be no trailing underground. The thing to do was to get some intelligence about how and where they would be moving Steve. It wasn't likely the VC would be keeping an American prisoner here in the Delta. They'd be moving him north. The best bet for a rescue would be while they were moving him. He explained all this to Eric, who reluctantly admitted they'd done all they could at the present location. Ray signaled his man to contact the C&C ship overhead and to send the Dustoff ship back to get its pilot. He and his men would stay on the ground and secure the plane until the Navy could recover it.

TWENTY-ONE

Binh Thuy, later that afternoon

The rotor blades were still coasting down when Eric climbed out of the helicopter and walked deliberately toward Navy Operations. When he pushed open the door marked "Lt. Commander Stuart Kelly, Operations Officer," Kelly was at his desk. Sid Kerr and another pilot, unknown to Eric, were standing over the desk, studying a map. It was obvious Eric was interrupting something. Kelly looked up to see a young Army warrant officer just off the flightline and still wearing his survival vest complete with revolver, survival knife and survival radio. Before he could say anything, Eric blurted out, "What are you doing about Steve Cooper?" It was a demand, not a question.

"See here," Kelly started.

Kerr stopped the Commander from making a fool of himself. "This is Eric Mohr, sir. He's Cooper's brother-in-law. He's also the Army pilot who went looking for him on the ground this morning."

Kelly immediately eased off. A hint of respect edged into his voice. "Come in, Mr. Mohr. We'll bring you up-to-date on what we've got going on so far."

Eric walked over to the desk, letting the door close behind him. The other men stepped aside to make room for him. The map they had spread before them was opened to the area where Steve's aircraft had gone down. The exact spot was marked in red. Other notations were on the map, some not familiar to Eric.

"To begin with," Kelly explained, "Search and Rescue has received no communications from Cooper's survival radio. We assume he was captured and is in the hands of the enemy. That fact was reported by Lieutenant Kerr here who observed Lieutenant Cooper being removed from his aircraft by what he believes to have been Viet Cong. Certainly if they were friendlies they would have contacted us by now and turned him over to us. We've put a P3 Orion in the air over the area. SLIR (side-looking-infrared-radar) surveillance will continue around the clock. The Orion will also monitor all radio traffic in the area with sophisticated scanners that should pick up any VC transmissions. If they move him above ground, or talk about him, we'll know about it.

"By midnight tonight a team of SEALS will be on the ground at the crash site. They'll blend into the terrain and monitor any enemy movements that might occur. The SEALS will also go into the tunnels that you and the Army Ranger located this morning. They'll follow them as far as they have to."

"What about the CIA?" Eric interrupted.

Kelly looked surprised. "The CIA?"

"Yes, sir. Don't they have contacts in almost all of the Vietnamese villages?"

"I'm not sure the extent of their penetration in that regard. It certainly couldn't hurt. I'll take care of it."

"Sir, I know the station chief in Can Tho. I think he's probably the guy we need to contact. If you'd like, I'll check with him."

Kelly saw the young warrant officer in a new light. His contacts and his thought processes seemed to be beyond that of a WO1 aviator. "That will be fine," he said. "Now if you'll excuse us, we've got work to do."

Eric was satisfied they were covering all the bases. He had work to do himself. He left the Navy office and walked back to Dustoff Operations. Once inside, he walked directly to Wade Daugherty's desk. Chris Sanders was in the office, along with K. J. Madison and Hank Harris. The three of them watched as Eric addressed Daugherty. "I need to borrow your jeep for a little while."

"Where are you going?" Daugherty asked. It was not a question, but a challenge. Daugherty had something on his mind.

"Can Tho." Eric said, matter-of-factly.

"Can Tho?" The tone was incredulous. "You can't. You're still First-Up."

"Look Daugherty," Eric responded, surprised at the anger in his voice. "Don't play games with me. I know you called Second-Up in as soon as Chris and I diverted to look for my brother-in-law. I need to go to Can Tho."

Daugherty had a smirk on his face. "Yeah," he said. "We called Second-Up in. It was because you deserted your crew."

"I didn't desert anybody. I went looking for a relative who was shot down and captured by the Viet Cong. Nobody else seemed able or willing to do anything. I left the aircraft and went to look because I had to."

"Your first duty is to your crew, Mr. Mohr. And you keep wondering why we haven't made you an aircraft commander."

That statement boiled Eric's blood. He looked around at Sanders, Madison and Harris. "There's four of you in here now. I'm sure Captain Scott is in his office. Let's get McElroy,

Dickson and Payne in here now and get this AC thing out into the open."

Daugherty started to object. Sanders halted him. "He's right, Wade. We owe it to him to make our objections to his face."

Daugherty resigned to it. "Okay, go get them."

Eric sat down to wait. The others scattered and came back within five minutes, bringing the remaining aircraft commanders with them. Only Payne was absent. He was finishing up a test flight.

They moved away from Daugherty's desk to an open area near the crew lounge. Eric leaned against the wall. A couple of the others sat down; the rest remained standing. "All right," Captain Scott said, "who's going to start this?"

"I will, sir," Eric answered.

Scott nodded. "All right."

"I've been in country for four months. During that time I've logged over two hundred combat hours, most of it at night on single-ship missions into unprepared landing sites. Not since the first week have I received any criticism of my flying, either constructive or otherwise. It seems to suit you all.

"You're short on aircraft commanders. You're having to juggle the duty roster constantly. There's two of us here who could easily help you fill that void—myself and Les Winters. Yet you say we're not ready. Maybe I can understand about Les. He doesn't like our mission and he really doesn't want to be an AC. But that's not true of me. Not only am I committed to the mission, but I'm doing a good job. Some of you guys don't think I'm ready for command. I want to know why."

There was some shuffling of feet, some staring at the ceiling. Only Scott, Harris and Daugherty looked directly at Eric. Scott was actually watching all of them. He'd stayed out of the conversations about Mohr because he had only flown with the

278

man once or twice. Each time, Mohr had been up to speed as far as he was concerned. No one spoke.

Eric looked at them one by one. "How come all of this criticism that I know goes on behind my back can't be spoken to my face?"

K. J. smiled. He'd asked Daugherty and Harris that same question just a day or two earlier. Whenever the subject of making Eric an AC had come up, they were the ones outspoken against it. Yet they offered no real reasons, only rhetoric. Eric deserved to hear their challenges. He hadn't heard them because they weren't legitimate.

"I'll tell you why," Harris began. "It's because you've got some kind of crazy notion you're too good to die. I don't see you taking the precautions necessary to save the lives of your crew."

"That's a bunch of crap," Eric responded. He was still surprised at the anger he felt. It was Steve's being captured that had angered him initially. He was on a roll now and decided to deal with everything that was festering in him. "I wear my chicken plate the same as the rest of you. I pull the armor plating on my seat as far forward as every one of you does. I hunker low in my seat when they're firing at us. I avoid the enemy locations reported to us. I carry several personal weapons on the back of my seat. I don't do anything any different than the rest of you do."

Several of the men looked around the room, catching each other's eyes and nodding. They knew what he was saying was true. Only Daugherty and Harris stood against him.

"I'll tell you what the deal is," Eric continued. "You guys are prejudiced against me because I'm an outspoken Christian. You don't understand me. You think I'm some kind of weird 'Jesus Nut' or something. Well maybe I am. I happen to believe the way I live and believe is a whole lot more normal than living in indifference to God, but that's your business. Each of you has to deal with God on his own terms." At this, Daugherty looked away, something like shame on his face. "But what I believe about God doesn't have anything to do with how I fly. Besides," he lightened up, realizing he wasn't winning any brownie points the way he was raving at them, "you ought to be glad I'm a Christian, Hank. You saw that invisible shield that saved our lives that night on the canal north of Cao Lanh."

"Well, yeah …" Hank began, then let it drop. He had no logical explanation for what had happened that night.

Scott saw where Eric had brought them. He took over. "Let's put it to a vote, men."

"I agree," said Chris. K. J. and Gary Dickson echoed the same sentiment.

Payne walked in about that time and K. J. explained what was happening. "We're voting on whether or not to put Mohr up for AC."

"With him here?" Payne asked. It was unusual.

"Yeah," K. J. answered. "With him here."

"All in favor of recommending WO1 Eric Mohr for aircraft commander status, raise your right hand," Scott said.

Several hands shot up immediately. Then, all the rest reluctantly followed.

"Congratulations, Mr. Mohr."

"Of course you've still got to get through my checkride," Rob McElroy added.

"Piece of cake," Eric said. "Thanks, fellows." Then turning to Daugherty he held out his hand. "Keys to the jeep, please." Daugherty reached into his pocket, pulled out the key ring and handed to it to Eric.

"I'm going to go with you," K. J. said. "Just where are we going anyway?"

"To see the CIA," Eric answered.

K. J. pursed his lips and nodded. "Okay," he said, as if it made perfect sense.

Eric drove like he'd seen the others do when in Vietnamese traffic—aggressively and with his hand on the horn. It took them thirty minutes to get to downtown Can Tho and another ten to find Russell Lamb's place. He parked in front, locked the chain around the jeep's steering wheel, and the two pilots walked up to the Lamb's front door. Eric knocked.

At first, there was no response. He knocked again, then stepped back out to the street and looked up toward the patio garden, wondering if they were outside and thus didn't hear him. He saw no one, so he walked back toward the door to knock again. K. J. waited near the street to keep an eye on the jeep. He had noticed a couple of Vietnamese kids across the street were showing undue interest in it.

When Eric approached the door again, he saw Mrs. Lamb in the shadows just inside the now open door. She had opened it while they were out on the street and stood waiting quietly as Eric came back up the walk. "Hello, Mrs. Lamb," he said.

"Please, call me Vanh," she said, inviting him inside. "And how are you, Mr. Mohr." Eric was surprised she remembered his name. They had only met the one time, when the Lambs had hosted the Bible study in their home. He looked back to see if K. J. was coming. Madison, shook his head "no" and waved Eric on. He wanted to keep an eye on the jeep.

"Mrs. Lamb—Vanh, is your husband home?"

"No," she said, smiling at him with the same rich smile he had noticed before. Again, her eyes radiated love. The Lambs certainly had something going for them.

"Do you expect him soon?"

"Soon," she nodded.

"Do you mind if I wait?"

"Soon may be hours, may be days," she said. Obviously to her "soon" was a relative thing.

"Okay, but I need to get a message to him."

"Business?" she asked.

"Well, it's sort of business *and* sort of personal," he said.

"Business I do not get involved in," she said. "Personal, I can listen and relay your message."

"It's my brother-in-law, Vanh. Do you remember I asked everyone to pray for him?"

"Oh, yes," she nodded as if she remembered.

"He was shot down today in the U Minh. The VC took him prisoner. I'm hoping your husband can help us find him."

"My husband is an executive with a Rubber Company," she said. "Why do you ask if he can help find your brother-in-law?"

Eric was at a loss for words. He had assumed everyone was correct in saying that Russell Lamb was the CIA Chief for the Vietnam Delta. An executive for a rubber company? Could that be a cover? Was it possible his wife didn't know?

"I was just hoping he might have some contacts. Would you at least please ask him? Tell him Steve was shot down near Kien Long and the Viet Cong captured him. They took him underground before anyone could get to him."

She nodded her understanding, and Eric turned to go. Vanh reached out and put her hand on his arm, stopping him. "We must pray for your brother-in-law's safe return," she said. Eric nodded. He intended to pray—a lot.

It was after dark when he and K. J. pulled up at Dustoff Operations. Eric went to retrieve his weapons and flight helmet from the aircraft he and Chris had flown earlier that day.

Someone had already removed them. Hopefully they were secured. They drove to the Navy mess hall for a quick meal, then to the BOQ. It was already getting cool again with the sun's disappearance. As K. J. drove around the perimeter, Eric thought about Steve and wondered where the VC were holding him. *Were they torturing him? Would he have any protection from the cold as the weather moved in again during the night?*

As the jeep pulled up to the BOQ, Nancy Pettis' door opened, and she looked out. When she saw it was Eric driving up, she stuck her head back inside and said, "It's him." Then she waved at Eric. "Eric, over here!"

He was irritated, tired and had a lot on his mind. He hoped she wasn't going to snag him in some long conversation about a Bible study or something along those lines. Reluctantly, he walked toward her. K. J. headed upstairs toward his room. When Eric got to Nancy's room, she swung open the door to invite him in. Inside the room were Mattie Hill, Lisa Sneed and Blake Sam. Mattie stood up to greet him. She took hold of his arm and pulled him into the room.

"Eric, we heard what happened," she said. "We want to pray with you."

Eric was surprised the word had spread fast enough for them to get together. He was also very moved. He sat on the bed, next to Lisa. "We really do need to pray," he said. "I think it's the only chance we've got." Then he surveyed the room, feeling a little overwhelmed by the support they were giving him. None of them even knew Steve. "How did you guys find out about it?" he asked.

Mattie answered. "Sid Kerr told us," she said. "Well actually, he told me and I told the others. We thought it would be good to offer you our support."

Eric nodded, looking around at each one of them. "It is good," he said.

They joined hands and closed their eyes. Eric began the prayer. *"Lord, You see all and know all. Somewhere south of here, Steve Cooper—a man who doesn't know You, but will some day— has been captured by the Viet Cong. We ask You to surround him with Your presence and Your protection. Let them not be able to lay a hand on him. Let them not be able to break his spirit. Let him know You are there with him and will protect him. Guide those who are searching for him in their search. Give us wisdom to know what we should do—what I should do to help."*

Each one prayed in turn. The prayers were simple, but powerful. There was the overwhelming feeling among them the prayers were not stopping at the ceiling, but were getting through to the Most High God, and that God would hear and answer. They became fervent in their prayers and in a way that can only be understood by those who have prayed through struggles together and seen victory. One by one their hearts were knit to one another and to Steve Cooper, the object of their prayers.

During a lull, Eric prayed again, this time for Gail and Emily, Steve's wife and daughter. He prayed they would be given a supernatural peace and that even before they found out about Steve's capture, he would have been set free.

How long their prayer time lasted, Eric didn't know. He only knew that at the end of it he was exhausted. He also was filled with peace. *Steve would be found.* He was sure of it. Because he knew God was in control and Steve would be found, when he went to his room, he fell fast asleep.

TWENTY-TWO

The U Minh

"Golf One, this is Hummingbird. Movement south of your location, sixty meters."

"Golf One, Roger." Chief Petty Officer Grant Stillwell was gaining a new respect for the technicians aboard the airborne surveillance post as he slowly turned his head toward the infrared sighting reported by the Orion. Stillwell was completely under cover in the dense foliage and would not have been seen by a Viet Cong soldier walking within two feet of him. The same cover that concealed him made it difficult to spot the objects of the sighting. He would have to move closer.

Moving in a southerly direction with the stealth of an Indian, Stillwell remained under cover of the jungle until he was approximately fifty meters from his previous location. He stopped and spoke into the tiny, bug-sized microphone clipped to his collar. "Hummingbird, Golf One, update?"

"Ten meters south, three warm bodies," came the response. The sound from the tiny earpiece in Stillwell's ear carried no further than his own hearing. Each member of SEAL Team Golf was similarly equipped.

Ten meters! The VC were close. This was the first sighting of human movement since the SEALs had staked out the location almost eleven hours earlier. During the night, members of the team had entered the tunnels and found evidence that someone had been dragged along one of the muddy corridors. At a point where the tunnel branched into several directions, they'd lost the trail. They attempted to follow each branch, but eventually ran into too many tunnels to cover. No sign of Steve or his captors had been found. The SEALs had come back topside and were now staked out at strategic points along all expected points of transition into or out of the area.

Silently creeping through the brush, Stillwell covered half the distance to the reported human activity, then stopped to listen. He heard a sound of movement, then saw them. Hummingbird had reported three warm bodies. He only saw two; then they were gone, apparently back underground. Quickly, Stillwell summoned another of the SEALs and the two of them located the tunnel entrance and slipped inside, their forty-five automatics drawn.

It was a tight crawl for approximately thirty meters, then the tunnel widened into an underground room. The room was empty, but there were signs of recent habitation. Tunnel exits left the room from all four sides.

Stillwell and his companion searched the cavern carefully. They found a spot on the ground where someone or something had apparently lain for some time. *Could this be where the Navy pilot had been held? If so, how long since he'd been there, and which direction had they taken him from there?*

Stillwell called for reinforcements. When the other SEALs arrived, they split into small groups and entered each of the tunnel corridors. Two men went back topside to try to locate and cover the above-ground exits. They reported in to the Orion.

"Golf team, who's topside?" the controller queried.

"Six."

"Nine."

"Just the two of you?"

"Roger."

"You've got company. I'm picking up several warm bodies fifty meters to your west, moving toward the river."

Fifty Meters! Golf Six radioed his teammates still in the cave, "Golf One, this is Six."

"Go ahead."

"Get up here. They're getting away!"

The other SEALS made their way back to the surface. The first ones to get above ground followed directions from the Orion controller, but by the time they got to the river, the Viet Cong had moved downstream. The controller had no reading on the kind of craft they used, except that it was gas-powered, as indicated by the emissions from an engine. Heavy foliage over the small river made the craft difficult to track, and within a few miles the infrared images of the travelers had blended with other images and were no longer distinguishable.

Steve Cooper knew he was on a river or canal in some type of boat. The cloth still covered his head and his hands were still tied behind his back. Since his capture, he'd had a couple of handfuls of rice forced into his mouth and a cup of water. His hands had never been untied to allow him to attend to personal needs, and he'd been beaten several times by his captors as they pushed or dragged him through underground tunnels. At times, he'd been extremely cold, and the circulation in his arms and legs was suffering.

Now they had him on some type of boat in a bamboo cage, barely large enough for him to fit inside. He heard water against the sides of the boat and the sound of the small gasoline motor that propelled them along. He had no idea how many guards were with him. His shoulder was in pain; his hands and legs were numb. He was barely conscious, but still thinking about escape. They were moving him from the area in which he had been captured. The further away he got, the less his chances of being rescued.

Several hours passed—hours in which Steve drifted in and out of sleep. Finally, he felt the boat run aground with a jar. His cage was picked up and transported over the ground, carried by men, grunting and breathing hard. Sunlight filtered through the cloth covering his head.

Time passed; he had no idea how long. He heard the opening of a door and shuffling of feet on a hard surface. His cage was set down. He heard his transporters move away and it grew totally quiet around him. Thinking he must be alone, he attempted to get into a sitting position, and worked to get his hands free. Rubbing his head against the side of the cage he was partially successful in dislodging his blindfold.

He was in a room with plywood-covered walls. Overhead, the roof was made of thatch. The floor was cheaply poured concrete. Methodically, Steve worked his hands against the side of the cage, attempting to work the ropes loose. He had little success.

Hearing noises, he stopped moving and waited. Several men entered the room wearing North Vietnamese Army uniforms. One of the men bent down and opened the door to Steve's cage. He and two others dragged Steve out of the cage. They jerked the covering off his head, rolled him over and untied his hands. He sat up and leaned against the cage, blinking his eyes against the light. He rubbed his wrists to restore circulation and observed the men warily. Gradually, his eyes became accustomed to the light.

An officer stood directly in front of him. "Lieutenant Cooper, you stink!" the man said. His English was accented, but precise. No argument from Steve. He did stink. He smelled of sweat and urine. He didn't know how long he'd been captive, but it seemed like days. He'd been allowed no personal hygiene, and virtually nothing to eat or drink. His mouth was parched; his throat was dry. Hunger pains gnawed at his stomach. His right shoulder tormented him. His wrists were rope-burned. Yet within him burned fire and hope. *He would get free.*

Without warning, a man stepped from behind the officer, and dowsed Steve with a bucket of water. It caught him totally by surprise, but he grabbed at what little ran down his face and tried to direct it toward his mouth.

The officer barked something rapidly in Vietnamese. The man with the bucket scampered out the door. The others stood glaring at their prisoner.

Within two to three minutes, the man came back with the bucket half full of water. He sat it down in front of Steve and stepped back. Steve looked at the men, gauging their intentions. Except for the officer, who looked at him with amused interest, their expressions were blank. Steve reached for the bucket and began drinking from it, expecting at any minute for someone to jerk it away from him. His hands could barely support its weight. With some effort, he put it down, bent forward and stuck his head in it. He cupped water in his hands and drank—slowly at first, then more hurriedly. It was river water, but it didn't matter. After a few swallows, he splashed water on his face and neck and wiped his face with his hands. It felt like about three days' growth of beard.

One of the men handed the officer a swagger stick. He poked at Steve with it and said, "That's enough. Back in your cage." Steve was too weak to fight, but at least they left the blindfold off and his wrists untied as he was stuffed back into the small cage like an animal. The officer barked orders to his men in Vietnamese and left the building.

The remaining men sat at a small table and began playing cards. Steve watched them, intent on discovering their weaknesses. There were four of them, all wearing sidearms. Each also had an AK-47, either draped across his lap or leaning against the table. There was no way he could overcome them in their present setting. Even if he did, he had no way of knowing who, what or how many were outside the room. He would have to wait for the right opportunity.

Somewhere in the hours that passed, Steve drifted off to sleep. He was awakened later by the officer who stood pacing outside his cage. Outside it had grown dark.

"Lieutenant Cooper, as you may have noticed, our comrades in the South have no facilities for maintaining prisoners. Many captives seem to die in their hands. For this reason we will be transporting you to the North where you will be treated humanely. However," he said, as he stopped his pacing and faced Steve, indignation in his voice, "your aggressive government is making it very difficult to transport you safely."

The officer resumed pacing. Steve was in pain from his shoulder and neck. He sat with his back against the side of the cage and closed his eyes. This angered the officer. He kicked at the cage and struck at it with his swagger stick. "Have you no respect for an officer who is trying to save your life?" he demanded. "Pay attention when I am talking to you!"

Steve could hardly stay conscious, he was so weak. He shook his head and forced his eyes to remain open. The officer continued. His English was excellent. Steve gathered he was well-educated. "Your government has put aggressors on the ground, presumably in search of you. Their aircraft fly overhead to monitor our movements. Perhaps they think they can rescue you. They will not succeed. He stopped pacing and turned to face Steve.

"You see this container we are forced to transport you in?" He whacked on the cage with his swagger stick. "It serves a very useful purpose. Six months ago, the Vietnamese People's Liberation Army found itself host to several American soldiers who were what you people call 'Special Forces.' These soldiers were challenging the freedoms in our country and had to be stopped. The officers from the People's Liberation Army decided these men should be taken to Hanoi, where the error of their ways could be clearly shown to them. They were transported in containers similar to this one." The officer was pacing again, back and forth, clearly enjoying the sound of his own voice, and the fluency with which he spoke English.

"American helicopters were sent to prevent the transport of these men. It was unfortunate. When the helicopters drew close, the untrained soldiers from the local populace simply pushed the containers in the river to avoid having them seen. The helicopters flew over, but no Americans were detected. They went on their way. The soldiers then waded into the river and lifted the containers back to the shore. Unfortunately, the men inside were no longer breathing." He turned and looked directly at Steve, making sure he had eye contact. "I hope they don't come looking for you while you are in transit. I fear they will." With that, he walked out, leaving only the guards. Steve was still not given anything to eat.

TWENTY-THREE

Navy Binh Thuy

Now that Eric had been made aircraft commander, Lieutenant Daugherty made sure he got plenty of duty time. To the other pilots, it was as if Eric's qualifications for being made an AC had never been questioned. The missions were piled on. Both the older pilots and the new pilots were scheduled to fly with him, and business went on as usual. There were routine missions, and there were hot ones.

Eric handled his flight duties professionally, as expected of a Dustoff aircraft commander. When on a mission, his mind was totally absorbed with the tasks at hand, the safety of his crew and the successful completion of the mission. His skills as a pilot grew, especially locating and landing in unimproved landing zones during the hours of darkness. Even Les Winters began to gain a respect for the Dustoff mission when he saw the dedication with which Eric and his crew went about the business of saving lives.

When he was not flying, Eric's sole focus in life was the rescue of his brother-in-law. He spent as much time in Navy Operations as Stu Kelly would allow. At night, he and the other

Binh Thuy Christians prayed as they had never prayed before for Steve's safety and release. They didn't know how the prayers were affecting Steve, but they hoped they would give him hope, and the captors would be inclined to treat him favorably. Most of all, they prayed the Americans would find him.

The situation at Navy Operations was not encouraging. Airborne surveillance had been used continually. Navy SEALs had probed the underground tunnels near where Steve had been captured. They'd found some indications of where he had been held early, but had followed all leads and had no idea where he was being held now. The consensus among the Navy people was that Steve, if he was alive, had been transported to North Vietnam.

There had been no word from Russell Lamb. Eric was now even beginning to doubt the man *was* a CIA agent. Perhaps he was, just as his wife had indicated, simply a businessman who had enough mystery about him for the Americans in the area to invent stories about him being the CIA Station Chief out of their own imaginations.

On a Tuesday afternoon, almost two weeks after Steve's disappearance, Eric received a double shock. He flew a mission to Vung Tau to deliver some equipment to the Army Maintenance Depot ship, the U.S.S. Corpus Christi, that was anchored in Vung Tau Bay. Upon his return, he went directly to Navy Operations to see if there was any word about Steve. Activity on the Navy ramp bothered him.

Equipment was being packed into large shipping containers, called Conexes, used to transport military equipment aboard ships. In the Operations office, his fears were confirmed. The Navy, both the Black Ponies and the Seawolves, were leaving Vietnam. The aircraft would be flown to Vung Tau and from there ferried to an aircraft carrier destined for the Philippines.

Eric protested. Kelly was sympathetic, but there was nothing he could do. The plans of the Navy Department could not be altered for one man, especially when there were no leads, no indications, no reasons to believe Steve would be located if the Navy remained in the Vietnam Delta.

Eric was angry, but he didn't know where to direct his anger. He feared it would be at God, yet knew that was not justified and also not a healthy thing to do. Whatever plans God had for Steve Cooper, Eric's being mad at God wouldn't speed them along. Nevertheless, he was angry. In the early hours of Steve's capture, Eric had been full of hope Steve would be rescued, that he would be all right. Now that hope was hard to hold on to.

Back at Dustoff Operations, he experienced his second shock. The 57th was moving to Long Binh. The Third Surg was shutting down. Navy Binh Thuy would be turned over to the Vietnamese Navy. It would all happen within two weeks!

"What's going to happen to the Delta?" Eric asked.

"We'll still be covering it," he was told. The 57th was moving to Long Binh, where it would share facilities with the 159th Medical Detachment. A crew would stage out of Can Tho each week on a rotational basis to cover the Delta. The Long Binh ACs and the Delta ACs would cross-train each other on their respective areas of operation. Steve was being abandoned!

At Mattie's place, Eric met with more bad news. No, the Donut Dollies weren't moving to Long Binh. They were going home. They, too, would be gone within two weeks. Eric's support group was being disbanded.

Eric was put to work in the supply room. Hank Harris was so short, he would not be the 57th's supply officer in Long Binh. That job would fall to Eric. He would be the officer responsible for making sure all of the equipment was packed properly and moved via convoy to the unit's new home.

The U Minh

Steve sat in one of the chairs at the small table where the guards read and played cards or dominoes while watching their prisoner. In front of him was a bowl of rice mixed with some type of soup. A cup of weak tea had been provided for him to drink. Across from Steve sat the officer, his arms folded, his legs crossed, a patient, thoughtful look on his face.

Steve ate slowly. He was weak and not sure he could keep the food down. He thought it ironic that when thinking about food during the early days of his captivity, he had envisioned himself eating ravishly, gulping down Big Macs, juicy steaks, fried chicken, mashed potatoes and gravy. Now, with the food in front of him, his weakness and shrunken stomach made it difficult to eat at all. He guarded the tea as if he might not get any more. The officer smiled when he saw that and motioned for one of the guards to put more tea on the table.

The guards were still there—four of them, heavily armed. Steve had been watching them every waking moment, waiting for some sign of distraction. The outer door was not latched. He could be through it in an instant. But how far could he get? Where would he go? It was not yet time to try anything. He'd have to gain some of his strength back.

When the rice and soup were gone, the officer leaned forward, looking Steve in the eye.

"I'm afraid I have some bad news for you, Lt. Cooper," he said. "We planned to move you north where the facilities might be a little more comfortable."

Steve wondered how he could lie so easily about the Vietnamese communists' treatment of their prisoners of war. Surely the man didn't believe Steve would receive any kind of favorable treatment in the north.

The man continued, "You would find it interesting to know that my comrades in the North have shown an unusual interest in you." He shrugged, as if it were nothing to him personally. "They have many American flyers at what your people call the 'Hanoi Hilton.' Why should they be interested in one more, especially a lowly Navy lieutenant?" It was obvious he was going to answer his own question. He sat back again in his chair and gestured with his hands as he spoke. "It seems that some of the ..." the officer hesitated, searching for the right English words to convey his meaning. When he found them, he spread his hands and nodded, obviously pleased with himself, and continued, "war doctrine people wish to learn of your Navy's use of the turbo-propeller-powered aircraft for the mission you call 'Close Air Support.'"

Steve said nothing. The man was obviously enjoying his ability to communicate so clearly in English.

"They have indicated to me," the officer continued, "it would be well if I saw to your safe transport to Hanoi. However, your Navy and your Army and even your CIA have been making it difficult for me to move you undetected. And now there is an interesting twist. We have learned they will soon be going home. Navy Binh Thuy is closing down."

Obviously, he was pleased at himself for being able to provide Steve with news of his own Navy's affairs. It was news he apparently thought Steve did not know. Steve let the officer believe the closing of Navy Binh Thuy was news to him. What did it matter? He was determined not to show any signs of weakness or discouragement in the man's presence. Because he already knew Binh Thuy was shutting down, it was easier for Steve to conceal the devastation the news actually had on him.

If the Navy was going home, they wouldn't be looking for him. He'd held on to the belief the Navy was doing everything it could to locate him and set him free. The idea of being totally on his own would take some getting used to. But he would still gain his freedom. The enemy was making a mistake now by feeding him. He'd build up his strength, and he would be ready for whatever opportunity presented itself.

The officer had more to explain, and Steve was glad to be out of the cage. So far, he had said nothing to his captors.

"We will simply wait until your Navy leaves the country before moving you to the North. I must find a place to keep you in the meantime. I'm afraid it will not be very comfortable. Since you will be with us for a while, I have arranged for some clothes for you to wear. You will also have your arms and feet in chains. Don't even think about trying to escape. You will be fed. I regret the earlier actions by my comrades in not seeing to your basic needs. After all, we are not barbarians."

He stood up to leave. Steve looked up at him, but did not stand. Two of the guards moved behind him and jerked him up out of his chair. They said something to him in Vietnamese, and motioned toward the officer. The officer smiled. "UCLA," he said, answering Steve's unspoken question about his command of English. "My sister lives in Seattle." He nodded to the men, who turned Steve around and started stripping him of his flight suit. The officer left.

TWENTY-FOUR

Navy Binh Thuy

Mattie Hill and Eileen Stewart had nearly finished packing and were nearing the end of what had been for them a
hectic day. One by one, people began to gather at their place
for final goodbyes. All day, the various units at Binh Thuy had
been packing and loading. The Navy was loading equipment
aboard an LST at the Binh Thuy River port. The 57th was
loading trucks for a convoy to Long Binh. The Third Surg was
almost ready to move, its patients all transferred elsewhere.
The Donut Dollies were packing their personal belongings for
transport to Saigon. For a while, it looked as if the group wasn't
going to have time to get together again.

When Eric arrived at the Donut Dollies' place a little after
nine, he found boxes and luggage stacked in the middle of the
living room floor. To his surprise, Sid Kerr was there. During
the past several weeks, Kerr had seemed detached and disin-
terested as far as Mattie was concerned. This had left Mattie
feeling hurt and disappointed and Eric relieved. He liked Kerr,
but doubted the man would ever become a Christian. Mattie
would get over the hurt from Kerr's rejection, but if she married him and he remained a non-believer, the hurt would last

a lifetime. Eric knew it wasn't his place to call the shots in Mattie's life, but as a friend and fellow Christian he didn't want to see her get hurt.

Lisa Sneed, Nancy Pettis and Blake Sam arrived at the trailer almost on Eric's heels. There was more involved in this group getting together than just final goodbyes. During the days since Steve Cooper's disappearance in the U Minh Forest, the small group of Christians at Binh Thuy had gathered together almost nightly to pray. It had become more than just prayer support for the downed flier; it had become a life channel for each of them. When they prayed together, they found reassurance and reaffirmation of their faith in God and His work in their lives. They each discovered a deeper level of communication with God, and had learned to become open and honest with one another. This type of fellowship was something none of them had expected to find in Vietnam and was evidence to them that God really did live in the midst of His followers. Now that they were going their separate ways, each was taking along some of the strength the group had obtained as a whole.

Eric and Blake Sam were staying in Vietnam; the others were going home. Sam had put in for a lateral transfer into Eric's Dustoff unit, the 57th Med Detachment. He would be moving to Long Binh to work as a flight medic for the remainder of his tour. The nurses were on their way home. Mattie Hill was going to Europe, compliments of the Red Cross. Eileen Stewart, Mattie's roommate, was returning to the United States, along with the other Binh Thuy Donut Dollies who lived in the trailer next door.

Sid Kerr had shown no desire to participate in the group's prayer meetings, though he'd been invited on several occasions. He shared their concern for Steve Cooper and he also felt Steve was being abandoned by the Navy. His purpose for coming to Mattie's on this last night in Binh Thuy was two-fold. He knew Mattie was attracted to him, but he also knew their philosophical differences were such that a permanent relationship wouldn't work out. He thought she was a nice kid and he didn't want to seem cruel or uncaring, but he just didn't want to encourage any emotional attachment. As a friend, he had come to say goodbye.

But he had also come expecting to find Eric Mohr. Kerr had information to share with Mohr which he felt might help save Steve Cooper's life. When Mohr entered, Kerr pulled him aside. He reached into his shirt pocket and pulled out a folded piece of paper.

"Last night, Stu Kelly and I met with one of the senior technicians from the P-3 Orion that has been patrolling the U Minh. Here is his name." He handed the piece of paper to Eric. "The Orion refuels at Bien Hoa once every twelve hours. The crew has information about Steve that Stu and I believe is worth following up on. Unfortunately, we can't do it. We're out of here tomorrow and there's no way the Navy is going to let us stay."

"What's this all about?" Eric wanted to know.

"They've been watching the area closely and have developed a theory about Steve."

"A theory?"

"Yeah. They think they know where he is and what the VC intend to do with him. They've been working with the CIA to get confirmation, and believe they're getting close, but they are frustrated because they can't get the brass to listen to them."

Eric stared at the name on the strip of paper. He began to feel the whole weight of Steve's rescue on his own shoulders. It would be difficult for him to get to Bien Hoa and make connection with the Navy crew. It was not like his days were his own. The next morning he was to accompany the convoy on its road trip to Long Binh. It would be an all-day trip, and there existed the possibility of an ambush along the way. Bien Hoa, he knew, was close to Long Binh. Somehow after the move he would have to find a way to get to the airfield and meet with the Navy crew during one of its refueling stops.

Kerr said his goodbyes, then left. Mattie tried to hide her disappointment, but Eric noticed a tear running down her cheek. He reached for and squeezed her hand. The others joined them, forming a circle and holding hands. One by one they began to pray, hoping the power in their prayers was making a difference with Steve, wherever he was. They also prayed for one another and for protection for Blake and Eric during the coming months.

When it was time to leave, Eric thanked them. "Please remember to keep Steve in your prayers. Our church back in Mississippi is praying for him. The church his wife attends in Meridian is also praying for him. Please pray for God to give us direction. Maybe this lead Sid just gave me will help us locate him."

Lisa, Nancy, Blake and Eric left together. They were twenty feet away from the Donut Dollies' place when the unmistakable sound of a mortar round whistled over their heads. With a loud explosion, it impacted the girls' trailer near the kitchen just to the right of the entrance door. It hit the exact place where they'd all been standing thirty seconds earlier. A second round was already whistling through the air as Eric and Blake raced toward the door. Smoke and debris filtered out of a gaping hole in the side of the trailer. Inside, the girls were screaming. The second round impacted a few yards away, just behind the second trailer. Eric jerked open the door and ran inside with Blake on his heels. Mattie and Eileen were huddled on the floor in the hallway, crying, covering their heads with their hands. They were almost hysterical.

"Come on!" Eric yelled, grabbing Mattie by the arm and lifting her to her feet. "We've got to get out of here!" Blake grabbed Eileen. A third mortar round impacted, this one closer to the hospital. The two men hustled the girls out of the trailer. The other three Donut Dollies—Mary, Gwen and Margaret—poured out of the trailer next door and joined them in the middle of the road. A few yards away, Nancy and Lisa stood transfixed as the mortars impacted beyond the BOQs, walking their way toward the hospital. Suddenly, a barrage of incoming mortars, rockets and small arms fire broke loose. The rat-tat-tat-tat of a machine gun joined the fracas. Eric and Blake herded the girls to the bunker near the west end of the Dustoff BOQ. The other girls put their arms around Mattie and Eileen to comfort them. They were all afraid. All three BOQ's emptied as the occupants fled to the bunkers on either end of the buildings.

Once everyone was safely inside the concrete bunker, Eric said, "Stay here!" and ran upstairs to get his weapons.

He met Chris Sanders coming out of his room. "Turn your light off and get down!" Sanders yelled. "Don't silhouette yourself in the door."

Quickly, Eric snapped his light off and grabbed his M-16 and M-79 from behind the door. A belt of ammunition for each hung on a nail in the wall. He felt for them in the dark and attempted to jerk them off the nail. They hung up as more rounds impacted outside and flares lit up the night sky. Eric stepped back inside his room and lifted the ammunition belts from the nail. An RPG exploded nearby and shrapnel raked his door. Outside he could hear people calling to one another and scrambling for cover.

Eric and Sanders bounded down the stairs together. "What's going on?" Eric asked.

"The VC," Chris responded. "They must have known we were leaving and wanted to get in some final harassment."

"Where are they?"

"They appear to be coming in from the Southwest, but I can't believe they're not going after the aircraft or the ammo dump."

Eric and Chris arrived at the bunker, and using it for cover, peered out at the perimeter fence a couple hundred yards away. Tracers from the guard towers swept outward toward the rows of concertina wire lacing the free-fire zone outside the main fence. M-79 rounds impacted beyond the wire. Eric didn't see any Viet Cong.

He slipped back around the side of the bunker and stuck his head in the entrance. "Everybody okay in here?" he asked.

A shaky female voice expressed the sentiment of them all. "No-o-o-o."

Another one asked, "What's going on out there?"

"V. C. trying to come through the wire."

"They can't get in here, can they?"

"I don't think so."

From the airfield came the sound of aircraft engines—OV-10s and helicopters. Sanders was standing a few feet away, his .45 caliber grease gun in hand. "Should we be over there?" Eric asked. Chris pointed at the empty parking spaces where the jeeps would normally be. Neither jeep was there. "It's not really an option," he said. "And I think we've got our hands full here." He nodded toward the bunker full of women. The other bunkers were filled with medical personnel—doctors and nurses from the hospital.

Any moment Eric expected to hear the OV-10s and Seawolf helicopters taking off to join the defense of the perimeter.

What he didn't know was that the aircraft had all been disarmed in preparation for ferry flights to Vung Tau. A few rockets had been located, but most of the ammunition was either on board the LST or stored in the underground ammo dump.

Abruptly, the sounds of the engines ceased, as if they had all been given a shutdown order. From off in the distance came the droning sound of a large aircraft high in the northern sky. Much of the firing on the perimeter died down.

"What in the world is that?!" Eric asked Chris.

"Puff," Chris answered.

"Puff?"

"Puff, the Magic Dragon, sometimes called Spooky. Wait and watch."

Within a few minutes, the aircraft was on station. It was an Air Force C-47, nicknamed Puff the Magic Dragon, flying overhead at an altitude of five thousand feet. Until it started firing, the airplane was invisible in the darkness. From out of that darkness came a deafening roar and three streams of red flame that moved back and forth across the ground as if each was a stream of red water coming from a high pressure fire hose. The flames were actually 7.62 millimeter tracer rounds fired from mini-guns through openings in the side of Puff's fuselage. The guns had multiple barrels that rotated, like a Gatling gun. Each mini-gun fired 6000 rounds per minute. Puff was the ultimate defensive weapon—out of sight and pouring forth computer-controlled firepower that could put a round in every six square-inch block of an area the size of a football field within a couple of minutes. Puff—utter devastation from the sky. It was the reason few American compounds were attacked by the Viet Cong.

The bunkers emptied as Puff began firing. The watchers were hypnotized by its firepower. The tops of the bunkers, favorite places for sunbathing in the daytime and eating cheese and sipping wine while watching far-off flares and firefights at night, became makeshift bleachers for watching Puff's awesome firepower demonstration. The sound put forth by the Gatling guns was a steady roar. Its stream of tracers moved back and forth across the free-fire zone outside the southwest perimeter, covering the ground with astonishing speed and leaving no area untouched. It was all over in minutes!

When the firing ceased, an eerie silence was left behind. Then, one by one, shouts could be heard outside the perimeter as the guards moved out to inspect the damage caused by Puff and to insure the attack had been dispelled. They called in the body count to the Sergeant of the Guard as they found the bullet-riddled bodies of Viet Cong lying where they had fallen.

This activity was anti-climatic. The tops of the bunkers began to empty as people left to assess the damage to their living quarters or the hospital. Except for the damage to Mattie and Eileen's mobile home and some of their personal belongings inside, damage appeared to be minimal. A couple of storage sheds had been hit, an empty wing of the hospital, the NCO club and a lot of dirt.

As a group, Eric, Blake, Chris and the five Donut Dollies made their way to the mortared trailer to inspect the damage and check the girls' personal belongings.

They were inside the trailer when a major explosion rocked its foundation, sending them reeling. Sanders was first out the door, with the others right behind him. The eastern sky glowed orange as explosions one after the other filled the night sky.

"Oh, my God, it's the ammo dump!" Chris was the first to figure it out.

"We'd better head for the airfield." Apparently, the attack on the southwest perimeter had only been a diversion.

"How are we going to get there?" Eric wanted to know. "There are no jeeps."

"At the O' Club. Somebody's got to be at the O' Club."

They both took off running. Blake hesitated a minute, then followed them. After all, he was now a Dustoff medic.

The O' Club had indeed been occupied by some of the Dustoff pilots and some of the engineers. When the mortars started impacting near the BOQs and the hospital, the club emptied. There were no nearby bunkers and the mortar activity was some distance away from them and heading in a different direction. Those that had been in the club simply stood outside watching the action as Puff subdued the infiltration attempt on the southwest perimeter. When the ammo dump blew, both the Engineer officers and the Dustoff pilots were spurred into action. The ammo dump was the engineers' responsibility. There was little they could do about it now. It had been built to be impenetrable. Obviously, that wasn't the case. No one in his right mind was going to go over there now and try to put the fires out. Ammunition was exploding in all directions. The only option left was damage control—get and keep the people under cover and don't let the fires spread.

The Dustoff pilots were thinking about injuries to personnel within the compound and about the security of their aircraft. Some of the medical personnel from the Third Surg were still on the base. The Dustoff unit had eight medics. The aircraft had to be protected and if there were injuries, the medics could help. Whatever it was that could be done wasn't getting done with them standing there. As the Engineer officers ran toward their headquarters building to marshal a plan, the Dustoff pilots piled in their jeeps to head for the airfield.

"Hey, hold up!" Sanders and Mohr yelled to them. They ran up to one of the jeeps, huffing and puffing and climbed in.

Both the jeeps sped away toward Dustoff Operations. Blake Sam was unable to attract the drivers' attention. He watched as the jeeps drove off, then jogged back toward the BOQ and hospital area.

Noise and confusion reigned, but so far there were few injuries. The dirt levees around the perimeter of the ammo dump did their job of containing ammunition that was cooked off from the heat and traveled on a horizontal plane. The sky continued to be filled with exploding shells and rockets and much of the encased ammunition sizzled off skyward. Construction dynamite added to the fireworks. Buildings offered little protection and there weren't enough concrete bunkers to afford everyone protection.

A command decision was made to evacuate the aircraft and to move the convoys to Can Tho to await first light. Air crew members gathered up their personal belongings and loaded them aboard the aircraft. Those traveling by convoy loaded their belongings into the jeeps and deuce-and-a-halfs. The Donut Dollies flew out in a Navy C-46. The MASH hospital left its buildings behind, but moved out onto the road with all of its personnel and equipment. By midnight, most of the military inhabitants of Navy Binh Thuy had left the base, leaving the fires and exploding ammunition in the ammo dump behind.

Can Tho

Russell Lamb had information for the Army pilot, Eric Mohr. He had planned to go to Navy Binh Thuy the next day to locate the man and pass along what he had learned. When sappers hit the ammo dump at Binh Thuy, the fire and explosions could be seen, heard and felt from Lamb's house in downtown Can Tho. He got in his Land Cruiser and drove toward Binh Thuy, hoping to locate the man he wanted to see. MPs stopped him on the road, telling him he didn't want to go any further because of the explosions. As he talked with them, he saw the aircraft taking off. Navy fixed wing aircraft, Navy helicopters, then the Army Dustoff helicopters, all taking off one behind the other and flying northeast toward Vung Tau and Long Binh. Lamb banged his fist against the wheel, thought of his options, then turned around. He'd have to find Mohr in Long Binh.

Five minutes after he left the MP checkpoint, the Dustoff convoy came through with Eric Mohr in the front passenger seat of the lead jeep. While the other pilots flew the helicopters to Long Binh, he had the privilege of spending a long night at Can Tho Airfield watching the Binh Thuy fireworks and the next day he would be taking the long trek up Highway One to Saigon and across to Long Binh in the front seat of a jeep.

TWENTY-FIVE

The U Minh

The Viet Cong's treatment of Steve Cooper improved under the supervision of the English-speaking, UCLA-educated NVA officer. Steve had given him the nickname "Jingles" because he reminded Steve of a classmate of oriental descent he'd had in school. The boy's last name was Jingles. Twice a day Steve was fed small meals, usually consisting of fish and rice. He was given water and occasionally tea to drink with his meals. The food was always brought in by two men. One kept his AK-47 pointed directly at Steve while the other placed the food on the floor.

His cell was a windowless room in a concrete block building. The door was wood and unbudging when he pushed against it. There was no heating or cooling and practically no airflow. Natural light and what little ventilation there was came from a gap between the ceiling joists and the top of the concrete wall. Through this crack, Steve could see enough light to tell night from day. At times, the heat became almost unbearable. During some of the early monsoon nights he was very cold. There was never a time when he was comfortable. Toilet facilities consisted of a small hole in the corner. His feet were chained together, but the chain was long enough for him to move around the tiny room to keep his circulation going. His hands were also chained, but at least they were in front of him and not behind. He slept on a small wooden bench and was thankful to have it, for it kept him off the cold, clammy floor.

No longer was he under constant guard. Apparently Jingles believed the chains and the concrete cell block were security enough. On several occasions, Steve had been taken out of the room to dine with the NVA officer. On these occasions, he'd been blindfolded so he had no chance to survey his surroundings. Except for the initial beatings in the underground caves and the deprivation of food and water those first few days, he was not subjected to any more torture. No doubt Gail, Lynn and Eric, perhaps others as well, were praying for him. Was it possible those prayers were being answered?

The thought of escape was always on his mind. But the opportunities were denied him. Jingles was determined to deliver the American pilot to his superiors in the North. He was taking no chances.

Before shipping to Vietnam, Steve had attended the Navy's Escape and Evasion Survival School near Pensacola, Florida. The school had prepared him for the possibility of capture and torture by the communist guerrillas. He knew that his first responsibility was to escape. During the training, it was demonstrated to the Navy pilots that the name, rank and serial number game wouldn't hold up if the North Vietnamese really wanted something from you. The NVA and the Viet Cong didn't abide by the Geneva Accords and could be cruelly sadistic in their treatment of prisoners. The first rule, therefore, was: "don't offer anything. If they did succeed in making you talk, do your best to avoid giving away military secrets. The average pilot wouldn't have access to any knowledge the Vietnamese didn't already know anyway. "Don't try to be a hero," they were told. "Stay alive, don't let them break your spirit, support one another, and escape when you can." That was the advice offered by the school cadre.

Fat lot of good it did here. There were no other prisoners. Escape was out of the question. Jingles had not tried to pry any military information out of him, implying that would be a job for the prison cadre in Hanoi. He seemed content just to practice his English on Steve.

At first, Steve resisted conversation with the officer, but the man had been patient and undemanding. He'd asked Steve a number of questions about the United States and the attitudes of the American people toward the war. Jingles said he'd been educated at UCLA and that he had a sister living in Washington state. *How could a man with such connections be an officer in the North Vietnamese Army?*

Steve's curiosity about Jingles' background finally led him to talk to the officer. He asked him how he rationalized his knowledge of the West, democracy and capitalism with being an officer in the Communist Army. Jingles smiled and looked at the lone guard who was in the room with them at the time, as if to satisfy himself the man couldn't understand English.

"A man does what he has to do," Jingles responded. "I do love my country. I believe it should be one country. As to the nature of the government, capitalism and democracy won't work in a country where most of the people are poor, uneducated, even illiterate."

Steve took exception to the man's statement. He knew the Vietnamese people, especially in the South, valued education and were not illiterate. He also knew capitalism and democracy offered the only hope for poor people to improve their lot in life. But he wasn't prone to argue the point. Instead, he took the opportunity to broach another subject.

"You are an educated man?" he asked.

The Vietnamese officer nodded.

"It appears to me you are also a man with some degree of human compassion."

The officer nodded again.

"Then let me go," Steve said.

"Not a chance," Jingles responded.

"Why?"

"You are an enemy of my people, a trespasser in my country, a war criminal."

"Surely you don't believe all of that propaganda. You know I'm just doing my job as you are doing yours."

"Do not compare us," Jingles said, anger now entering his voice. "I am in my own country. You are not defending your own country. You have committed acts of aggression in my country. For these acts you must be punished."

Steve sighed. *It was the standard communist propaganda line.* He had hoped Jingles didn't really believe it.

"Besides," Jingles continued, a grin on his face, "getting you to Hanoi is worth a lot of money to me, perhaps even a promotion." He stood up and motioned to the guard to take Steve back to his cell. The blindfold was put over his head and Steve was led back to the small concrete enclosure.

On the Road to Long Binh

After crossing the Bassac River on the ferry, the 57th Medical Detachment convoy started up the highway to Long Binh. The going was slow due to the condition of the roads and traffic. Water buffalo, motor scooters, bicycles and over-loaded buses traveled the highway, often blocking the progress of the military convoy. MP escorts went ahead of and behind the Dustoff convoy, their jeeps equipped with mounted machine guns. The chance of an ambush seemed remote in the open terrain. Rice paddies lined both sides of the road. It was only when going through the villages that Eric felt uneasy.

They arrived in Long Binh before dark. K. J. Madison greeted Eric as the jeep pulled up in the Long Binh Dustoff area. "Hey, buddy. You ready for a meal, a shower and a place to sleep?"

"You bet. In that order."

"Come on. I'll help you get settled. Where's your stuff?"

"In the back of that deuce-and-a-half." He pointed to the first truck in the convoy.

"Let's get your personal gear and take it over to the BOQ. Then we'll get something to eat. You like Tuna on Toast?"

Eric looked at him sideways.

K. J. shrugged. "That's what we're having."

Later in the mess hall, Eric sat eating with K. J. and Gary Dickson. "So what's it like here, guys?" he asked.

"The tactical situation is pretty hot," Dickson answered. "The 159th lost a bird up at An Loc this morning. They recovered the crew, but the bird's still up there. Maintenance went up to try to recover it and the VC had set up a .51 caliber machine gun in it. The maintenance officer called in air support and the Air Force sent a couple of F-4s up there to obliterate it."

K. J. picked up the story. "The NVA are moving in from Cambodia on a push to Saigon. They've captured An Loc and are threatening Tay Ninh and Lai Khe. The 17th Cav is putting Americans in on the ground. It's not like the Delta."

"Have you guys met Tom Zerbe or Brian Patton?"

"Yeah, they're both aircraft commanders. Zerbe is the Operations Officer. I think Patton is out on a mission."

Eric had another question. "How far is it to Bien Hoa?"

"Bien Hoa?" K. J. asked. "Why do you want to know about Bien Hoa?"

"I have a lead on where Steve might be."

"Your brother-in-law? You think there's a chance he's alive?"

"I know he is. The Navy thinks he's still in the Delta. But they're not sticking around to try to get him out."

"What can they do?"

Eric dropped his fork and raised his voice. "It's not like going into North Vietnam," he said. "They saw him taken captive. They tried to locate him once. They gave up. Now they're just pulling out, leaving him there!"

K. J. attempted to settle Eric down. "It's not like he's the only POW we've got over here. It's just personal to you because you're related to him."

Eric turned in his seat and gave K. J. an exasperated look. "Yeah, it's personal to me. But it ought to be personal to every one of us. It could be you down there; it could be me. There shouldn't be anything to stop us from trying to get one of our guys back."

"You went in yourself and had a look," Dickson said. He'd meant to stay out of it, but found the subject too volatile to leave alone. "You came back empty-handed. What kind of miracle do you expect them to pull off?"

"It might just take a miracle," Eric said quietly. "At least I believe a miracle can happen."

Holding the end of his fork between his thumb and forefinger, Dickson toyed with the food on his tray. "I believe miracles can happen, too."

Eric looked at him in disbelief. "Yeah?"

"You're not the only one who believes in God."

"What are you talking about?"

K. J. watched the dialogue between the two younger pilots with interest. This was going somewhere.

"I'm a Christian, too. I grew up in a Pentecostal Holiness Church."

"You're kidding," Eric said. Dickson had done absolutely nothing since Eric had known him to indicate he was a Christian. "How come I didn't know that? How come you've been so quiet about it?"

Dickson seemed eager to explain. "I figured a long time ago that if I was on fire for God, the Devil was always on my case. If I was living for the Devil, God was on my case. So I found a middle ground, where I don't bother either one of them."

"You must not know your Bible very well," Eric said.

"What do you mean?" Dickson asked, defensively. K. J. appeared interested in Eric's comment, too.

"In Revelation, Jesus told the church He wished they were either hot or cold, but because they were neither, He would spew them out of His mouth. I think I'd be afraid of getting spewed out of God's mouth."

Dickson was quiet. K. J. pursed his lips and nodded. This talk about religion was beginning to make him uncomfortable. It was time to change the subject. "So what's Bien Hoa got to do with all of this?" K.J. asked.

"The Navy has a P-3 Orion flying surveillance over the U Minh. The crew says they have a theory about where Steve is being held and what the NVA plan to do with him. The Orion crew refuels at Bien Hoa. I want to talk to them."

"You'll have to clear it with the Old Man," K. J. said. "And I don't think that's going to be easy. The 159th is taking a beating. They need us flying ASAP. Plus, we've got to put a crew back in the Delta tomorrow. You're going to be getting all the flying you ever wanted." He stood up and picked up his tray. "But look on the bright side," he said.

"What's that?" Eric wanted to know.

"Here they fly mostly in the daytime. They're supporting Americans and most of the operations are conducted during the daylight hours." That was a welcome relief. Eighty percent of the flying in the Delta had been at night.

The U Minh

From beneath a rain-drenched canopy of trees near a small unnamed hamlet east of Long My, a Vietnamese man watched the activity within the compound. Twice a day soldiers carried food and water into the small concrete building near the VC command post. From the command post an NVA officer stepped out and looked into the sky, as if to wish away the rain. A driving wind bent the tops of the trees and dislodged debris from the village trails. The bamboo cage had been brought from its hiding place and was now sitting beside the prisoner's habitat. They would be moving the American soon. The man slipped deeper into the jungle and found the trail to Vinh Quoi. He had to get word to the American CIA. It would be worth many piasters.

Can Tho

Russell Long kissed his wife goodbye and drove to the Can Tho Airfield. He looked at his watch as he turned the Land Cruiser onto the road that would take him to the Air America terminal. The Turbo Porter would be there in half an hour. He had alerted the Saigon Station Chief he would need a vehicle to take him to Long Binh.

Long Binh

Eric was on the duty roster with Brian Patton, his former roommate from Fort Sam Houston. Patton and the other III Corps ACs had been told to get the Delta Dustoff ACs up to speed in the III Corps AO as soon as possible. They were staging out of Tay Ninh West to cover an assault toward the Cambodian border. Here it wasn't a First-Up, Second-Up situation. Instead several aircraft were committed for mission support each day. As they departed Long Binh, Patton took Eric on a short aerial tour around Long Binh, pointing out the 24th Evac, the refueling area at Plantation and some of the high traffic areas where they really had to stay alert for other helicopters. Upon arriving at Tay Ninh West, they refueled, then found some shade where they would wait near the helicopter for the assault to begin.

Gary Dickson was assigned the first week in the Delta. He took with him one of the 57th's peter pilots, Kelly Smith. Dickson's crew left Long Binh early and were at the Can Tho Airfield by eight o'clock. After checking in with the Operations Officer at the 119th Assault Helicopter Company headquarters, Dickson was shown a small building near the south end of the airfield which the Dustoff crew could use for its temporary staging area. In it were four bunks, a card table and a refrigerator. The building was not air conditioned, but had windows all around and several fans to stir up the air. The crew set about making it their home for the next week.

Tay Ninh West

ARVN troops were moving up the road toward Loc Ninh, with Cobras providing gun cover and the American Air Cavalry providing airlift support. Brian Patton and his crew were following the assault as it moved northeastward, available for any Dustoff missions called in—ARVN or American, it didn't matter. Further west, another Dustoff crew was at Lai Khe, covering troop movements to try to retake An Loc.

Ten clicks up the road in the shadow of Nui Ba Den (the Black Virgin Mountain) one of the helicopter gunships was shot down. The enemy had literally fired down on the aircraft from the mountainside above as it flew along the valley floor.

The gunship's two crewmembers were alive. They were seen exiting the Cobra and heading for nearby underbrush. A Huey slick attempted to pick them up, but was chased away by heavy fire from the mountain. Covey 23, the Forward Air Controller working the assault called for Dustoff and Patton and Mohr responded. The FAC then brought in some A-1 Skyraiders, the "Sandies," to take out the guns while Patton and Mohr located the Cobra. On his FM frequency Covey 23 instructed the Dustoff crew, "I'll give you a mark with white smoke in just a minute. Let me get these Sandies on that gun location on the mountain."

"Five-Nine, Roger," Patton responded. The adrenalin was flowing. Unlike so many of the night missions Eric had flown, this one was laid out before them in panoramic view. They could see the FAC in an O-2 Cessna Skymaster circling slowly over the valley as he directed the two World War II vintage Douglas Skyraiders on a bombing run on the mountainside. Ahead of them, a formation of Hueys was on a long approach to an LZ that lay west of the road. The twisted wreckage of the Cobra came into view as the Dustoff ship skirted the edge of the mountain.

"Covey Two-Three, this is Dustoff Five-Nine," Patton radioed. "No need to mark the pickup point. We have the Cobra in sight."

"Roger, Five-Nine. Proceed at your discretion. I've got two more Cobras heading back this way if you want to wait for them."

"We'll let you know," Brian replied. He was flying. It was his AO and he was the aircraft commander for this mission. Eric poised with his hands near the controls, ready to do anything that was needed. The Cobra lay to the left of a winding road. The crew was nowhere to be seen. Patton dropped low over the road and slowed the aircraft. All four crewmembers were searching the bushes. Apparently, the FAC and the Sandies were keeping the VC on the mountainside occupied, for the Dustoff crew was not being fired upon.

"There they are!" Eric yelled as he saw two men in Army flight suits step out onto the road waving their arms.

"Got 'em," Patton replied. He bottomed pitch and hauled back on the cyclic to slow the Huey further. "Bringing the tail left," he said. The road twisted and he had some small trees he had to avoid.

"Tail clear left," came the call from the back.

"Everything green," Eric said as he monitored the instruments. It wouldn't have made any difference. They were going to land anyway.

Brian put the Huey down within twenty meters of the two men. They ran toward the aircraft and jumped in the back, assisted by the crew.

"Ready to go, sir," the crew chief called.

"Coming up," Patton said and lifted the Huey to a hover. Immediately it settled back to the dusty road. Eric, who had been looking to the right to make sure they cleared the trees, jerked his head back around in time to see Brian look over at him with a strange look on his face. His eyes rolled back into his head, his mouth dropped open, and he slumped forward over the controls.

It took a second for Eric to realize Patton had been hit. They had not heard any rounds hitting the helicopter. Eric grabbed the controls and yelled over his shoulder to the medic, "Danny, get Brian! He's been hit!" Eric pulled pitch, shoved the cyclic forward and accelerated out of there. As soon as he cleared the trees, he made a sharp right turn and raced toward Long Binh. Danny Young, the medic, popped the seat back release on Patton's seat and pulled the pilot's seat backwards into the cabin. He jerked off the pilot's helmet and felt for a pulse. He couldn't find one. He also couldn't find a wound.

"I think he's dead, sir," he said over the intercom.

"Dead!" Eric yelled. "He can't be dead! Do something to revive him."

"We're trying, sir!" Together, Young and the crew chief released the pilot's seatbelt and pulled him onto the cabin floor where they could work on him. Danny removed Brian's chicken plate to start CPR. That was when they saw the bullet wound—a single round right into the heart. It had apparently come in through the helicopter window and over the top of the bullet-proof vest. A freak shot, at a freak angle, that caught the pilot right in the chest.

It was a little over forty miles to Long Binh. Twenty to twenty-five minutes any way you cut it. Eric called Dustoff Operations to let them know he was headed for the 24th Evac and that Brian Patton had been shot. He didn't realize it, but he was crying. Once again, the war had come too close to home. This wasn't just another American pilot, this was his friend. It couldn't be true. He prayed, *God don't let him be dead.* He pushed the Huey as fast as it would go. He pleaded with the crew to revive him. The whole time, Brian Patton's blank face stared serenely and unseeing at the ceiling of the Huey's cabin. For him, the war was over.

A crowd had gathered at the 24th Evac helipad by the time Eric approached. Bernie Johnson, the 159th's CO; Brad Duncan, the 68th Med Group Aviation Officer; Tom Zerbe, Brian and Eric's classmate; and the other ACs and pilots from the 159th and the 57th who weren't out flying missions were all there. Like Eric, they did not want to believe that one of their own had been killed.

As the helicopter touched down, the doors were jerked open. The men on the ground cleared the way for the hospital crew and their gurney, feeling helpless as they watched their comrade unloaded. He appeared lifeless and they all knew their worst fears were true.

Wade Daugherty and K. J. opened Eric's door and motioned for him to get out of the helicopter. He was obviously shook, as they themselves would have been. Rick Payne, the Maintenance Officer was there to fly the aircraft back to Dustoff Operations. Rick took Eric's flight helmet and climbed up in the Huey's right seat as Eric was led off to a jeep by the other pilots.

Eric felt a sense of detachment, as if he had been an observer while someone else had watched his buddy die, had taken off from the road beside the mountain and flown the Huey back to Long Binh. Brian Patton was among one of the closest friends he'd had since joining the Army. How could this have happened and why hadn't Eric's protective shield extended to cover Brian?

They were in the crew lounge later, all of them, quiet and subdued when Captain Johnson came in with the word. Yes, Patton was dead. It had been a single gunshot wound to the heart. A freak thing. The bullet had come in at an angle above the chest protector. The doctors figured Patton never knew what had hit him. Eric knew better, having seen the look of surprise and anguish on Patton's face just before he'd collapsed. Patton knew he had been hit, but like the others, just couldn't believe it. It was not like they had come under a barrage of fire and one of the rounds had found its mark. It was a single round, a freak accident, a lucky shot on the part of a Viet Cong, who probably didn't even know his round had found a target.

Slowly, the men filtered out of the room. Eric had no desire to go anywhere. He was sitting by himself in a chair along the wall when Les Winters came in. "Hey, buddy," Les said. "You all right?"

322

Eric looked up at him, saying nothing. Then someone stepped forward from behind Winters—Russell Lamb.

"Somebody here to see you," Winters said.

Lamb sat down in a chair beside Eric.

"I understand you've had a rough day," he said. His eyes, as before, were kind, caring. Eric nodded.

"I know you may not feel up to it," Lamb said, "but I've got some information about your brother-in-law that might help us recover him."

Eric looked at the man without saying anything. He was still numb. He didn't want to hear anything that would give him false hopes.

"I know where he is," Lamb said. "At least I believe it's accurate information."

"You're the second one that's told me that this week," Eric said. "What's going on?"

"Who was the other one?"

"A Navy flier. He told me an Orion P-3 crew knows where Steve is and what the V.C. plan to do with him. He said it was just a theory, but that I should talk to them."

"Where are they?" Lamb wanted to know.

"They fly into Bien Hoa once every twelve hours for fuel. I'm not sure where they're stationed."

"Clark Air Base, in the Philippines," Lamb interjected.

"Anyway, I've got a name." Eric pulled his billfold out and retrieved the piece of paper Sid Kerr had given him.

"Let me see that." Lamb took it from him. The name meant nothing. Lamb stared across the room, gathering his thoughts. A plan was coming together.

"I'll go to Bien Hoa," he said. "I can wait there until the crew comes in and find out what they know. We've already been interchanging information with Naval Intelligence on this matter."

"So you *are* CIA," Eric challenged.

"Who said I wasn't?"

"Your wife."

"Good for her." He patted Eric on the knee. "Remember, my boy, God's got your brother-in-law in His hands. Apparently your prayers are being answered." He stood up to go.

"I was beginning to wonder," Eric said. "This afternoon was pretty devastating."

"I imagine so." He held up the piece of paper. "I'll be back in touch. We've got to move swiftly on this thing. I think they're about to move him."

Lamb left, but Winters lingered. He pulled out a chair and sat down. "When you go after your brother-in-law," Winters said, "count me in. Remember, I used to be a grunt."

"Thanks," Eric said. "I will."

TWENTY-SIX

The MACV Compound, Saigon

Russel Lamb went to see the CIA Station Chief at Saigon. "I need to see David Perry, Jim."

"David Perry? The Naval Intelligence Attaché? What's going on, Russ?"

"I've been gathering intel regarding some American POWs in the Delta. The Navy has an Orion covering that area. I believe they have information I need to complete my assessment."

James Dalton, the Saigon CIA Station Chief, was suddenly interested. He'd not been aware Lamb was working on anything related to prisoners. "This is not an official operation, is it, Russell?"

Lamb smiled. "It's just something I came across … a long shot. It probably won't turn up anything." He knew Dalton would want in on it if there was a chance of visibility in Washington. Lamb intended to give this thing to the Army if it panned out. He knew just the team who could pull it off. It would be too visible an operation for the agency anyway. "Just get me through to Perry," he said.

Dalton hesitated, then picked up the phone. They were on his turf; he could control the shots. It took three calls, but within an hour he'd arranged a meeting with Captain David Perry, Naval Intelligence. Dalton arranged for Perry to come to CIA headquarters. That way he could stay in on it. Lamb, quietly amused at Dalton's political maneuvering, said nothing.

When Perry arrived, Lamb got right to the point. "David, there's a P-3 Orion patrolling the U Minh." He reached in his pocket and pulled out the name Eric Mohr had given him. "This man is one of the crewmen aboard. I want to talk with him."

"What's this about?" Perry wanted to know.

"The Navy lost a flier a few weeks ago, an OV-10 pilot. He wasn't recovered, even though SEALs were brought in. The VC took him underground. I was asked for help."

Jim Dalton swallowed his tea wrong and started coughing. "Who asked you for help?" he asked, after he'd recovered.

"The man's brother-in-law is an Army Medical Evacuation pilot who was stationed in the Delta. He feels the Navy has given up on finding the pilot. He asked me to help; I put out a few feelers."

"How did he know to come to you?" Dalton wanted to know. Lamb didn't answer his question. Dalton pondered a minute, then asked, "Do you think you have something?"

"I don't know," Lamb responded. "That's why I need to talk with the Navy crew."

If Perry knew anything about it, he didn't let on. "Let me make a few calls. I'll find out when the Orion crew is due in."

"Use my phone," Dalton said, "it's secure."

Twenty minutes later, Perry had it arranged. "O-five-thirty tomorrow morning. The south ramp at Bien Hoa. The Orion's tail number is seven-two-five."

"Thanks, David."

"Don't mention it. Where are you sleeping tonight?"

"I don't know. I'll stay at the Lotus, I guess."

"Nonsense. You'll stay at my place. I'll arrange a driver for you in the morning." Just like that, they squeezed Jim Dalton out of the operation.

Bien Hoa, the next morning

Lamb was at the airport when the Orion's landing lights appeared out of the darkness and the ungainly aircraft landed. The Orion's unique appearance, accented by the huge dome mounted above the fuselage, made it easily recognizable as it taxied to the transient ramp for fuel. Lamb and his driver drove across the ramp to meet the plane. When the crew emerged, the CIA man was standing near the exit ramp.

"Kennedy?" he asked as several men deplaned.

"He's still on board." They pointed toward the plane. The parking ramp was a secure area. If the man was there, he had security clearance.

Lamb walked up the steps and peered inside. A man sat flipping switches and studying gauges at the electronics console that occupied almost one entire side of the aircraft's interior.

"Kennedy?"

"That's me."

"I'm Russell Lamb, Central Intelligence Agency. Can I talk to you?"

"Sure. Have a seat."

Kennedy was obviously a technician. He studied the console, ignoring the visitor for the moment. Lamb waited. Finally the man looked at him. "I'm here about Steve Cooper," Lamb told him.

"CIA, huh?"

"That's right."

"Who sent you?"

"Actually, nobody sent me. Some of Cooper's buddies heard you had some possible information about him. I've had a lead or two myself. I want to find out if what you have correlates with what I have."

"I can't believe somebody took me seriously."

"Yeah, I know what you mean." Lamb knew the game. Getting information was his profession. This man wanted to tell him, but he wanted to build it up a little, stress the genius of his discovery. That's okay. Russell would play the game with him.

It took only fifteen minutes and feigned interest in some of the Orion's gadgets along the wall. The two men bent over a plexiglass encased map of the Vietnam Delta as Kennedy explained the theory he and the other technicians aboard the Orion had developed.

In light of what Lamb already knew, their theory was amazingly accurate. They knew the hamlet where Steve was being detained. They knew about the other prisoners, or at least suspected where they were. They didn't know who Colonel Nguyen was, but they knew he was from the NVA and that he was responsible for moving prisoners to the North. Then Kennedy dropped a bombshell. He knew the timetable and the transportation.

"You see this port here?" He pointed to a place southeast of Soc Trang where the Cai Lon River flowed into the South China Sea. Lamb nodded. "We've tagged a junk that makes regular runs from that port to Hanoi and back. It's typically a twenty-one day round trip. The boat left Hanoi six days ago. It's four days out."

Lamb was interested. "What do you mean you 'tagged' it?"

"Trick of the trade. Just like sonar guys map the sounds of various submarines, we airborne surveillance guys have ways of identifying certain infrared patterns put out by a particular vessel. We mark it; the computers follow it. We can do the same thing with people when the conditions are right."

"How did you locate this hamlet?" Lamb wanted to know. He pointed to the place where he himself had recently learned Steve Cooper was being held.

"We put a bunch of pieces together, and suddenly the puzzle started to look like a picture. Here let me show you." He bent over the map. "See the concrete hut here?" Lamb nodded. "Unusual for that area, don't you think?" It was true. Lamb said so. "It's got no windows. It's too small for storage. It's at the edge of the hamlet under trees. We found four more like it in this group of hamlets east of Long My. Then we noticed the bamboo cages nearby. They're mounted on poles, like if a bunch of guys were carrying a sultan or something with the poles on their shoulders."

"We found this VC cadre," Kennedy continued, "complete with an NVA advisor. We started watching. Between the infrared, the photos and the sound monitoring, we put the picture together. They're holding prisoners in each of the five concrete bungalows. The NVA guy visits each of them on a rotational basis."

"How'd you tie the boat into this?"

"History. We know the boat has been making regular trips. We looked at the location of the bungalows and tried to find a pattern that would tell us why they were located where they were. Look at this river." He pointed out the Cai Lon as it meandered across the mangrove swamps toward the eastern coastline. "See these tributaries?" Lamb nodded. "They each lead to the Cai Lon. VC traffic is heavy on them at night. They are too small for the PBRs to get into, so the sampans move freely."

Kennedy sat back. "The rest is theory," he said, "But my bet is that there are five American POWs who will be transported down those tributaries to the Cai Lon River, then down the river to meet the Junk. They'll travel at night and hole up in the daytime."

"I think you're exactly right," Lamb told the technician. "I just learned about the NVA advisor. He's Colonel Ky Nguyen. Educated in the States and on the rise in the North Vietnamese military. He was apparently sent to the Delta to recover these prisoners. The North Vietnamese feel they can exploit prisoners taken in the south in a different way than the ones they capture in the North."

"Who are the other prisoners?" Kennedy wanted to know.

"Crewmembers from a PBR that was captured up the river from Rach Gia a few weeks ago."

"More Navy guys, huh?"

"Yes. Apparently the North Vietnamese don't understand our 'Brown Water Navy' tactics and want to learn more about how we operate. They probably figure they can get this information from these prisoners."

"Do you have a plan for getting them?"

"No, not yet," Lamb admitted. He stood up to go, offering his hand.

"Thanks, Mr. Kennedy. You've been a big help."

"Don't mention it, sir. I'm just glad somebody is going to do something about those guys. They're pulling us off this patrol at the end of the week."

"You mean you won't be overhead if we need you when attempting a rescue?"

"Not unless you do it in the next three days. I guess you've got to, anyway. Four or five days max and those guys are on their way to Hanoi."

"What if we wait until they load them on the junk, then let the Navy intercept them?" Lamb wondered.

"They'll be dead ducks," Kennedy assured him.

"Why?"

"Why do you think they're transporting them in bamboo cages? If anyone approaches them while they're on the open water, those cages go overboard. No prisoners, no evidence!"

"They could drown them on the rivers, too," Lamb observed.

"Yes, that's right."

Long Binh, later that morning

"You really know where he is?" Eric found it hard to believe what Russell Lamb was telling him. Even he had begun to think it was hopeless.

"The Navy's intelligence matched what my contacts told me. I believe we have him located, but that's just part of the story."

"Yes, I know. Rescuing him will be pretty risky, not just to any rescuers, but to him as well."

"Unfortunately, I don't have the necessary assets, and the Navy is not buying the story. They've effectively pulled out of the Delta. Their official position is that Steve Cooper is already in Hanoi."

Eric shook his head in disbelief. "Who's running this war, anyway? It seems that every high level command decision we hear about is stupid."

"I tend to agree," Lamb said. "Unfortunately, it appears the war is being run from Washington."

"Well, I'll get him out."

"Don't worry. You'll be in on it," Lamb replied. "But there's an ace in the hole."

"Who?"

"Hamilton Ray."

"You mean the Special Forces advisor, the guy with the Vietnamese Rangers?"

"That's him."

"Do you know where he is?"

"I will tonight. Can you get to Can Tho with a helicopter?"

"One way or another. I'll either clear it with the CO, or take one off the ramp."

"I think it would be best if you clear it with the Old Man. It's Aubrey Scott, isn't it?"

"Yes, sir, but he's getting so short that Captain Bernie Johnson from the 159th has effectively taken command of the two units that now make up Long Binh Dustoff."

"Let's go see them."

A few minutes later, Lamb and Mohr were in the Long Binh Dustoff CO's office.

"Absolutely not!" Aubrey Scott raged. "We have a medevac mission to support and too few resources to do it with. You're not Search and Rescue. Let the Jolly Greens do it."

"Sir, there are no Jolly Greens in the Delta. They're all up north," Eric told him.

"Well, it's not our mission. We're not equipped to handle it, and you are not qualified."

"But, sir …"

"No!"

Bernie Johnson interrupted. "Wait a minute, Aubrey. You haven't even asked Mohr if he has a plan."

"Well, do you?" Scott spat out.

"Yes, sir—a partial plan, sir. It involves Major Ray and his Special Forces."

"Who is Ray?" Johnson wanted to know.

"Army Special Forces guy," Scott told him. "He's an advisor to the South Vietnamese Ranger Battalion in Long Xuyen province. We've worked with him before."

"Does he know his stuff?"

"He's good. Been here forever."

"I say we rotate Mohr to Can Tho. Let him coordinate with the Rangers. If they need a ride, we can classify it as a rescue mission. Might help your career along if he pulls it off."

"Yeah, but what if he loses his ship? How are we going to explain that?"

"Casualty of war. It won't be the first one we've lost."

Mohr listened to the two COs working it out. He silently prayed that God would intervene on Steve's behalf. He looked at Russell Lamb and noticed his lips moving, too, his eyes looking up. He was bombarding the heavenlies as well. Eric still marveled at God's faithfulness. A CIA Station Chief was a Christian and he was here helping Eric find and rescue Steve. That was a miracle in itself.

Scott was coming around. "Who are you planning to take with you?" he asked.

Eric didn't hesitate. "Les Winters."

"Winters!"

"Yes, sir."

"Why him?" It was obvious Scott didn't think too much of the idea.

"He volunteered to go. He's a former infantryman. He's older and more experienced than I am. He might see things I don't."

"When has this got to happen?" Scott asked.

Lamb answered. "Within four days, five at the most. We'll probably have a better chance when they're moving them. At least they should all be together."

"We. Does that mean you're in on this?" Scott asked.

"Wouldn't miss it for the world," the CIA man answered.

Johnson made a command decision that took the pressure off Scott. He turned to Eric. "You're on the duty roster tomorrow night. I need you to fly that schedule. You can sleep in the next morning, then you and Winters go to Can Tho that afternoon to relieve Dickson and his crew. Let Operations know who your medic and crew chief will be."

"Yes, sir!"

Mohr and Lamb left the CO's office before either CO could change his mind. Outside, Eric thanked Lamb for his help.

"Don't mention it. I'll see you in Can Tho day after tomorrow. I'll locate Ray and try to get him there. We'll need to have a planning session that night."

"Okay. See you then, and thanks again." Lamb nodded and walked toward his borrowed jeep.

Long Binh Dustoff, the next day

During the day, Eric worked in the supply room. The two supply sergeants, Massey from the 57th and Hill from the 159th were deciding which items to keep and which to turn in through Operation Keystone, the newly instituted procedures for eliminating waste and duplication as equipment was prepared for shipment back to the States or for transfer to the Vietnamese. The paperwork stack was overwhelming, and Eric shuffled through it halfheartedly, finding it difficult to keep his mind on business. He had talked to Winters the previous night, right after Russell Lamb left. Winters made no move to back out—said he was looking forward to the mission.

Winters suggested a crew chief and medic. Because of his former life as an enlisted man, he spent time with the enlisted crewmembers when off duty and had a better rapport with them than most of the pilots. He suggested "Turk" Smith as the crew chief and Johnny Hartman as the medic. Eric was satisfied with Smith. He was on an extended tour and handled himself well in a tight situation. His was always the cleanest and best maintained aircraft in the fleet. Hartman was a good medic, but a little belligerent at times. Instead, Eric decided to take Blake Sam along as their medic. Sam was new to Dustoff, even new to combat, but during his short time with the Dustoff unit, he had gained the respect of the other, more experienced medics. Eric wanted him for another reason: the assurance of prayer support.

All day long, two duty crews worked with the ARVNs and the Air Cavalry as they pushed their way north toward An Loc. Each ship made several dropoffs at the 24th Evac, each time severely overloaded because of the ARVNs who climbed on board when they made a pickup in a hot area. As much as they didn't want to, the crews had started having to use electronic cattle prods to dissuade hangers-on when the aircraft was pulling out of a hot LZ, grossly overloaded.

Each time Eric heard a Huey land at the hospital helipad, he thought of that first day when he, Patton and Zerbe stood with Captain Duncan watching the Dustoff ship land and drop off a wounded patient. The newcomers had been so excited that day, anxious to get their share of the action. Now Patton was dead. The remaining two had each seen more action than they cared to think about in a lifetime. They were different men now. Each had aged the equivalent of a few years in just the few months since they'd arrived in Vietnam. Losing a friend will do that to you. Eric had lost more than one. Would they be able to recover Steve? Hamilton Ray and Russell Lamb would be there to help. So would Les Winters,

Turk Smith, Blake Sam and Ray's Rangers. Lamb thought they might also have help from the Navy Orion, if it was still allowed to patrol the area. He was leaning on his Naval Intelligence contacts to try to insure that they would have that help.

The afternoon passed slowly. Finally, it was time to preflight for the night shift. Thanks to some intervention on the part of Bernie Johnson, Eric was to have the entire crew he was taking to the Delta together for the night's missions. Normally, during this transition period for the Delta Dustoff ACs, the other pilot would have been a III Corps aircraft commander.

There were no missions on the board when they came on duty. The early part of the evening passed quietly. A little after 11:00 p.m., Eric and Les were in the pilots' lounge playing a game of eight ball. Tom Zerbe sat on the old leather sofa, reading a copy of *Flying* magazine in the dim light of the table lamp. Rob Powers and Mike Nichols, two of the 159th's pilots, occupied the stools at the bar in the corner, drinking beer and reliving the day's action near Lai Khe.

Eric bent over the table and lined up a shot he thought he could make—the nine ball in the corner pocket. It would be a tricky shot to make without disturbing the eight ball. He called his shot. Winters leaned against the wall, waiting for Eric to miss. He had a chance to clean up the remaining three solids, all of which were in playable positions.

Captain Johnson, the CO, walked in and looked around. He watched Mohr take his shot, then left without saying anything. Mohr's body english failed to coax the ball into the pocket. At least he didn't scratch. As Winters chalked up his cue stick, the phone rang. Zerbe picked it up, listened for a second, then announced, "You've got a mission, guys." He put the phone receiver down and returned to his magazine. As

Mohr and Winters ran out to the alert helipad, Powers and Nichols began racking the pool balls for a game of their own.

The crew arrived at the helicopter just ahead of the pilots. Turk Smith untied the rotor blades and rotated them perpendicular to the fuselage. Blake Sam opened the left side pilot's door and removed the fire extinguisher from its mounting bracket on the floor just inside the door. He pulled on his flight helmet, plugged its microphone cord into the ICS intercom system and went to stand fire guard beside the engine compartment while the pilots started the engine. Mohr, in the left seat, plugged the cord from his flight helmet into the ICS, put his flack and survival vests on and fastened his seatbelt and shoulder harness. Meanwhile, Winters climbed in the right seat, flipped the main fuel switch on, rotated the throttle to a point just below the flight idle detent and yelled, "Clear!"

The crew chief and medic both echoed, "Clear!" and Winters pulled the starter trigger, bringing the Huey to life. The smell of JP-4 filled the air as the ignition igniters crackled with the high-voltage spark that set fire to the fuel being dumped into the turbine engine's combustion chamber. When the turbine engine speed reached 40 percent, Winters released the starter trigger and rotated the throttle to the high side of the flight idle detent. After checking the oil pressure and temperature gauges, he rotated the throttle full open and using the toggle switch on the head of the collective pitch lever, beeped the rpm to 6600. Mohr, who was totally strapped in by now, placed his hands on the cyclic and collective on his side of the aircraft and wiggled them to indicate he was ready to take over the controls. Les released his grip and started putting on his own survival equipment, helmet, seatbelt and shoulder harness.

"You guys ready?" Mohr asked over the intercom.

"Ready left, sir."

"Ready right."

"Coming up."

Winters was still buckling his seatbelt as Eric lifted the Huey to a hover, turned it into the wind and eased the cyclic forward. The Huey began moving over the ground and with a shudder climbed away from the Dustoff helipad.

Eric rotated his ICS switch to position three and keyed the FM radio. "Ops, this is Seven-Four. What have you got?" Less than two minutes had passed since the phone call to the pilots' lounge.

"Dustoff Seven-Four, we have four wounded on a Navy river boat on the Vam Co Dong River north of Ben Luc. They are in contact. I have the coordinates when you're ready to copy."

Eric looked at Winters who now had his helmet plugged into the intercom and was turning around to face forward after sliding the armor plate on the right side of his seat into place. Winters nodded to indicate he had heard the conversation. He removed the grease pencil from the shoulder pocket of his flight suit. Eric keyed his mike again. "Ops, this is Seven-Four. Go ahead with the coordinates and the contact frequency."

"Okay Seven-Four. The Coordinates are xray-sierra-five-seven-zero-eight-one-one. Contact River Rat Three on Fox Mike thirty-six-point-four-five." As the RTO supplied the information, Winters used his grease pencil to write the coordinates and the FM frequency on the lower right-hand corner of the windshield.

"You got it?" Eric asked on the intercom. Winters nodded.

"We got it, Ops. Seven-Four out."

"Seven-Four, this is Dustoff Operations." It was Captain Johnson's voice. "We're working on getting you some guns."

"Roger," Eric replied. He knew there were no Cobras left in III Corps, except the ones flown by the 17th Cav's gun platoon, call sign "Blue Max." There couldn't be but about eight of them left, the way they'd been getting blown out of the sky around An Loc, Lai Khe and Tay Ninh. If there were no Blue Max's, Eric would have liked to have Navy gun cover from the Delta, but those guys were all gone. The Old Man had to try for gunships, but he and Eric both knew this mission would have to go without guns, if it went at all.

After taking up the heading that would intercept the river Southwest of Saigon, Eric called the Air Force at Bien Hoa for flight following.

"Parrot Control, this is Dustoff Seven-Four off Long Binh. We're headed for ..." he leaned over the console to read the numbers off the windshield on the other side of the cockpit, "xray-sierra-five-seven-zero-eight-one-one."

"Dustoff Seven-Four, this is Parrot Control, squawk one-two-seven-four and ident." Eric nodded to Winters, who dialed in the transponder frequency and pressed the ident button.

"You're radar contact, Dustoff Seven-Four, four miles southwest of Long Binh. It looks like two-hundred-forty degrees and thirty-one miles will put you over your target."

"Thanks, Parrot."

Eric took up the new heading, his mind racing ahead, trying to sort out the details of the mission. A boat on the river in contact at night provided an interesting set of challenges. The night part didn't bother him. In the past six months, he'd logged over five hundred hours at night. Most nights, he made between ten and twelve landings to jungle clearings, rice paddies and other unlit, unimproved landing sites. It was just part of the job. Tonight there was a high layer of clouds and no moon. The first part of their flight would take them right over the southern part of Saigon, creating havoc with their night vision. Within a few minutes, those lights would be behind them and the pilots would have to rely on small visual cues and highly-developed night vision to carry out the mission. Eric wasn't worried about his night vision, but knew that Winters had avoided flying at night as much as possible. His lack of recent experience at night could easily be a liability on this mission.

Eric wondered how Winters felt about flying with him. *Did he subscribe to the belief that some of the other ACs had that Eric flew like he was invincible and believed he couldn't be killed?* Winters had flown as Eric's peter pilot before, but never on a hot mission. He glanced over at Winters, trying to gauge by the look on his face how the man would respond under fire. He wondered if Les' insides were in knots.

As if responding to Eric's thoughts, Les asked him, "Want me to fly?"

"Yeah. You got it."

Les put his hands on the controls, wiggled them slightly. "I've got it."

"You guys okay back there?" Eric asked.

"Yes, sir." It was a subdued response.

"What are you guys thinking?" Eric didn't want to give way to the fear nagging at the corners of his mind. He knew too much about the mission. They'd have fifteen minutes or so to think about it en route. He couldn't let his mind be idle, couldn't let their minds be idle.

Blake was the first to answer him. "I was thinking about a mission last week that Johnny Hartman flew up by Tay Ninh."

"What about it?" Hartman was a medic with the 159th. Eric was beginning to know the guys.

"It was a hoist mission. He rode the jungle penetrator down to pick up a Sandy pilot who bellied in after getting shot up. The guy didn't have enough strength to strap himself to the seat, so Johnny rode down to make sure he got on the JP and stayed there. They had to come up through the trees and they got banged up pretty bad by some tree limbs. Johnny said it was worse than getting shot at and that he never wanted to do that again." The intercom was quiet a few seconds, then Blake added, "And that was in the daytime."

Eric didn't comment. He dimmed the lights on the instrument panel, leaned his head against the back of the seat and closed his eyes momentarily.

Turk Smith was staring at the lights of Saigon. "It's so weird to be this close to a big city, yet on our way to a medevac in the boonies," he said. Nobody answered. "Don't get me wrong," he continued. "I'm glad to be flying. It was boring back there. Nothing to read, nothing to do but play cards. The guys back there … their conversation never seems to get beyond cars, dope or women. At least here we're doing something."

"You got that right," Eric said. Winters remained silent. Eric opened his eyes and glanced at the heading indicator. Winters was keeping them right on course.

Suddenly, the radio came to life. "Dustoff Seven-Four, this is Operations."

"This is Seven-Four. Go ahead." Eric sat up. The lights of Saigon were now behind them.

"Seven-Four, you're cleared to contact the boat commander, River Rat Three, on his tactical freq. There'll be no guns. The Old Man says to be careful, and if it's possible, you should wait until the mission is secure."

"Dustoff Seven-Four, Roger." Eric caught the significance of the words "you should." It meant the CO hadn't given him an order to fly the mission without gunship support. Captain Johnson's position was not an easy one. He was caught between protecting his crew and getting the job done. SOP said they couldn't attempt a hot mission without guns. SOP had been written when things were different, when gunships had been plentiful. Americans were on that boat. Guns or no guns, the wounded men were counting on the Dustoff crew to get them medical help. The entire time he had been in Vietnam, Eric had never known a Dustoff aircraft commander to refuse a mission involving Americans because it might be dangerous. He wasn't about to be the first one.

Eric switched to the new FM frequency, but before calling the boat, he checked in with Parrot Control on UHF.

"Parrot, this is Dustoff Seven-Four. What's our current position relative the pickup coordinates."

"Your destination coordinates are at your twelve o'clock and eight miles, Seven-Four."

"Roger, Parrot. Thanks." To Les, Eric said, "What about artillery? What's the artillery sector around here, anyway?" He was beginning to realize how much more he had to learn about III Corps. The Delta, he knew by heart.

"If you want to take the controls, I'll look it up," Les said.

Eric took the controls and Les dug in his flight suit pocket for the little book that had the day's frequencies and call signs. Meanwhile, Eric called the boat commander. "River Rat Three, this is Dustoff Seven-Four."

The response was immediate. "Dustoff Seven-Four, this is River Rat Three, over." Eric could hear heavy machine gun firing in the background.

"We're inbound your location, about five minutes out. Can you give us an update on your situation?"

"Roger, Dustoff." The man was shouting. Eric turned down the volume on his ICS. Why did people always shout into their microphones when talking to helicopter pilots? "We're in the river and the boat is adrift. They hit our engines with an

RPG. We're taking fire from the north bank. Mostly it's small arms fire, but they have a grenade launcher. We're also getting some sporadic fire from the south bank, but we're slowly drifting away from that threat. We have four wounded men—two of them critical, over."

Using the small overhead map light with its red lens cover, Eric looked at his map. The man had referred to north and south banks instead of east and west. That meant they were past the bend in the river.

"How far past the bridge are you?" Eric asked, noting a highway bridge just before the river turned due west.

"I'd estimate about three klicks, Dustoff."

"Roger, stand by."

He turned to Les. "What about the arty?"

"I've got the freq," Les replied.

"Okay. Just a second and you can give them a call." Eric switched back to the FM radio. "River Rat Three, we'll be off the frequency for a couple of minutes getting artillery clearance. Listen for us. We'll be coming up the river from the East."

"Roger."

Eric told Les to make the artillery call. He searched the darkness below for signs of the river and the bridge. While Les was using the FM radio to contact the artillery advisory center, Eric flipped his ICS switch to UHF to get an update from Parrot Control. "Parrot, this is Dustoff Seven-Four. Where do you show us?"

"I show you now just about on target, Seven-Four. Maybe two clicks east."

"Roger. We'll call you on the way back out."

"Roger, Seven-Four. Be careful down there."

Eric clicked his mike twice, then looked over at Les to see how he was doing with the artillery clearances. Les was writing something on the windshield again with his grease pencil. Not good. *Come on, where is that river? ... There it is!* Eric banked slightly to the left and decreased power to start a descent. They'd been cruising at a comfortable fifteen hundred feet.

"We're okay," Les said. "They're firing north of us, but nothing in this area and nothing between here and Long Binh."

"At least something's working for us. Get me back on the River Rat freq."

Winters dialed in the frequency. Eric contacted the boat captain. "River Rat Three, this is Dustoff Seven-Four. Is there any chance of you getting ashore?"

"That's a negative, Dustoff. We have no power."

That must have felt awful. Adrift with no power—people shooting at you from both sides. "You guys familiar with a jungle penetrator?" Eric asked.

"That's affirmative, Dustoff."

During the conversation with the Navy boat, Eric continued his slow descent. He never saw the bridge, but the river was flowing east and west. He figured the bridge was behind them. He maneuvered the helicopter over the river, which he could pick out in the darkness only because its texture was slightly darker than that of the terrain on either side. He leveled off at 500 feet, continuing to follow the river until it led them to the boat.

"Les, kill the lights," Eric said. Winters reached up to the overhead panel and turned off both the position lights and the rotating beacon. No reason to give Charlie an easy target to shoot at.

The river took a slight jog to the north, then turned back west. Just beyond that point there was tracer fire. Red AK-47 tracers were coming from several positions along the north bank of the river. Green M-16 tracers and the unmistakable flaming orange baseballs from the .50 cal were originating from a point in the river. Eric judged the river to be about a hundred feet wide at that point. The boat was almost midstream.

The FM radio crackled in Eric's ear. "Dustoff Seven-Four, this is River Rat Three. We can hear you, but can't see you."

"We're running dark. Can you give us your position lights?"

"Might as well. We're already sitting ducks."

"Hold them for now. Wait until I give you the word."

"Roger, Dustoff."

Things were starting to happen fast and Eric realized he had not briefed his crew.

"Okay, guys, you know the routine." Eric spoke as if he had done this dozens of times. He couldn't let the crew know it was a first for him. He willed his voice to sound calm and full of confidence.

"Communication will be extremely important. Turn your intercoms to 'hot mike.' Turk, you run the hoist and keep me posted on its progress the whole time. I want to know how far down it is. I want to know when it's on the deck. I want to know when someone is on the JP. I want to know when it's coming up, how far up it is. Just like we've done in training. I need constant chatter from you guys. Blake, keep your head out the door on your side. Don't be afraid to talk to me. I need to know where I am over the boat. I need to know what's going on. Don't worry about calling incoming fire unless somebody gets hit. We can't do anything about that. Les, you keep your hand on the cable cut switch on the pedestal. If anybody yells, 'Cut the cable' don't ask questions. Jerk up the cover and flip that switch. Turk, you've got a switch, too. You can use it if we get snagged, but don't do it if we've got guys on the hoist unless we're going down. Les, you watch the vertical speed indicator. Don't let me get into a descent without me knowing it. Any questions?"

"No, sir."

"No."

Only Winters was silent. Mohr looked over at him, and Winters shook his head. He moved his left hand to the cable cut switch. His right hand remained close to the cyclic. Eric had no idea what the man was thinking. *Was he going to come unglued, or was this just old stuff to him? Could he fly the mission better than Eric could? No time to find out now.*

"Les, you turn your ICS to 'hot mike', too. I'm going to try to find the wind direction and turn into it. Talk to me. Tell me everything I need to know, except about incoming fire. Turn the panel lights down." Winters dimmed the lights.

Even with the hostile fire being aimed at their pickup site, Eric began to feel the peace inside he had learned to recognize as the supernatural calm from the Holy Spirit. It was a welcome relief from the fear he had felt just a few moments earlier when he had time to think.

This peace was more than just confidence in his abilities and that of the crew. The crew was an unknown. This crew had never flown together as a crew before tonight, and had certainly never faced this kind of mission before. The fact that it was going to be a hoist mission over a drifting target at night, with the enemy firing at them, meant this would be more difficult than anything any of them had ever tried before—at least it was more difficult than anything Eric had ever done. But there had been other things that had seemed impossible only months before. Now those things were under his belt. A lot of what the Dustoff crews did routinely probably seemed impossible to most people. The mission had to be done. They were the ones who had to do it.

Guns would be nice. Something to neutralize that fire on the north bank like Steve in his OV-10. He couldn't think about Steve now. They would get through this. Tomorrow they would get Steve. Tonight they had to do this.

They were only a couple hundred yards from the boat. Eric keyed the FM. "Give me your lights, Three. We're coming overhead blacked out. Do you know the wind direction?"

"It's out of the northwest, Dustoff, about eight knots. Here are the lights."

"Okay," Eric said. "We see them. I don't know if you can hold your position, but if you can, try to hold it steady down there."

"Okay, Dustoff. We've got anchors out and we're turned into the wind. Come up over the stern if you can."

Eric double clicked his mike as he slowed the Huey's forward motion. He brought it to a hover just behind the boat, then eased forward slowly. He estimated the helicopter was about fifty feet above the boat deck. To go any lower would create so much rotorwash they wouldn't be able to manage the jungle penetrator. Eric was vaguely aware of tracers coming toward them from ahead and to their right, but he tuned out everything except the boat on the water below them and the chatter that was already beginning to come from the crew. He knew the Viet Cong were probably throwing everything they could at the sound of the helicopter, but he doubted they could see it. He only hoped they would guess that it was higher or lower than it really was.

To avoid the brightness from the tracer fire, Eric looked toward the south shore and picked out a tree that was taller than the rest. He would use the tree as a visual reference to help him maintain his position over the boat. He could no longer look down and see the boat, which was directly below him. That angle of view gave him a much too limited perspective, making it impossible to hold the helicopter steady over the back end of the small boat. He had to depend upon the crew's verbal instructions, the relative position of the tree in his peripheral vision and a steady hand. He was sweating and realized he was unconsciously holding his breath for seconds at a time. Flexing his fingers, Eric forced himself to breathe deeply. He was tight all over, which made it difficult to keep a steady hand on the controls. He relaxed his grip on the cyclic, holding it tenderly between his thumb and fingers, his hand resting on his thigh. With his left hand, he eased a little friction on the collective to help overcome the tendency to fight it up and down. Electronic interference could be heard in his headset as Turk rotated the hoist boom outward and began lowering the cable. Suddenly, he remembered the static electricity.

"River Rat Three, let the JP touch the boat before you grab it," he radioed. Letting the jungle penetrator touch the boat first would discharge the static electricity build-up associated with lowering it.

"Roger," Three said.

"Hoist going down, sir. Move forward. Hold it. Hold it. Forward. You're drifting left. That's it. Ten feet. You're coming left again. Easy. Easy. Back to the right. Now forward just a little. That's it. Twenty feet." It was impossible to tell who was talking. Eric responded to every instruction as gently as possible. If he ever needed a smooth control touch, it was now.

"Move it forward, sir!" Turk cried. "We're losing the boat."

Eric nudged the chopper forward slightly, then immediately countered his action, realizing the helicopter was moving forward too fast.

"That's it. The hoist is on the deck ... oh, great. Some sucker grabbed it and got shocked." (So much for the warning.) "Hold it still, sir, they're strapping them on. There's two of them. You're doing fine. A little to the right. That's it. Hold what you got. I'm giving them a little slack. Hold it. Forward a little. Okay, we're bringing them up."

Eric kept the reference tree in his peripheral vision. He concentrated on keeping his hand steady. He felt himself tightening up again. He couldn't help it. He wanted this to be over. He was afraid to breathe. Sweat was running down his forehead into his eyes. He felt the Huey drifting right even before he heard the warning.

"We're drifting right, we're drifting right! Watch it. Come left, come left! Okay, bring it back, bring it back. They're off the boat." Blake was doing most of the talking. Turk was out on the skid, the hoist control box in one hand, his other extended toward the upcoming load.

"Twenty feet." It seemed to take an eternity. "Ten feet. Five feet. We've got them!" Blake scrambled over to help Turk swing the two men on board and Eric felt the helicopter dip as their combined weight shifted the helicopter's center of gravity to one side He moved the cyclic slightly to the opposite side to counteract the shift. He let out his breath, then took another deep one, which he subconsciously held again. It was too quiet in the back. "What's going on back there?" he demanded. "Talk to me!"

"We've got them both on board, sir," Blake told him.

Eric nosed the helicopter over, allowing it to accelerate. He added power to climb and turned towards the lights of Saigon. They'd been over the boat for two minutes, maybe three. It had seemed like hours. Not one round had impacted the aircraft, though tracers had flown all around them.

"What have we got, Blake?" Eric asked.

"They're both alive, Mr. Mohr, but in shock. I've got to get IVs started. They're both bleeding pretty badly. Here, Turk, put this on that guy's shoulder." He interrupted himself to give the crew chief directions on helping with the wounds. "See if you can stop that bleeding. Sir, we need to get these guys to the 24th Evac as soon as possible."

Obviously, the medic had his hands full with the two men they had on board. Eric called the boat. "River Rat Three, this is Dustoff Seven-Four. My medic tells me we need to get these guys to the hospital. What's the condition of your other wounded?"

"They're okay, Dustoff. Not so bad. We don't want to do this again. You take care of those guys. We'll take care of the other two."

"Okay, we'll be back for them. It'll take us thirty, maybe forty minutes. Wish we had some guns to help you with those Viet Cong."

"Roger that, Dustoff. River Rat Three, out."

"You've got it," Eric said to Les.

"I've got it." Winters said. As he came on the controls, Eric released them. At the same time, he tried to release the tension in his body. It wouldn't go away.

"Nice flying," Winters commented.

"Thanks," Eric said. The man was a second tour aviator. A seasoned flier. Just not a Dustoff pilot. It was a high compliment, and Eric recognized it as such.

The flight path home was obvious. The lights of Saigon were spread out before them. Long Binh and the 24th Evac were just beyond the city.

It was quiet in the back as Blake and Turk worked to stabilize the two patients. Eric switched his ICS selector to UHF. "Parrot Control, this is Dustoff Seven-Four off our pickup site, en route to the 24th Evac."

"Dustoff Seven-Four, radar contact," came the controller's calm reply. It seemed ironic to Eric that night after night he communicated with a guy sitting at a radar scope at some secure site at Air Force Binh Thuy or Bien Hoa Air Base, while he was flying in and out of places where there was a real war going on. He wondered if the Air Force controllers had any feel for what the Dustoff crews were doing whenever they disappeared off the radar scope only to reappear again a few minutes later. He was glad they were there. If for some reason the helicopter didn't come back up, the Air Force would know right where to send help.

"You need a heading to Long Binh, Seven-Four?"

Eric smiled, his first light moment since the eternity ago when all he was thinking about was putting the nine ball in the corner pocket without sinking the eight. That seemed like a different part of the world in a different life. "Negative, Parrot. We can see the lights of home."

"Roger, sir. Tell me when you have the hospital in sight. By the way, you might try recycling your transponder. It appears to be intermittent."

It was always intermittent in this bird. Eric would write it up again. It would get bench checked again and be certified okay, then put back in the aircraft only to be intermittent again on another flight. It would have to break completely before anything would really be done about it.

Eric switched the FM radio back to the Dustoff frequency. "Dustoff Operations, this is Seven-Four, estimating the Twenty-Fourth Evac in fifteen minutes with two critically wounded Americans." It was just a few days earlier that he'd flown Brian Patton into that hospital helipad. In fact, that had been the last time he'd landed at the 24th Evac. *Was that a lifetime ago, or just the other day?* Brian was gone. He still hadn't gotten used to it.

"Roger, Seven-Four. We'll notify them. Does this complete the mission?"

"Negative. We've got to make another trip. There are two more patients on the boat who weren't critical."

"Roger. What's the tactical situation?"

"Say again, Operations. You're breaking up." The RTO got the message. He didn't ask the question again.

In the back of the Huey, Blake Sam worked steadily on his patients with Turk assisting him. One of the men had a sucking chest wound and was struggling from loss of blood and oxygen. Blake applied a plastic bandage to seal the puncture. Turk helped him wrap it. They started an IV. It took several tries to get the needle in the man's veins in the vibrating helicopter.

The other man had shrapnel wounds all over his chest, neck and shoulders. He also had a bad cut on the side of his face. One of his shoulder wounds had been bleeding from an artery and Turk had stopped the bleeding with a pressure bandage. They got an IV started in this man, too, just before Winters told them he had the 24th Evac in sight.

Les made an uneventful landing at the hospital helipad. The emergency room crew was there waiting for them. Because these were American patients, two doctors and two nurses met the helicopter.

While the patients were being unloaded, Eric looked at the fuel gauge and mentally calculated the time it would take them to get back to the boat, pick up the other two wounded men and get them back to the hospital. It would be close on fuel, but they could do it.

As the Dustoff crew arrived back in the vicinity of the patrol boat, Eric called them on their tactical frequency.

"Dustoff Seven-Four," came the reply, "we've made it to the shore and we're by ourselves now."

"You mean there's nobody shooting at you?"

"No, sir. They just ran out of ammo or guts or something. I guess they figured if they couldn't kill a Navy boat and couldn't blow up an Army helicopter, they might as well quit before they got in some real trouble." It was typical of the lighthearted joking that was often part of the post-action letdown from a tension-packed situation.

"What's your location like?" Eric asked.

"Well, sir. I know you don't like to land that thing, but we found you a Huey-sized clearing the south side of the river. You say the word, and we'll give you a flare."

"I'd rather have a strobe light, if you have one," Eric replied. A flare would blind them to the surroundings and limit their night vision. Eric much preferred a small strobe light as a marker.

"Ten-Four on the strobe," came the reply. Almost immediately, Eric saw the strobe ahead of them.

"Strobe in sight," he said. "Tell me about the LZ."

"No obstacles, Dustoff. It's an open field. If you'll swing around to the south and land toward the river, it will keep you away from the bad guys' last known location. Land just south of the strobe and you should have no problem."

"Okay," Eric said. "Coming around." He made a circling motion with his hand to Les, indicating he should set up a pattern to take them to the strobe light on a northerly heading.

The landing and pickup were uneventful. Les Winters did a fine job of making an approach to the flashing strobe light. When the patients were aboard, he departed over the river and turned toward Long Binh. Eric was content to let Les fly. He'd had enough for one night.

After dropping the patients at the hospital, the crew flew to the Plantation fuel dump for fuel, then back to the Dustoff ramp. They were relieved when Operations told them there were no more missions pending. After landing, Eric sat in the helicopter for a while to unwind. Les went off to the latrine. Turk and Blake got a bucket of water and washed the blood from the canvas litters and the cabin floor. Eric was still sitting in his seat when they finished and walked off toward the enlisted crew lounge. A few minutes later he got out and walked up and down the ramp between the rows of revetments where the Dustoff helicopters were parked to stretch his legs. He thanked God they had been able to save at least two lives and had made it through the night unscathed. He shook off a chill as the night breeze blew through his sweat-drenched Nomex. He turned toward the now dark pilots' lounge. A shower and a bunk would feel good.

I've got a fine crew to take with me to get Steve, he thought. *If they can work together like they did tonight, we can do anything.* It was a confidence booster he needed.

TWENTY-SEVEN

Saigon, the MACV Compound

Chief Petty Officer Grant Stillwell was uncomfortable in the air conditioned Navy offices of the MACV compound in the northern part of Saigon. He had no sooner reached his new assignment as an advisor with the Vietnamese River Assault and Interdiction Division (RAID) 71 at Tan An, when word reached him to meet with Captain Perry, the Saigon Chief of Naval Intelligence—ASAP. An Air America helicopter was dispatched to transport him to Saigon.

Captain Perry didn't keep the SEAL waiting long. As Stillwell entered the captain's spacious office, he observed the carpeted floor, oak furniture and tasteful appointments. It was a stark contrast to the living conditions he and the other SEALs encountered in the field. None of that mattered to Stillwell. Perry was a high-ranking, rear-echelon officer. Let him have his cushy environment. Stillwell preferred the field any day.

"Have a seat, Chief." Captain Perry extended his hand, gesturing to one of the two leather seats that sat across from his desk.

Stillwell sat on the edge of his chair uneasily, his eyes surveying the room as if to mark the exits and identify any potential
danger spots. The Navy he knew was a far cry from that found
in Saigon.

Perry leaned back and adopted an easy manner with the
SEAL. He hoped to put the man at ease. "Grant, the reason I
asked you here is to help me out with a touchy situation."

Stillwell nodded. That's what SEALs were for.

Perry continued. "There's a POW situation in the Delta. I
believe you already know something about it. Last month, a
Bronco pilot went down a few klicks south of Vi Thanh and
was captured by the Viet Cong. I understand you and the rest
of SEAL Team Golf attempted to find him, but the Vietnamese had taken him underground."

"Yes, sir." Stillwell explained. "They created a diversion, then
took him down river on some type of craft. We had eyes in the
sky, but they weren't able to follow the trail. We lost him."

"I understand," Perry said. He wanted to make sure Stillwell wasn't on the defensive. "The Orion crew working with
you that day continued to patrol the area. In subsequent weeks,
they developed a theory about where the man is being held."

Perry stood up and stretched his back. He walked over to
a window that overlooked a courtyard below. After a quick
survey of the courtyard and the office windows across the way,
he turned back to face Stillwell. Leaning against the window
sill, he said, "He's not the only Navy prisoner we believe is being held in the Delta. Approximately three weeks before the
Navy pilot was captured, we lost a PBR crew near Rach Gia.
At first, we thought they had all been killed. Now we believe
some, perhaps all, of them are prisoners."

Looking Stillwell in the eye, he said, "We dropped the ball
on this one, son. The Navy chain of command has refused to

acknowledge that we still have prisoners in the Delta. They're too busy standing down and moving units back Stateside to deal with it."

Perry had anger and disgust in his voice. He wasn't coming across like "the brass," but like a field officer. Stillwell remained silent. He was an NCO in the presence of a field grade officer.

Perry pushed his "father-son" routine to its next level. He walked around and sat in the chair beside Stillwell. He searched the NCO's face, looking for the anger and determination he hoped was there. "The Army and the CIA have scooped us on this one. They're going in. But I don't believe they've got the expertise to pull it off. That's why I've offered your assistance."

Stillwell spoke for the first time since the Captain began his explanation. "Sir, you know SEAL Team Golf has rotated back to the States. There's only me and Jerry Bush left."

"I know that. I know you've been assigned as an advisor with RAID 71 and Bush as an advisor with RAID 70. Where is he? My Tho?"

"Yes, sir."

"I've arranged for you and Bush to be assigned TDY to Can Tho for a few days. The CIA Station Chief there is putting together a team to intercept the prisoners as they're being transported to Hanoi. He has intelligence information. He has an Army Special Forces Major and a couple of Vietnamese Kit Carson Scouts. He also has an Army helicopter crew."

Stillwell flinched at the last bit of news. He didn't have a lot of respect for what aviators could do on the ground, much less Army Aviators.

"You may know the aircraft commander," Perry continued. He's a medical evacuation pilot, the captured pilot's brother-in-law, Eric Mohr. I understand he helped in the ground search right after the man was captured."

"That's right, sir. I didn't meet him, but I heard about him. He had guts."

"Time is of the essence. The word is they may start moving the prisoners tonight, tomorrow night at the latest. The chopper that brought you here will take you back to Tan An to get your gear and to My Tho to pick up Petty Officer Bush. The pilot will then take you to Can Tho. When you get there, the man you want to see is Russell Lamb. He lives downtown, but I expect he'll be at the airfield. Look for the medevac helicopter."

"Yes, sir."

Stillwell left Captain Perry's office full of doubts. It sounded like his kind of mission, but it was a mission for SEALs, not for a hodgepodge mixture of unqualified people from various branches of military and civilian life. Two weeks earlier and he would have still had his team.

The U Minh, near Long My

The dank, musty cell was becoming like a coffin. A few feet to move in each direction, no light, no heat, no cooling, no ventilation, little exercise, not enough food, filthy clothes, no water for bathing—it was all taking a toll on Steve Cooper's health. Amazingly, something just the opposite was happening to his mind and to his soul.

He had not given up on the idea of escape. There were simply no openings. Jingles had eliminated the opportunities. The only escape was in his mind, which he kept occupied with plans for escape and with thoughts of what he would do when he was finally free. That he would be free, he never ceased to believe. To think otherwise would have been fatal. But something else was happening to Steve's mind. Things that had seemed so important before, began not to matter. What mattered was seeing his wife and daughter again, being a husband and a father. But there was more. He began to think about God. Somewhere during an agonizingly long night, he came to the realization that God was beyond his figuring out. But God *did* exist. Steve didn't know how he knew that, but he did. He knew that not only did God exist, he also knew that God cared about him in the same way He cared about Eric, about Gail, about Lynn.

The moment Steve came to the realization that God was God and what happens to Steve Cooper matters to God, something *did* happen to Steve Cooper. It happened in the depths of his soul, in his heart and in his mind. It started as a small warm spot in the center of his chest and radiating outward. He had been cold, but the warmth spread through his entire body until he was warm. Something else happened. He didn't know how to describe it at first, it was such an unfamiliar feeling. It was peace—a supernatural peace. Not only peace, but assurance: everything would be all right! He somehow knew it.

He drifted off to sleep and when he awoke, the peace was still with him. He was summoned to talk with Jingles. When he greeted the NVA officer, Steve had something almost like a smile on his face. It must have shocked Jingles. He was supposed to deliver Steve to Hanoi in reasonably good mental condition. Had the prisoner cracked?

Steve didn't know any Bible. He had no explanation for what had occurred. He only knew something had happened and Jingles had no ultimate control over him. He was in God's hands.

All Jingles had on his mind was to tell Steve he would soon be on his way to the Hanoi Hilton. He had him fed, then sent him back to his cell.

TWENTY-EIGHT

Can Tho Army Airfield

Rain pelted the tin roof of the small building where they were all gathered. Near the runway, the wind sock stood straight out one moment, danced around the pole the next, then changed directions like an NFL running back. A heater in the shack would have been welcome.

Stillwell came inside, his rain gear dripping on the floor. He took off his rain hat, pulled the tiny radio earpiece out of his ear and removed the headset. "We've got commo," he announced, "but with all of this rain, our eyes in the sky may not be able to do us much good."

"Has there been any movement from the prison compounds?" Lamb asked.

"No, sir. But we don't expect them to move until after dark."

Dark was two hours away, less, if the rains continued. They weren't ready. The first problem the group encountered after getting together was an elementary one: who was in charge? The CIA was represented by Russell Lamb and a South Vietnamese counterpart. The Navy was represented by two SEALs, now in advisory status and separated from their team, Grant

360

Stillwell and Jerry Bush. There was an Orion crew overhead, compliments of David Perry's ability to bend a few rules.

The Army contingent consisted of Special Forces Major Hamilton Ray, a man who had been in Vietnam for more than eight years and Eric Mohr's Dustoff crew consisting of Eric, Les Winters, Turk Smith and Blake Sam. Accompanying Ray were two South Vietnamese Kit Carson Scouts, the Vietnamese equivalent of Special Forces Rangers.

After a short conversation, they all conceded leadership to Major Ray. He was the ranking military officer and would therefore command the expedition. He picked Grant Stillwell as his "1st Sergeant." Mutual respect was gained and they all set about planning the mission based on the sketchy information they had.

The boat from Hanoi would reach the coast just off Xan My Thanh by midnight. The sampans carrying the prisoners had roughly fifty-four nautical miles to travel before they reached the coast. At six knots, that would take them nine hours. The boats might be able to make eight knots.

There were so many logistics problems to be solved. Where should they intercept the sampans? How would they get there? If the helicopter came within earshot of the Viet Cong, it would alert them and the prisoners might be dumped overboard. What weapons should they use? An ambush would endanger the lives of the prisoners.

Stillwell came up with a plan. It was a SEAL plan, and some of the others weren't sure they could pull it off. But, what choice did they have?

Near Long My

As darkness approached, Colonel Nguyen thanked his ancestors for the rain and saw to the preparations of getting the prisoners underway. He had confidence in his plan to move them to the South China Sea during the night. With the clouds and rain, overhead surveillance by the Americans in their sophisticated airborne observation posts would be severely hampered.

Knowledge of the transfer was limited to Nguyen and his chain of command in the North. Even the guards would not be made aware of the transfer until a few minutes before the prisoners were loaded on the boat. Five sampans had been allocated. They would travel separately, and each would begin from a different starting point. Four of the boats would have two veteran Viet Cong guards each. The Navy lieutenant's boat would have three. The rendezvous point had been carefully chosen in a desolate area six kilometers south of the river mouth. The trip to the coast should take no more than eight hours. Nguyen was ready. Within an hour, he would have his prisoners underway.

Can Tho Army Airfield

To the SEALs, the Special Forces major and the Kit Carson Scouts, the rain was an asset. It would mask their movement, muffle any inadvertent noise and hopefully lull the sampan crews into a false sense of security. For Eric and his crew, the rain was a major hindrance. Transporting the team to a place near their intended intercept sight would be difficult in the restricted visibility. There would be no one to guide them into a safe landing using any of the normal methods to mark an LZ. The pilots would have to descend into the darkness, feeling their way down, every pair of eyes watching for trees, bushes or dead limbs that could tangle with one of the rotors or poke a hole through the bottom of the helicopter's fuselage. They would have to find a suitable spot and it would have to be the right one. To move the helicopter when the sampans were within earshot would give away their presence and could easily mean death to the prisoners.

To Russell Lamb, the weather was a hindrance to communication. He had a spotter near the village. He would be depending on radio relay through the Orion. Stillwell and Bush would be severely limited in their options if they were not able to get sampan position reports from the Orion.

It was getting dark, almost time to go. Stillwell checked in with the Orion. "Hummingbird, Golf One, commo check."

"Golf One, this is Hummingbird. I've got you five by."

"What's the status?"

"We have some movement. It's difficult to make it out because of the rain, but our guess is it's going down."

Eric was standing beside Stillwell. "Ask him what the weather is like."

Stillwell passed along the question. "Hummingbird, our helo pilot wants to know about the weather."

"There are scattered showers throughout the Delta. Intensity varies. An overcast layer between 4,000 and 6,000 feet blankets most of the area, but we're getting some breaks in the overcast down south."

Sillwell relayed the information.

"Ask him about the visibility below the clouds," Eric said.

Stillwell asked and then passed the answer along to Eric. "He says he doesn't know. They're not flying below the clouds. They picked up information about the bottom of the cloud deck from observation posts at Rach Gia and Soc Trang."

Eric nodded. His own weather briefing through Army channels had been much more succinct. It was simply, "Don't fly!"

It was time. The team loaded into the Huey and Eric started the engine. The SEALs were dressed in their full combat gear and carried a variety of weapons, including silenced Beretta pistols in waterproof carrying pouches. Major Ray's favorite weapon was a 12 gauge Winchester pump shotgun. He wore two belts of ammunition across his chest comanchero style. The belts were filled with 12 gauge double aught buckshot. The Kit Carson Scouts carried M-203s, a combination weapon consisting of an M-16 and an M-79 grenade launcher mounted on the same stock. If Russell Lamb had a weapon, he didn't display it. The flight crew all carried their normal personal weapons. For Eric, this consisted of a World War II vintage .45 caliber handheld machine gun, commonly called a "grease gun," and his Army issue .38 caliber Smith & Wesson revolver. Les Winters carried his .38 caliber revolver and an M-2 carbine. The other two crewmen carried M-16s. There were also two AK-47s, complete with 30-round banana clips, hanging on the back of the two pilot seats. These were captured Viet Cong weapons that the helicopter crew carried in addition to their M-16s.

As they departed Can Tho, Eric noted the winds. They were strong and out of the north. This would be a factor when they landed near the Cai Lan River. The lower part of the river passed through rice paddies, all of which were flooded due to the recent rains. Though the banks of the river were mostly lined by trees, there would be landing sites a few hundred yards away. The trick would be to find one that wasn't standing in three or four feet of water.

The U Minh, near Long My

They handled him roughly, put him in the cage, lashed the door shut and hurriedly transported him to the river. Within twenty minutes, Steve Cooper was moving down river in a sixteen-foot-long sampan powered by a small gasoline motor. Two guards sat in front of him, alert and ready for danger, their AK-47s poised to fire at the slightest provocation. Behind him, another guard manned the tiller. His weapon was close at hand. A steady rain chilled the night. Visibility was hampered by rain and fog. It was one of the darkest nights Steve had seen. His hands and feet remained bound. As the craft made its way down the river, Steve's thoughts were on God and his family. No longer doubting that God would deliver him, his only questions were "where" and "when."

South of Can Tho

Leaving Can Tho, Eric picked up the highway to Soc Trang, intending to follow it to the "Wagon Wheel," the point where seven canals fanned out from a single point near the village of Phan Hiep. They flew at 500 feet with the helicopter's external lights off. Normally, helicopter pilots avoided the Wagon Wheel. It was such an obvious landmark that flying over it invited target practice from Viet Cong marksman loitering in the area. Tonight, it wouldn't matter. It was dark; they were blacked out. Let the VC shoot at the sound, if they wished. They weren't likely to hit anything.

Eric needed the Wagon Wheel for navigation. From it he would depart south, southwest, following a parallel road and canal that would lead him into the heart of the U Minh and on an intercept of the Cai Lon River.

Earlier that afternoon, Eric and Les had labored over the map and finally picked a spot near the river that appeared to be high ground with few trees. Between there and the river, a few hundred meters north, a thick stand of trees would offer concealment. There would be no radar contact with Paddy Control tonight. They were too low for radar and desired to keep radio transmissions to a minimum.

Eric strained to pick out landmarks through the rain-swept windshield, while Winters followed their progress on the map. Small cooking fires from the indigenous population offered the only relief from almost total darkness. When they left the road fifteen klicks south of the Wagon Wheel, there was nothing but darkness.

They found the river, at least what Eric thought was the right river, and that led to an argument. Eric was sure it was the Cai Lon. Les, who had been following their progress on the map, wasn't so sure. There were several small rivers in the area and multiple canals. In the darkness and with the limited visibility, the rivers all looked alike. To solve the problem, Eric flew east until they picked up the glow of lights from Soc Trang. Then they turned slightly southeast until they picked up Highway 1 on its way to Bac Lieu. From that point, they flew southwest along the highway until they came to the bridge over the Cai Lon. They followed the river northeast to the place where they intended to land. The extra searching cost them half an hour—time they really didn't have to spare.

The map showed a small lake just west of their intended landing site, which the pilots intended to use as a landmark. They found the lake and Eric made a turn to the south to set up a downwind pattern. When he turned back into the wind, he lined up on a spot east of the lake. As they approached the area, Eric eased off power and slowed his forward speed. All eyes were outside the aircraft, searching for obstacles. There was nothing but darkness below them, making it impossible to determine if the fields below were clear. Eric continued the approach, losing altitude slowly. Les sat forward in his seat, his hands near the controls. Dare they use the landing light? They would have to.

Eric checked in with Hummingbird to see if they had a position on the sampans. Kennedy, the technician responsible for first locating the prisoners, gave the helicopter crew an unconfirmed position report. A target he believed to be the lead boat was just passing the small village of Tu Trac, eleven kilometers away. Winters turned on the landing light. The field below looked wet, but there was no standing water. Eric eased the Huey down to a point just above the ground. Turk got out on the skids to talk him down the last few feet. As Turk jumped to the ground, his feet sank ankle deep in mud, then found solid ground beneath the top layer.

"Ease it down, sir," he coached. "There's mud here, but it appears to be only surface mud."

Slowly, Eric eased down on the collective pitch lever, transferring the helicopter's weight from the rotor system to the skids. When he felt the Huey settle, he eased in power again to lift it out of the mud to see how it responded. The Huey came unstuck easily. Eric eased it down again, then lowered the collective until the full weight of the helicopter was on the ground. The skids spread slightly, sunk approximately six inches, then stopped. The bottom felt solid. Winters turned off the landing light and Eric rolled off the throttle.

The SEALs, with Major Ray and the Vietnamese Scouts went to check out the river bank. Lamb and his counterpart stayed with the helicopter crew while they secured the aircraft.

If the eleven kilometers was correct, they had approximately an hour and a half before the first boat would be coming through. It was enough time, but barely.

On the Cai Lon River

The sampans moved steadily down the river, traveling near the shore, using the overhanging trees as shelter from the rain. Remaining beneath the trees also diminished the possibility of observation from above.

Steve's hands were tied in front of him, allowing him to explore the construction of his bamboo cage. The cage was cramped, its interior approximately two feet wide by four feet long by four feet high. Steve barely fit in it seated, his legs at an angle in front of him. Slowly, so as not to alert the guards to his movement, he explored the cage's floor and its sides, looking for weaknesses. The bamboo was woven together to make up the individual panels, but the panels were lashed together with rope. A sharp knife could sever the strands, but there were multiple strands to cut and it would take some time to get through them all. Unfortunately, the panels weren't just lashed at the corners, but the full length of each joint was bound by multiple wraps of the rope. Getting out would take some doing.

It was a moot point. Steve had no knife. Finally, he settled back in his cage. He was weak, but the peace of God was still with him.

The SEALs worked swiftly to get set up. They were in the water and virtually out of sight when the helicopter crew and the intelligence agents slipped into the woods to the place where Major Ray stood guard.

The Scouts positioned themselves along the river bank so that they had a field of fire covering a wide area. They were a few feet back into the woods to prevent being seen from the river. Ray instructed the civilians and the helicopter crew to stay out of sight and to remain quiet. They would be the back-up if things went wrong. If the plan went well, they wouldn't be needed until the prisoners were safely on the shore. Then it would be the medic's turn to see to their needs.

Hummingbird obtained a sighting on the two lead sampans and passed the word along. They were spaced approximately fifteen minutes apart on the river. That was great because it would allow enough time between boats if the rescuers could avoid any shooting.

Eric's heart was pounding in his chest. He had confidence in the SEALs' plan, but there was so much that could go wrong. They had no idea whether Steve was in the first boat, the second, third, fourth or fifth. To everyone but him, the rescue mission was the same, regardless. They were there to rescue all five Americans. Only Eric was single-focused on Steve. He knew it was wrong to feel that way. It was callousness toward the others and certainly not the way God wanted him to feel. Nevertheless, he was so determined that Steve would not be left behind in Vietnam that all of his physical, mental and spiritual energies were directed toward making sure Steve escaped the hands of the Viet Cong.

This whole thing could be a false alarm. Maybe the sampans weren't carrying prisoners. Maybe the rendezvous with the Junk offshore was fictitious. Maybe there were men on the boats, but Steve wasn't one of them. A thousand possibilities existed. It didn't matter. They were committed now.

Eric took stock of the immediate situation. The conceal-ment was professional. Even his own crew had blended into the dark shadows of the mangrove trees that bordered the river. The SEALs were in the water, totally out of sight and confident they had both sides of the river covered. Their trap was simple—a net stretched across the river just below the water's surface. Its purpose was to foul the prop, to stop the boat. They were using a common fishing net, something that would not arouse suspicion. They had two of them—a spare in case it was needed. As the guards worked to free the net, the SEALs would overtake them, subdue them and move the sampan to the shore, where the others would quickly remove the prisoner's cage and get the boat, cage and prisoner out of sight before the next sampan came along. No shots were to be fired. If they had to resort to shooting, the SEALs had silenc-ers on their Berettas.

The sounds of the night were muffled due to the steady rain that continued to fall. Birds and other forms of wildlife were relatively inactive. Beneath the trees, very little of the rain was actually reaching the Americans, yet it was a cold night. Eric was fidgety, restless, uncomfortable. He wondered how the SEALs, the Ranger and the Kit Carson Scouts could remain so still and quiet.

The sound of a boat's tiny gasoline motor cut through the night. It sounded to Eric like a small camp generator accom-panied by a burbling sound. The boat was close when they first heard it, because the sound did not carry far in the dense, humid air. Eric was tense, his eyes searching back and forth between the locations where he believed the various members of the team were hidden. Did they hear it? Were the SEALs ready? Were they out of sight from the river?

It didn't take long to find out. The sound grew louder, the boat emerged from the darkness. Abruptly, the engine quit. It gave out a gasp, then died. Immediately afterward came the sound of Vietnamese curses.

It was over in thirty seconds. Eric heard muffled sounds, saw flashes of movement. There were scraping noises and quiet whispers. The sampan was pushed across the river toward Eric and the others. The Scouts waded out into the edge of the river and helped pull the boat toward shore. Eric was one of the first to grab the handles on the cage. "Come on, guys," he said. "Let's get this out of here." The cage was heavy. Eric and his crew lifted it and carried it on their shoulders to a point beyond the trees while the Scouts and CIA agents disposed of the sampan.

Eric slashed at the ropes securing the cage sides with his survival knife. He couldn't cut them fast enough. Les started cutting on the other side. They got the door off, reached inside. The man they drug out was nearly unconscious, but he was alive. It wasn't Steve.

Eric looked over his shoulder toward the river. He was disappointed, ready to capture the next boat. He left the crew to attend to the freed prisoner and hurried back into the woods. He tripped over something, fell flat on it. It was a body—one of the Viet Cong guards. His throat had been slashed. It hadn't occurred to Eric what the SEALs would have to do with the guards. He got up, wiped blood from his hands on his pants, and slipped back into his hiding place.

The sound of the next boat came almost too soon. This one was traveling on their side of the river. The SEALs had gotten their net spread back across the river in time and were hiding in the shadows. The propeller snagged, the engine died, the guards bent over it, were suddenly and quietly jerked into the river and disposed of, their bodies thrown upon the shore. Eric ran toward the sampan and grabbed at the cage. There were fewer men to help lift it off the boat this time. They half rolled it, half drug it up on the bank. The man inside was crying, "Oh, God! Oh, God! Oh, God!" Eric didn't wait until they got it beyond the woods to start slashing at the ropes that held it together. Russell Lamb and the Vietnamese man with him, assisted, and within a couple of minutes they had managed to get one side of the cage cut free. The man kept crying over and over, "Oh, God! Oh, God! Oh, God!" Lamb kept assuring him that it was all right, that they were Americans, but he wouldn't be quiet.

"Shut him up, guys," Major Ray told them. "We can't afford for the next boat to catch us by surprise. We have no idea how far down the river it is."

Eric reached in and grabbed the man by the shoulders, pulling him out of the cage. The prisoner responded by grabbing Eric in a bear hug, almost pulling him to the ground. Eric shook himself free and looked the man in the face. He was a small, dark-headed man, obviously not Steve, but obviously glad to be free. They helped him walk toward the helicopter where Les, Blake and Turk were tending to the first prisoner. Both men were manacled. Turk searched the tool box he had stored under the aircraft seat and brought out some cutters so he could free their arms and legs.

Eric and the CIA men went back to their river hideouts to wait for the next boat, while Les, Blake and Turk tended to the needs of the freed prisoners.

It turned out to be a long wait. So long in fact, they began to wonder if more than two boats were traveling the river that night. Stillwell attempted to put in a call to Hummingbird, but was unable to raise the Orion crew. They waited for what seemed an eternity, but was in fact just a little over an hour. Finally, the sputtering sound of a sampan motor drifted through the night. Eric noticed it had stopped raining.

This time when the boat's propeller snagged the net, the engine didn't stop right away. Instead, after stopping the boat's forward motion for only a few seconds, it tore through the net. The guard in front grew wary of a trap and stood up, holding his AK-47 in a ready position. The man in the back of the sampan raised the long shaft with the propeller on the end of it out of the water, leaving the engine running. He saw that something was wrapped around the shaft and needed to be untangled. He looked quickly around him for signs of danger, and seeing nothing, hit the engine's kill switch. At that moment, the two SEALS rose up out of the water on either side of the boat and grabbed for the guard's legs. The one holding the AK-47 fired off a couple of quick rounds, then dove for the center of the boat. He grasped the gunwales on either side of the boat with his hands and started rocking. Before either SEAL could get to him, he managed to rock the boat over on its side, tumbling the cage overboard.

"No!" Eric cried and ran toward the water's edge. The Kit Carson Scouts quickly took out the two Viet Cong guards, firing a couple of short bursts each from their M-203s. If the next boat was close, the element of surprise was gone.

Eric waded into the water's edge, attempting to dive for the cage. Hamilton Ray grabbed his shoulder, restraining him. "Let the SEALs do it," he said. "They know what they're doing."

Eric watched hopelessly as one at a time, the SEALs came up for air, then dove back down to the river bottom, attempting to locate the cage and set its occupant free.

Suddenly, the sound of another boat was upon them. The sampan rounded the corner, its guards with rifles poised. They saw the figures on the bank ahead and swept the bank with several long bursts from their AK-47s. The Americans and South Vietnamese dove for cover.

Eric was in the water. He huddled close to the bank, under some bushes. His weapons were on shore. He didn't know where the SEALs were, but they weren't in sight.

The sampan crew moved closer, watching the disabled boat in front of them. They obviously could see there was no prisoner cage, no Viet Cong in the boat. A couple of bodies floated in the water. It took them a while to put the puzzle pieces together because of Colonel Nguyen's secrecy. These guards had not known other prisoners were being transported on the river ahead of them.

On the bank, Hamilton Ray and the Kit Carson Scouts waited. Ray had his shotgun. He was anxious for the boat to get closer. With two quick rounds, he would be able to eliminate these guards. But, he didn't know where the SEALs were, or what they were planning. Were they still searching for the underwater prisoner, or had they given up on him and were moving in on the other boat?

Tense moments passed in which nothing could be seen clearly by either party. The Viet Cong didn't know what they had stumbled upon; the American ambush party couldn't account for all of their people.

The Viet Cong helmsman made a mistake and killed his engine. There was absolute silence. It was so quiet, Eric was sure the VC would hear him breathing.

A small thud and a gasp broke the silence. The Viet Cong manning the tiller of the approaching sampan twisted on his feet, then fell headfirst into the river, the victim of a silenced Beretta round. His comrade, afraid and not seeing the threat, started raking the river bank on both sides with his AK-47. Ray silenced him with two rounds of buckshot from his shotgun. From inside the cage they heard the sound of a man crying.

Eric started swimming toward the boat. He bumped into a floating body. He brushed it aside, thinking it was one of the Viet Cong guards. Then he saw the face. It was Grant Stillwell, a gaping bullet hole in his forehead, his lifeless eyes wide open and staring.

Frantic, Eric pushed Stillwell's body toward the shore and thrashed his way toward the sampan. He reached it just as Jerry Bush popped up out of the water near the bow.

"They got Stillwell," Eric told him.

"What?!"

"He's over there." Eric nodded with his head toward Stillwell's body, which was drifting toward the shore.

Bush said nothing, grabbed the bow of the sampan and started swimming, pushing it toward the shore. In the darkness, it was difficult to see what other damage had been done, but there was still a live prisoner in this boat. For the one at the bottom of the river, it had been too long.

Eric and Bush pushed the boat up against the shore. Ray, Lamb and the Scouts lifted the cage out and carried it the short distance through the woods to the edge of the field. As they climbed out of the river, Eric and Jerry Bush dragged the sampan with them.

Bush surveyed the carnage. "We'll have to move upstream," he said. "Hopefully, the next boat was out of earshot."

"What about the guy down there?" Eric cried. It could be Steve, or Steve could be the one they had just rescued. He had to find out. He ran toward the helicopter. When he got to it, he found Les Winters crouched in front of the cage. He had just finished cutting loose the door. The man inside was crying, huddled against the back of the cage, afraid to come out. Les talked to him in soothing tones, assuring him that everything was all right. Eric stuck his head in the cage. He couldn't see in the darkness! He grabbed at the man's shoulders, attempting to pull him out where he could see him. The man shrunk back.

"Come on, Les," Eric pleaded, "give me a hand."

Winters reached in and helped Eric drag the man out of the cage. It wasn't Steve. *No, God!* Eric cried in his heart. *Don't let that be Steve at the bottom of the river.*

If their intelligence was correct, there was still another sampan, another prisoner. One more chance. They couldn't blow it. Stillwell was dead. He was a major part of their team, the most capable and the most qualified to do the kind of ambush they were attempting. Eric jogged back toward the river. At the river's edge, he encountered Jerry Bush dragging Stillwell's body out of the river.

He pushed Stillwell's body up to Eric. "Here," Bush said. "Take him. I'm going to try to recover that other prisoner."

Eric pulled the lifeless body of Grant Stillwell up on the bank. Bush turned to dive back under water. They both heard it at the same time—the sound of another sampan. Bush aborted his plan to recover the submerged prisoner and pulled the spare net out of the pouch slung over his shoulders. He began unfolding it and tossed one end to Eric. "Take this," he said. "We don't have time to string it. Grab that end and start swimming up river with me. Stay near the shore and stay low. We've got to try to get around that bend up there and stop them before they see this mess."

Eric swam hard upstream while Jerry Bush crossed the river, swimming and unwinding the net as he went. The boat was almost upon them by the time they rounded a small bend in the river. They would have to hold the ends of the net and stretch it tight across the water in order to snag the prop.

Eric crouched low in the water, held his breath and waited. He couldn't see the SEAL in the darkness, but could feel his strong pull on the other end of the net. The boat plodded toward them, its form taking shape out of the darkness. It was on Eric's side of the river, very near him. Eric's heart was pounding. What should he do? He sank deeper back into the bushes and willed himself to blend into the darkness. His breath was now coming in short gasps and he was almost certain the VC would hear him as soon as their motor stopped.

With a jerk, the net was snagged out of his hand. It did its job of snarling the propeller and the engine coughed and died.

There were two men in front of the boat! Two men in front and one on the back. Yet, there was only Eric and Bush to handle all three guards and Eric wasn't armed. Nor was he capable of the kind of hand-to-hand combat the SEALs had done. Did Bush still have his pistol? Where were the others?

When the boat's motor stopped, Bush swam underwater toward it. He was out of Eric's sight and Eric had no idea where he was or what he planned to do. He only knew they had stopped the boat and he wanted to believe the prisoner in the cage on that boat was Steve.

The sampan's helmsman was scarcely three feet away from Eric. Had it been light, or had the man known to look under the bushes, he likely would have spotted Eric. Eric had to take this man out and hope Bush would handle the others. He didn't know what kind of help the members of their party who were on the shore could give. Eric hoped they had heard the boat approaching and had heard its motor stop. This was not working according to any plan. There was no plan. They'd have to deal with what they had and hope God was watching and would help and protect them.

The rear guard was bent over the motor, struggling to free the propeller. Eric lunged at him from out of the bushes and grabbed for his ankles, throwing him off balance. The man kicked at Eric, then fell overboard on the opposite side of the boat. As he did so, he rocked the boat. The two men in front rose to their feet and raised their rifles to fire at Eric. When they stood, stabs of flame from the shore sprayed toward them as the Kit Carson Scouts opened fire. Both Viet Cong were hit and fell into the water, tilting the boat even more. The combined weight of all three men falling out of the boat on the deep water side, tipped it over so that the prisoner cage slid toward the edge of the sampan, then rolled over the side and into the water. Eric jumped and tried to grab it, but was unable to stop its fall. Not another cage in the water!

Quickly, he dove under the Viet Cong sampan, and grabbed for the survival knife fastened to his survival vest. He bumped into the cage and started hacking at the ropes with his knife. He could see nothing, but thought he heard or felt the SEAL on the other side of the cage doing the same thing. He could feel the man inside the cage struggling to break free. His lungs bursting for air, Eric shot toward the surface, gulped a quick breath of air, then dove back under the water's surface. He'd never been comfortable in the water. Now the murky darkness terrified him and the inability to breathe was pushing him toward the brink of panic. But he had to set this prisoner free before he drowned.

Frantically, Eric searched in the black water for the cage. It had slid further toward the center of the river, and was now in deeper water. He'd no sooner gotten a hand on it than his body cried out for air. It would have to wait. He slashed at the ropes, cutting first one, then the other. How many were there?

Why was his knife so dull? Why were his arms so tired? He had to breathe.

Turning loose, Eric shot up to the surface. As his head broke out of the water, another head shot up nearby. It was Bush. "I've nearly got him!" Bush cried. Eric sputtered, gasped, shook the water out of his nose and submerged again, kicking himself toward the bottom. He found the cage, searched with his hands for the strands he had cut, then found the remaining ones and went to work. His hands got tangled up with the SEAL's hands, then Bush moved to the other side of the same panel and began slashing much more effectively through the ropes with his knife. Seconds later, they had cut enough to pry a small opening between the cage's panels.

Bush continued to cut away the ropes, while Eric reached in and grabbed for the prisoner. His hand grabbed the prisoner's hands, manacled together. He pulled. The prisoner, his body weight buoyed by the density of the water, followed easily. Eric pushed against the side of the cage with his feet as he attempted to pull the man through the opening. He didn't know how much longer he would be able to stand the crushing pain in his chest, the demand for air. Bush pulled at the man's legs and together they slipped him through the small opening and quickly shot to the surface.

Eric burst out of the water, choking and gasping for breath. Heaving, he tried to drag the now lifeless body toward shore. The Navy SEAL, trained in underwater tactics, was in control of his facilities. He grabbed hold of both Eric and the prisoner and started swimming with them toward the shore.

Hands grabbed for them. "Blake!" Eric yelled, his voice revealing signs of panic. "Blake! He's not breathing!"

"We've got him! We've got him!" The voices were firm, but calm, as the seasoned veterans, Russell Lamb and Les Winters took over. They pulled the prisoner onto shore, where Blake Sam immediately began mouth-to-mouth resuscitation and CPR. Turk Smith began pushing on the man's chest, while Blake continued to breathe life-giving air into the man's lungs.

Eric plopped down beside them. *It was Steve they had rescued, but his body was lifeless!* While the medic and crew chief worked on him, Eric began to pray. A hand was on his shoulder. At first he didn't notice, but then felt the power as Russell Lamb, the Can Tho CIA Station Chief, joined Eric, the Warrant Officer Aviator in petitioning God for the life of Steve Cooper, the Navy pilot.

Blake Sam, the medic, worked over Steve's body, willing it to life. Blake Sam, the Christian, prayed between breaths. "Come on, breathe!" he demanded, then took another deep breath and bent over to put his mouth over Steve's. From deep within Cooper's body a lung full of water was expelled, almost catching Blake full in the face. It didn't matter. With the expulsion of the water came breath, with the breath came a heartbeat. Steve Cooper was alive!

He coughed and choked for almost a minute, spitting up water and drawing deep breaths into his lungs. Slowly, he became aware he was alive and there were people all around him. He raised his head. The first face he saw was Eric's.

"Eric?"

"Steve!"

Cooper looked around him, taking in the American's faces, and it began to dawn on him the effort behind his rescue. He looked back at Eric. "God does answer prayers, doesn't He?" Steve said.

It took Eric a few seconds to grasp what Steve had just said to him. Then he smiled, "Yes, He does, Steve! Yes, He does!"